How dare David close her out this way?

Slamming the door after his retreating figure, Annie tore up the stairwell and into her bedroom. In a kind of frenzy, she stripped off her dress, her sandals and panty hose, and then stormed into the bathroom and started a tub of hot water running. Her eyes were hot and dry, and her breath came in short, angry gasps. It took several moments before she was aware that someone was leaning on the front doorbell.

She didn't remember grabbing a robe, going down the stairs or unlocking the door so David could burst in. She only knew that he was kissing her all over her face, wild kisses that tasted of her tears and his agony. The smell and feel and taste of him engulfed her.

"Annie, my Annie, I need you." The words were torn from him, raw and full of pain.

Somehow they climbed the stairs, his arms still locked around her.

Bobby Hutchinson was born in a small town in interior British Columbia in 1940. Her father was a coal miner, her mother a housewife and both were storytellers. Learning to read was the most significant event in her early life.

Bobby married young and had three sons. Her middle son was deaf, and he taught her patience. She divorced after twelve years, and worked at various odd jobs. She later remarried and divorced again, writing all the while, mostly romances. She now has had more than forty books published, most of them Harlequin novels. She's currently working on a few more projects. Bobby has four enchanting grandchildren, and another on the way. She lives alone in Vancouver where she runs, does yoga, meditates, bikes, works out at a gym and writes every day.

BOBBY HUTCHINSON

REMEMBER ME

Silhouette Books

Published by Silhouette Books

America's Publisher of Contemporary Romance

SILHOUETTE BOOKS

ISBN 0-373-51210-4

REMEMBER ME

Visit Silhouette at www.eHarlequin.com

Printed in U.S.A.

CHAPTER ONE

"WILL HE REALLY make the cage and the birds disappear, Annie?"

Seven-year-old Maggie balanced her narrow behind on the very edge of her seat, round blue gaze fixed on the spectacle unfolding before her on the stage, squeaky voice full of wonder.

"It looks that way, Mag." Annie Pendleton's whispered response went unheard by her small companion, because now the magician was gesturing at children in the front row, inviting them to join him onstage.

Annie swallowed against the sudden constriction in her throat. What was going wrong with her? Her heart was hammering and she could feel perspiration dampening her palms.

"Come on up here and hold this cage down for me, won't you?" His baritone voice was gentle, full of humor, filling the auditorium. It was amplified by the small microphone Annie could see clipped to the open collar of his casual blue denim shirt, and it seemed to reverberate in her head.

What was it about this man?

Unlike the other amateur Vancouver magicians who'd appeared this afternoon, this one—The Sorcerer, he called himself—wasn't wearing the magician's traditional uniform of top hat and tails. He had on jeans and comfortable loafers, and his shirtsleeves were rolled up his forearms. He was probably a few years older than Annie's thirty-four years. He was attractive, but not startlingly handsome.

So what was he doing, affecting Annie the way rock stars affected teenyboppers?

Children were thronging from their seats now, eager to be part of the fascinating activity onstage, and The Sorcerer was arranging them around the twittering canaries' cage, which sat on an ordinary wooden table.

"Go on up there, Maggie," Annie's son, Jason, urged, but Maggie shook her head vehemently, making her long blond braids fly.

"You go, Jason. You go. I'm scared."

Jason groaned, torn between wanting to be close enough to study the spectacle about to unfold, but convinced he was far too old and jaded at thirteen to join "kids."

"It's just magic. There's nothing to be scared of, for Pete's sake, Maggie. Go up and see what's goin' on for me, please?"

But Maggie's round blue eyes were threatening to pop from her skull, and she shook her head as the other children ringed the bird cage, their hands overlapping on its surface. The Sorcerer held his hands in the air, staging the illusion to come.

"I bet the table has a false bottom, Mom, so the cage just drops inside."

Thirteen-year-old Jason didn't bother continuing his scoffing explanation to his mother. Jason had read every book on professional magic he could get his hands on, and he wasn't about to be fooled by any of this amateur stuff. He'd done his annoying best all afternoon to explain each trick to Annie and Maggie as it was being enacted...and had successfully spoiled the illusions for everyone within hearing distance.

"There isn't room, Jason. You can see underneath from here." Annie made a concerted attempt to sound normal.

This was the final act of the amateur magic show and Annie had been relieved that the afternoon's clumsy performances were finally coming to an end.

It was hot and stuffy, and her neck had started to ache by the time The Sorcerer was scheduled to appear. Maggie and Jason were becoming restless on either side of her.

Then this man had strolled casually onstage, and from that moment on Annie and the rest of the Saturday afternoon audience had paid close attention.

It was obvious right away that despite his casual garb, The Sorcerer was a consummate magician. During the first part of his act, he'd smoothly made scarves appear and disappear, pulled a small white squawking pigeon from the depths of an empty box and retrieved with a butterfly net a small army of white mice from the seemingly empty air in front of him.

Clever sleight of hand, but with it he had presence, a sense of timing and rapport with his audience the other performers had lacked.

And this trick with the bird cage was unusual, if he was actually going to make it disappear with all those kids holding on to it. In the third row from the front, Annie tried to look away from the stage, focus her gaze anywhere except on the magician.

The fact was that this Sorcerer was having a peculiar effect on her. A distinct chill shuddered its incongruous way down Annie's neck and back, a chill that had little to do with the clever tricks being enacted on the nearby stage, and everything to do with the uncanny feeling of familiarity she'd experienced from the first moment the tall, dramatic man had ambled out from behind the dusty stage curtains and taken command.

"It's done with fishing line, I bet it is," Jason concluded once again.

A middle-aged woman in front of them turned and glared, and then shot Annie a look that suggested she do something about Jason and his comments.

But Annie was impervious. Her attention was still riveted to the man onstage as he held both arms high in the air, and with a sudden loud exclamation, brought them down.

The bird cage disappeared, and a collective roar of amazement issued from the group of children who'd been resting small hands all over its surface.

"Humph." Jason made a noise like a balloon deflating, and his red-brown hair stood on end as he sat forward on his chair, brows beetled together in a concentrated effort to figure out what was really going on.

Annie narrowed her eyes and studied the commanding figure on the stage, unconsciously frowning herself. Her heart was pounding in an unnatural rhythm, and she felt confused, a confusion that had nothing to do with the trick, and everything to do with the man performing it. She was shivering, and yet the air in the auditorium was warmer and stuffier than ever, with its evocative reminders of yesterday's sweaty bodies and years of smelly gym shoes.

You've never seen that man before, you know that, she silently reprimanded herself, wiping cold, sweaty palms in slow motion down the sides of her red cotton skirt.

Then how, from the very first instant, had she instinctively known exactly how he'd turn his body...like now. She anticipated that slight arrogant tilt to his leonine head an instant before it occurred...and there, she knew the exact way his strong, clean features mirrored amazement and delight at his own sleight of hand, subtly making him one with his audience, projecting the impression that he was having as much fun as they were.

In his deep, shadowed eyes Annie also knew for certain that warm blue lights flickered like candle flames, that kindness and bottomless compassion were reflected in the dark irises.

Rubbish, she admonished herself. She couldn't even see his eyes from where she sat.

Ah, but she knew their expression as well as she knew the soft and voluptuous rounded lines of her own body.

She recognized his long-boned, rangy shape with its deceiving muscular strength. She remembered the way his wide, narrow mouth tilted in a wicked grin, the way it was tilting now.

How could she know these things about someone she was certain she'd never seen before? A mild form of panic made her heart pound and her breath come in shallow gulps.

This whole thing was ridiculous.

"How did he do that, anyway?" This time, the puzzled query came from Jason, poised on the edge of his seat. Maggie had been clapping her hands with delight, along with the rest of the audience.

Annie felt familiar, unaccountable pride and admiration mix with the other confused emotions racing through her consciousness.

He had such presence. He'd always been able to hold children in the palm of his hand, command their attention from the first instant he appeared among them. It was one of the innumerable things about him that delighted her, his love for children.

It was what made him such a fine doctor.

The thought had almost evaporated before she examined it, dissected the discrepancy there, and shuddered again.

Always when, Annie? And how do you know what kind of doctor he is?

Before, an impatient ribbon of rebellious thought insisted.

When before? You've never laid eyes on him until today.

She swallowed hard, aware that her face was burning hot now, her fingers trembling.

Suddenly he made a dramatic gesture, and out of nowhere, the bird cage appeared and settled in his right hand, its silver paint sending shards of light glancing outward from the strobes overhead.

Jason expelled his pent-up breath in a long whoosh of admiration and wonder.

"Jeeze, that's ace. I never heard of any trick like that before, making it disappear and then come back out of thin air. Did'ya see that, Mag? Mom, you're going to interview this guy for your research, aren't ya? He's ace. Hey, Mom, when ya talk to him, find out for me how he did that trick, will'ya please? Jeeze, that's excellent." Jason slid back onto his chair, shaken completely out of his role as debunker of magic.

The Sorcerer set his cage back on the small table, smiled his crooked smile, bowed to his clapping audience and disappeared behind the dingy curtain.

The brown velvet closed behind him, and something totally unexplainable happened to Annie. As if the light at the core of her being had been switched off, utter desolation swept over her, an ancient, searing loneliness in her soul so intense and hurtful she had no armor against it.

Hating herself and feeling an utter fool, but unable to stop the onrush of puzzling emotion, harsh sobs rose in her throat and Annie began to weep, frightening Maggie and absolutely horrifying her son.

AN HOUR LATER, sipping iced tea in the familiar jumbled order of Cleo Fowler's kitchen, Annie felt embarrassed and apprehensive as Jason related the entire afternoon's drama in minute detail to his mother's best friend.

"And so help me, Cleo, I never heard of any prestidigitator..."

Cleo rolled her eyes heavenward, and suggested, "Can't you just say magician, Jason? Just say magician, for Lord's sake. I'm a simple, uncomplicated woman and it's easier for me to follow you if you use one-syllable words."

"Any—any—sorcerer—" Jason supplied triumphantly. "That's what he called himself, see. Sorcerer. I mean, he actually made a bird cage disappear, with a dozen kids holding on to it. Honest to, honest to goodness, he did. It's a super trick, Cleo. And it made Mom bawl like anything, didn't it, Mom? Man, I never thought you'd start to bawl about something like that. I mean, it was outrageous and all that, but still...cryin' over it..." Jason's recently unpredictable voice suddenly shot into a higher octave and he screwed his freckled face into a masculine grimace of horror and distaste at the memory of his mother's embarrassing fit of tears.

In a no-nonsense tone of voice he well recognized, Annie said, "Isn't it time for your paper route? Go home and fold your papers, Jason. I heard the van deliver them a few minutes ago."

Rolling his eyes in an exact parody of a habit his mother had, Jason ambled toward the screen door leading out to the wide porch.

"Can't you just say when you guys don't want me around, Ma? I mean, don't...prevaricate, okay? I mean, I'm old enough to handle the unvarnished truth. I'm not an adolescent anymore. I'm a teenager, Ma."

"Jason." There was a definite steeliness in Annie's voice this time, and her son speeded up his exit.

"He's driving me nuts," Annie said, staring at the door he'd slammed after him. "I've let him go too far, and now he's driving me crazy."

Cleo agreed. "Single mothers like us shouldn't have to cope with precocious teenage kids," she sympathized. "There ought to be a good home we could send 'em to until they turn twenty. And just think, I've still got the girls to live through all that with, and I'm barely over thirty.''

Actually she was thirty-two.

''Anyhow, school starts in another week, so that should help,'' Annie said.

Cleo nodded, making her mop of soft, prematurely white hair look more than ever like dandelion fluff as it floated and resettled on her well-shaped skull. She turned her astute green gaze on Annie, noting the unmistakable silver tracks of dried tears on her friend's flawless skin, and the hint of pallor under the apricot tan.

''So what's up, pal?'' she demanded. ''Why fits of weeping over some dumb magic show, huh?'' A look of concern passed over her angular features, and she added, ''Hey, it's not your back again, is it?''

Cleo banged an exasperated hand down on the table between them. ''Damn, I knew you shouldn't have been lugging Paula around like that yesterday morning. That kid may be only three but she weighs a ton.''

Annie shook her head. ''It's not my back, Cleo. My back's been fine for quite a while, apart from the odd twinge, and anyhow, it's not carrying kids around that affects it.''

Cleo's eyebrows rose.

''So what did happen this afternoon?'' she demanded with quiet persistence. ''What happened to that famous Pendleton control, huh?'' Her eyes widened. ''Hey, you didn't have another call from Michael, did you? Honestly, you'd think when your son's father has been invisible for all these years, he wouldn't have the nerve to start bothering you again about wanting back into the kid's life.''

''He hasn't called for two weeks now, Cleo. No, it wasn't Michael, either, that set me off, although heaven knows I wish he'd take a one-way flight back to India and stay there. It was just, it was...'' Annie stammered, and felt herself flush. How could she explain that wrenching gut reaction to a total stranger that even now made her stomach twist with anxiety? For no known reason? A man she'd never even met?

''It wasn't anything, anything...physical today,'' she lied, taking a long, slow sip from her tall glass, and then meeting Cleo's curious, steady expression with a helpless shrug.

''Or maybe it was entirely physical,'' she confessed with a long, drawn-out sigh. ''The simple truth is, I really don't know what came over me. I don't have the foggiest clue why I started crying, and I feel embarrassed as hell about it. It had something to do with that magician, some absolutely stupid feeling I had that I'd known him somewhere before. Not just casually known him, either.'' Annie slumped back into the wooden chair.

"Well, do you? Know him, I mean?"

Annie shook her head. "I know for certain I've never even met him, Cleo. I mean, the rational part of my brain knows that. It's this other feeling that..." Her words trailed off and her forehead drew into a frown. "Anyhow, why should that make me start bawling?" Annie paused, her soft brown eyes reflecting puzzled exasperation. "I've never felt remotely like that before, and I don't want to ever again. It's... disconcerting. Weird. Besides which, I'm going to have to meet him now, in the flesh, because I phoned yesterday when I got the tickets and made an appointment to interview him next week." With one slender finger she traced the ring her glass had made on the Arborite tabletop, and added, "I found out he's a pediatric surgeon at Vancouver Regional Hospital, named Dr. David Roswell, when he's not being The Sorcerer. The way I feel right now, I'd phone and cancel the interview, but you know what a hard time I've had to locate a decent magician to talk with for this next book I've got planned. And this guy was exceptional. He was really good."

"Jason certainly thought so," Cleo remarked, still studying her friend. "And Jason's about the most knowledgeable kid I've ever met when it comes to magic shows."

Annie nodded, a tiny grin masking the worried expression in her deep brown eyes. "Yeah. It was because of Jason's fascination with magic that I originally decided to do this book. He does know a lot about it. I figured once or twice today that the three of us were going to get tossed out, he was so vocal about how all the tricks were done."

"I told you to let the kids sit by themselves," Cleo teased. She paused, and then asked with disarming casualness, "How old do you think this Dr. David Roswell would be? Was he good-looking, tall, sexy? What? Give me a verbal sketch here."

Annie gave her a narrow-eyed, warning look. "The next thing you're going to ask is, did I notice a wedding ring?"

Cleo, not at all abashed, demanded, "Well, how old was he? Just take a guess. And yeah, did you happen to notice if he wore a ring? I know you're not interested in romance in the least, Annie, but think of me. I have to consider the potential of every single male we come across. I'm a tough case for any matchmaker, let's face it, and I haven't any intention of growing old without a sexy man to keep me company, even if you intend to."

"Cleo, you're impossible." Annie grinned all of a sudden, an infectious grin that lifted her winged eyebrows over her deep-set, wide eyes, making them sparkle with mischief and gamin deviltry. Annie's grin was contagious, and as always, it drew an answering fond smile from Cleo.

"Let's see now, this candidate was about thirty-eight, forty maybe, and yes, you could say he was good-looking." Annie's lighthearted tone belied the sudden acceleration of her heart as, without effort, her brain formed a clear picture of David Roswell.

"He's tall, slim but strong, long arms and legs, good broad shoulders, crisp dark brown curly hair, a lopsided smile and sort of...aristocratic features. Thick eyebrows, really nice blue eyes."

"Aristocratic? You're as bad as that son of yours with words. What the devil is aristocratic supposed to mean?" Cleo interrupted, but Annie ignored her.

"And no, Cleo, I didn't look for a ring. But when I interview him on Tuesday," she forced herself to add, "I'll be sure to sound him out about his feelings concerning gorgeous divorcées with collections of kids." Annie was grateful that Cleo seemed unaware of the effort behind her lighthearted nonsense.

"Only two kids of my own," Cleo corrected. "The others are here part-time, on loan, seven-to-five, weekdays. Make that clear whenever you're advertising me, lady. And let's skip the 'gorgeous,' shall we? Say I'm witty, say I'm faithful, say I'm amazingly good in bed...if I remember how after all this time...but gorgeous I'm not."

Annie smiled at Cleo's matter-of-fact assessment, but it was a strained smile, and Cleo noticed this time and stopped her bantering.

"Don't worry about this thing today, Annie," she said softly, reaching across to touch Annie's hand. "Sounds to me like you just had a severe attack of what they call déjà vu or something. Everybody has experiences like that now and then. Maybe this guy just reminded you of someone you knew when you were a tiny girl, someone you don't consciously remember knowing, some doctor your mom took you to or something. That happens sometimes. I remember hearing..." Cleo launched an involved story about a friend of one of her aunts recognizing someone unlikely at a funeral, and Annie finished her lemonade, nodding vaguely now and then but not really listening.

The image of a tall, lean man with intense blue eyes...she absolutely knew his eyes were that certain royal shade of deep blue, and she refused to wonder again how she knew...kept getting in the way of Cleo's husky, animated tones.

When the story ended, Annie got to her feet.

"I have to go, Cleo. Thanks for the drink. Pop over later if you feel like a coffee. I'll be home all evening as usual. I've got to work."

"Maybe after Maggie and Paula are asleep."

"Jason will come over and baby-sit for them if you like," Annie promised. "He'll be watching TV anyhow. They're doing reruns of *Star Trek*, and he can watch here as easily as next door. Besides, you always have better snacks than we do. Quote."

Cleo reached out to put a staying hand on Annie's arm. "You sure you're okay, friend? You're kinda pale. If you feel like company, you know you and Jason are always welcome to stay for supper. I've got a tuna casserole..."

Annie smiled at her generous neighbor, and shook her head.

"I'm fine, Cleo, honest. And thanks, but I really do have to get some work done. The synopsis on this magic book is due in two weeks, and all I have so far are a dozen scraps of paper with notes on them."

And an upcoming interview with a man she dreaded meeting.

She made her way down the rickety back steps, across the wide expanse Cleo optimistically called a lawn with its sandbox and swing set and wading pool, to the small gate in the high wooden fence that connected her property to Cleo's.

The lots in this older section of Vancouver were large, and Annie's back garden was a private, shaded welter of flowers, shrubbery and huge weeping willows.

Jason earned spending money by taking desultory care of it for her, mowing the lawn and giving the flower beds random attention, but his thirteen-year-old ambitions didn't extend to intensive neatness or dedicated gardening. Thus the yard had a careless, casual appearance she loved, as if no one interfered unduly with nature's whims.

She walked slowly up her own backstairs, in better repair than Cleo's because she'd hired a workman last fall to replace the rotted boards with new ones, and unlocked her back door.

A long, deep, indrawn breath revealed the myriad scents of living, the pleasant muted yesterday smells of cooking, the echo of the flowery cologne she habitually wore, the more pervasive sad perfume of the lilacs she'd placed on the narrow hall table.

She glanced down at a pair of filthy, ragged sneakers and a tattered jean jacket tossed just inside the door and she grinned.

Add to all those aromas the definite tang of a half-grown boy who hated soap and water, and you had the unique essence of the Pendletons' habitat.

Home. Annie never entered without experiencing a rush of warmth and wonder that she'd managed to actually buy this house for herself and Jason. Her fifth children's book, a tale of medieval demons and dragons, had unexpectedly sold its fanciful way out of bookstores and gone into a second and then a third printing, selling not to the children she'd intended it for, but to college students suddenly intrigued by all things medieval.

It didn't make her rich by any stretch of the imagination; her mortgage was a constant concern, and a writer's income was anything but predictable. But since then, three other books had also sold reasonably well, and now there was even a slender balance most of the time in her bank account—at least, on months when she didn't have to pay the orthodontist.

Life was stable, pleasant and she was a self-supporting, proud single mother. Annie planned to keep it that way.

She wandered through her well-equipped kitchen, on down the narrow hallway to the winding staircase. Halfway up, a window overlooked Cleo's backyard, and she smiled down at the foreshortened figures of Paula and Maggie, busy enacting some housekeeping game of their own in the wooden playhouse Annie and Jason had devised for them.

Having Cleo Fowler and her kids living next door had been the best bonus possible in living here.

The huge, skylighted study she'd created by having workmen knock out the wall between two bedrooms was to the left at the top of the stairs. Directly ahead was an old-fashioned segregated bathroom, with the toilet in one small room and the bathtub and sink in another. To the right was her bedroom. It still felt strange to have the entire top floor to herself.

Jason had taken over the large finished room in the basement last fall, the day he'd turned thirteen.

"I'm not a kid anymore, Mom, scared of the dark. We both need more privacy," he'd declared, and Annie remembered now the confusion of emotions his words had caused her. Baby son had become small boy, and boy was fast becoming man. It was a progression she wasn't ready for. Yet.

Annie turned into the study, her mouth twisting in acknowledgement of the controlled chaos inside the door. The room was exactly the way it always looked when she was busy on a book. Cleo had described it as a bird's nest mixed with an egg beater.

The flecked gray wool rug was littered with scraps of paper and reference books and notepads. Scribbled notes were also tacked in haphazard fashion to the huge cork bulletin board along one wall, along with pictures torn from magazines, addresses, reminders to herself, and the most recent colorful, crayoned drawings Paula and Maggie had made for her.

Annie studied them for a moment and a wistful smile came and went. Paula's artwork was a mélange of three-year-old scribbles and lines, but

Maggie's drawings were always of families, mother, father, and two children, stick arms joined, happy smiles bisecting round balloon faces.

Cleo joked about finding a man, but Maggie's drawings were silent and heartrending reminders that the little girl longed for a father figure in her life.

Dear old Mags, Annie thought as she moved to her worktable. If only dreams came true just from wishing.

The computer shared space with used teacups and assorted crumbs, and over the back of her comfortable chair hung the old grey T-shirt she pulled on against the chill of early mornings or late nights. The opposite wall held matted snapshots of Jason and Paula and Maggie, framed cover art from her published books and a coveted review *Maclean's* magazine had given her most popular book.

This room was the core of her home, the place where Annie worked and dreamed and spent most of her time. It was her surrogate womb, she had once told Cleo.

Now she sank into the padded desk chair in front of the computer, staring blankly at the dark screen. She'd worked there for several hours this morning, losing track of time as always, and then had to race to get ready to take the kids to the magic show as she'd promised.

She glanced up at the wall, at the huge face of the clock Cleo had given her last Christmas. Five hours ago. Only five short hours had passed since she'd last sat here. Such a minuscule span of time. Yet something had changed deep inside of her during those few hours; something had tugged at curious buried strings and made them resonate. It was disturbing.

There'd been a break in the even cadence of her comfortable life, a crack like the terrifying chasm an earthquake might create, and it both scared and angered her. She didn't want surprises. She didn't want upset.

Making an impatient noise deep in her throat, she chose a diskette from the plastic container beside the machine and inserted it in her computer, forcing her attention on the familiar messages that appeared, giving the automatic commands that would access her work.

The world outside this room could disintegrate and reform without her being aware, as long as she had her work—or so she'd thought until today.

For the rest of the August afternoon, as the late summer day dwindled and the sky overhead took on the hues of evening, she tried to center every ounce of attention and energy on the preparation of her book outline.

But just beyond her conscious thought, somewhere above and behind her in the deepening gloom, disturbing questions without answers lingered like specters, hovering and waiting to pounce the instant she relaxed her guard.

Questions like who was David Roswell, and how could she possibly remember how it felt to be loved by a man she'd never met before?

CHAPTER TWO

DAVID ROSWELL, still thinking about an intriguing conversation he'd just had with a colleague over lunch, strode down the hall to his office a few minutes after 1:00 p.m. Tuesday afternoon.

He thrust his outer office door open in typical energetic fashion and burst into the small room like an unleashed energy force, making the woman sitting on a hard wooden chair beside Phyllis's desk jump, and then leap to her feet. Phyllis was obviously still out on her lunch break.

"Sorry." He smiled in apology. "Didn't mean to startle you. I'm Dr. Roswell. How can I help you?"

Annie had spent the past two days convincing herself that whatever reactions she'd had to this man were pure imagination.

It took an eighth of a second, standing three feet from him, to realize how wrong she'd been. Her entire body signaled awareness. He seemed to exude an electric force that radiated outward and connected with her own aura.

Trying to control the sudden trembling in her legs and arms, the dryness in her throat, she drew in a deep breath and prayed her voice would have some semblance of normalcy.

"Hello, Dr. Roswell." Not too bad, only a trifle shaky. "My name is Annie Pendleton. I arranged with your secretary to interview you this afternoon."

Damn. Some kind of reporter. If Phyllis had mentioned this, David certainly didn't remember. And in typical fashion, he'd neglected to even look at the daily reminder on his desk. Now Phyllis would have to get hold of Calvin and let him know David couldn't break off early as he'd planned to have a quiet dinner with his old friend. There was also that consultation, and those overcautious parents he wanted to reassure, and now this interview would take a good hour or so of an already overloaded afternoon.

Besides, he'd have to be careful what he said until he found out who she worked for. There were several publications that were blistering in their objections to organ transplants, especially those involving children.

"I phoned last Friday, and your secretary said to come in today at one...."

This Annie Pendleton had a nice voice anyway, he decided. Soft, mellow, with a shy, endearing quality to it. She seemed a trifle nervous for some reason.

"Of course, Ms Pendleton. C'mon in here, have a seat...."

She was suddenly convinced he was covering up the fact that he'd totally forgotten about the interview, and a flash of unreasonable anger flared in her.

She'd spent the past two days and nights thinking of nothing else but him, and he hadn't given her a single thought.

Annie, you dope, why should he? she chastised herself in an effort to be rational. *The man's never even met you. His secretary arranged the whole thing. You know that.*

"Can you give me some clues as to what this will be about?" he was asking with a charming grin. "Is it to do with that TV interview I did about organ transplants for children?"

Organ transplants? Damnation. He really didn't know who she was or why she was here, despite the careful briefing she'd given that woman on the phone when she set up the interview. So his snippy secretary hadn't told him anything about it.

Had Phyllis told him what this was all about, David pondered?

Probably, but if she had he'd simply not been listening. At any rate, this woman looked and smelled delightful—some light floral scent he must have smelled before, because it was familiar.

He rubbed a distracted hand through his hair, feeling the way it curled down over his shirt collar at the back. He needed a haircut, but that was nothing unusual. There was never enough time for things like haircuts. And he knew without any doubt that he smelled of antiseptic soap, with an undertone of disinfectant.

He grinned suddenly. She wasn't interviewing him for bachelor of the year. Why the sudden concern about his admittedly roughshod grooming?

"This isn't to do with medicine at all, Dr. Roswell. It's about magic. You see, I write books for children. I'm planning one about magic, and I wanted to interview a magician."

He expelled his breath in a relieved sigh. Magic, huh? This was going to be enjoyable after all. "Why not just call me David, and I'll call you Annie. Let's make this informal, all right?"

She nodded, trying not to look straight into his eyes because when she did, she found herself stammering.

"All right, ah, David." Swallowing hard, she fell back on the carefully prepared introduction she'd gone over and over the night before when she ought to have been sleeping.

"My books are usually aimed at the nine-to-twelve age group, and have to be absolutely accurate. Kids that age are fascinated by magic, and I wanted to talk to you about your magic act last Saturday, at Thompson High School auditorium?"

David sat back in his chair and relaxed.

"So you were at that benefit show on Saturday, Annie? Weren't those kids a great audience?" It gave him a subtle sense of pleasure, using her name. Besides, it suited her perfectly.

Annie. Simple and unpretentious. Intimate and easy. He repeated it to himself. Annie. Not the formal Anna, or the cool Anne. Just Annie.

"The organizers tell me it was quite successful financially, that show," he remarked. She had soft hair, he mused. Hair the color of...he tipped his head to one side a little, considering the exact shade.

"I was there, yes. I—enjoyed your performance. You're an excellent magician, doct...ah, David." She was uncomfortable using his first name. It made it much harder to maintain the emotional distance she felt she needed between herself and him.

Oak, he concluded with a sense of satisfaction. She had hair the shade of oak, that same lush richness undershot with gold and a bit of red that the best wood displayed. It must be quite long, because she had it wound in a plump knot at the back of her head, with soft wisps curling before and behind small ears.

"I'm very much an amateur," he assured her. "Magic is a combination of skill and showmanship, and I'm wise enough to know my limitations." He winked in a conspiratorial way. "I concentrate hard on showmanship."

"But you also do illusions that aren't ordinarily performed by an amateur," she persisted. "That bird-cage disappearance, for instance. My son was really impressed by that one. He has dozens of books on magic and neither of us could locate anything like that trick in his books."

So she had a son. He felt let down, and realized he'd been assuming she was single.

"The bird-cage illusion actually originated with a French magician called Bautier de Kolta, who died in 1903," David explained, watching Annie take out a yellow spiral notebook and begin jotting in it as he spoke. "Two well-known American magicians, Carl Hertz and Harry Blackstone, also presented the bird cage in their shows early in the 1900s. And currently, Harry Blackstone, Jr. does a version of the vanishing bird cage in his act. I saw him perform it several years ago, when a medical conference I was attending in New York coincided with a worldwide gathering of The Magic Circle.''

Blackstone's interpretation wasn't the one David used, however.

She was scribbling with furious intent, and he took the opportunity to study her. He liked the tiny frown of concentration between her winged eyebrows, the length of the gold tipped lashes as she bent over her notebook.

She looked up and caught him at it, and her eyes and his locked for an instant. She looked away, determined to get through the questions she'd prepared. Staring into David Roswell's eyes wasn't going to help any.

"How did you learn the bird-cage trick, David? Wait. First tell me how you began doing magic. What made you start learning? Aren't sorcery and medicine mutually exclusive?'' she queried with a small smile, watching him tip his head a little to the side, knowing just the way his deep blue eyes would change with gentle humor as he answered her question.

He deliberately skipped the first question and went on to the others, hoping she wouldn't notice.

The bird-cage illusion should have been beyond his skills. But he'd read about it, found a limited description of technique in an old, tattered book and been able to master the whole thing with amazing ease, making the illusion entirely his own. Even he didn't fully understand how a complex illusion other magicians were puzzled by should come like child's play to him.

He never revealed the secrets of the bird cage, and he wasn't about to now, no matter how beguiling he found Annie Pendleton.

He told her only that he had a weird kind of superstition about the trick, as if it were an heirloom to be passed from father to son and guarded with care. Not that he had a son.

"Actually magic and medicine have a great deal in common, Annie, particularly so-called mystical magic,'' he began, leading her off the track of the bird cage.

"Mystical magic relies on a combination of hope and fear, which are the same emotions that send modern-day patients to visit a doctor. Mystical magic was the handmaiden of sorcery, witchcraft, alchemy, all of which have contributed in some way to modern medicine.''

He was accustomed to lecturing, she noted. His deep voice was devoid of awkward pauses, even and flowing, full of confidence and that ability she'd recognized last Saturday, the knack of commanding the attention of an audience.

He sat forward, interested in what they were discussing, his long-fingered, scrubbed-looking surgeon's hands resting on a closed file folder. The nails were cut short and square. He wore a ring with a green stone on the small finger of his left hand, but he had none on his ring finger.

"The amateur magician of today is a long way from practicing mystical magic, however. The kind of magic I do is known as entertainment magic, providing amusement through interesting deception."

"How did you get interested in magic?" she asked again.

Maybe he was married and just didn't wear a ring.

"Oh, that started about the same time I developed an interest in medicine."

She had plain silver drop earrings suspended from pierced earlobes. With that coloring, he mused, she ought to wear only gold.

"My interest in magic started with a book my uncle Edward gave me for Christmas when I was ten. It came with a box of tricks, and I bored everyone nearly to death with my bungled attempts at making things disappear." He laughed at the reminiscence, and the sound made her smile. His laugh was deep and hearty, and it was just the way she'd known it would sound.

"When I wasn't smoking out the house with some concoction that had gone wrong, I was driving Uncle Edward crazy bungling a card trick," he added. "But you must have gone through the same trials if your son is interested in magic. How old is he?" he asked.

She was aware once again of his voice, a rich, deep voice, with a resonance of ironic humor that evoked a memory she couldn't quite hold on to.

"Jason's thirteen. Actually I had two kids with me on Saturday. They both considered your act the high spot of the day," she managed to say.

"Your own kids?" he queried with what he hoped sounded polite, detached interest. He was surprised for a moment at her having a teen-age son. He'd have guessed her too young.

"Only one of them is mine. I'm a single parent, and so is my neighbor, so we usually combine the gang for outings." Annie felt the heat of embarrassment slide up her neck and over her face. Fool, she chastised herself. He's not interested in your marital status. Whatever had made her volunteer that bit of trivia, anyway?

But David considered it anything but trivial to know she wasn't married, and Annie knew it by something in his eyes. In tandem, her glance and his went down to her left hand, to its naked third finger. She met his gaze and felt hot color burning her face, and just as quickly draining away beneath his steady scrutiny.

"I'm glad they liked my act," he said, bridging the awkward moment. "Kids are difficult to impress these days because magicians have become so good. There's television's Doug Henning, there's David Copperfield, Harry Blackstone, Jr. Each of them brings a vastly different viewpoint to their performances, too. What particular slant on magic will your book have?"

"It's not a how-to book," Annie explained. "It's fiction, the story of a physically handicapped boy who learns to do a trick that hasn't been done for centuries, one that has baffled magicians over the years. There's an element of the supernatural, of mystery."

Now that was a coincidence for you. David thought of the bird-cage illusion, of how close her idea was to what had actually happened to him, almost as if she'd picked the idea for the book right out of his mind. It was uncanny.

He decided to dismiss that reaction as ridiculous. He concentrated instead on how alive her eyes became when she described her writing, shining behind that curtain of thick lashes.

"The biggest problem I'm having is finding an illusion that's conceivable, but not easy to execute. Like your bird cage."

"I can see that would be a problem, all right." He knew she was hinting, and he regretted having to refuse her. But the bird cage was his and his alone.

They exchanged a smile that admitted each knew what the other was thinking, and David went on studying her.

Lush was the word for her hair and lashes, all right. Lush was the best word for the rest of Annie as well, he concluded. She had sun-stained skin that refused to pale to nothingness in the cruel fluorescent light overhead, and the modest mint-colored shirtwaist she wore did nothing to hide full breasts and generous hips beneath its prim buttoned-up front.

"Have you written many other books for youngsters?" he asked, not paying as much attention to what she said as to what his roving eyes were observing.

Trim waist. Wonderful legs, crossed at the knee and sheathed in skin-toned hose, so narrow at the ankle he was sure his thumb and forefinger would fit like a bracelet.

"...and with the fifth one, I just got lucky. It was published almost the very week that the board game Dungeons and Dragons became so popular, and the same group that was fascinated by the game began to buy my book. This one will be my ninth."

She stopped speaking abruptly, and he met her forthright, deep brown eyes with a trace of guilt, conscious of having been looking anywhere but at her eyes. An unexpected wave of sexual need swelled in him, so intense and throbbing and full that he was grateful for the concealing desk between them.

"Have we met somewhere before?" he asked with a sudden frown, and Annie watched the vertical line appear between his thick, dark brows, waited for and then saw that one eyebrow tilted in a question mark as the other lowered, just as she'd known it would.

She shivered, feeling goose bumps cover her arms and legs and lift the soft hairs on the back of her neck.

"No, I'm quite certain we've never met," she said with firm emphasis, avoiding his puzzled glance and beginning an inventory of objects littering his cluttered desk, because a ridiculous feeling made her certain she was telling a lie.

Files, with papers bulging out, two Styrofoam coffee cups with black sludge in the bottom of each, and, half hidden under loose papers and an open medical book, a smooth, polished alabaster egg resting at a crooked angle in a silver cradle, all reminders of those diverse interests of his, sorcery and science.

No framed photos of wife and children.

"Funny, I just have this weird feeling I know you from somewhere...." David realized after he'd said it how trite such a line must sound, and for a moment he, too, was flustered.

"I've a lot of books about magic, if you care to..." he blurted, and then was even more flustered. He'd been about to invite her to his apartment, to browse through the library of esoteric and ancient volumes he'd collected over the years, a library he was proud of having.

He realized in time that it might sound like an invitation to view his etchings. "Tell you what," he amended. "I'll look through them and see what I can find that might work for your book. Most illusions are variations of ancient deceptions, going back to Egyptian times, and there are very few that haven't been documented. But I'll see what I can find, if you like."

"I'd really appreciate that," Annie said sincerely. "I've been using my local public library branch, and the best area seems to be the children's section. The adult stacks have a book or two on Houdini, one on Mother Shiptons's prophecies, and that's about it. My son has more reference books than they do."

"Give me a number where I can reach you, and I'll see what I can do," he promised, and she did, writing her home number on the pad he handed her.

For the next ten minutes, Annie asked technical questions about the paraphernalia magicians used and where they obtained it.

At that point, a tall, austere-looking woman in her late sixties poked her steel-gray head in the door, looked with disapproval at Annie and snapped at David, "I'm holding your calls, but you're running late again, Doctor," before she disappeared.

Annie leaped to her feet, but David waved a staying hand. "Relax," he commanded. "That's just Phyllis. Her mission in life is to run mine for me. I've told her before she's far too obsessed with time," he commented with the half smile Annie had been waiting for without being conscious of it.

"Really, I must go. I have stayed too long," she assured him, and he got to his feet, moving from behind the desk to stand beside her. He came far too near. She moved several steps away.

"Thank you very much. You've been super, giving me all this information," she gabbled, thrown off balance by his physical proximity and the devastating effect it had on her. Every pore was aware of him; her hands ached to reach out and touch him.

She moved another step toward the door, and the sudden awareness that she was leaving, that she probably wouldn't see him again, swept over her with shattering effect.

He followed close behind as she fumbled for the door handle, and then he reached out a hand to shake hers in a gesture of farewell.

It was such an ordinary, everyday movement; yet she had to lift her own hand by force of will, make herself put it in his, deal with the tumult of having him so near she could smell the faint odor of his body, the warm, clean man odor, peculiarly his, that lingered in her memory in some mysterious fashion.

"I enjoyed this past hour, Annie." He smiled, a different smile this time, a whimsical smile, just a bit uncertain, as he held her hand.

Touching him was agony. It reaffirmed all the messages her emotions had been telegraphing, that this man somehow affected her as no other had done in her entire life, and she was compelled to look up, deep into his eyes.

He held her warm hand an endless moment too long, aware that her hands were rather wide and strong, that the skin on the back of her fingers felt soft and smooth.

"I'll call you soon, with that information I promised," he was saying as she all but wrenched her hand free and struggled to open the door.

She hurried through the outer office, oblivious of the curious glances Phyllis was giving her, intent only on escape before she disgraced herself the way she had at the magic show the other day by bursting into tears like an idiot.

It wasn't until she was in the hallway that Annie realized David was still close behind her.

"Annie, Annie wait..." he started to say, and she turned around, just as a woman's teasing call sounded from farther down the hall.

"David, you dope, where were you last night? I thought you promised me you were coming to Jenna's party," the slender dark-haired nurse scolded, sweeping past Annie as if she were invisible, and putting a familiar, restraining hand on David's white-coated arm. "I know eligible bachelors are at a premium in Vancouver, but playing this hard to get is ridiculous," she went on, smiling up at him with beguiling beauty.

Annie's heart felt as if it were about to stop beating. She felt a powerful rush of primitive fury, and for an instant she contemplated grabbing the nurse and flinging her away from David.

In another instant, Annie's brain cataloged what was happening to her, and she was appalled at herself. She was jealous, she was having a fit of violent jealousy over a man she hardly knew.

Saints in heaven, what was happening to her? She'd never been truly jealous over any male in her entire life.

Feeling anger and shame combine in a white hot rush, she whirled around and hurried a few more steps down the long, green painted corridor. When the first stab of pain shot through her neck and back, she ignored it.

But a moment later, a cry of agony she couldn't suppress was torn out of her to echo down the hallway. The pain was so sudden and extreme that even her vision blurred beneath its onslaught, and she staggered as if she'd been drinking, lurching to the side and catching herself by placing a hand on the wall.

It was her back—the old, dreaded, familiar pain that spread through her neck and shoulders and head. She'd thought it was gone, this persistent torment that had recurred at just such unexpected moments as this, all through her life. She gasped as the spasms shot down her arm, up into the back of her head, deep into her spine.

Over Betty's head, David was frowning, conscious that something was happening to Annie, but unable to pinpoint exactly what it could be.

Then he heard the cry, saw Annie stagger and, wrenching his arm away from under Betty's proprietary grip, he moved with the speed of an athlete down the corridor.

He was barely in time to catch her before she fell, and she was only dimly aware of his arms encircling her as the torment grew and engulfed her.

CHAPTER THREE

THE WORDS PENETRATED Annie's foggy brain in a persistent stream.

"Can you describe the pain? Is it constant or intermittent? Is it like the thrust of a knife, or dull? You say you've had these attacks since early childhood, Annie. Is there ever any warning, perhaps a difference in color of your surroundings, a buzzing in your head, a sense of unreality? Who's your family doctor? What medications has he prescribed for this in the past?"

David's rapid, professional questions were endless, and Annie, stretched out on a narrow, wheeled bed in the corridor near his office door, wished between spasms that her stupid problem had occurred anywhere in the western hemisphere but here, that she'd had this attack in front of anyone but him.

Nice going, Annie.

She answered his questions, aware every horrible second of being prone and helpless, of feeling stupid and vulnerable when she'd wanted above all to appear professional and capable to him.

There was a coffee stain on the front of his white coat that she hadn't noticed before, and she tried to center her attention on it, attempt the relaxation techniques that one of the endless list of specialists she'd visited had suggested as a last resort when these attacks occurred.

Annie heard Phyllis's irritated voice announce from somewhere overhead and behind her bed, "I have Dr. Simpson on the line now, Dr. Roswell."

David moved away, and Annie felt profound gratitude that her old family doctor had been in his office this afternoon. At least he'd confirm what she'd been gasping out for the past twenty minutes—that the pain was not life threatening, it had no known medical origin, and it usually went away by itself after an indeterminate number of hours.

Relax your toes, relax your feet. Relax your ankles, your calves, your knees...

Aghh. A moan escaped despite her best intentions.

When the pain was at its worst like this, it felt as if her neck were breaking, as if her spine were cracking in two.

"Dr. Simpson agrees that a strong muscle relaxant will give you some relief," David was saying, and the nurse who'd been hanging on his arm and flirting a short while before was now sponging Annie's arm with antiseptic, efficient and oozing professional concern.

Annie wanted to object—she'd had these shots before, and they'd turned her into a vegetable for hours.

"I don't want…"

But she had to close her eyes and bite her tongue against the pain as it swelled, reaching a nauseating crescendo. She panted and felt perspiration break out on her forehead. The minor prick of the needle in her upper arm barely registered.

"I want to go home," she managed to say next. "There's no need to keep me here, I want to go home. Now." She opened her eyes, and stared straight up at David.

He was bending over her, one arm resting beside her shoulder on the narrow cot, and she felt a ridiculous happiness for an instant, just having him this close to her.

He was frowning, and his blue gaze looked concerned and puzzled as he met Annie's eyes.

A tiny muscle around her mouth jerked as she strove to stay in control.

Then Annie could feel the drug beginning its numbing journey through her veins, and she felt a desperate, urgent need to escape this place before her eyelids grew heavy and sleep overcame her as it always did as a result of this shot.

She didn't want to fall asleep here in the corridor, helpless in front of Phyllis, in front of the dark-haired nurse. She didn't want to be vulnerable in their presence. She wanted to go home.

"Did you drive over, Annie? Where's your car? Is there someone I can phone to come and get you, a…friend, perhaps?"

David was unaware of holding his breath in tense anticipation for the time it took her to answer. She was lovely. There had to be a male friend, a lover. There wasn't time to wonder why he cared, why it should be an urgent matter to him.

"Nobody except my neighbor, Cleo, and she's taken all the kids camping till tomorrow," Annie said with a dejected tone to her voice. She could feel herself beginning to slur the words, too. "Please, just call me a cab. I'll arrange about my car…"

"Nonsense." The plan had formed the instant she answered, and he acted on it. "Phyllis, arrange a special permit for her car. What make is it, Annie? It's in that lot at the side of the building? See that security understands it will be there until tomorrow at least. And Phyllis, have the attendant in the underground park bring my car to the side entrance. Nurse, find me a wheelchair.''

Everything was growing vague and distant in a pleasant, giddy way, and the torture in her neck had dulled now to a blissful, almost bearable ache.

She heard David issuing instructions, canceling appointments, and she paid little attention. Everything was receding, getting farther and farther away, less real to her.

Soon she was going to be asleep, and the reluctance she'd felt moments before no longer mattered at all.

Annie gave a wide yawn as the nurse helped her slide off the stretcher bed. Then she was strapped into a wheelchair and pushed down the corridor.

A polished silver-gray car, roomy and sleek, was parked close to the curb, engine running. With the nurse's help, Annie struggled in, drawing the rich leather upholstery smell deep into her nostrils.

She watched the young driver slide out and David come hurrying over, tugging on a tweed sport jacket and handing the boy a large tip and a word of thanks as he slid in behind the wheel.

A muted protest sounded deep inside, but it didn't reach her lips. It was just too much trouble.

Sinking back into the luxurious gray seat, expelling a huge sigh, Annie closed her eyes, willing to let whatever fate was in control carry on as if everything was normal.

"Hey, sleepyhead, you have to give me your address," his voice was saying.

Even with her eyes closed, she could envision the way the beginning of a smile was tilting the corners of his wide mouth, the way an eyebrow arched with gentle humor. He was watching her. She could sense his gaze, but she didn't mind. She loved having him look at her.

After a moment's thought, while a tiny frown creased the smooth skin in the middle of her forehead, she slowly, with great effort, repeated the numbers and the street.

"Gotcha." David reached across her, grasped the seat belt and drew it over her prone form, snapping it in place and allowing his hand to graze the satin skin of her arm before he jerked away and in one easy gesture guided the car free of the curb.

For Annie, there was no memory of time between that moment and the next, when she came out of sleep and became aware of David's hands unlocking the belt around her, his strong arms half lifting her out of the car in front of her house.

"We're here, Annie. Do you want me to carry you?"

"No, I don't. I can walk by myself," she protested with groggy dignity.

He took in the defiant tilt of her rounded chin and the hazy confusion in her sleepy eyes. She stumbled a bit when her shoes touched the sidewalk. With an amused half laugh he looped an arm around her waist, and even through the effects of the drug she shivered at that contact.

"I'm sure you can, but just let me help a bit. Neck all right?" he inquired, distressing her because his lips were close to her ear.

The burning sensation in her back was still intense, but the pain was far-off, and she told him so as she struggled to control her knees and make her feet go where her brain ordered. They progressed inch by inch up the cement path to her front door, and then Annie fumbled for endless moments in her straw handbag for her key. She finally located it with numb fingers and handed it to David.

"Can you unlock it please?"

"Sure can." It was more difficult than he'd anticipated, however. When he released his hold on her the slightest bit, she began to crumble in slow motion toward the ground. Finally, with a sigh of relief, he managed to release the lock, and he half carried her in, looking around for somewhere to put her. There was a huge, soft sofa in the living room to the right of the door.

She gave him a sleepy, friendly grin as he laid her down and tucked a pillow beneath her head, and with a supreme effort, she drew her legs up one by one so they rested on the sofa.

Her shoes were still on, and David hesitated, then struggled with the straps on her high-heeled sandals, muttering an oath under his breath as they defied his best attempts. Finally he settled for inching the straps over her heels without undoing them. He dropped the shoes on the floor.

"I thought magicians were good at undoing things," she mumbled, and David laughed at the unintentional innuendo of her words.

"I guess I haven't practiced much on women's shoes," he confessed, and she nodded as if that made perfect sense.

"Are you going away now?" she said next, and the intense anxiety in her voice and eyes surprised him. "I know you must, but I wish there was more time..." Her voice trailed off into a mumble.

He had been planning to return to the hospital right away. By now, Phyllis would have canceled his most urgent appointments, but there was always paperwork to catch up on, and of course the dinner date later with Calvin. He hadn't told Phyllis to cancel that.

For some inexplicable reason, he decided to stay a while. He deserved to play hooky once in a while, and today was that once, he assured his conscience.

He walked back into the entrance hall, down the short passage that led to the high-ceilinged kitchen, searching for a phone. There was one on the spacious counter.

"Phyllis? Listen, cancel all my appointments for the rest of the day." He listened, and added, "Yeah, cancel dinner with Calvin, too, please. I know he won't be too happy, but do it anyway and don't bitch at me, okay? Oh, and Phyllis, call the Quinlins, Carrie's folks, and ask them to meet me in the coffee shop tomorrow morning at ten and I'll give them all the details about her surgery."

He hung the phone up and looked around. Nice, homey kitchen, really well equipped. He'd bet Annie liked to cook. The place had an efficient yet warm feeling to it, and there were well-used utensils hanging over the stove.

Why had he suddenly decided to stay here? Well, he rationalized, Annie shouldn't be left alone. The powerful relaxant he'd administered would affect her for at least another few hours, and it was possible that she might try to get up, fall and hurt herself.

And that was a crock, he admitted with a twisted, honest grin. He wouldn't be here if she were a man, or anyone at all except Annie, because there was no real danger.

He walked back into the living room and studied the lines of her face against the pale rose pillow. Her eyes were closed. A pang of intense emotion clenched at his insides.

She was desirable, stretched out limp like that. Her skirt had ridden up above her knees, and her long legs were curled to one side, her arm folded beneath her. Soft tendrils of hair, a rich red-brown streaked with golden highlights, had come loose from the knot on her neck and lay in disarray across her ear and shoulder. Her skin was flushed a bit, and he had the most intense desire to lean over her, stroke his hand across her cheek and smooth the hair away from her face, just to test its silk texture on his fingers.

What the hell's getting into you, Roswell? You're a doctor, and technically, she's your patient. That's why you're here, remember? You're responsible for her well-being, which doesn't include sensuous stroking when she's half asleep, for Pete's sake.

Sound asleep, he corrected, looking at her again. Annie's breasts rose and fell beneath the pale green dress, and she sighed.

There was a knitted afghan in shades of rose and blue across the sofa back, and he hurried to shake it out and cover her with it, neck to toes.

When that was done, he moved away, undecided again as to what he should do next.

Annie's home was welcoming and cheerful, quiet, with pleasing mixtures of bright colors scattered here and there. Purple and rose and blue throw pillows hugged the couch where Annie lay, and a wall of shelves held books and small objects. Blue venetian blinds at the windows contrasted against muted cream walls and a darker blue rug.

David wandered over to the stereo, curious about the tapes arranged on the rack over the machine. The mixture of musical tastes represented was a vivid reminder that Annie had a teenage son: Michael Jackson and Ravel's "Bolero." Men Without Hats and Glen Campbell. Willie Nelson and Prince, Neil Diamond and Lori Anderson.

A few muttered words from behind him brought his attention back to the woman on the sofa.

"...hear the birds. Is that a mockingbird in the apple tree?"

David strolled over to her. It was obvious she was dreaming. But when he drew close, he realized her eyes were open, and seemed to look straight up at him, the pupils dark and dilated.

"Are you awake, Annie?" he queried in a soft voice. "Do you mind if I play some music?"

Annie could hear him, from a far distance, asking her about music, but it was difficult to separate the dream from reality because his voice blended with the other voice she could hear. Present and beyond were fading into each other.

Something strange was happening to her, strange indeed. Her eyes were open, and she understood for brief seconds that she was in her own living room, but it was as though a movie screen stood between her and the reality of her home, as if she could watch the movie and act in it at the same time.

Then the images grew too strong to resist, and her living room faded, and she was young, in love, in some far distant place.

SHE WAS SO GLAD to have him with her this afternoon. Overwhelming tenderness for the man walking close at her side, holding her hand, filled her heart with joy. She loved him, and it made her happy.

It was a summer afternoon. Bird song filled the air along with the smell of earth and growing things. Now and then a pungent farm odor from the small holdings that lay along the fertile loops of the river made her wrinkle her nose, but even that had an earthy appeal.

Wildflowers bloomed, and the air was heavy with summer's warmth.

"Hear...music?"

Her lover's question wasn't clear, but she turned her face up to his and smiled into his deep blue eyes.

"It's just the birds, and the wind in the trees," she murmured. "Remember, darling, this is where we sat and had our lunch that other afternoon."

She gave him a shy glance, full of meaning. They'd lain there naked under the sheltering trees, as close as it was possible to be, and moved in each other's arms, moved in each other's bodies, until the world shattered and erupted in hot ecstasy, and she'd cried out and held him there inside her with her legs, and then wept afterward, and he'd stroked her tears away with his tongue.

She loved him with an intensity that frightened her, and as she looked up into his beloved face, she felt a foreshadowing trace of pain and fear that formed a constricting band around her heart that made her struggle to escape the dream. But it was woven in firm tendrils around her, and she couldn't escape its fabric just yet.

"Love, don't go, will you?" she begged him.

THE PASSIONATE WHISPER, the disconnected sentences she spoke were no doubt part of her dreaming, and David stood over her, observing the naked longing on her face, unable to look away from the tenderness and passionate feeling mirrored there.

Who was she seeing with eyes so heavy with love? Who inspired that devotion on her features, that soft moistness around her full, parted lips?

He felt strong emotion well in him, a feeling that might have been jealousy, and he dismissed it with impatient reason. Surely her dreams were private, and he should respect them as such.

"You won't go yet, beloved? You'll stay with me until night comes?" Her whispering voice was husky, heavy with a sensuousness that captivated him.

David couldn't stop himself. He bent over her, and placed his lips on hers, a light caress, almost innocent, allowing only his lips to touch her, but needing in some obscure way to make his presence known to her, to woo her away from that dream lover who held her captive.

He felt the heat of her, the petal softness of her lips against his own. He could detect a faint acid vestige of the drug he'd given her on her breath, along with a sweetness only Annie's.

She felt his mouth, locked in her dream, and she knew only that the lips on hers were those of her lover, her soul companion, and there was nothing else in the world she wanted or needed or desired. Only him, only his love. Forever.

"Sleep well, Annie. I'll stay until you wake up," David whispered, straightening, tugging the afghan closer around her shoulder, stroking a knuckle lightly down her flushed cheek.

It had taken a definite effort of will to take his mouth from hers. He shoved his hands into the pockets of his trousers, walked over to the window and stared without seeing out at the overgrown greenness of the backyard. Kissing her that way had left him unsettled, a trifle guilty, but excited as well.

He wanted to know her, know the real, waking Annie. He wanted to strip away the social mask he'd seen her wear that afternoon when she was interviewing him, locate instead this passionate, fiery woman she became in her dreams. He wanted to kiss her when she was awake, when she knew it was him instead of some damned fantasy.

He gave a deep sigh and a small, rueful smile crept across his mouth as he searched the recordings for one he'd noticed of Zamfir playing the pan flute.

The eerie, haunting music filled the room, and David chose a book at random from the shelves and settled himself in a comfortable armchair near the window, where he could glance over at Annie.

A thought occurred to him, and he smiled again. Magicians about to create an illusion often referred to putting their audience under the "fluence." The woman sleeping there had David Roswell under her "fluence," and he wanted to be part of the illusion of love she'd created in her dreams.

He would be part of it. He settled back and waited without much patience for her to awaken.

CHAPTER FOUR

ANNIE NOTICED SHADOWS creeping into the corners of the room.

She'd opened her eyes a moment before, but the delicious lassitude that filled her body and her mind made it impossible to move quite yet. And really, there was no need, was there? A sense of utter relaxation, of thick and heavy peace permeated her being.

"Annie? Are you awake?"

The deep, questioning male voice seemed a natural part of her waking at first, but as she grew more aware, surprise filled her.

"David? You stayed here this long? How late is it, anyway?" She cleared her husky throat and squinted at the evening shadows, raising her head with caution, anticipating pain. But there was only a dull ache as she wriggled to a sitting position, moving the afghan away from her body and tugging down the skirt of her crumpled green dress. Then she stretched her legs out to flex their cramped muscles.

He was over by the window, in her favorite armchair, and she was grateful that he allowed her these waking moments in relative privacy.

"It's..." He glanced at his wristwatch and his voice registered his own surprise when he said, "Hey, it's nearly seven. You slept four full hours. Is the pain gone?"

Annie again moved her head first one way and then the other. A relieved half smile touched her lips and she nodded. "Completely gone," she said on a long, relieved sigh.

He got up and came over to her, and she noticed that his suit jacket was now off, his tie hanging loose at his open shirt collar, the cuffs on his off-white shirt rolled to his forearms. The dark, curling hairs on the back of his wrists made a sharp contrast with the pale cotton fabric.

A wave of shyness rolled over her. There was an intimate feeling about being here with this man after he'd watched her sleep. He must have covered her with the afghan. He'd taken her shoes off; she did remember that much.

She'd been dreaming, a weird, crazy dream, undoubtedly caused by the drugs. But her brain was beginning to function again, and she gave him a puzzled look. "I'm grateful, but there wasn't any need for you to stay with me, David. I would have been fine on my own."

He nodded agreement, and his wide mouth tilted upward at the corners. A quizzical expression came into his eyes.

"You probably would have been fine, yes. The simple truth is I wanted to stay." His glance slid away from her to take in the details of the room.

"I enjoyed being here. You have a comfortable home, Annie. I took the liberty of using your tape deck and browsing through your books. It's not often I have a chance to just laze away an afternoon." His smile was conspirational and warm.

Annie frowned up at him, trying to make sense of it all and failing. He must have had appointments today with others besides her, things that demanded his attention, and yet here he was, looking relaxed and perfectly at home in her living room.

She reached up to brush away a tendril of hair and realized that she must look a complete mess. The careful chignon she'd fashioned was undone, any makeup she might have had on must be gone, and her dress was a wrinkled wreck.

"Besides, I'm starving," she blurted out, and he laughed as if he'd guessed the rest of her thought pattern.

"That's proof positive that you're feeling better," he teased. "Now that you mention it, so am I hungry." He hesitated an instant, and then said, "Shall we go out and find a restaurant?"

Annie stood, testing her body and finding it back to normal.

David seemed much taller when she wasn't wearing heels.

"How do you feel about leftover lasagna?" she said with impulsive zeal. "I've got some in the fridge. I could heat it up in the microwave and make a salad."

"Are you certain you feel like doing that?"

She nodded and he smiled with pleasure. "Sounds great to me. As long as you let me help. I'm not bad at making salads, if you steer me toward the ingredients and a sharp knife."

"Give me a minute, and I'll be right back." Annie headed for the stairs, calling over her shoulder, "I think there's a cold beer in the fridge if you'd like."

Did he drink beer, she wondered? *He liked wine.*

Halfway up, she paused for a moment, staring out the landing window at Cleo's darkened house and wondering what in hell she was doing, inviting a man she barely knew to stay for dinner. She hadn't had a man at the dinner table for—how long?

Well, no big deal, she rationalized. Leftovers, Annie, just leftovers.

No candles, no wine, no spiderwebs. What made her think he liked wine?

Look, idiot, you owe him. He drove you home, took care of you, took off your shoes and covered you up.

A wispy memory of lips brushing hers with urgent softness came and was gone again before she could pin it down. She shook her head and three pins fell out on the carpeted stairs, reminding her of what she was supposed to be doing.

She hurried up to the bathroom and let out a groan when she caught sight of herself in the full-length mirror.

Fifteen minutes later, dressed in worn jeans and a bright red patterned rayon shirt tied in a knot at her waist, feet bare, Annie entered the kitchen. She'd washed her face and left it clean of all but pale lipstick and a touch of mascara. She'd brushed her hair and braided it, letting it hang in one long, thick plait down her back.

David was standing at the counter, a drawer open in front of him and an unopened bottle of beer in his hand.

"Can't find the opener to save my soul," he said, turning toward her. He looked her over with unabashed interest. "You look different," he added, studying her naked face, letting his gaze rove over the snug jeans and casual blouse. "You look about fifteen years old."

"Sir, this is the real me," Annie said with an attempt at flip humor, hoping he didn't notice the flush of color she felt at his words. "That other outfit was just a clever disguise." She located an opener, handing it to him without meeting his eyes, then turned away and started taking things out of the fridge. "I'm a peasant at heart."

"You enjoy cooking," he said. It was a statement rather than a question.

Annie smiled at him over her shoulder. "I sure do. If I didn't, heaven knows what it would cost me for take-out food for my kid. Teenage boys have appetites that have to be witnessed to be believed."

"So I've heard. I still can't believe you have a teenager."

"You don't have any kids?" The question was out before she could censor it.

He shook his head. "My wife didn't want any," he explained, and then added with deliberate casualness, "My ex-wife, that is. We've been divorced for four years now."

Overwhelming relief engulfed Annie, and she bent down and started pulling lettuce and green onions out of the vegetable tray so he couldn't see her face.

"How about you? How long have you been alone, Annie?"

She stood, avoiding his eyes, and plunked the salad makings on the counter.

"Always," she said in an even tone. "I decided not to marry Jason's father at all. So you see, I'm not a divorced single parent. I'm a single parent, period."

"And do you sock everybody who asks you why you decided to stay single?"

She looked up at him in surprise, unaware of how belligerent she'd sounded. Humor deepened the blue of his eyes as well as the tiny wrinkles surrounding them, and she had to smile back at him as he took the leaves of lettuce and started rinsing them under the tap.

"You know, hardly anyone's ever asked me why? Most people want to know if I get any support money."

"So why did you decide to stay single?"

He was persistent. Annie took a knife out of a wooden holder and started peeling an avocado. Her forehead creased in a frown.

"It's hard to explain. I was in love with...with this guy named Michael McCrae..."

Why was it always difficult for her to even say his name?

"Or thought I was. He was an engineer, five years older than me. I wasn't a kid at the time, either. I was twenty-one years old. He wanted the baby, wanted me." A shiver ran down her spine, remembering. "And the worst part was I didn't decide not to marry him until the day before the wedding."

"Deserted at the altar. So he was a touch annoyed with you." Once again, it was more statement than question. She glanced up and found David watching her.

"Yeah, you could say that he was a bit put out, all right," she said with ironic lack of emphasis.

"What happened?"

Michael had been more than angry. He'd been furious, livid. His absolute rage had terrified her. When he had finally understood that Annie meant what she said, that she had no intention of ever marrying him, he'd launched a vicious court battle for custody of his still unborn baby that had lasted until Jason was born and well over a year old.

"He fought me for custody. The thing was, I felt that it wasn't so much because he wanted the baby. It was simply that he wanted to hurt me any way he could."

His actions had underlined for her the rightness of calling off the wedding. Michael had illustrated the very things Annie had begun to sense about him; that underneath his quiet surface, there was a deep possessive strain, a jealousy and potential for violence in Michael's nature that frightened and repulsed her.

"He fought me for five months before Jason was born, and a full year afterward. Thirteen years ago, that was quite unusual, a biological father fighting for custody of an unborn child. I often think he might have had a much better chance now than he did then." Annie kept her tone as impassive as she could, hiding the deep and bitter hurt that still lingered over those long-ago memories. "Anyway, he lost. Thank God."

It was significant that she didn't say instead that she'd won. There hadn't been triumph for her that day after the court decision, only profound relief. And physical terror such as she'd never experienced before or after. The scene in front of the courthouse that afternoon twelve years before was still fresh in her mind, the horrifying moment when she'd come, by accident, face-to-face with Michael.

"Bitch, you cheating bitch, I'll kill you for this."

The murderous rage in his eyes was seared forever into her soul. He'd lunged toward her, and grabbed her by the shoulders. She'd felt his hands digging deeper and deeper into her flesh, sensed the muscles in his arms contracting, and with awful certainty she'd known that he was going to shake her like a rag doll, until her neck snapped.

Adrenaline surged even now at the memory, and the knife in her hand slipped, just missing her fingers.

David swore and took it from her.

"Let me do that. I'm quite good with knives. We surgeons have to practice on salads before they turn us loose on people." He smoothly sliced a tomato into thin pieces and when he spoke again the light, teasing note was absent from his voice.

"I'm sorry, Annie. I didn't mean to upset you. I had no right to pry."

She shrugged with an attempt at nonchalance that failed. "I didn't have to answer you."

The astonishing thing was that she had answered. It had taken Cleo well over a determined year to uncover the things Annie had just told David.

"True." He nodded, and began chopping the lettuce while she found a wooden bowl and rubbed its inner surface with a cut garlic clove.

"Maybe that stuff you injected me with was actually truth serum," she teased. It took real effort to move away from those memories of the past.

He shook his head. "Nope, we sorcerers never have to resort to anything like that. We just cast a spell—nothing to it—and from that moment on, we see and know all.''

Annie smiled at his banter, even as she ackowledged the ironic truth in what he said. She actually felt as if David had cast some sort of spell over her and could see into her heart. She'd been aware of it from the very first moment she saw him up on that stage, and now the feeling intensified.

When she took plates and cutlery to set the table in the dining room, David motioned to the small wooden table under the kitchen window, where Annie and Jason normally ate, and said in a plaintive tone, "Can't we have dinner right here? I have this thing about kitchens. We always ate in the kitchen when I was a kid and I loved it."

So she wiped off the battered wooden surface and used the everyday straw mats. Dusk became darkness outside, and Annie twisted the venetian blinds shut, encompassing the two of them in the warm and cozy room.

Deliberately she turned their conversation to books, and then to music, and as she served their meal, David related amusing stories about magic tricks he'd attempted and failed at with spectacular and funny effect. He told of wild things that had happened during performances. He described for Annie the ingenious ways magicians had of covering mistakes and making them appear part of their act.

He made her laugh and he laughed with her. Their laughter filled the room, the easy spontaneous delight of two people who find the same ridiculous things amusing.

And as time drifted by, Annie found herself filing away the things he revealed about himself, almost as though they were souvenirs she could take out and fondle again when this strange evening was over. Would she ever see him again, or was this all they'd ever share?

"Let's move into the living room where it's more comfortable for coffee and dessert," she suggested, not daring to think beyond the moment.

Together they cleared away the dishes and stacked them in the dishwasher. He helped her carry the coffee tray she prepared into the living room, and they sat on the sofa, the tray between them on the low coffee table.

"When I came to your office today," Annie ventured as she handed him a bowl of ice cream smothered with her own preserved brandied cherries, "you said something about a TV interview, which had to do with heart and liver transplants for children. Is that an area of medicine you're particularly interested in?"

She watched as he swallowed a mouthful of the dessert, tracing the strong muscles in his throat with her eyes.

"Yeah, Annie, it sure is." He stirred cream into his coffee. He sat forward on his chair, setting his bowl down. His voice took on a new intensity.

"Not performing the operations. I don't have the training or the skill for that. But teams of skilled professionals are available as soon as the facilities are in place here. At the moment, B.C. has no provincial budget for such procedures, and the kids needing them have to go out-of-province. But there's also the problem of donors, you see. There has to be a major educational campaign, and that, too, takes money."

"Do some of your patients need these operations, David?"

His face was bleak for a moment. "They sure do. Four kids right at the moment. They'll all have to go out of the country if they're going to have the operations they need to live."

Both he and Annie forgot their dessert as David explained the stress and almost overwhelming strain such trips placed on both the children needing them and on their parents.

"I'll give you an example. There's a patient of mine, this little kid named Charlie Vance. He's nearly three. His folks live in a small town in interior B.C. called Enderby, and his dad's a truck driver. They don't have much money. Charlie was born with a liver disorder, and his only hope is a transplant. You've probably seen Charlie's picture in the daily papers, because his folks have no choice but to exploit his cuteness and his plight in order to raise the formidable amount of money required to take him to a U.S. medical center for treatment. They have another baby, a little girl, and it looks as if she's inherited the same problem Charlie has."

Annie made a despairing sound in her throat at the unfairness of such a destiny.

David nodded. "Can you imagine the agony these young parents go through, having to exploit one desperately sick child just to raise money for a procedure that ought to be available here...will be available if the mills of government ever decide lives are on an equal level with roads? And the only thing the Vances have to look forward to is going through the whole damned procedure all over again with their daughter, because I can't promise those parents that when baby Angela's condition demands a transplant as well, we'll be able to perform it here at home."

David's voice was bitter but resigned. "Chances are they'll just have to undergo the same media exposure, the same demeaning hands-out-for-donations performance that they're going through right now for Charlie."

Annie felt shaken. She'd read the articles in the papers, looked at the appealing photos of children like Charlie. She'd even donated money to such causes, without ever once personalizing the experience, or questioning why a child should be in such a begging situation. Her ignorance made her feel ashamed.

The depth of David's caring was evident in every word, and his passion was revealed through his voice, the way he leaned forward, the graphic motions his hands made as he spoke.

"We need the facility desperately, and we need it now," he concluded. "The feeling among most of the hospital board is that there's no real urgency because there aren't hundreds of kids standing in line to use it. There are relatively few in relation to the other problems we treat. But every day of delay for those few like Charlie means that their chances for life grow slimmer, their families' chances of survival as a unit grow fewer."

Annie was silent, thinking over what he'd said, and also what he hadn't had to say. It was obvious David Roswell loved his job more than anything else in his life. There was none of the detachment she'd have expected in him, none of the distancing she'd always heard was essential for a doctor dealing with high-risk patients. He cared and he showed it. He was open and honest and vehement in his convictions.

Her soul responded, *Hasn't he always been this way?*

"Did you always want to be a doctor, David?"

He was gulping coffee that had to be stone-cold by now, and he waved away her offer to reheat it.

"You mean did someone give me a little doctor's bag the way my uncle did that magic kit?" He shook his head and laughed. "I think being a doctor is born in some people, like having six toes or a white streak in your hair for no reason. As far back as I can remember, I knew I'd be a doctor. There was never any question in my mind."

"Did you come from a large family?" The need to know about him was insatiable, and he seemed willing to answer her questions.

"Nope, I was an only child. I grew up in Toronto, and my parents were professional people. Dad was a research analyst for a chemical company, and my mother taught high-school English. So in many ways I was fortunate because there was enough money for education, and they were supportive of me in every way."

"They must be very proud of you." Annie thought for a moment of how bitter and disappointed her mother had been with her until she achieved some success at writing. That disapproval and the pain it had caused her had made Annie vow that whatever Jason did with his life would be fine with her. That awful, crushing sense of parental disapproval wouldn't ever be part of her son's life if she could help it.

David had finished his dessert, and now he carefully put the bowl and spoon down before he looked over at Annie.

"My parents died several years ago in the Mexican earthquake," he explained. "They used to go to the same isolated resort every year, to an old hotel run by a family they'd come to love over the years. The roof collapsed, and mostly everyone was killed. Their bodies were finally uncovered about a week later."

"David, I'm sorry." The words sounded inadequate. Annie could imagine that having both parents die suddenly must have been awful for him.

David was as open about his feelings as he'd been about everything else she asked. "It was a shock at the time. I miss them, but it's exactly what they'd have wanted, given a choice. They both had a horror of being old and helpless, and they were very much in love even after all those years of marriage. This way, neither had to suffer losing the other."

This time his smile was enigmatic, with more than a trace of sadness, and his eyes seemed to caress Annie's face as he added, "They misled me, you see, those parents of mine. Because of them, I grew up believing that marriage was a wonderful institution. When mine failed, I wasted a lot of time trying to figure out where I'd gone wrong before it finally dawned on me that my parents' relationship was the exception rather than the rule, and that more often than not, marriage simply doesn't work. Nobody's fault."

Marriage wasn't something Annie felt she could discuss with any expertise at all, but his conclusions about most marriages were basically the same as hers.

"I was an only child, too," she confided. "My father died when I was eleven, and my mother never remarried. From what I remember, their relationship was nothing like the one your parents had, but it was workable. I had a good, solid childhood."

"And you were never tempted to even try marriage after that first time?"

Annie shook her head. "Nope."

"That's unusual. You're a beautiful, sensual woman, Annie. You obviously love children. Don't you ever get lonely?"

His voice had deepened, and Annie's heart began to pound, at the intimate tone as well as his actual words.

"Of course I do," she said, and her voice was ragged despite her efforts at control. "But I'm aware that not everyone's cut out for marriage. You said as much yourself. I'm not—I know that. Besides, how many marriages do you know of that are happy, besides the one your parents had?''

He looked distressed, and reached a hand out and laid it on her bare forearm, showing her how tense her body had become. She was also aware of his long, smooth fingers touching her skin, making every nerve ending come alive with a sensation almost painful, and causing the delicate hair on her forearm to stand on end.

"Annie, I'm not criticizing you. I'd never do that. I'm simply trying to understand. I want to know you better, that's all.''

Wasn't that exactly what she wanted as well—to get to know this man who managed to stir such confused responses in her?

She made a conscious effort to relax. "Sorry. I guess I'm paranoid about this marriage thing. There's a lot of pressure when you've got a mother with traditional values constantly lecturing about how hard it is to raise a teenage boy without a strong man around. She's spending a year in Florida with a friend, and believe me, it feels like a parole not to have her watching my every move with Jason.''

This time his voice was cool and cautious. "And there isn't a man around?'' He didn't quite meet her eyes this time.

A tiny, delighted smile flickered across her lips. She sensed by his attempt at nonchalance that the question was important to him, and a glad rush of joy surged through her, knowing that it mattered.

"No," she said. "There isn't a man around.''

Time pulsed, and pulsed again.

"I'm glad, Annie.''

David drew his breath in and let it out again in what could only be a relieved sigh. Silence fell between them, a charged silence during which Annie repeated his three simple, complicated words in her head...I'm glad, Annie...and reflected on the strangeness of having him, sitting beside her...and on the conviction that being with him this way was right.

"This afternoon I found several of the books you've written over there in the bookcase," he remarked after a while. "I didn't have time enough to read them thoroughly, but what comes through is how well you remember what it's like to be a child. You manage to incorporate fantasy and reality in a believable way. It's no wonder your books sell, Annie.''

She flushed with honest pleasure and thanked him just as the phone in the kitchen began to ring.

"Excuse me, David.'' She answered it, still smiling.

"Annie, I hope I'm not disturbing you," the familiar male voice said, and she stiffened and turned away from the living room.

"But you are disturbing me," she said in a low, passionate tone. "I've told you a million times that I don't want you to call here, Michael."

And why did he have to call now, at this moment? It was almost as if she'd somehow initiated this call just by mentioning his name earlier. Frustration filled her, and the impotent anger and unease that talking with Michael McCrae roused in her churned her stomach into a knot.

His tone was quiet and patient. "I apologize, but you do see that going through you is the only rational way for me to arrange to meet my son, Annie. Whatever you feel about me, Jason is my son, and I want to get to know him. With your full approval."

Annie knew that this new, quiet, reasonable persona Michael had adopted since he'd reappeared in her life was all a clever act designed to lull her into acquiescence.

"This isn't a convenient time," she insisted with stubborn emphasis.

"Then you set a time and place, and I'll meet you and we can talk this thing through." A deep sigh sounded over the wire. "Please, Annie. I don't want to have to go through another court battle with you. Think what it would do to Jason. He's not a baby this time."

"I'll..." She turned and shot a glance into the quiet living room, knowing that David had to be overhearing her end of this conversation, hating the uncomfortable situation Michael was forcing on her, hating the need to deal with him at all.

"I'll think it over and let you know. That's the best I can do."

"You have our number, Annie. Call anytime at all."

She hung up and when the connection was broken, realized that the palms of her hands were sweating. She rubbed them down the legs of her jeans and drew in a deep breath, expelling it bit by bit before she made her way back into the other room.

David was just sliding a tape into the deck on the stereo, and soft music filled the room.

"Everything all right?" he queried, and she knew his penetrating glance was assessing her strained features and the new, stiff movements of her body.

"Sure, everything..." She paused. Within her was the unreasonable, overwhelming conviction that she shouldn't ever lie to this particular man, but her private nature made it impossible to confide in him any more than she'd already done tonight.

Besides, it was embarrassing. How could she blurt out any more of the convoluted tale of her association with Michael McCrae, explaining that for twelve blessed years, he'd all but disappeared from her life?

After the trial, he'd gone to India on assignment for the engineering firm he worked for, eventually taking an Indian woman as his wife. He'd stayed on and on. As the years passed, Annie had slowly come to believe she'd never see him again, and it gave her an immense feeling of relief.

Then, for some inexplicable reason, Michael had returned to Vancouver three months ago. And, like a bad dream, the whole problem of access to her son had started all over again, started with phone calls like this one, with Michael wanting to share part of Jason's life.

After all these years. He had no right, no right at all.

"Annie?" David came over to her and put a hand under her elbow. "You're pale again. Not feeling dizzy, are you? Your neck's fine?"

She forced a wide smile, hoping it didn't look as phony as it felt. She looked into David's clear blue eyes and wished with all her heart that her life was just beginning right here and now, that there wasn't any Michael to contend with, that she was free to just...belong...to this man.

But life wasn't that simple, was it? There were no brand-new beginnings, unburdened by baggage from the past.

"I'm fine, David," she insisted. "Everything's fine."

"Good," he said. And then his other arm came around her and he drew her into his embrace. She felt her body come into contact with his, separated only by clothing, and a part of her mind registered how well their spaces still fitted each other. She absorbed the welcome warmth he exuded, and she knew this was the only place in the entire world she longed to be at this particular moment.

At any moment.

He slid one hand up her back, along her neck and under the heavy braid, fingers tender, playing along her scalp.

"Annie," he said, as if saying her name pleased him.

He studied each detail of her face, unhurriedly, questioningly, and then he bent his head and his lips covered hers.

CHAPTER FIVE

AT FIRST HE ONLY BRUSHED her mouth with the tenderest of kisses, soft, elusive, tantalizing, as questioning as the look he'd given her a moment before. But with the full meeting of their lips, the caress changed. His arms tightened around her and a low groan rose in his throat.

Annie's lips parted in eager welcome, and suddenly they were locked together in a scalding, drugging embrace, his lips and hers moving with hungry need, intent on discovering every way possible of tasting, teasing, shaping to suit and delight the other.

Annie's body filled with heat, softening and melting against him, and it was glorious to feel the ripe hardness of his erection against her belly.

Mindless, she moved her hips in cadence with the rhythm pounding through her blood, the rhythm of his tongue thrusting and withdrawing, plunging deep into her mouth with sweet, hot abandon.

As unexpectedly as it began, the kiss ended. Annie wasn't sure which of them drew away first. She knew only that she was standing on legs that trembled, a few feet away from him. His hands were on her shoulders, his grip almost painful, and he looked at her with eyes still clouded with desire.

"Lord," he whispered, his voice hoarse. "I want you, Annie. I want to take you right here on the floor, right now. I don't understand how this could happen so fast, but it has."

His words sent a shudder coursing through her, because it was so exactly what she wanted as well. But the tumult of emotions he roused in her were too new, too complex. She felt as if an integral part of her might shatter, irreparably, if the depth of feeling he roused was taken to its sensual limit tonight.

She didn't have to try to put the feeling into words, because he pulled her into his arms for one last, quick hug, and then, obviously reluctant, dropped his arms and with deliberation stepped away from her.

"Because of that damned injection, you're still technically my patient tonight," he said with rough irony. "And I don't seduce my patients." A rueful grin came and went. "But I'm severing our professional relationship as of this moment, Annie. After tonight, I give you fair warning, we're simply man and woman." Again his crooked smile played across his lips, but Annie knew he meant every word. "You'll have to find yourself another doctor, Ms Pendleton."

He turned and retrieved his tweed jacket, still tossed over the sofa arm where he'd left it earlier, and shrugged the garment on with careless grace.

"I'm leaving now, because I can't promise I'll be this honorable for even another five minutes."

At the door, he leaned toward her and brushed a light kiss on the tip of her nose.

"Thank you for supper, Ms Pendleton. Will you be home tomorrow?"

She nodded.

"I'll call." He gave her a formal little bow.

He was gone then, moving with the litheness that was somehow familiar to her.

Annie stood in the open doorway until the engine of his car purred to life. The night was star-studded, the neighborhood quiet until, a few blocks away, a fire truck began wailing, its undulating cry slowly receding as the taillights of David's car disappeared down the street.

She closed the door as if doing so took all the energy she possessed.

IT WAS A FULL WEEK before David kept his long overdue dinner appointment with Calvin Graves.

If David were to describe his old friend, he'd begin by saying the man had incredible energy. Calvin was fifty-six, but it would have been difficult, David always thought, to pin any age on his small-boned, tidy frame.

Tonight, as always, he was impeccably groomed and tailored in a charcoal-gray pin-striped suit and a silky white-on-white shirt. He'd looked askance at David's comfortable, albeit crumpled navy pants and well-worn tweed sports jacket. Calvin shook his head.

"I'm going to have to drag you forcibly to my tailor, David. Clothes may not make the man, but you must at least have heard the expression 'dress for success.'"

David had given him a deadpan look. "And you must have heard about rough cut stone. Give it up, Calvin. I'll never make the pages of *Gentlemen's Quarterly*."

They were meeting tonight only because Calvin had appeared at the office that afternoon and insisted. He'd all but dragged David off to this small but elegant French restaurant hidden away on one of Vancouver's downtown side streets. Calvin prided himself on always knowing the best new place to eat before it became popular—and thus no longer attractive to him.

Calvin had finished his typical ritual with the waiter, finding out what fish was caught that day, what exact spices the soup contained, and precisely which vintage of wine was best to complement the meal.

It usually drove David crazy to sit through the performance. In his opinion, it was a pretentious act, and it irritated him when he was out with Calvin.

But tonight, David hadn't noticed. His thoughts were all for Annie, just as they'd been every spare moment of the past seven days. Soft music was coming from the overhead stereo speaker, a French Canadian chanteuse whose husky tones reminded him of Annie's voice. There was a trace of the same shyness he'd noticed that first day in his office....

"...wondered what your opinion was on the hospital board's decision to cut back spending on the administrative level?"

David looked at his friend with a blank expression.

"Sorry, Calvin," he apologized as the waiter arrived with the soup. "I was thinking of something else."

"Apparently." Calvin's face creased in an ironic smile. "You've been woolgathering this way all afternoon. What's up, David? Tough case? Want to talk about it?"

Calvin was a renowned cardiologist who'd been in semiretirement for several years. He now accepted only those cases that intrigued him, or those that brought him the most recognition because the patients were well connected in the community. Calvin was a rare blend of medical doctor and sharp businessman.

"No, no," David assured him. "Nothing to do with work."

"Then it must be a woman," Calvin joked, and David had to smile at the outright amazement on Calvin's face when he answered, "Yes, as a matter of fact, it is a woman. Her name's Annie, Annie Pendleton. I met her a week ago."

The relationship between the two men was complex. Calvin Graves had taken an interest in David when the younger man was still an intern, and in important ways, he'd influenced David's career over the years, always in a positive manner, always in a way that negated any sense of David's being indebted to him, although David was well aware of the favors Calvin had bestowed on him.

There was an unpaid debt between him and Calvin Graves. It wasn't a conscious, nagging awareness that kept David awake at night. It was simply an acknowledgement that no one helped another's career or investment portfolio to the degree Calvin had helped David's without there being repayment somewhere along the line.

Their relationship had changed as time passed from that of student and mentor to the status of friendly equals, and then by a curious twist of fate, changed again to that of relatives through marriage. It was through Calvin that David had met his ex-wife, Sheila.

Sheila was Calvin's niece, and the older man had been pleased when the two young people married—although he'd tactfully hidden most of the disappointment he felt six years later when they divorced.

"It's sad. The combination of doctor and lawyer was ideal from a career standpoint," was all he'd said to David. "It's unfortunate you couldn't go on with it, just as a business arrangement."

David had told himself later that the remark couldn't have been as cold and heartless as it sounded, even taking into consideration the fact that Calvin and his niece had no strong emotional bonds. Perhaps it was just a comment on the fact that Calvin had never married. In fact, Sheila had referred to Calvin more than once as a cold fish.

So it wasn't exactly old family ties that kept David from discussing with Calvin the other women who'd wandered in and out of his personal life since his divorce.

Well, he amended, maybe it was partly out of respect for Sheila. Their divorce had been as amiable and good-natured as that legal procedure could possibly be. Sheila was a litigation lawyer, and her firm had handled the details for both of them.

Neither Sheila nor David harbored any ill will toward the other. Their marriage had simply run down, like a clock nobody cared enough to wind, with Sheila pursuing her legal career and David focusing his life around medicine. Heaven knew either career could eat a person's time and energy, leaving nothing to give a marriage.

But it hadn't seemed honorable at first for David to mention the women he casually dated to Sheila's own uncle.

However, years had gone by since the divorce, and Calvin of course knew that David hadn't taken any vows of abstinence. But neither had David deliberately introduced or discussed any of his women friends. Until now.

"Pendleton, Pendleton," Calvin repeated, as if he were tasting the name. "Don't think I know anyone with that name. What does she do, David? Is she in medicine?" Calvin took a long, judgmental sip of the white wine the waiter had poured moments before, and pursed his lips in grudging approval.

"She's a writer. She writes children's books. She has a thirteen-year-old son, and she's warm and funny and bright..." David struggled to find the words that would best describe Annie, and felt that none of them were adequate. "You'll have to meet her."

Calvin nodded, his penetrating pale gaze on David's face. "Who was this Pendleton man she was married to?" he inquired, taking an experimental bite of the mushroom-and-spinach salad.

"She's never been married."

The bare statement of fact, Calvin's slightly raised left eyebrow and disapproving expression gave David just an inkling of the type of reaction Annie must have encountered over and over, and it disturbed and angered him.

"For crying out loud, Calvin, plenty of people these days choose to be single parents," he exploded, unaware of the amazement his outburst created.

David was normally the most even-tempered of men, and Calvin noted his reaction with interest, and hidden concern.

"There's absolutely no social stigma attached to it anymore."

"Of course there isn't," Calvin soothed. "You mustn't be so defensive, David. I'm not exactly a prude. In fact, I'm looking forward to meeting your, uh, Ms Pendleton."

There was charged silence between them for a while.

"Isn't this an unusual hot dressing on the salad?" Calvin chewed with the slow appreciation of a gourmand.

David had already wolfed down half his bowlful without tasting it at all.

Calvin's calm voice went on commenting on the food, his manner relaxed and at ease so that gradually, David relaxed, as well. For the rest of the sumptuous meal, nothing more was mentioned about Annie.

Over coffee, they discussed local politics and the disturbing cutbacks the government was making in health care. Inevitably, the subject touched on David's pet project, the heart and liver organ transplant unit at Vancouver Regional Hospital.

"There are long-term plans to set up the unit sometime in the next five years, but nobody I know of is really pushing the plan, either in Victoria or here on the hospital board. Which means it could easily get shelved and we wouldn't get financing for who knows how long," David complained.

It wasn't the first time the subject had been discussed between them. Calvin listened, as always, and not for the first time, expressed his views.

"There's only one effective method of making changes, David, or of getting the specific things you want, like this heart and liver transplant unit. You can't rely on others to do it. If you care enough to make changes, you know the route, through the governing body of the hospital, which in turn has the ear of the Ministry of Health.''

Calvin sat on numerous committees, and had a quiet finger on the pulse of hospital administration. Although he kept a deliberately low profile, David suspected he also had a great deal of influence in many political areas.

Calvin enjoyed pulling strings, manipulating power from the back room. David often thought of Calvin when he watched documentaries on the invisible men behind the scenes in politics.

"I've mentioned before," Calvin said with offhanded detachment, "that it wouldn't be at all difficult to get you an appointment as Advisor to the Board, and from there it would be simply a matter of time and opportunity before you became a junior board member."

David's answer was long-standing and automatic.

"Thanks, Calvin, but no thanks. Hell, I'd have to invest in a whole new wardrobe just to attend meetings."

Calvin smiled at David's attempt to take the sting out of his refusal. As always, the political machinations of the hospital were the last things David wanted to be involved with. He was busy enough with his practice, never mind taking on a whole new sphere of problems.

"Well, your wardrobe would be a drawback," Calvin teased. "But you really should give the idea serious consideration this time, that is, if you're sincere about wanting to implement that transplant unit. I'm afraid that what you said about it getting shelved is all too probable. Will you give me your word that you'll at least think it over?"

Surprised, David glanced up from pouring rich cream into one last cup of coffee. Calvin sounded much more emphatic about the subject than he ever had before, and David found himself wondering with a trace of suspicion if perhaps the entire evening had been a way of leading up to this particular discussion.

It wouldn't be the first time Calvin had quietly pushed his young friend in the direction he thought best for him to go. And that tactful pushing had always been very much to David's benefit.

A little boy with huge brown eyes, a boy named Charlie Vance, filled David's mental vision for a second. He saw Charlie's trusting wide smile, symbolic of a personality persistently cheerful despite incredible physical restrictions and pain that would have destroyed a lesser spirit long ago.

The child was only one of several. There were others out there like Charlie. The unit David envisioned would at the very least simplify their lives, allowing them to undergo treatment here at home. How he wanted that damned facility.

Calvin was still waiting for an answer. David looked across at his old friend and said, his tone devoid of humor, "All right, Calvin. I promise you I'll give it some serious thought."

Calvin was wise enough to drop the subject then. He ordered them each a snifter of excellent brandy, and launched into a good-natured argument about free trade.

But before long, David couldn't resist a surreptitious glance at his watch. Would it be too late by the time he got home to give Annie a call? She'd mentioned that she often worked long past midnight.

He found himself bolting his brandy and wishing impatiently that Calvin would get a move on.

"ANNIE? HI, IT'S DAVID. I hope I didn't wake you."

"Not a chance. I'm finishing this synopsis at last."

Her heartbeat accelerated right on cue, and she knew the pleasure she felt at hearing his voice was reflected in her voice. "I've been up here in my study ever since Jason went to bed." She glanced up at the wall clock. It was past one, and just as usual, she felt mild amazement that four hours could pass without her knowing.

"Heavens, I didn't realize how late it really was. But I think I finally managed to get this outline right, anyway," she remarked with a contented sigh, leaning back in her chair and trying to get the painful kink out of her shoulders.

"I was out with Calvin Graves for dinner. I just got home," David told her. "He's the friend I mentioned to you the other day."

"I remember." She got up, pulling the telephone cord with her as she moved the short distance to the window. She pulled up the vertical blind so the dark night sky and the rooftops of the neighborhood were visible. "Did you have a good dinner? Where'd you go?"

It still amazed her that she was able to chat with him in this casual way. They'd learned a great deal about each other in just one short week, Annie reflected. The initial intensity had never lessened between them, but they were more comfortable in their conversations.

And to her relief, most of those conversations had taken place on the telephone. David's job was a consuming one in terms of both time and energy, and for now, Annie considered that a blessing. She remembered all too well the overwhelming passion his kisses had evoked, and the promise he'd made her, that from that first memorable evening on, there would be no holding back as far as he was concerned.

Which seemed to put the ball in her court, and she wasn't at all certain about that. Annie had built a fortress around her heart in the past years, a barrier sturdy enough to withstand persuasive attack from outside. There had been several determined, attractive men who had set out to court her despite her reticence. Because of that reticence, maybe?

And that fortress had also managed to withstand the more insidious demands of her normal, healthy woman's body as well as the crippling loneliness that came like a virus every so often to torment her.

Her reaction to David had been so unexpected, so intense, that she was thrown off balance. But during the past days, she'd had time to reflect, time to regroup and make a firm, cautious decision to go slowly.

He'd called her often, beginning the very morning after that first real meeting. He'd taken her out for lunch one afternoon, and dropped in two nights ago for a few hours. Jason had been home that evening, and at first he'd been awed and excited at the prospect of meeting "The Sorcerer."

But after the first hour, the evening had disintegrated. It was no fault of David's. It was Jason. He'd come very close several times to being out-and-out rude that evening, leaving Annie furious with him as well as puzzled by the encounter. Jason was normally as polite and well mannered as a thirteen-year-old could manage.

"Why did you act that way, Jason?" Annie had inquired with open anger after David left. "You were smart mouthed and rude, and David was my guest. There's no excuse for rudeness. I won't tolerate that kind of behavior."

Jason's eyes were dark and resentful. "I just figured he'd be different than that," was the only mumbled explanation the boy would give. Annie had ordered him to bed, but she still didn't understand what was going on in Jason's head.

Annie listened now as David described the restaurant and the meal, smiling at his witty, sometimes wicked descriptions of the patrons and the serving staff. As usual during these telephone conversations, the content didn't matter to her half as much as the cadence and pitch of his baritone voice.

She sank back into her chair, closed her eyes, and let that voice become her universe. But her eyes snapped open and a pang of anxiety went through her when he said after a few minutes, "Tomorrow's Saturday. I'm not on call this weekend, so I'd like to take you and Jason out for the day if you haven't made other plans."

The uncomfortable first meeting between Jason and David was vivid in Annie's mind. An entire day spent trying to control Jason's unpredictable behavior would be difficult for her at best. She'd be on edge, forced into a role of diplomat and peacekeeper between the two males.

Drat her ornery kid. Why had he chosen David, of all people, to resent?

"I'm sorry, David," she heard herself saying. "I've already asked Cleo if she wants to come with me and take all the kids down to the park for the day," Annie improvised, praying her friend hadn't made different plans.

"Mind if I join you, then?"

Annie swallowed hard. What could she say to that?

"No, not at all, except it might not be much fun for you. You do realize we have three kids between us? Cleo's girls are still pretty small..."

"Hey, Annie, slow down. I like kids, remember? And healthy ones are exactly what I need at the moment to take my mind off work."

She'd done it this time. There was no way out.

"All I can suggest, then, is that you wear something washable. You're bound to get spilled on," she warned, and he laughed, a low, pleasing rumble of sound.

"I'll meet you down at Stanley Park then, say at the entrance to the zoo, at what? Eleven in the morning too early?"

"Great," Annie said with phony heartiness, and the moment he hung up, she dialed Cleo's number in a frenzy, hoping this was one of those nights her friend was propped up in bed, engrossed in some book or other. Thank heavens Cleo was a voracious reader and a nighthawk as well.

"Cleo, I'm in a mess. Please tell me you and the kids can come to the park tomorrow morning," Annie blurted the instant the phone was lifted on the other end.

"Do you often get these uncontrollable urges for our company at 2:00 a.m.?" Cleo sounded wide-awake.

"David wants to spend tomorrow with me and Jason, and..."

"He wants to spend the day with you, and you're inviting us along? Annie, my friend, have you taken leave of your senses?"

"I can't handle this alone. I told you how Jason acted the night David was here. I can't bear the thought of a whole day with that rotten kid of mine being either silent or snotty by turns."

Cleo was silent for a long moment.

"I have to say I think you're making a big mistake here, Annie," she finally said. "If you're going to go on seeing this guy, the best thing you could do would be to force the two of them to work it out, without any buffering from you. Or me, for that matter. That's what the psychologist from Parents Without Partners advised at that lecture I went to, the one about single parents forming new relationships."

"Yeah, well, I'm not that brave. In fact, I'm plain old chicken about this. So will you come?"

"The other thing you haven't considered," Cleo went on, "is that you're taking an awful risk, letting that gorgeous hunk of masculinity get a good look at me in a pair of shorts. My legs are my best feature, remember, and I did happen to catch a glimpse of Dr. Roswell through my front window that evening he came over. He is a hunk, capital *H*."

"I noticed," Annie said with dry humor. "Maggie told me you sat at the window the better part of an hour with your binoculars trained on my house. I'll have to chance even your magnificent legs in this," Annie sighed. "Now come off it, Cleo. Say you'll come before you drive me frantic."

"Of course I will. I'll even bring a large kerchief to tie around your kid's mouth if the going gets rough."

"Cleo, you are a true friend," Annie sighed. "Seriously bent, but a friend all the same."

"Yup," Cleo agreed, adding in a different tone, "You know what's wrong with old Jason, don't you, Annie?" Her voice was gentle.

"No, quite frankly, I don't know. This one's got me flummoxed."

"Well, when was the last time a man sent your blood pressure soaring? When was the last time you cared enough to see someone more than twice, or introduce him to your kid?"

"I see what you mean. You figure Jason senses this damned reaction I have to David, and he's plain old jealous?"

"Something like that, but more complex. Kids are superquick to pick up on emotions in their parents." Cleo was quiet again, and then she said abruptly, "Have you thought any more about letting Jason meet Michael and his wife?"

Annie had confided in Cleo long ago about Michael, and she'd told her friend about the ill-timed phone call from him the first night David was over.

"I suppose you figure I ought to give in on this," Annie said with more than a trace of irritation in her tone. "I suppose you're gonna tell me that Jason might feel a lot more secure around men if he actually got to know his own father."

She found herself wishing for an instant that she'd never told Cleo anything. How could an outsider understand?

But then she was ashamed of herself. Cleo was truly her friend. She'd proven that many times. And maybe, Annie forced herself to consider, just maybe Cleo could see something here that Annie was missing.

"Yeah, I guess I do feel that," Cleo was saying now. "Every kid wants to know who his parents are, both parents. Jason's no different. You told me Michael sounded calmer, more mature than he was when you knew him. He's been married quite a while to this Lili, you said.

Maybe it would be good for Jason to get to know them. And with Michael pressuring you about it, well, it just seems maybe it's meant to be, but then, what do I know? You're the only one who really can decide.''

Cleo's voice became wistful. "Heaven knows I'm the last one who should be handing out advice. I have no idea what I'd do if that bum who fathered my girls turned up again and wanted to see them. I can't say whether I'd let him or not.''

Johnny Fowler, according to Cleo, had been lovable, handsome and fun, but he'd proven as well to be dishonest and totally irresponsible.

The day after Cleo had told him she was pregnant with their second child, Johnny had said he was driving to the store for a pack of cigarettes and hadn't been heard from since. He had taken the car, cleared out their meager bank account and helped himself to a diamond ring Cleo had inherited from her grandmother.

Cleo had managed, somehow, to survive, and it never failed to amaze Annie that she harbored very little bitterness about the hand Fate had dealt her. She often referred to herself as an incurable optimist, and Annie had to agree with that assessment.

They made the arrangements for the day ahead and ended the conversation. Annie took a long, hot bath and went to bed, but hours passed and she still lay awake, tangled images of Michael and David and Jason chasing one another through her thoughts.

"MOM? HEY, MOM, wake up.''

Jason's voice and the smell of fragrant coffee finally penetrated the foggy dream Annie was having. She opened her eyes with difficulty to find her son standing by her bed balancing a tray and grinning at her.

She dragged herself to a sitting position, gave a huge yawn and straightened the oversize T-shirt she wore as a nightgown.

"Morning, kid.'' She squinted toward the open window. "Gosh, it's broad daylight out there. What time is it?''

Jason settled the tray on her knees, rescuing the mug of coffee before it slopped over.

"Nine-thirty. You work really late again last night, Mom? You sure were out of it. I called you before but you didn't move a muscle, so I figured the only solution was breakfast in bed just this once.''

His eyes, exactly the same shade of soft brown as Annie's, twinkled at his joke. The truth was, he brought her breakfast in bed almost every weekend morning.

Annie smiled at her redheaded son, and took stock of the tray. It held a fried egg, over easy, just the way she liked, two slices of buttered toast and a carefully peeled and sliced orange as well as the coffee.

Ever since he was barely able to reach the countertops, Jason had been cooking and bringing her these breakfasts in bed. His first efforts had been pretty bad, but Annie had praised them and pretended to enjoy them, touched at the effort he'd made to please her. It had paid off, because now her trays were wonderful to wake up to.

His efforts made her feel pampered, and her delight made Jason feel proud. It had become a wonderful tradition.

"So how does it feel to be in junior high school, kid?"

School had started the week before, and Jason had made the transition from elementary to junior high.

"It's okay, I guess. It's funny to go from being the biggest guys in the school to being the runts again, though."

Annie smiled in sympathy, and they chatted about his teachers and his hopes about making the junior rugby squad. She sipped her coffee, and as they talked she wondered how best to introduce the plans for the day. She chewed her toast and forked up the egg, while her son sipped his own mug of chocolate, sitting on the wicker chair by her bed.

"We're going down to Stanley Park this morning, with Cleo and the girls," Annie finally announced with casual aplomb.

"Hey, neat. There's a new baby whale in the whale pool. Can we watch the show? I've got my own money."

"I suspect so," Annie said, adding, "David is meeting us at the entrance to the zoo at eleven, so I'd better finish this and get my act together."

"That doctor? Dr. Roswell? He's goin' with us?"

Annie was certain Jason knew exactly who David was, but she nodded anyway.

"Yup, that doctor. Alias The Sorcerer, remember?" she added with forced heartiness. "He's meeting us there, and we'll all spend the day together."

Jason set his empty mug on the tray, avoiding Annie's eyes. "Maybe I'd rather not come along after all, if that's okay, Mom. Larry and I figured maybe we'd work on his model today."

Annie felt exasperated. "Jason, I want you to come with us and that's that. I know you've taken some kind of weird dislike to David, but I can't see any reason for it. He particularly mentioned wanting to get to know you better."

"Yeah, well that's his problem. Do I have to come?" Jason's voice was martyred.

"Yes, I'm afraid this time you have to come."

His mouth curved in mutinous, silent rebellion, and Annie sighed with irritation. "Jason, I simply don't understand what's going on here. Clue me in, okay?"

Mute, he stared off into the middle distance, and she knew there wasn't any way to get him to talk when he was in this mood. Annie sighed again and finished her food in silence, the atmosphere between them strained as they got ready for the day.

STANLEY PARK was one of Vancouver's landmarks. A verdant thousand-acre peninsula jutting into Burrard Inlet, it contained beaches, picnic areas, playgrounds, swimming pools, as well as the zoo and the public aquarium, and it was already well populated this warm September morning by Vancouver residents who found it a great place to get away from it all.

It seemed a miracle when Annie found a parking place almost right away in the lot closest to the zoo entrance, and the little girls in their crisp cotton shorts sets tumbled out, with Jason following much more slowly, trailing far behind Annie and Cleo.

In an untidy group, they made their way through the crowd, and with uncanny precision, Annie picked out a tall male figure lounging against a low stone wall that bordered a pond where elegant swans floated to and fro.

He was waiting, just as he'd promised he would.

The trees, the sound of birds, the water...a flash of something that had to be a dream filled her senses, and for a brief instant, she knew that this man had waited for her in a setting very much like this, time after time.

And to Annie, the crowd was gone. The chattering of Maggie and Paula no longer penetrated the private world she inhabited.

She knew only that the greatest love she'd ever known was embodied in that tall waiting figure, and she had to go to him, just as she had gone so many other times.

With a smile full of joy, a radiance that brought stares and answering wistful smiles from those around her, she hurried toward him.

CHAPTER SIX

"I FEEL LIKE A PERVERT around the two of you," Cleo complained hours later, sipping the coffee Annie had bought from the nearby vending stand.

It was three in the afternoon. They'd toured the zoo and the aquarium, taken the girls for rides on the miniature train and eaten hot dogs and fries washed down with soda.

Annie and Cleo were sprawled on a grassy knoll, watching David and Jason. The two males were tossing a Frisbee in the field nearby, while Maggie and Paula provided an enthusiastic backup retrieval system.

"I feel like a pervert," Cleo declared, "because every time you and that hunk of man look at each other, it's like an X-rated intimate encounter." She sat up and crossed her legs Indian fashion so she could prop her coffee on one bare knee.

"The vibes between you two are hot, Annie. As in sexual. But then I suppose you might have suspected that without my telling you?"

"Has anybody ever mentioned that you're not exactly a subtle conversationalist?" Annie asked with sweet sarcasm, her eyes always on David, now sending the Frisbee flying across a wide expanse so Jason had to run hard if he were to catch it. "You have a definite tendency to go straight for the jugular, friend." Annie's tone was light and teasing, but her cheeks grew hot beneath their tan, because Cleo had pinpointed what Annie knew to be true.

Try as she might to keep everything casual, there was an impossible-to-ignore undercurrent of strong emotion between herself and David. It was disconcerting to find out that others were aware of it.

Cleo was undisturbed by Annie's comments. "It's best to bring things like this out in the open," she said with complacent ease. "Just in case you've hibernated for so long you don't recognize good old sexual vibes anymore, I figured I ought to mention it. And you have, you know, Annie. Hibernated. For all I know, you'll mistake good, honest desire for premature hot flashes or something, and this whole thing will be ruined. As your friend and advisor, I can't let that happen, now can I?''

She crumpled the plastic cup and tossed it at a nearby garbage container. "Actually this is giving me back my faith in pure, unadulterated romance," she went on, flopping back on the grass and folding her arms under her head. She narrowed her eyes at the blue and cloudless sky and smiled.

"It's like that song, remember the one about some enchanted evening, meeting a stranger and knowing you'll see him again and again?"

Though Cleo pretended to tease, there was an undercurrent of wistful envy there as well.

"That day after the magic show, you told me something weird happened, Annie, that you felt as if you'd known him before, remember?"

Annie nodded. How could she forget?

"And seeing the two of you together today, even I get the damnedest feeling that you belong together." She squinted up at the blue of the heavens, her shock of white hair dramatic against the green grass, her voice thoughtful.

"Ever think that for all the scheming we do, Annie, we really haven't any control over destiny, that the whole thing is planned out on some master computer somewhere long before we're even born?"

"Mommy, Paula's going to have an accident."

From a distance, Maggie's piercing voice carried clearly to several families picnicking nearby, causing a faint ripple of laughter, which Maggie ignored.

"She has to go right now, Mom, and she won't let me take her, either." Maggie was panting as she tugged her roly-poly younger sister up the incline. The two of them stood over their mother's prone body, waiting with impatience for Cleo to take action.

Cleo rolled her eyes and sprang to her feet. "Straight from the mysteries of the universe to the reality of the bathroom. From the sublime to the ridiculous, that exactly describes being a mother. C'mon, kid, and be sure you hold it till we get there." She swung the curly-haired Paula up on her hip and hurried off in the direction of the public washrooms.

Mission accomplished, Maggie plopped her skinny bottom down beside Annie and heaved a huge, loud sigh. Annie couldn't help laughing, because Maggie so often gave her the impression that Cleo's household would collapse if Maggie didn't manage it.

"Mag, you're a case." Annie looped an affectionate arm across the girl's shoulders and planted a kiss on her blond head. "Tired, peanut?"

Maggie shook her head vehemently. "We're havin' the best day, aren't we, Annie?"

Annie smiled down into Maggie's round blue eyes. "We sure are. I'm glad you're having fun, honey."

"I like him lots, that David guy," Maggie declared, with a decisive nod of her head. "He said we could call him David. But he's The Sorcerer, too, y'know, Annie. He knows magic and everything. Wasn't it neat at lunch when he made my hot dog disappear and then it came out of Paula's shoe?"

Annie nodded. "Yup, that was a neat trick all right." David had charmed the girls silly with his sleight of hand, and even Jason had looked as if he were enjoying himself every now and then, until he remembered he wasn't supposed to and deliberately assumed his glum look again.

Maggie sighed again. "I think he ought to marry you, Annie."

Annie swallowed hard. "What makes you say that? Marrying is serious stuff, Mags. And anyhow, why me? There are lots of other ladies around."

"'Cause he likes you better, silly," Maggie said with matter-of-fact innocence. "He likes us all, but he likes you best."

"Did, umm, did David tell you that?"

The child shook her head again. "Nope."

"Then how do you know?" Annie put her nose down against Maggie's.

Maggie drew back and gave her a look she reserved for imbeciles. "I just know, Annie. 'Cause he looks at you all the time, same as they do on TV when the man likes the lady and then he kisses her."

"I see," Annie managed to say. She stared down at the innocent face for a long, thoughtful moment.

First the mother, now the daughter, somehow both aware of whatever this thing was between her and a man she'd known only a short while.

What was it that made the two of them seem emotionally transparent to Cleo, to Maggie?

To Jason? She had no doubt Cleo had pinpointed the problem when she suggested Jason was plain old jealous of whatever he sensed between herself and David, if it was as evident as this to everyone.

Irritation sparked in her, and an old deep-rooted fear. She didn't want this complication in her life just now. She didn't need it.

Against her will, her eyes were drawn once again to the tall, lithe figure off in the field, laughing and leaping high in the air to make a difficult catch Jason had just pitched, and try as she might, Annie couldn't stop the telltale warmth that spilled through her just at the sight of him.

He'd finally come back to her....

The fleeting wisp of memory was gone before she could pin it down. But something deep in her responded, something in her knew that it was so, even while her rational conscious mind rejected it.

It was simply ridiculous, she chided herself.

Annie scrambled up, clasping the grubby paw Maggie held out to her and pulling the child to her feet.

"Let's go have a swing, what d'ya say, kid?"

"Yeah, I'll beat you to the swings, Annie." Maggie dashed off to the playground nearby, and Annie followed at a slow trot.

"I'm beating you, Annie." Maggie's shrill voice floated back as she ran hard for the swings.

Two rambunctious boys, three or four years older than Maggie, were racing with wild abandon from one set of swings to the next, grabbing the ropes and giving the wooden seats a mighty push so that the six swings were all in frantic motion within minutes.

Annie, her mind still on David, saw them pull the nearest swings back and heave them as hard as they could, and at the same moment, she saw Maggie dashing along, her head turned back toward Annie.

"Maggie, look out..."

"I beat you, I beat..." the child chanted, at the same instant Annie screamed the warning. The swings came flying forward, with Maggie directly in their path.

Annie leaped ahead in a desperate attempt to reach Maggie in time, but one of the wooden seats connected fully with the girl's forehead an instant before Annie could snatch her away.

The dull, sickening thunk of the blow mingled with Maggie's sharp, startled cry of pain as Annie grabbed for the girl and missed, barely deflecting the second swing as it also came hurtling toward them.

Maggie went flying up and then down again, tossed forcefully to the ground. Her skinny little figure, clad in bright red shorts and a gaily patterned T-shirt, lay sprawled motionless, like a discarded scarecrow on the hard-packed earth below the swings.

"Maggie! Oh, sweetheart—"

Annie flung herself down beside the child, noting the bright blood surging and then seeming to erupt in a torrent from a long, ugly gash just above Maggie's left eye.

The girl was unconscious, eyes half closed and rolled back far in her head. Was she even breathing?

Annie opened her mouth and hollered as loud as she could, the only name she could think of.

"David, David, come quick...."

She peered in the direction of the open field, to see if he'd heard her, but other people were hurrying over, crowding around in a tight packed knot, and someone yelled, "Hey, this kid's hurt bad. She's bleeding. Someone better call an ambulance...."

"Stay back," Annie ordered, her voice loud and fierce. "Get back, do you hear me?" She sounded so forceful that the people crowding in actually moved away again, muttering but giving her and Maggie room.

A bolt of white-hot pain shot through Annie's neck and shoulders, and she gritted her teeth against its intensity.

Not now, please not now....

"David," she screamed again. "David, David..."

One moment she was alone, and the next David was kneeling on Maggie's other side, fingers on the child's pulse. Maggie's eyelids were fluttering, and a faint whimpering sound came from her throat.

"What happened here?" he said with calm control.

"The seat on the, the sw-swing, David. It hit her head."

Annie gulped and David's eyes moved from their intense study of Maggie, meeting Annie's stricken gaze for an instant before his attention returned to the swift and thorough examination he was conducting on the child.

The pain in Annie's neck eased a little, and a cold sweat broke out on her body.

"It's okay, love, don't look like that," David said, too low for the onlookers to hear. "She'll be fine. There's always more blood than an injury like this warrants," he assured her. "Did she lose consciousness immediately?"

Annie nodded, trying to release the tightly held air trapped in her chest, trying to relax the knotted muscles in her neck. It felt as if a vise were squeezing tighter and tighter, constricting her breathing, pain escalating...

David's here, he's a doctor, she told herself. Everything will be all right because David's here. Like a mantra, she repeated the words in her mind.

Jason came hurrying over just then, carrying the black medical bag David must have sent him to get. He quickly handed it over and then came to kneel beside his mother, taking her hand in a gesture that was comforting to her.

Annie squeezed the grubby, warm paw hard, then said, "Honey, please go find Cleo. She went down to the washrooms with Paula. But try not to scare her, won't you, Jason? Just tell her...tell her..."

Annie's voice trembled and faded.

"Should I just say Maggie got a little bang on the head, and you and the doctor are here with her?" he queried, and at Annie's nod, he tore off.

By now, Maggie was awake and wailing at the top of her lungs, and it seemed the best sound Annie had ever heard. David's medical bag was open, and he was sponging off the deep gash in her forehead with a square of cotton and liquid from a small vial, chatting to her all the while.

"Want to sit on Annie's knee while we put a bandage on your head?" he asked at last, and after a second, Maggie stopped sobbing and gulped out a shaky "Yes, please."

He lifted the child with care and set her in Annie's lap while he secured a temporary dressing to the cut.

Annie's arms trembled uncontrollably as she held the fragile little body against her. How easily, how quickly, a child could be damaged.... Her love for Maggie and her fear mingled in a wrenching tumult of feeling.

With a final check of her pulse rate, David stuffed his equipment back into his bag and was snapping it shut by the time Cleo came hurtling through the crowd.

Her face was drained of color, but she did her best not to show alarm in front of Maggie. She knelt beside Annie, and the women transferred the girl from one lap to the other.

Cleo cuddled Maggie with one arm and grabbed for Annie's hand with the other. She squeezed it tight, needing support as she turned toward David, her green eyes begging him for reassurance.

"Is she, do you think there's any danger to her eye..."

"None at all. She's going to be fine, Cleo," he interrupted, his calm voice and easy reassuring smile causing an immediate response in the fingers gripping Annie's hand.

Cleo relaxed a trifle, her shoulders losing their tense stiffness as David went on, "She's going to need a couple of stitches, however, to close that gash, and we should take some X rays to make sure there's no other problem. We'll take her over to the clinic right now in my car, Cleo. Maybe you could take the other kids home in yours and wait for us there, Annie? We won't be long."

Annie nodded, and the quick smile he gave her warmed her heart.

"Maggie was unconscious for a very short time," he told Cleo, "so you'll have to keep an eye on her tonight, just in case of concussion, but you can probably do that at home. There's no need to admit her unless the X rays indicate otherwise.'' He got to his feet and reached out to help the two women up, one after the other. His hand was strong and comforting around Annie's cold and perspiring fingers.

IT WAS AFTER NINE that evening before Annie and David were alone together at last.

She'd brought Jason and Paula home and gotten them involved in helping her make pizzas out of a wild assortment of leftovers and odds and ends of cheese and cold meat she dug out of the fridge. Jason was touching in his attentiveness to the little girl, answering the same questions about Maggie's accident over and over, reassuring Paula that her mother and sister would soon be home, making her giggle at his antics with the pizza dough.

Watching them, Annie was reminded that just that morning, Jason had acted like a naughty child when she'd told him the plans for the day. She'd wanted to throttle him.

Now, a few short hours later, he was being mature and supportive in a way that foreshadowed the strong man she hoped he would someday become. It was confusing, trying to keep current with a boy growing up.

If his swiftly changing moods were difficult for her to understand, she mused as she watched him, they must be doubly difficult for Jason.

She flexed her shoulders and kneaded the warm yeasty smelling dough she'd mixed up, aware of the intense burning in her shoulder that had been there ever since the accident that afternoon. But at least the pain in her neck hadn't gotten out of control this time. It was there, a smoldering ache that stabbed her now and then, making her catch her breath.

David brought Cleo and Maggie home, and they all ate the hot pizza picnic fashion in Cleo's kitchen, so that Maggie could rest in her own bed. By now, Maggie was feeling a bit pleased at being the center of attention, but she was also prone to quick fits of tears.

Cleo gave her a hot bath and let her sit at the table with everyone for a short time, but soon Maggie's eyes drooped and her head nodded.

"Can I carry her up to bed for you?" David asked, and Annie felt a pang of tenderness go through her as the strong man lifted the fragile child in her pink flannel nightgown and trotted her upstairs. Maggie's arms were twined around his neck.

The accident had somehow bridged any awkwardness the women and children might have felt about having David included in such a homely scene this early in their friendship with him.

The fact was, he'd charmed the little girls, and charmed Cleo as well. Paula, shy but determined, demanded to sit on his lap after dinner, and when Maggie woke up for the second time, feeling sick, she accepted his presence beside her bed.

Cleo raised her eyebrows at Annie as David loped up the stairs to tend the child. "Think he's got a twin brother?" she whispered as she passed Annie's chair. "I wish."

It was a pleasant, intimate gathering. Only Jason had been quiet, eating fast and then hurrying away to deliver his papers.

As soon as Cleo's kitchen was tidy, Annie suggested she and David go back to her house. Cleo needed time alone with her children, and Annie found herself longing for a few private moments with David.

"Coffee?" she suggested as they came in the back door and she turned on lights.

"Sounds great," he agreed.

"With brandy?" she suggested, tossing her blue sweater on a chair and filling the drip coffee maker.

"Sounds even better," he said with a grin.

David ambled around the kitchen as she gathered up mugs, cream and sugar, a tray. He spent long moments looking at the dramatic prints she'd framed and hung on one wall, modern, cheerful studies of kitchen utensils and herbs and sunflowers.

"I like this one," he said after a moment, and she glanced up from filling the sugar bowl. "It's different from the others. Is it an old family picture?"

It was different. In fact, the picture he was studying would have looked quite out of place among the modern prints she'd grouped on the other long wall, so she'd decided to hang it by itself in a narrow space near the door to the hall. Usually no one noticed it there but her.

It was a small, simple watercolor of a thatched roof farmhouse in the country. Annie liked to think the scene was right after a rain, with fresh-washed fields stretching off in the distance and an orchard of apple trees beginning to bloom pink in the background, rambling down a slope with a wide river just visible in the distance. The colors were muted, misty green and gold and blue seeming to run together in the favorite fashion of some of the French Impressionist painters.

"I found that in a junk shop down on Water Street years ago, and for some reason it appealed to me." Annie was waiting for the last of the coffee to drip through, and she slid the pot out an instant too soon. Coffee dribbled over the counter and she swore under her breath, adding without thinking, "I guess when you live in a city, there's always a part of you that longs to return to the country."

"Did you grow up in the country, Annie?" He was still studying the picture, hands tucked into the back pockets of his jeans.

"Heavens, no. I've always been a city girl. I hardly know one end of a cow from the other," she said with a laugh, picking up the tray and leading the way into the living room.

"When you said that the scene makes you long to return to the country, I just wondered," he said, one eyebrow lifted quizzically as they sat down side by side on the sofa.

She had said that. A stab of irrational irritation with herself niggled at Annie and she forced it away. Her mind was playing tricks on her, had been ever since the day of the magic show.

There was the recurring dream she'd been having about walking through farmland beside a river, for instance. Perhaps it had originated with the picture on her kitchen wall, but it seemed strange she'd never dreamed it before now. And she was irritable these days, which wasn't like her.

Well, she rationalized, today her vague irritation was no doubt a result of this mild but persistent pain in her neck, combined with the trauma of Maggie's accident.

"Has Maggie had a similar accident before, a bad blow on her head?" David queried.

"Not that I know of, and I'm sure Cleo would have mentioned it. Why do you ask?"

David shrugged. "When I was taking her up to bed tonight, Maggie asked if I remembered that other time she banged her head. She seemed to be convinced I'd treated her then as well. It was probably just a child's imagination, and a result of the shot she had for the stitches, combining to make her a bit muddled."

Annie nodded agreement and poured them each cups of steaming, strong coffee, adding generous dollops of brandy. They sipped, and almost at the same time they both relaxed, sinking back into the cushions and expelling mutual sighs of relief.

They caught each other's eyes then, and both of them started to laugh without a single word being exchanged. The incongruity of the day's happenings suddenly struck them both funny.

"Some nice relaxing day you had, huh, away from the hospital and all that chaos," Annie teased. Then she sobered. "It meant a great deal to have you there, David, caring for Maggie. I was so darned scared. I thought for a moment her eye was going to be damaged." Annie shuddered. "I'm afraid I'm not very rational when one of our kids gets hurt."

"You're very close to Cleo and her children, aren't you?" he inquired in a tender tone, and Annie nodded.

"Very, especially Maggie. I love both the girls, but Mags could easily be my own child. I felt it the moment I met her, which was the day Jason and I moved in here. And Cleo is like a sister to me. Even though she had so little to spend on groceries, Cleo came over that first day with a big tuna-noodle casserole for us, and I asked her and the kids to share it with us."

The details of that meal suddenly made Annie giggle. "Cleo'd been so excited about our moving in that she forgot to put any tuna in the casserole."

David laughed with her, and Annie went on, "That was three years ago. Paula was just newborn, Cleo's husband had walked out on her only months before and they sure didn't have much to go on. Cleo's a strong, brave woman, though. I watched her pull herself together and start a day-care center to support herself and the kids." Annie paused and thought for a moment.

"I do feel this particular bond with Maggie, though," she admitted. "Probably because I was like her when I was a girl, a weird combination of bold and timid, outgoing and introverted."

"You still are that way," he said, and Annie caught her breath as his fingers touched first her hair, and then slid down her cheek, stroking her skin, outlining her ear, making her shiver.

"You're as bold as hell at times, like when it comes to protecting the kids. I heard you order that crowd today to stay back out of the way." His index finger was resting just beside her lips, and now he used it to outline them, tracing their full shape slowly once, and again. His eyes followed the movements of his fingers, and his voice came from deep in his chest, a low thoughtful rumble.

"But when it comes to this, to lovemaking, I think you're timid. I can feel you holding back, trembling. I can feel you wanting me, and still resisting it." His words were wistful. "Can't you let yourself trust me? Trust whatever this is that's happening between us, let it grow? It's neither trivial nor ordinary, Annie, not to me." His finger journeyed back across her lips. She shuddered, and his hand cupped her chin, then released it when she resisted the gentle pressure he exerted.

Nervous, she reached out toward the low coffee table for her cup, wincing as pain shot through her shoulders and down her back, forcing herself to ignore it, to hide it from the man beside her.

"It's just that I need to go slowly, David," she said as she sipped the now lukewarm coffee. "I'm...I guess I'm out of practice," she joked with feeble humor. "I'm not used to this yet."

The truth was, she was terrified of being in his arms. The passion he roused made her lose any control that might have existed, and that loss of control frightened her.

"We've got plenty of time, Annie. There's no hurry." He studied her for a moment, and then he frowned.

"Your back is giving you problems again, isn't it?"

She opened her mouth to deny it, and said instead, "How'd you know?"

"You move differently when it's hurting. Your eyes change. They get darker and sort of glossy, and I can see the strain in your face, the way your jaw tightens."

She attempted a shrug and aborted the movement with a gasp when a spasm of white-hot pain shot once again through her neck.

"Damn it. Yes, yes, it is bothering me, but it's something I've had all my life in varying degrees, so I try not to think about it. It started this afternoon again when Maggie got hurt."

"Would you agree to a thorough evaluation if I set up an appointment for you with some friends of mine?" David didn't wait for the denial that would follow the quick negative shake she gave her head at the suggestion. She'd been through the same thing before, and she had no desire to submit to still another round of medical testing.

Before she could say no, he went on, "We're learning new treatments all the time. Diagnosis is better than ever before. I know you've already gone through careful testing. Your doctor told me he'd sent you through the whole business several years ago. But if there's even a remote possibility something could be done for you, it's worth another try, don't you think? Nobody should have to live with pain." The compassion in his eyes reminded her of his role as physician.

"I'd like you to think about it at least. Will you, Annie?"

She was spared an answer. The back door opened and slammed, and Jason yelled excitedly, "Hi, Mom. Hey, Mom, guess what? Mrs. Thompson wants me to take care of her budgie while she goes..."

Jason appeared in the doorway to the living room, his denim jacket half on and half off, his bright hair standing on end. The torrent of words stopped in an instant when he saw David, arm still looped around Annie's shoulders.

The animation faded fast from Jason's mobile features. His expression became stiff and remote. "Sorry, Mom. I didn't know you still had company," he mumbled.

"David's not company," Annie said, more sharply than she had intended. She tried to moderate it. "Why don't you get a glass of Coke and come talk with..."

Annie's invitation stopped in midsentence. Jason had already turned away. He was opening the door to the basement, and before she could call to him, he hollered belligerently, "You oughta warn me when you're having your boyfriend over, Mom. I'd make myself scarce so you could be alone to make out."

He slammed the door shut with enough violence to shake the house. Annie heard his footsteps pounding down the stairs.

A moment later his bedroom door also slammed, and then there was silence.

Annie felt her face burn with embarrassment. She couldn't meet David's eyes. Jason's words had made her self-conscious and horribly angry and ashamed of her son all at the same time.

"I'm sorry. He's not usually this way," she stammered, and then blurted out, "Damn that kid. I'm afraid he's jealous of you, David."

"Of course he is," David agreed. "It's natural he would be. You've been alone with him for a long time." He paused, and then added, "You know, Jason talked about his father quite a bit today. Does he see him often?"

Annie's entire body stiffened with shock and she gaped at David.

"Jason talked about... But that's impossible. Jason has never even met his father. What on earth could he say about him?"

David was frowning at her, confused.

"What do you mean, never met him? Jason's never met this Michael McCrae?"

Annie shook her head. "Michael went to India shortly after the court case when Jason was a baby. He stayed there until three months ago. Since his return, I'm certain he's never been in touch with Jason. What on earth did Jason tell you about Michael?"

"Let's see. He told me his father was a famous engineer, that he'd built three important dams in India but that now he was back in Vancouver for good. I naturally assumed he and Jason spent a lot of time together."

Annie slowly shook her head. Why did she have the unwelcome feeling that she was being shoved against her will these days, in directions she didn't want to go?

"What Jason told you is technically correct. Michael is living here now, with his wife. But I haven't allowed—I haven't agreed to their meeting or to Michael spending time with Jason."

David, watching her face said, "I see. Still, the boy must think about it a lot, Annie, because he talked about his father several times today. He also said McCrae had been a wrestler at university, and that he,

Jason, is also in a wrestling club at the community center. He even knew how many matches his father had won years ago.''

David gave her a lopsided grin. ''In fact, I had the distinct feeling that Jason was letting me know that he's a pretty tough guy, like his dad, and not to be messed with. That he was warning me off you, maybe.''

Annie was astounded. ''I didn't know he was even interested in all that stuff about Michael. He must have gotten hold of some old yearbook from the university. And my mother goes on a lot about Michael. She never forgave me for canceling the wedding. I just can't believe this,'' she stammered. ''Certainly he's asked me about Michael, more in the past months than ever before, but he hasn't talked to me that much about him…'' Her voice trailed off as she admitted to herself that Jason's questions about Michael had always annoyed her, so she'd been short-tempered about answering.

Kids were smart. She guessed he'd just stopped asking her and found ways to learn about his father himself. It made her feel as if her own son was becoming a stranger, hearing all this from David.

''Sometimes I think I don't know the first thing about raising kids,'' she remarked in exasperation. ''Maybe I ought to take a course or something.''

David was sympathetic. ''I've never even had kids, Annie, so there's a hell of a lot I don't understand about them, either. And my ex-wife used to accuse me of not knowing the first thing about women, even after living with her for six years. So I'm anything but well qualified at kids and women. But if you decide to give me a chance, I'll try my best with both of you. With Jason, and with you.''

You don't have to try at all with me, David, her heart answered. *I'm yours, whether I can accept it or not, whether you realize it or not. I've been yours from the beginning.*

Before the beginning.

Her mind snapped back in gear.

''I'll have to have a long and honest talk with that boy,'' she said, more to herself than to David. It wasn't going to be easy, either. Jason was her son, but it seemed that whether she wanted it or not, he was also his father's son.

''Speaking of talking to people, there's a cocktail party this Thursday that I've been railroaded into attending,'' David was saying. ''It's a business obligation of sorts, and it will probably be as exciting as watching paint dry, but it would give me a chance to show you off, as well as introduce you to Calvin. Would you come with me, Annie? We could get through it fast and then go somewhere quiet for dinner.''

"You make it sound worse than a visit to the dentist," she said with a weak grin. "With the promise of ice cream later if I behave."

"You got it," he confirmed with his charming, lopsided smile. "Will you come?"

She looked at the lines of his face, and recognized the complications of the question. He was moving them away from her familiar ground, from the privacy of her insular world to the scrutiny of the much larger arena his work entailed. Perhaps it was a test of sorts, for both of them. It took courage to venture there with him.

"Yes, I'll come," she said after a moment. The simple word seemed to echo in her head after she'd said it. Yes, and yes, and yes again.

She was amazed to find she wanted to go with him. Her reward was the pleasure his blue eyes reflected in the soft light from the lamp in the corner, and the kiss he planted full on her lips.

She allowed it to go on much longer than she had intended, but at last with reluctance, she pulled away.

"Jason..." she murmured in apology. "He's liable to come upstairs for something, and I'd rather not..."

"Yeah," David said, and he moved back on the sofa, putting distance between them. "Yeah, I understand, Annie."

There was a faint trace of constraint and disappointment in his voice, however.

She felt guilty. To bridge the moment, and because it was something she wanted to know, she said, "Tell me more about Calvin Graves, David. If I'm going to meet him on Thursday, I ought to have some sort of road map to go by. What's he like, what kind of man is he?"

Annie listened as David sketched his friend in words. "Calvin's image conscious, always perfectly groomed." David smiled and added, "He's forever threatening to send me to his tailor. I'm afraid clothes never mattered all that much to me."

David's casual disregard for style was one of the things Annie found endearing about him. She'd always had reservations about men who relied on clothing to convey an impression of themselves. She didn't say so now, though. It would sound like a criticism of Calvin.

"Did I tell you that Calvin was my former wife's uncle? It was through knowing him that I first met Sheila."

Annie was surprised and also in some obscure way, disturbed by the disclosure. She hadn't realized that the men's relationship was as complex as that. "Was he upset when you divorced, then?"

The man had every reason to hate her on sight, considering.

"Not on a personal level, no. He and Sheila had never been close. From a professional standpoint, however, I think he felt Sheila and I suited each other. I think I told you that she was a lawyer, and Calvin figured that was a great combination.''

Annie was beginning to suspect that she and Calvin Graves might have very different outlooks on life, and the thought of meeting him began to make her nervous.

"I'll pick you up at seven on Thursday," David confirmed as he was leaving a short time later.

"I guess I should wear something pretty fancy?" Already she was mentally sifting through her closet, choosing and discarding from her rather meager supply of dresses suitable for a cocktail party. Maybe she'd have to buy something, and she hated shopping.

Already she was having second thoughts about getting herself into this.

David was holding her in his arms in the darkened hallway, and now he kissed her hard before he answered. There was a smile in his voice.

"I'm about the last person you ought to consult about what to wear." His lips grazed across her ear, and he whispered, "Don't you know by now that all I want to do is take off whatever it is you're wearing, Annie?"

It was all she could manage not to start undoing buttons on the spot.

CHAPTER SEVEN

"Ooops...EXCUSE ME. I didn't spill any of that on you, did I, dear? How awfully clumsy of me."

"No harm done," Annie lied as she swiped at the darkening stain the red wine had left on the sleeve of her brand-new off-white dress. She held on tightly to the stiff smile she'd worn ever since she and David had arrived half an hour before at the opulent mansion on Marine Drive.

She tried to pretend polite nonchalance as the sleek and lovely woman gushed over David while keeping a precarious grip on the wine-glass she'd just spilled on Annie.

"Merv Kanmill introduced us at the Christmas party. You do remember, don't you, David? I'm Gillian Fraser."

"Hello, Gillian. This is Annie Pendleton."

Gillian's adroitly made-up eyes slid across Annie and then returned to rape David's features.

"Nice to meet you," she murmured, taking hold of his arm with her free hand and adding without a pause, "Come with me, David. There's someone over here you simply must meet."

David tried to tug Annie along with them, but she held back, and she caught the helpless glance he shot her as he was propelled away, Gillian's talonlike fingers secured around his forearm.

Annie wriggled her fingers at him and winked, trying to pretend she didn't mind one whit being left alone in the middle of this roomful of strangers. The truth was, she did mind, something awful.

Five minutes after walking into this huge chandeliered room, she'd begun wishing that she'd never agreed to attend the cocktail party with him, and that feeling had escalated with every succeeding moment.

The large group was comprised of people who either seemed to be intimate friends, or at least knew of one another by family name or political connection. It was a slick, plastic "in" group, and Annie felt decidedly out.

She was familiar with many of the faces present. She'd seen them before in the society and gossip sections of the daily papers. She'd just never wanted to meet any of them in person. Their world and hers were poles apart.

"Hello there. You must be Annie Pendleton."

The well-modulated male voice came from just behind her, and Annie turned toward it. Relief flooded through her for a giddy moment. At least whoever this was, he knew her name and he'd be someone to talk with for a few minutes.

"How do you do? I'm Calvin Graves," the well-dressed small man explained, giving her the faintest of faint smiles and extending a polite hand. "I saw you arrive with David, but he seems to have disappeared, so we'll simply have to introduce ourselves."

"He's just over there." Annie gestured to the group surrounding David, and then added, a beat too late, "How do you do? David's mentioned you several times." She remembered all her faint misgivings about this man, and found herself hoping that none of them were well-founded.

He seemed formal, a bit old-fashioned, perhaps? Should she call him Doctor? Mr. Graves? Calvin?

He didn't enlighten her. In fact, he barely touched her hand with his own before he withdrew it. He was not the hearty handshake type. Annie was also becoming aware that his pale, cool eyes were taking in every detail of her face and hair and clothing, and registering not one sign of approval or warmth.

It didn't make her feel at all comfortable.

"David tells me you're a writer, Annie. I may call you Annie, may I? Children's books, isn't that it?"

Was there something patronizing in his tone, or was this damned party simply making her paranoid?

"Annie's fine. Yes, I write fiction for kids. I'm working on one about magic at the moment. That's how I met David. I needed to talk to a magician and attended one of his performances at a school one afternoon. I found out later that he was a doctor masquerading as The Sorcerer. You're a doctor, too, aren't you?"

Damn, now he was making her babble.

One precise nod. "Semiretired, yes." He took a careful sip of the martini he held and swallowed with deliberation.

Uncomfortable silence formed a pool in the midst of the party clamor around them.

"You and David have known each other a long time," she finally commented, more to bridge the awkwardness than anything else.

"Yes. We've been close friends for years, even though we're in the unusual situation of being at opposite ends of our careers. Mine is winding down, and his is accelerating. Which is exactly as it ought to be.''

He paused a long time again, seeming to consider his next statement with care before he said it. Each word was precise, though devoid of emotional emphasis as he went on, ''David is a gifted young doctor with unlimited potential, but of course I don't have to tell you that. I'm sure you're aware of his capabilities. He's mentioned his aspirations to you, of course?''

Annie nodded, feeling a little confused. ''The organ transplant unit at the hospital—yes, he did tell me about it. I hope the funding becomes available. It sounds like something the city needs.''

''These things are never easy to achieve, you understand. They never happen by accident. They require hard work and a great deal of cooperation, as well as a dedicated man to hurry them along. And the right connections, of course. David has the potential, the charisma, to make quite a difference, and of course when he succeeds... Well, my dear, it's quite possible he might have a future in politics. Who knows?''

''I'm sure I don't,'' Annie said, mystified by the conversation. It was as if he was talking to her on several different levels, with undertones of meaning she wasn't sure she understood. Could he be hinting that she wasn't quite good enough for David?

''I understand you have a son.'' The rapid shift in subject confused her still further.

''Yes, I do. Jason is thirteen.''

''Hmmmm.''

The noncommittal sound made Annie's hackles rise for some unexplainable reason. What was that sound supposed to mean, exactly?

''A difficult age, thirteen,'' he said with pursed lips.

What the hell was she supposed to make of any of this, when it came down to it? Annoyance and apprehension mixed into the knot that had been in her stomach ever since she'd arrived.

She didn't like this man.

Calvin Graves was the kind of person who made her feel she must have food stuck in her teeth and smudged eye makeup. He also made her feel as if she wasn't quite bright enough.

It was disappointing, but David's friend just wasn't the sort of person she could ever feel comfortable with. He had all the warmth and animation of a two-day-old salad, and she had the definite impression that he was weighing her on some private scale and finding her wanting. Well, she didn't have to stand here and let it go on any longer.

''If you'll excuse me, I think I'll wander over there and get some food,'' Annie said with a final, polite, strained smile.

She moved away fast. She was loading a tiny plate with lobster mousse and chilled shrimp and caviar, swearing under her breath, when a warm hand slid around her waist.

"Get rid of that stuff quick. I'm gonna feed you, but not here. We're getting out of here right now," David breathed into her ear.

"Thank heaven," she sighed. With casual aplomb, she abandoned the overflowing plate on one of the side tables and with her hand tight in David's soon found herself reclaiming the exotic shawl she'd borrowed from Cleo and being whisked out the door. Three people intercepted them on the way, and David somehow managed to slide past while still being polite and friendly.

Annie caught a glimpse of Calvin Graves talking with a group of dark-suited men near a stairwell. He glanced their way and made an imperious, beckoning gesture at David.

"David, a moment please—"

David waved with utter nonchalance and kept right on toward the door. Annie felt wicked triumph as the door closed behind them.

Take that, Calvin Graves. One mark for the girl from the wrong side of the tracks.

Freedom at last. The night air was salty and damp, and when the thick door had closed behind them, the sounds of the party inside had all but disappeared.

"Run for it, before somebody comes after us," David ordered in an urgent whisper, and they fled like children up the driveway and along the street. Annie started to giggle. It was incongruous to be running away from such an elite gathering.

When they were safe in the car, David laughed with her, and then he leaned back into the seat and whistled a long, low expulsion of relief.

"Lord, I can't stand these things. I don't know why I ever let Calvin talk me into coming tonight."

Annie wriggled her feet out of her high heels and sighed.

"He came over and introduced himself to me, you know, just after that woman with all the teeth dragged you away," she said. "Who was she, anyway?"

"Gillian the barracuda." David groaned at the memory and started the engine, pulling away from the curb with a roar. "On second thought, better forget I called her that. She's the wife of a prominent politician."

He grinned. "You know, I could tell she hated you on sight, Annie." His voice deepened in that intimate way that always thrilled her. "Because you're beautiful and young and soft and sexy and absolutely ravishing in that dress, and she is none of the above."

"Because I was there as your date, more likely." She'd noticed plenty of speculative looks coming her way from women tonight, and it certainly hadn't been her dress that had attracted them.

Not that there was anything wrong with the dress she and Cleo had shopped for most of last week. It was a short, classy white crepe that skimmed down her body and subtly hinted at her generous curves. It felt as sensual as she hoped it looked, but the party had been crawling with outfits that screamed "designer label" and probably cost thousands of dollars.

No, the female attention had been just because of David.

"You must be on Vancouver's most eligible bachelor list, Dr. Roswell. Or did you pose for some calendar you haven't told me about?" The acerbic words were out before she could consider how they might sound.

He laughed. "Not that I'm aware of, on either count."

She knew he was looking over at her, and she kept her attention on the traffic and buildings flashing past outside the car window. Her face felt hot because she realized her statement made her sound jealous and petty.

Well, damn it, she was jealous. Insecure as well, because until tonight she hadn't given any thought to the type of people David knew and felt comfortable around. She'd been too overwhelmed with the feelings he stirred in her to consider the other people in his life.

People like Calvin Graves, for instance. And that elite group of socialites back there.

Writers like her who earned a living but never set the literary world on fire didn't ordinarily rub shoulders with retired doctors, directors of hospital boards, or politicians and their wives.

If tonight was any indication of what that was like, Annie hoped she'd never have to again, either. They seemed to her to be an insular, self-centered lot.

"I'm glad you had a chance to talk to Calvin," David was saying. "I've mentioned you a lot over the past couple of weeks, and he's been eager to meet you."

It sounded natural and friendly when David said it. Why had the actual meeting set her teeth on edge? She struggled with a suitable, polite response.

"It was, umm, interesting, meeting him. He certainly speaks highly of you. He mentioned the transplant unit and how important it was to your career. I got the impression he expects great things from you," she ventured, looking over at his profile in the dim illumination from the streetlights outside and wondering all of a sudden just how much influence Calvin might have on David.

Annie knew for certain that she'd never find much common ground with that cold little man. Any common ground at all, she corrected, and shivered.

David frowned. "I'm afraid Calvin is inclined to be ambitious, not for himself but for me. He's been great at advising me to make certain career moves over the years, and his advice has always been good. Calvin's hobby is taking up causes, and he's making this transplant unit his priority issue at the moment. In fact, he's got some wild scheme for getting me on as an advisor to the Board of Directors at the hospital."

The ambiguous conversation with Calvin slowly began to make more sense to Annie. She'd been right in suspecting that Calvin was warning her off. He obviously had plans for David's career that didn't include a single mother who wrote little books for kids. He probably had the premier's daughter all picked out, she thought with malice.

Another thought struck her. Was Graves the sort of man who automatically considered Jason a bastard because she'd never married? His enigmatic attitude when she'd mentioned Jason seemed to suggest it.

She swallowed the deep anger that attitude always aroused in her and did her best to keep her voice even and casual.

"Is that what you want, David? To be on the Board of Directors, to get involved with the political structure of the hospital?"

His slight shrug was noncommittal. "Actually I hate meetings and hospital politics, but I guess I'd be willing to do whatever it takes to get the unit I want in place and operating, and as Calvin says, the Board is the logical first route."

It was becoming clear to Annie that Calvin Graves had been warning her tonight that there wasn't much room for her in David's future.

They were heading toward the downtown area, crossing Granville Street Bridge.

"Where are we going?" Annie felt the safest thing to do was change the subject, because she couldn't trust herself when it came to saying nice things about someone she didn't like.

"To the restaurant I went to that night I was out with Calvin. The food is great, and it's quiet, and I've been wanting to take you there."

Annie wished they were going to McDonald's instead, because she was pretty certain Calvin Graves didn't eat there.

"SO WHAT HAPPENED NEXT? Where did you go after this wonderful meal at the restaurant?" Cleo demanded.

She and Annie were sitting on the floor in Cleo's living room the next morning just after 10:00 a.m., surrounded by children of varying ages and a mad assortment of toys and kitchen utensils and old junk the kids seemed to love.

Cleo was comforting an eight-month-old baby girl named Lisa, and Annie was adjusting three-year-old Aaron's pants after a recent trip to the bathroom.

"Oh, we drove over to David's apartment," Annie replied, helping Aaron fit an assortment of shapes into a holder, cradling the tiny boy between her outstretched legs and saying, "Look, love, this one's a star. Where does it go? Good boy, that's exactly right." Annie planted a smacking kiss on Aaron's cheek.

"David has a place in one of those anonymous apartment buildings off of Oak Street. Expensive, well cared for, all the same, all decorated by the guys who do dentists' waiting rooms. He's got beige and brown and some glass blocks. And a nice fireplace that doesn't look as if he's ever lit it."

Without looking at Cleo, she added, "And please don't assume anything intimate happened after we got there, because it didn't."

Cleo threw her hands up in dramatic disgust. "I wasn't assuming, I was hoping, for gosh sakes. Talk about wasting precious time! How much longer do you plan to keep this relationship platonic, anyway? How will you ever know you're suited if you don't go to bed together? And what the hell did you do at his apartment if you didn't do...*that*?"

Annie ignored the first set of questions. "You've heard of conversation, haven't you? We talked. He showed me his library of books about magic, and helped me choose some that would help with this book of mine. I looked them over this morning, and they're exactly what I needed. There's even an obscure illusion he found for the kid in my book to do."

Cleo shook her head at such a colossal waste of time.

"Then we had coffee and talked some more, and then he brought me home. End of evening."

Cleo gave her a look. "Don't snow me, pal. There has to be a part of this you're censoring. I know it."

It hadn't actually been that uneventful. There'd been an intense interlude in David's arms, on his comfortable brown couch, when their "platonic" relationship had come close to changing into a passionate affair.

David had been the one who held back.

"I won't be put in the position of seducing you, Annie, of feeling as though I've brought you here with some sort of goal in mind. I'm falling in love with you. You must know that," he'd said, in a calm way that was much more effective than a passionate outburst might have been. And she'd known by the look in his eyes that his body and his senses were just as inflamed as her own.

"When the time comes, when it's right for you, we'll make love."

All the same, there'd been subdued anger and impatience in his voice. I'm falling in love with you, he'd said.

Those words kept her awake most of the night, and they'd managed to keep her from working that morning, which was why she'd finally abandoned her computer and sought out Cleo and the children.

She'd found in the past that holding Cleo's babies always made her feel better, no matter how serious the problem.

Was having David love her a problem?

Not in itself. It was what she longed for, deep in her soul, because she loved him as well.

But there were many complications. There was Jason and his irrational resentment of David, for instance.

Last night had also illustrated graphically that Calvin Graves could be a problem. And, as David sensed, there were her own deep-seated reservations about entering any long-term relationship with any man. For the tenth time that morning, she tried to explain to Cleo how she felt.

"I've been alone all my adult life. People become more set in their ways as they get older. It would be insane to get into something, and then end up alone all over again, with a broken heart as well as a resentful kid."

Cleo listened and for once didn't comment.

Annie bent her head and pressed her lips against Aaron's sweet-smelling baby hair, and a hot, evil stab of pain in her neck made her gasp and flinch. Beads of sweat formed on her forehead.

"Your back's acting up again, isn't it?" Cleo frowned as she handed Annie a mug of coffee and led Aaron over to the low table where the three other toddlers were making things from Play-Doh.

"Yeah. It's bothered me off and on ever since that first day I met David, and it's been getting worse ever since, for no reason at all. And now David's set up a whole battery of appointments and tests for me with every back specialist in town, beginning next week." Annie gave a disgusted sigh. "I'm not thrilled about it, but he seems to think some medical wizard might be able to help."

She sipped her coffee, and then blurted out in a low voice, "It's probably the best idea, though. You know, Cleo, there are times when I'm scared stiff I'll end up a bedridden invalid because of this stupid thing with my back." She felt tears well in her eyes, and she fought them, disgusted with herself for letting her deepest fears erupt.

Cleo was too wise to offer platitudes. "If you feel that's even a remote possibility, then you have to explore every avenue available in order to find treatment," she advised in her no-nonsense way. "And I can't think of anyone I'd trust more than David to help you."

The phone rang, and Cleo went to answer it in the other room, where she could hear over the babble of children's voices and babies' cries.

Annie talked to the group around the table, admiring the shapeless, lumpy objects they displayed with innocent pride, but her thoughts were a confused jumble.

Cleo's faith in David was well-founded. He was a person who invited trust, both as a man and as a doctor. Therefore, she ought to have confidence in their love for each other, right? Enough confidence to make love with him without reservations.

But it wasn't David she doubted, an inner voice reminded her. It was herself.

Cleo came back into the room excited. "Guess what? That was a guy with a three-month-old baby boy," she explained. "Same thing happened to him as happened to me. His wife walked out on him and his kid. She hasn't been heard from since the baby was two weeks old. The guy's name is Don Anderson, and he says he went on till just lately believing she'd come back. I remember doing the exact same thing, even leaving the door open when I went out somewhere in case Johnny wandered back. Anyhow, Don's over that finally, and now he needs day care for his son, starting right away. He's a cop. He says his holidays and sick time have both expired and he's got to get back to work. And he's finally given up believing she'll come back to him and the baby."

Cleo gave a sound intended as a laugh, but it came out more sad than amused. "I read the other day that there's actually just as many deserted fathers as there are deserted mothers these days. Can you believe there's no dating game to match us up?"

"Did you agree to help him, Cleo? Can you manage one more child, especially such a tiny baby?"

Cleo nodded. "Yeah, I'm sure I can. I can always get a couple of high-school girls to work for an hour or two in the afternoons if things get too hectic. But it's a little complicated because he works shifts, so the baby'll be here overnight every third week. He says he'll supply a crib."

"Make sure you charge enough extra for the inconvenience of having the baby here overnight," Annie warned. "I know you. You're liable to take one look at that sweet little baby and offer to take him for fifteen years or so for free."

"Nope," Cleo said. "After Mag's accident in the park, I started thinking about how important it is to have some sort of emergency fund put away. Sure our medical costs are covered in B.C., but what if the whole thing had been more serious than it was? Say she'd, Lord, I don't know—" Cleo shuddered. "Say Maggie'd lost an eye or something. If she'd needed treatment not available here, or even extensive dental repairs maybe? I simply wouldn't have had the money. So I'm starting to put away a little bit off each check, just in case. It helps me sleep better at night."

"I know exactly what you mean," Annie said. "I used to be terrified of having the dentist tell me Jason needed braces or something, back when we were really poor. Now I do just what you're doing. I keep a special fund just in case."

Annie went back to her quiet house shortly after that, and forced herself to sit in her chair in front of the computer and at least try to get a start on her second chapter.

She finally gave up trying to write, however; it was one of those rare days when nothing triggered the free flow of words.

She turned the computer off in disgust and started reading instead, choosing one of the books David had loaned her.

It was a history of magic down through the ages, beginning with ancient Egyptian lore, and she was soon engrossed in it.

For the rest of the day, while she munched a peanut butter sandwich for lunch, while she nibbled crackers and cheese late in the afternoon, she methodically skimmed her way through one after the other of David's books, not only looking for illusions and facts and ideas that might be helpful with her own book, but also reading with the need to learn more about the man who had collected these books and studied them, the man who had practiced the illusions described until he was adept at performing them.

She was beginning to understand just how much determination and practice were necessary before even the simplest illusion could be performed with any degree of competence, and her respect for David's skill as a magician as well as a new insight into just how determined he must be grew with every page she turned.

Sorcery had introduced her to David. Reading his books made her feel that she was getting to know a special part of him.

When Jason came home from school, she showed him some of the books. He paged through them, and Annie became engrossed again in a fascinating account of how modern illusions had almost all evolved from ancient times.

"I'm going down to the kitchen to make a sandwich, Mom," Jason announced. "Maybe I can read some of these before you give them back, okay?"

"Sure. Don't eat a whole loaf of bread. I'll make supper in about an hour."

Jason clattered down the stairs, and Annie was once again drawn into the world of illusion. The phone rang once, and Jason must have answered downstairs, so Annie went on reading.

"Mom?"

She looked up. Jason was standing in the doorway, and there was something about his expression that got Annie's full attention.

"Yes, Jase?"

"There was a man on the phone just now. He..." Jason's hands were curled into tight fists at his sides, and he was flushed and breathing hard, as if he'd been running.

Annie suddenly knew exactly what he was about to say, and she also knew that it was inevitable that this happened sooner or later. She ought to have expected it, prepared for it.

"It was my father on the phone, Mom. Michael McCrae, my my biological father. How come you never told me he's been calling here and wants to see me, Mom?"

Annie felt her abdomen grow tense with apprehension, and hot anger and outrage rose in her throat. Michael McCrae had absolutely no right to do this to her.

"I didn't know he wanted to get to know me." Jason's eyes were full of blame. "You shouldn't have kept the whole thing secret from me, y'know, Mom. You never talk about him or anything with me, and I mean, can't you understand?" His voice squeaked out of control. "He's my...my father, for cripes sake. I have a right to know about him." Jason's face was crimson.

The raw emotion contained in the statement struck terror in Annie's soul. Jason didn't sound anything like a child making childish demands. He sounded mature and outraged, like a person demanding what he knew to be his birthright.

He sounded like an angry adult, and the person he was angry at was her. She wished now that she'd discussed with Jason the things David had confided, the confused facts Jason had gathered somehow about Michael.

But she hadn't.

She'd thrust it to the back of her mind instead, hoping that if she ignored it, it might just disappear.

It had been both foolish and dangerous of her. She saw that now as words burst out of her son, words that must have been building inside of him for a long time.

"Even people who get divorced, like Frankie's parents—they got divorced—well, he still gets to see his father. He knows where he lives and what kind of guy he is and everything."

Jason's voice was intense and trembling. "Y'know, I used to think maybe my father was in jail or he'd done something awful?" Jason's dark brown eyes looked wounded, and Annie felt like weeping.

"I figured he must have, because you never would talk about him at all."

Annie gathered her wits and tried to explain. "Jason, your father was in India until just recently. You always knew that. I didn't realize...I guess I thought there's absolutely nothing about your father to be ashamed of. You have to understand, I...I just didn't know until, until just recently, that you even thought about him that much." Annie felt as if her heart were being torn in two.

Jason stood there, fists clenched at his sides. "So then why don't you want me to see him? He said on the phone just now that he'd like to get to know me. Why don't you want me to get to know him?"

Annie didn't know what to say. The deep-seated feelings she had about Michael McCrae were far too complex and even irrational to put into any words her son might understand.

Once again, as she had more and more often in the past few weeks, Annie felt her life slipping out of control, felt herself pressured into things she wasn't certain about, forced into facing a situation she didn't want to experience.

But looking at her son's contorted face, hearing the raw pain and troubled confusion in his voice, she had no choice but to face this.

"It's complicated, Jason," she heard herself saying. She felt defeated and old. "You and I have a pretty stable, happy life. It...it could make life a lot more difficult if your, your...father...got involved."

"I don't get it." He was looking at her with such cold accusation in his eyes. "How could knowing my dad make things different around here? You and I live here. I'm not even saying I want to go live with my father, Mom."

Jason, live with Michael? The thought had never crossed her mind, but now that he'd tossed it out, Annie began to wonder if her son didn't toy with the idea now and then.

A new and different apprehension came alive in her, and it made her much more impatient with Jason than she'd intended because it stirred overwhelming fear inside of her.

"I don't want to discuss this right now, Jason."

He didn't revert to the child who accepted her decisions, complaining sometimes, but recognizing her authority as his parent. Instead he stood planted, firm, frowning at her, and the new determination in his gaze, the patent lack of trust in his expression, frightened her more than she'd thought possible.

What had become of the little boy she knew and loved, the little boy who trusted and loved her more than anyone else in the world? He'd disappeared in the space of a phone call.

All Jason said now was "I want to see my father, Mom."

And then he stood there, stubborn, unmoving, waiting for her to give in to him.

CHAPTER EIGHT

"YOU CAN GET DRESSED NOW, Ms Pendleton, and then I'd like to see you in my office, please."

Annie waited for Dr. Kendrick to close the door before she climbed stiffly down from the examining table. During the past three days she seemed to have done little else but climb on and off examining tables.

Assorted doctors had performed endless tests and examinations, poked and prodded and questioned. Many of the procedures they put her through resembled medieval torture more than modern diagnostic medicine, and she was convinced the ever-increasing pain in her neck was being amplified by the medicine men who were supposed to be interested in curing it.

But this morning, the endless tests were finally over. Dr. Kendrick was the doctor she'd seen first, the coordinator of the series of tests David had arranged for her to have, and Kendrick was also the one who would give her the results of the whole, pointless—in Annie's estimation—series of tests.

Moments later, sitting in the comfortable and rather worn chair in the older doctor's office, Annie was disappointed but not surprised at his diagnosis.

"I hate to admit this, Ms Pendleton, but after all these disagreeable things we've put you through, we can find absolutely no physical cause for this pain in your neck."

The balding, pleasant-faced man frowned and toyed with a paper-weight beside the fat file folder with Annie's name on it.

"Now just because the pain you feel isn't life threatening and doesn't seem to have a physical origin related to injury, don't think I'm suggesting for a moment that it doesn't exist."

He tipped his chair back and folded his hands over his generous middle. "It causes you discomfort, and that's all that matters. However, we doctors tend to prefer a concrete reason for everything, simply because if we understand the origin of the problem, solving it becomes less difficult. With your particular problem, we are unable to pinpoint any cause, so therefore we'll deal with the pain itself."

He paused again and seemed to study her before he continued.

"Pain of this sort, pain which we consider psychosomatic in origin, for lack of any better label, can sometimes be controlled in much the same way we control physically-based pain."

"With prescription drugs," Annie supplied with a dejected sigh and a grimace, as bolts of white hot misery shot through her neck.

It seemed as if her body were taunting her, underlining the doctor's words in ironic counterpoint.

Psychosomatic pain. Was he hinting that she needed a shrink?

All of a sudden she felt rotten, drained and frustrated and angry, because after hours of submitting to every stupid test under the sun, still no one could say what was really wrong.

Some part of Annie had gone on hoping that David would be right, that new diagnostic techniques would reveal a physical reason for the persistent agony that plagued her. She'd been hoping that somewhere in the annals of medicine there would be a cure.

Now she felt utterly defeated. Dr. Kendrick was telling her, gentle as could be, that the real cause of this infernal thing was mental, that she was doing this to herself for some unknown reason.

"Sometimes we recommend drugs, but not exclusively," Dr. Kendrick was still explaining. "There are other methods that don't have the side effects drug therapy often does. There's biofeedback technique, for instance, and auto suggestion, often effective in controlling the discomfort. Another method is hypnotherapy. Many of my colleagues don't agree with me on this issue, but I've had remarkable results from patients who've tried hypnosis."

He gathered together pamphlets that described each system and scribbled several numbers on a paper and handed it to her.

"Read all the information. These are the places you can go to learn biofeedback. There's a center on Broadway, if you want more information, stop in there and pick up some pamphlets. If you decide to try hypnosis, then Dr. Steve Munro is the hypnotherapist I most often recommend. Think it over and then let me know. Whatever you decide, I'll arrange an appointment for you promptly."

Annie took the papers and stuffed them into her handbag, feeling as if the time she'd spent on the tests had been wasted.

It would be, if she walked out of here and let it go at that. She might as well waste a bit more and at least try this hypnosis thing, she decided on sudden impulse. She might as well explore every avenue available, because her neck wasn't getting a hell of a lot easier to bear.

"Make an appointment with this Dr. Munro for me, please," she instructed, and Kendrick immediately used the intercom and told his nurse to arrange it.

"He has a cancellation tomorrow at ten. Will that be convenient?"

Annie hadn't expected it to be so soon, but she agreed. The appointment was made, and she got to her feet.

Dr. Kendrick did, as well. He reached across the desk and shook her hand, his lined face a mixture of regret and resignation.

"Thank you for all the trouble you've gone to on my behalf," Annie said, giving him a strained smile. After all, it wasn't Kendrick's fault that nothing had been solved by all this. He'd done his best for her.

"My dear, I wish we could have helped you more than we have," he said with a rueful sigh. "We tend to believe that modern medicine is far advanced, but personally, I believe we're still in the sandbox stage, not even in kindergarten yet. There's so much we don't know. Will you let me know if the hypnotherapy helps at all?"

Annie was skeptical about even trying it. She knew precious little about hypnosis, but she nodded anyway and walked out into the brilliance of a sunny Vancouver day, struggling to throw off the depression and frustration she felt.

She was meeting David at a small café nearby for lunch, and she wanted to be cheerful and upbeat for him, despite the negative results of the assessment he'd arranged. She didn't want to spend the brief time they had together complaining.

David spent enough time with those who were depressed and ill during his working hours, she lectured herself. He didn't need more of the same from the person who loved him—who hadn't told him yet that she loved him. She'd only admitted it to herself that very week, while she was waiting for some procedure and had plenty of time to think.

Well, damn it all to purgatory, when had she had time alone with him to tell him anything lately?

She lifted her free hand and irritably massaged the base of her neck, the place where the pain seemed the worst.

Psychosomatic. If that was true, then she had to be a real nut case, creating this kind of problem for herself.

And if this was all some warped product of her imagination, she ought to be bloody well writing Stephen King-type horror stories instead of children's literature.

If she was disturbed mentally and didn't even know it, she was no fit partner for David, either, was she?

She strung together a pithy group of the worst words she knew, and repeated them under her breath until she felt better.

DAVID FELT as if he'd never manage to escape from his office in time to meet Annie for lunch as he'd planned. Two telephone calls came just at the last moment. Both were from parents anxious about children who were slated for surgery, so David spent precious moments explaining exactly what was going on with their kids.

When he finally hung up after the second call, he instructed, "Phyllis, absolutely no more calls. I'm not here to visitors. In fact pretend I'm not here at all. I'm leaving as soon as I grab my jacket."

He washed his hands and doffed the white lab coat for his light tweed sport jacket, squinting at himself in the mirror over the sink. He still hadn't found time for a haircut, and his hair was now curling far below his shirt collar.

Well, what the hell. At least it wasn't falling out the way it was for some guys his age. He shoved his damp fingers through the sides of his hair, smoothing them back, and promptly forgot all about haircuts as his mind went to his luncheon with Annie.

She'd have the results of the assessment by now. He was eager to find out what George Kendrick had recommended.

Bull. He was just eager to be with the woman he loved.

He was thrusting his arms in the sleeves of his coat when Calvin walked through the doorway into the office.

"Well, seems I caught you just in time. How are you, David?"

"Great, Calvin. And you?" David forced a grin and shook the hand the other man proffered, but inside he felt a little irritated. Why did it seem as if everything conspired against his time with Annie?

"I've been trying to get in touch with you so that we could talk. I came by hoping you might be free for lunch today. There're several matters I need to discuss with you before that dinner meeting on Friday. You do remember agreeing to attend that meeting, David?"

David had forgotten all about agreeing to attend the damn thing.

"I'll be there," he promised. "But as far as today goes...well, the fact is, Calvin, I'm meeting Annie in a few minutes."

"I'm sorry to be insistent, my boy, but there are matters that I absolutely must talk over with you. Today."

David couldn't help but suggest, "Well, then, would you care to join us for lunch, Calvin?"

He found himself hoping that Calvin would refuse, but the other man considered it for a long moment with his head tipped slightly to the side, and then nodded, rather as if he were doing David a favor.

"Actually I suppose that will be fine, David. I have a meeting at two this afternoon, but until then I'm free."

David couldn't stop the rush of disappointment and irritation he felt at Calvin's acceptance.

"Fine, let's get out of here then. The café is just three blocks from here, so we might as well walk."

It was a small and petty rebellion against the older man. David knew perfectly well that Calvin was less than enthusiastic about walking anywhere except out of his car and onto a golf green, where he immediately rented a motorized cart.

Calvin drew his mouth down in disapproval, but he didn't say anything. David was forced to shorten his long, impatient strides to match his friend's more sedate pace once they reached the sidewalk, and it simply added to David's impatience to have to creep along amidst the bustling crowds as Calvin went on and on about this committee, that association, the need for courting some official.

David saw Annie when they were still half a block away, and his heart opened and his soul lifted at the sight of her.

She was wearing a vibrant yellow dress, sitting at one of the outside tables with her chin propped on her hand, her body not relaxed but tense, waiting for him.

It pleased him that her waiting was visible to him. Her gleaming hair was caught up in a rich, high knot at the back of her head. She was wearing sunglasses, but David knew she was watching the crowd, watching for him.

He also knew that she stiffened a trifle when she saw Calvin beside him. She hid her reaction well, however, and smiled a welcome when they drew closer to the table.

"Hi, Annie. You remember Calvin." David did his best to convey subtle apology in the simple greeting, and she slid her glasses to the top of her head and took the limp hand Calvin extended.

"How nice to see you again," Calvin said with a jovial smile. "I hope you don't mind my joining you. I'm afraid I appeared in David's office at the last moment and he had no choice except to invite me."

David drew up two chairs and sat down close beside her.

"Of course I don't mind," Annie lied, and when Calvin turned his attention to the exuberant young waiter who'd appeared at his side, David gave her a quick, reassuring wink and then leaned over and planted a slow, luxurious kiss on her full, red mouth.

He regretted the impetuous action when fullness and heat surged in his groin, making him shift in his chair.

But he loved the way her eyes softened and slow color rose in her cheeks. She glanced over at Calvin, who was now drilling the waiter over precisely what kind of mustard they used in the sandwiches. If it wasn't Dijon, Calvin insisted they leave it out. He ignored the kiss as if it had never happened.

"I'll have deviled egg on whole wheat, and iced tea," Annie ordered when the waiter turned her way, and David, disinterested in food, simply said he'd have whatever Calvin had ordered.

It turned out to be a good choice; German beer with a fat ham on rye, but while they ate, David grew more and more uncomfortable.

Calvin was acting as if Annie wasn't present at all, and she was sitting silent, not eating, not talking.

Even though David understood his friend's single-minded fixation on getting things in order and settled, still he resented the way Calvin narrowed the conversation to include only himself and David.

"I think it's time we moved ahead as planned on your campaign, my boy. Summer's over, which means everyone's back in harness. The first general meeting of the hospital board is less than three weeks away, and it's time to concentrate on strategy. There are several social functions coming up that I feel you absolutely must attend. The first is a black-tie dinner, I've already arranged for invitations...."

"You remember I mentioned that Calvin wants me to campaign for the position of advisor to the Board of Directors at the hospital," David explained to Annie, using one hand to eat his sandwich. "I've more or less agreed." He reached across the checked tablecloth and grasped Annie's cold fingers in his, giving them a reassuring squeeze and holding on when she tried to pull away.

He wanted contact with her, but he also wanted Calvin fully aware of his feelings about Annie. He wanted to force his friend to acknowledge her.

"Now the other area we have to address if this is to work is that of public support. Television interviews, newspaper coverage, that sort of thing."

David wished Calvin would shut up. He wanted to know how the morning's assessment had gone for Annie. He wanted to sit in the sunshine and the open air and simply enjoy being with her, tell her how pretty she looked in that daffodil-yellow dress.

He didn't want to be bothered today with publicity, or black-tie dinners that he knew would bore him cross-eyed, or anything else Calvin considered earth-shattering enough to discuss here in the sunshine on a hot fall afternoon.

But it was also unfair to agree to play the game and then leave Calvin out there doing it alone, wasn't it?

When he'd made up his mind to go ahead and let Calvin put the machinery into operation, David had thought of the meetings he'd have to attend, the hours of precious time that would be taken up with sense-less politicking, and at first he'd told himself he couldn't go through with it.

But then he thought again about perhaps being in a position to influence the power makers into allotting funds for the unit. Most of all, he thought about Charlie and his baby sister, and he'd given Calvin the go-ahead.

David had always been a man who made decisions quickly and surely and stuck by them, but he already regretted this one.

Calvin subsided finally, looking more than a little grumpy at David's obvious lack of interest.

David noticed Annie had been unable to eat even half of her sandwich. He still had her hand trapped in his, and now she glanced at her watch, extricated her hand and stood, looping her purse over her shoulder and wincing, then taking the bag in her hand instead.

David guessed that she was in pain again. There was something else as well, some tension in her that he couldn't identify.

"I've got to go, David. I...have a lot to do this afternoon. My editor will be phoning around two."

He'd been foolishly hoping that they could linger until Calvin was forced to leave, and then salvage something out of the day for themselves. Feeling as if their time together had been ruined, David stood as well.

"I'll walk you to your car," he said, and when she began to protest, he ignored her and turned to a disgruntled Calvin.

"I won't be long. Order me a coffee, would you?"

When they were out of earshot, he swore. "Damn Calvin and his persistence. I wanted to be alone with you, Annie. How did the tests go?"

He'd be phoning Kendrick, but he wanted to hear her reaction.

"About what I expected." She told him the details, careful to hide her own disappointment at the inconclusive diagnosis. She skipped the psychosomatic bit and the suggestions about hypnosis. They could discuss that later.

He was holding her hand in his; the sun was bright, and they were together. Everything else was unimportant now.

The parking garage where she'd left her car was nearby, and she paused outside the entrance. "My car's just inside on the first level. Don't bother coming in." She couldn't help adding with a touch of malice, "Calvin will be getting impatient."

"To hell with Calvin. I'll see you tonight. It might be after nine because I've got a late meeting," he explained, leaning forward to kiss her, not trusting his body's reactions should he take her in his arms on the busy street and hold her tight against him the way he wanted to.

He waited while she retrieved her car, and he paid the attendant when she presented her ticket.

She smiled and blew him a kiss as she drove out into traffic.

He watched her drive away, and then, with a reluctance he'd seldom felt before, he made his way back to Calvin.

ANNIE HAD STRETCHED the truth a little in order to escape. Her editor had said she'd call, but no time had been set.

Gritting her teeth as she inched her way through heavy traffic and along the busy streets toward home, Annie couldn't shake the anger and outrage Calvin Graves had once again managed to stir in her.

How dare he horn in on one of the few times she and David had managed to arrange to have lunch? How dare he act as if she were the intruder, and not him? How dare he usurp their precious hour together with his blathering about meetings and dinners and appointments?

Lord, she didn't like that man. She'd have to tell David sooner or later, explain that she didn't ever want to be in Calvin's company again. How could David...

Her train of thought came to an abrupt end as she pulled up in front of her house, turned off the key and sat motionless as she reasoned through what she'd been thinking.

What right did she have to be critical of David's choice of friends? What if David had acted this way about Cleo?

She pushed the idea away, telling herself how warm, how vibrant and friendly and nice Cleo was compared to Calvin.

Honesty made her stop short again. The simple fact remained: Cleo was her friend, and David had done his best, gone far out of his way, to accept her friend.

Calvin, for whatever complex reasons, was David's friend.

Surely she owed him the same courtesy he'd given her—an honest attempt to accept the other people in his life.

Damn it. She banged an angry fist against the steering wheel. Damn it all to Hades and back again.

Was this what being half of a couple meant? Wasn't this the thing she'd been avoiding by staying single and apart all these years, this compromising of her instinctive feelings? Was it worth any amount of compromise to be in love with David, to have his love in return?

Her mind, her heart and her soul answered without a single hesitation, immediate, deep and irrefutable.

Yes and yes and yes.

She loved David, and that was that.

So she'd simply have to try harder with old Calvin Graves, wouldn't she?

Feeling weary to the very bone, she got out of the car and went into the house, then put the kettle on and made a pot of tea to take up to her workroom, where she turned on the computer.

She stared at the words on the screen, trying to get out of her own way so the story could continue. If only there was secret knowledge buried inside of her, the way there was inside of her young hero.

Annie's proposed book was about a boy named Seth, born with a deformed arm and hand, who would become fascinated with magic.

Although he could only perform the simplest of tricks because of his limited dexterity, in his dreams Seth saw himself performing one specific, complex illusion, a trick he couldn't remember ever having witnessed.

He would visit the Magic Store, a strange, musty hole-in-the-wall establishment that proved to have every magic book ever written, but when he tried to find a description of the dream trick in books, or locate a magician who performed it, Seth would realize that no one had ever heard of it.

The illusion would become an obsession to the boy. Although he remembered the essentials, there would be portions of the trick missing from his dream, parts Seth knew he could figure out if only he could truly practice magic.

If only he weren't handicapped.

The eccentric old magician who ran the Magic Store would insist that Seth stop talking about why he couldn't do magic, and just see himself doing it the way he did in his dreams.

Seth slowly would begin to try. By the end of Annie's book, real magic would happen.

By believing absolutely that he could perform the illusion, and reaching a point in his mind where he no longer doubted in any way, Seth would do the impossible.

Annie skimmed the outline, locating the scene she was developing.

She'd been working for over an hour, using pure force of will to shove everything but the story out of her mind, and after a while she'd even managed to block out the insistent ache in her neck. She was typing in a furious rush when the doorbell sounded, and she swore with disgust.

She ran down the stairs and threw the door wide, wanting to get whatever it was over with fast. Two uniformed policemen stood there, and between them was her son.

"Mrs. Pendleton?"

Jason's face was a tight mask, rebellious and closed.

"I'm Constable Marsh, and this is Constable Stevens. Could we talk to you for a few minutes?"

"Come in," Annie managed. When they were in the hall she shut the door and turned, terror making her whole body stiff.

"What...what's happened?" She looked at the policemen, and then at Jason, but he let his glance slide away from hers.

"We caught your son and one of his friends an hour ago sneaking into a movie theater downtown, without paying. We'd already been notified that they'd done the same thing at a different theater, earlier today."

"But today's a school day," Annie said. "He's supposed to be in school." She realized how stupid that sounded, but she couldn't seem to grasp what was going on.

"I thought he was in school," she heard herself repeating like an idiot.

"Exactly," Constable Marsh confirmed.

Constable Stevens took over. "Jason assures us that he's never been in trouble before. Is that right, Mrs. Pendleton?"

"Yes. I mean no, he never has. And it's Ms Pendleton." Her brain was beginning to function again, but she was out of her depth here. "Is Jason...what will happen..."

"We found him committing an act of juvenile delinquency. And of course you're aware that the downtown theater district isn't a healthy place for a kid as young as Jason to be hanging out."

Annie actually felt as if she might faint.

"Because he hasn't been in trouble before, however, the police aren't going to press a charge in this instance. But should he come to our attention again, we would take him before a juvenile court."

Annie realized she and the officers were talking as if Jason wasn't right there, listening to all this.

"Jason?" she questioned.

She looked at her son. His freckles were standing out against the whiteness of his skin, but he wouldn't meet her eyes or deny what was said.

Juvenile court. Delinquent. It was a nightmare.

"Our suggestion to Jason is that he make some effort to repay the theater, perhaps by volunteering to do several hours of work for them, cleaning up or something."

"Yes, yes of course," Annie agreed. Jason still wouldn't look at her, still stood immobile between the officers. Annie felt as if they'd all been standing there for hours like that, and she wanted these men to go, to walk back out the door and leave—leave her alone with her son, so they could work this out somehow between them, so Jason could tell her what had really happened.

At last, they did. They left a card with their names on it, and said to call if she had any questions. The door closed behind them, and still Jason stood unmoving.

"Jason?" Annie's voice was trembling, but she couldn't seem to control it. "Jason, why? Why did you do a thing like that? You have your own money, you're allowed to go to movies on weekends. But to play hooky, to sneak in...I never thought you'd..."

Do something like this, Annie's mother used to say, voice trembling with deliberate pathos. I never thought my own daughter would do something like this. To me.

The whole time Annie was growing up, over every smallest transgression, that had been her mother's cry. Every large one as well, including that one last time when she'd refused to marry Michael, when she was pregnant and already in disgrace.

Her mother had said then exactly what Annie had been about to say to Jason.

"Come in the kitchen and we'll have a glass of milk and talk about this," Annie substituted, her tone as reasonable as she could manage.

But Jason shook his head. His face was shuttered. He brushed roughly past Annie and a moment later, the door to the basement opened and slammed.

Fury exploded inside of her. She raced over to the door, tore it open, and shrieked like a madwoman at his disappearing back, "You get back up here, young man, if you know what's good for you. Don't you dare walk out on me, do you hear? I want to know what you think you were doing today."

He stopped and turned, and came inch by inch back up the steps. When he reached the top, he looked her in the eye for the first time, and she could tell behind his mute show of bravado that he was afraid and alone. Behind the thrust out lip and the rebellious eyes, a frightened child was hiding.

Annie melted.

"Oh, Jase..."

She reached out, took his shoulders in her hands and drew him toward her to hug him, but he pulled violently away, moving behind the table as if it were a shield and she were the enemy.

"Jason, what's going on? I don't understand any of this. What's happening to you? You're changing. I don't feel I know you anymore."

He seemed to be holding his breath, but then it let go in a torrent of words that started low and intense, and increased in volume as his boy-man's voice traveled from bass to squeaky soprano and back down again.

"It's not me, Mom. You can't just blame me for everything around here. You do things, too, you know. You promise things and then you never do them. All you think about is your stupid boyfriend these days. You never think about me anymore, or do what you promise."

It took willpower, but Annie controlled her own voice. "What have I promised and not done, Jason?"

He sounded so angry, and his words tore at her. His control evaporated, and tears began rolling down his cheeks. His voice rose to a shriek.

"You promised me you'd see about letting me meet my father. You promised and then you never did it, and I hate you, you know that? I hate you, hate you, hate you."

He knocked over a chair on his flight to the back door, and by the time Annie could make herself move, he was out the back gate and running down the alley.

There was no way of ordering him back this time, and she couldn't have anyway, because her sobs were choking her.

CHAPTER NINE

THE TROUBLE WITH RAISING a kid on your own, Annie told herself as she struggled for control, was that you had only yourself to blame for the mistakes you made.

And you had to wait alone for him to come back when he ran away like this.

Half an hour had gone by since Jason slammed out the door, and she'd just managed to stop crying. She blew her nose hard and filled the coffee maker.

There was a sharp, familiar tap on the back door and Cleo came in, giving Annie's arm a sympathetic squeeze and acknowledging in silence her tearstained face and reddened eyes.

"The kids heard Jason having a fit a while ago, and they said he ran off down the alley. Maggie followed him. She said he's gone over to Jeff's place. So I called Jeff's mother and acted real casual. I said that Maggie was looking for him, and she assured me the boys were downstairs watching *Star Trek*, just so you know where he is."

Annie breathed a sigh of relief. She'd been trying to decide what she ought to do to find him.

"Thanks." The tears she'd managed to stifle now rolled down her cheeks all over again. She used her hands to wipe them away and sniffled.

Cleo handed her the box of tissues. "I figured I'd come and have coffee with you before we head for the bridge."

It was an old joke between them. Early in their friendship, Cleo had gone through a particularly bad time, with one calamity right after another. One morning, she'd burst into Annie's kitchen and collapsed in tears, announcing hysterically that she was fed up with it all, that she couldn't take anymore, she was about to jump off the nearest bridge and be done with the whole mess.

Annie had suggested they have a cup of coffee first, and then she'd drive Cleo to the bridge. After all, somebody had to bring the car home and feed the kids lunch.

They'd ended up laughing like a pair of maniacs, and then they'd talked over Cleo's problems and come up with a temporary solution.

Now Annie managed a shaky smile.

"Jason's getting harder to manage every single day," she said in a small voice. "The police were here. He skipped out of school and sneaked into a movie without paying. Two movies, in fact."

Cleo took mugs from the cupboard and filled them from the coffee-pot.

"Two, huh? Jason never does anything by halves. Well, I did that a couple of times when I was a teenager, not sneak into movies, but skip out of school. I was mad at my mother."

"He's mad at me because I haven't let him meet Michael."

"I figured it was probably something like that."

"I told Jason I would, and I've been putting it off. I guess I have to call McCrae and get it over with."

Cleo sipped her coffee. "I guess you do."

Annie shuddered. After a moment, she said, "You know those doctors I saw this week? Well, their diagnosis was that there's nothing wrong with my neck. According to them, the pain is psychosomatic. And after this fiasco with that kid, I'm ready to accept that my head is on crooked."

Cleo snorted. "So what do they know? I actually had a doctor tell me the same thing about childbirth. What I thought was pain was purely psychological, he said. I was having contractions, no pain allowed, thank you very much."

Annie met her friend's eyes. "The thing is, maybe they're right about me, Cleo, because I do feel like a psycho about this Michael McCrae thing. I get physically sick when I have to talk to him on the phone. I can't bear the thought of actually meeting him face-to-face. I actually have nightmares of him chasing me with intent to murder. Why should a middle-aged man I haven't seen in years affect me this way? Maybe I am a bit mental. After all, why should I still feel so emotional about him?"

Cleo shrugged. "Who knows? Maybe after you do meet him again, you'll find out it isn't as bad as you thought. Sometimes we build things up in our heads, and they're really not as bad when they happen."

Annie gave her a baleful look. "Don't feed me that, Cleo. Usually they're worse."

The back door opened, and Maggie stuck her head in, the bandage on her temple now reduced to a giant-size Band-Aid. She was wearing her prissy, managing expression.

"That man's at our house with his baby, Mommy," she announced. "I'll tell him you're coming right now, okay?"

"Never a dull moment," Cleo sighed. "That's my deserted father with his kid. I better go convince him I'm a stable, responsible human being, which isn't going to be easy." She got up and followed her daughter out the door. "Let me know if there's anything I can do."

The telephone began to ring, and Annie called a hasty thank-you after Cleo and lifted the receiver.

It was Jason. "Ma, I'm over at Jeff's house. I figured you might be worried." He was doing his best to sound offhand and tough, but the tension was there.

Annie kept her tone as even as she could.

"Under the circumstances, Jason Pendleton, I think you'd better come home right away."

"Whatever," he said in a bored, gloomy voice.

"No whatever about it. Home, now."

She'd sit him down and they'd have a long, honest talk.

BUT SOMEHOW IT DIDN'T WORK. They sat, Annie talked and Jason did little more than nod and grunt a few times.

There was no way she knew of to make a thirteen-year-old talk when he chose not to. He nodded when she said he was to apologize to the manager of both theaters and offer to work off his debt. He nodded when she said she would not have him bully her, his mother, through misbehaving, into doing what he, Jason, wanted her to do.

And, she concluded—and this was much more difficult—despite what Jason thought, she'd meant to keep her word about getting in touch with his father. She would phone, tonight, and set up a meeting, for tomorrow if that was possible.

But the final decision about that was still hers to make, not Jason's. "If, for any reason, I feel it's not a good idea to involve Michael McCrae in our lives, I expect you to accept that without giving me a lot of grief over it," she said.

He met her eyes for the first time. "That's not fair," he stated flatly.

Annie came near to losing her temper all over again.

"Fair or not, that's the way it's going to be. I happen to be the adult in this family, and I still make the rules."

He rolled his eyes and went off to his room without another word.

DAVID PHONED LATER that evening, and talked fast because he was stealing the time from a meeting he was supposed to be in.

"Annie, this infernal thing is running late. In fact, it looks for all the world as if it's going on into infinity. I want to see you, but I had the feeling today you were really tired. Instead of coming over tonight, how about having a real, honest-to-goodness date with me on Saturday night?''

Before she could do more than smile at the idea, he hurried on, ''I'll spring for chocolates, flowers, wine and a fancy dinner, with dancing thrown in as icing on the cake. I'll even get a haircut,'' he promised with rash abandon, and she laughed, the first time she'd really laughed that whole long, miserable day.

David touched her heart without even trying.

''Get a haircut and the deal's off, buster. Don't you know it's that romantic, untamed hair that I fancy?''

Disappointment mingled with relief when she hung up. Much as she would have liked to see David that night, she'd about had it.

She put the next phone call off as long as possible, but finally she forced herself to dial the number her son had scribbled all over the pad beside the phone. Michael McCrae answered, and she made arrangements to meet him and his wife on Thursday afternoon, being as brisk as she could.

Thursday was tomorrow.

Annie hung up the phone, wondering what was wrong with her head. She had to go to the hypnotherapist in the morning, and now she was committed to meeting this man she detested in the afternoon. It wasn't going to be one of her better days, for sure. But then, neither had today been anything but disastrous.

As if she could scrub off the residue of the day's calamities, she ran a tub of hot water and rubbed soap on a cloth and then all over herself, over and over again. She was in bed and asleep by ten-thirty.

SHE REALIZED it was a dream, because part of her knew she was lying in bed asleep while it happened. Her right hand was outside the covers and cold. But another part, just as much her, just as real, was in another place. Another time.

The whitewashed room was small, the walls were thick stone. There were two windows. There was a fireplace on the inside wall, and the stone chimney formed the division between the kitchen and the room where she now sat in a comfortable rocking chair, holding a sweet-smelling, dark-haired child and singing her to sleep.

It was evening, a late summer evening. The soft rosy light coming in the windows would soon give way to darkness. The cow was milked, the chickens locked in their shed for the night.

She was alone. She was lonely, but there were worse things than loneliness.

The child's father was gone, had been gone for a long time now, almost since the war began, and it was a tremendous relief to her. She didn't miss him, even though she had to work hard to keep the small farm in order, even though she was often frightened when she felt rather than heard the far-off booming of the guns and thought about what would happen if the fighting came closer.

So far, they'd been lucky in this tiny hamlet.

The child stirred against her breast, and she bent and put her lips to the velvet cheek. This child was the best thing that had come out of her marriage. She ought to put her in the bed, but there was such comfort in the feel of the small, warm body.

Suddenly there was a knocking at the seldom-used door at the far end of the room.

Alarmed, she got up with the child cradled in her arms, moved into the small adjoining bedroom and laid her carefully in her bed.

Then, heart hammering, she hurried to the door and opened it, just a crack. These were troubled times.

The man, the tall foreign man, smiled at her in apology, and it seemed as if her heart would pound its way out of her chest as she looked up at his face. His eyes were a deep and smoky blue, like the sky over the Seine just before the darkness fell, and there was a sadness in the lines of his face.

Her fear had evaporated as soon as she looked into his eyes. She wanted to stretch out a hand and smooth the lines away.

Annie moved in her sleep, her cold hands grazing her cheek, and the part of her that was dreaming thought the face was his and it confused her, just for an instant, in the time it took to cross the boundaries of the dream and come half awake.

She'd been in that dream before. It was familiar. She remembered the path below the house, beside the river...

Moments later, she slept again, and the dream was forgotten when morning came.

AT NINE, waiting in Dr. Steven Munro's unpretentious office, Annie felt nervous and out of place. She wished with all her being that she'd never agreed to this appointment.

The waiting-room receptionist was a plump, motherly woman and the whole place had an air of casual messiness. Magazines were scattered in haphazard disarray across a battered table, and there was a blue-

and white budgie in a cage in the corner, hopping from perch to perch and shrilling out indecipherable noises.

The atmosphere reinforced Annie's feelings about hypnosis in general; that there was nothing professional about the process, and that it could hardly result in anything that would benefit her miserable neck pain.

She came close to walking out after she'd waited ten minutes past the hour set for her appointment, but just as she was making up her mind, the woman at the desk smiled and said, "Steve will see you now."

Steve? Annie's expectations were well below zero when she walked into the inner room that, just as the rest of the place, looked more like a cozy, messy, artist's study than a doctor's office.

"Hi, Annie. I may call you Annie? I'm Steve. We're pretty easygoing around here. That's my wife, Edith, at the front desk."

He wore an ash-stained electric-blue tie, wide and garish, and a green shirt that clashed with everything else. His sleeves were rolled up past his elbows. His jacket was slung across a chair and his pants bagged at the knees and backside. He was short and stocky, and it was hard to say how old he was. He wore small reading glasses on a blue string around his neck. His bushy black hair was receding, his nose was large and his soft, dark eyes could have belonged to a young child. They were gentle, questioning, and they seemed to take her in and accept her without criticism.

It was impossible to be nervous around Steve Munro, and Annie felt the tension begin to flow out of her as he motioned her to a seat on a battered gray couch along one wall.

To Annie's surprise, he knew without referring to any chart exactly why she was there, the nature of her neck problem and the tests that had been done during the past days.

Steve Munro did his homework, and it restored Annie's confidence somewhat.

He chatted about the weather, asked her what she worked at, and seemed fascinated by the idea of her being a children's writer. Finally he said, "How much do you know about hypnotherapy, Annie?"

"Not much at all," Annie confessed. "Practically nothing, in fact. I know hypnosis is used as a magician's trick at times, but beyond that..."

"It sounds like a lot of mumbo jumbo to you?" he inquired with a crooked grin that revealed a chipped front tooth. She felt herself flush.

"Yeah, pretty much." No point in lying. He might as well know from the beginning that she was dubious as hell about this whole thing.

"Well, I thought the same until a few years ago. I was trained as a clinical psychologist, you see, conventional, formal, emphasis on scientific method, reverence for Freud and the rest of the big boys." He smiled at her, an endearing, humble smile. "Unearthing subconscious material and bringing it to the surface where it can be dealt with works. We all know and accept that." He strolled around the room as he talked, and Annie decided she liked his voice. It was deep and musical, at odds with the unassuming figure it came from.

"Trouble is, analysis is a long, expensive process. I found myself wanting a shortcut to the inner mind, and along with a lot of other people in my field, I started studying hypnosis as a tool that would speed up the process."

"It's a fairly new idea, isn't it?"

"Nope," he declared. "Hypnosis is as old as Methusela. It's been employed as a tool since the beginning of history. There were famous sleep temples in ancient Greece and Rome, and the priests used hypnotic procedures. Many passages of the Bible refer to it. The British Medical Association in 1955 and the American Medical Association in 1958 gave hypnosis official sanction. Even old Freud, at the end of his long career, stated that hypnosis, because of its efficiency, was the key to helping people. My attitude has always been, if a thing works, use it. So I learned hypnotherapy."

"And do you find it effective?"

"Yup." There was total conviction in his answer. "I've used it for years now, and I'm convinced it's helped countless patients." He collapsed like a boneless puppet into an armchair every bit as battered as the couch, facing Annie.

"What we'll attempt to do for you, Annie, is instruct the subconscious mind to relieve that pain in your neck, and maybe also we'll be able to uncover some reason for it that you've decided to bury deep in your memory, some trauma that you don't remember at all."

"Is that what you think I've done, suffered some awful experience and then shoved it out of my awareness?"

He shrugged. "It's certainly possible."

"I doubt it. My childhood and adolescence were pretty ordinary and easy." Annie was still dubious. "But I'm willing to give this a try, so do me and let's get it over with," she said in a tone of resignation, settling back stiffly on the couch and closing her eyes.

Munro's laugh was big and musical.

"Not so fast. You're too quick for me. This isn't a shot in the arm. Let's talk a bit more first. I have to lead up to this a bit slower. I'm a slow sort of guy. Tell me why the thought of being hypnotized scares you witless."

Annie opened her eyes and stared at him. "But I didn't say that it did."

He grinned. His teeth were stained from smoking. "If it doesn't, so much the better. Most people have a deep fear of hypnosis, of giving up control to someone else. They worry about losing consciousness, not knowing what's happening, having the hypnotist plant macabre suggestions in their poor minds."

It was uncanny, but he was describing exactly the half-formed concerns Annie had been trying to ignore.

For the next half hour, Annie listened again and asked questions as Steve dispelled every one of the fears she hadn't wanted to put into words.

"First of all, you don't lose consciousness the way you do when you're sleeping. You enter a deeply relaxed state, and you begin to focus more and more inwardly. You'll always be aware of me guiding you to some degree. But your conscious and subconscious mind are in control, not me."

At last, when every one of her questions were answered, he casually suggested she stretch out on the couch and relax.

Annie found she was tense and shaky again when they reached this part of the procedure, but Steve's deep, resonant voice instructed her to concentrate only on her breathing and its rhythmic pattern: in, out, in, out.

"Relax your scalp," he went on, and continued with all the muscles of her face, neck, shoulders, and on down her body, until Annie was only aware of a deep, tranquil sense of total peace.

"This process will become easier and easier to accomplish as our sessions go on," he reassured, and she could feel herself silently agreeing. It was such a pleasant, floating sensation, such an untroubled place to be.

He took her to an imaginary garden, a place of placid beauty, and used the various senses, one by one, to experience the scene. She smelled a rose, saw the rainbow of colors before her, heard the gentle song of birds and the trickle of water from a nearby stream.

By now Annie felt more than half asleep, comfortable, warm, lost in a wonderful daydream as he had her imagine pure, clear white light flooding through her, cleansing her, before he led her to examine her body from outside herself.

"The pain you experience in your neck is visible as a hard, red knot. Concentrate on untying that knot, Annie. Smooth it out, see it uncurl, and watch the red give way to healthy pink. The pain is going, and each time you concentrate on this image, it will diminish more and more.''

Annie followed the suggestion. It actually seemed as if the nagging discomfort diminished.

"We're going to travel backward now, Annie. As I count backward you will envision the years of your life and travel down them, back to childhood times.

"Thirty, twenty-five, twenty..."

"WHAT WENT WRONG? Why did I just come out like that?''

Annie was sitting up again, having a cup of tea Edith had just brought in.

She was beginning to anticipate the wordless shrug Steve used so graphically. "Haven't got a clue. It happens. Next time will be easier, and the next easier still. That is, if you decide to continue.''

The hypnotic session had ended abruptly when Steve was guiding her somewhere through her early twenties. She'd suddenly felt a strong urge to escape the images he was encouraging, and she'd promptly opened her eyes and sat up.

"I don't want to do this anymore," she'd announced with childish determination.

"No problem," Steve had said agreeably. "We made good progress anyway for a first session. How's your neck?''

Annie rolled her head from side to side, waiting for the shaft of pain that always accompanied the movement. There was a faint discomfort, but the sharp knifing sensation that had been there when she arrived this morning was gone.

"Why, it's lots better.'' She gave him a grateful smile. "I definitely want to try again, Steve.''

"Great. I want you to take these tapes home with you and use them. They're deep relaxation tapes. Try them a couple of times a day and always end with the auto suggestion I gave you for your neck. Next time, they'll make the hypnosis easier because you'll be able to relax much more quickly. Make a date with Edith, and we'll have another go.''

When she walked out of the building and retrieved her car, she was astonished to find that she'd been gone two and a half hours. There was time for a quick lunch at a muffin spot, and then she made her way across town to the area where Michael McCrae had an apartment.

Annie checked the address she'd written down the night before, and tried to subdue the anxiety this forthcoming meeting aroused in her.

She still wasn't at all sure what it was she needed to know about Michael McCrae or his wife, and the peaceful calm she'd felt after the hypnotic session disappeared when she found the street she was searching for.

It was an old neighborhood, prestigious at one time, but now all the stately old mansions had been converted to apartments. Tall oak and cedar trees still lined the boulevard like sentinels determined to keep out intruders.

She felt like an intruder. She should have insisted they come to her. But wouldn't that be worse, having them in her home?

And how was this wife of Michael's, this Lili, feeling about meeting a woman who'd borne Michael's son? Wouldn't she be resentful? Annie thought of someday meeting David's ex-wife, and shuddered. Lord, this was awful. It couldn't be anything but awkward and embarrassing for all of them.

Annie pulled in under the trees and parked her car, staring up at the three-story monolith behind the stone fence.

We're on the main floor, Michael had said.

Annie walked up the wide steps and a surge of nausea rolled over her as she pushed the doorbell.

The door opened almost immediately.

"Please, won't you come in? I am Lili." The woman smiled and put out a narrow hand, taking Annie's in a welcoming grasp and drawing her into the hallway.

Lili was perhaps forty, dark and exotic. Her long hair was drawn back in a high knot, and she wore black pants and a silky patterned blouse.

Annie noticed that her narrow feet were bare, the toenails painted a soft rose. There was something vulnerable about those bare feet, and Annie felt a little less nervous for a moment.

Although she wasn't beautiful, Lili gave the illusion of both grace and a kind of humorous vivacity. If she felt any animosity toward Annie, she hid it well.

"It's most kind of you to come here. What do you prefer I call you?" Lili's voice was well modulated and pleasant.

"Oh, just...call me Annie." She swallowed and did her best to smile, but her palms felt wet and her heart was racing in a crazy rhythm as a tall male figure came around the corner from another part of the house.

"Hello, Annie. Thank you for coming." The deep male voice was Michael's.

It was the moment Annie had dreaded most, the first time she'd seen him since the scene in front of the courthouse all those years ago.

I'll kill you for this, you bitch....

Annie almost panicked as he put out a hand toward her. She curled her fingers into fists and pressed them into her sides. She couldn't bring herself to touch him.

It was an awkward moment. He dropped his hand, but went on smiling at her.

Annie forced herself to look full at him, and it shook her to see traces of her son's face reflected there, in cheekbones, the way the ears were shaped, the set of the jaw. It shocked her, that physical resemblance. And it galled her to have to admit that Jason was indeed his father's son.

But Michael was different from her memory of him. He was older, certainly; he'd been twelve years older than Annie, which made him...she added rapidly as they moved through the hallway, the two of them drawing her with them into their home.

Michael was now forty-six. He looked his age. His rather long, straight hair was peppered with gray and there were deep lines running across his forehead. But it was a nebulous air of tranquillity about him that Annie found foreign.

Michael had been a quiet man, but certainly not tranquil.

"Please, sit down." Lili seemed to glide instead of walk, and she gestured to a deep armchair. Annie slid down into it, facing the sofa where Michael and Lili took seats side by side, close together.

There was a tray on the low table separating the seats, and Lili leaned forward, indicating a coffee carafe and a teapot.

"Would you care for something to drink?"

Annie began to refuse, but changed her mind. It would give her something to do with her hands.

The pain in her neck was there again.

"Coffee, please," she said, and Lili poured some into a delicate china cup and set it in front of Annie.

After the cream-and-sugar ritual, there was a long moment of silence. Now Annie was afraid to lift the cup in case her trembling hands spilled the hot liquid.

"This is really difficult for you, and we appreciate your coming here, Annie," Michael said at last, as if it were a formal speech he'd rehearsed.

Annie's nervousness turned to sudden anger, and her voice was hard-edged and spiteful. "I had no choice. You deliberately forced the issue by talking with Jason on the phone that day."

He stayed calm. "It wasn't planned, it just happened. He answered, and I couldn't hang up. I want to get to know him. He said the same thing about me.''

Annie's emotions choked her. She reached for her cup and took a gulp of the coffee, but she had to force it down her throat. She set the cup back on the table with a clatter.

Lili was sitting motionless, her dark eyes going from her husband to Annie. How much had Michael told her about the things that had happened between them? Annie wondered. How honest was he capable of being?

"Why now, Michael?" she burst out. "Why now, after all these years, why come back and bother me now? I've raised Jason. What makes you think there's a place for you in his life?"

She understood that she was deliberately trying to hurt him, to cause him pain, but she didn't care. "You and your wife have no children. What makes you think you even know how to relate to a young boy like Jason? I thought I made it plain years ago that I preferred to raise him alone."

The Michael she'd known long ago had no gift for introspection. He'd had a volatile temper, and he would have quickly met anger with anger. He'd been stubborn, determined, and certainly not given to expressing feelings in words.

She remembered his animal strength, the way his fingers had dug into her shoulders, and she shuddered, glancing involuntarily at his large hands. Lili was holding one of them, and it reminded Annie of the way David had held her hand not long before, aligning himself with her instead of with Calvin. That gesture of affection angered her even more. Michael didn't deserve love, certainly not from Jason.

"Years ago, you hurt me and I guess all I wanted to do was hurt you back," he said after a long pause. "I'd like to think I've grown up since then." There was strain in his voice.

Annie guessed that Michael still wasn't good at expressing emotion in words. The amazing thing was that he was trying.

"Back then I wasn't thinking of Jason as much as I was wanting to just pay you back."

Annie nodded, an angry pulse hammering in her ears. She'd always known his lawsuit was vindictive.

"I'm older now, Annie. Maybe a little wiser?" He raised an eyebrow, and attempted a smile. "I'd like to think so, and it's thanks to my wife. She's helped me understand a lot of things. Oh, I don't pretend to know much about a thirteen-year-old boy, but I'm anxious to learn. Lili and I simply want to be part of Jason's life, be his friends, if that's possible. We're not trying to take over as parents, or anything like that. We're just ordinary people, leading ordinary lives. We'd never undermine you in any way, if that's what you're concerned about."

Until now, Lili had been quiet. In her soft, slightly accented voice, she said, "Please, if there is anything you wish to ask me, Annie, feel free. I will have close contact with your son if you allow him to know us, and if there are problems with my being from another culture, perhaps we could discuss them now?"

Her openness was disarming. What could Annie say? There wasn't anything about Lili she objected to, except that she'd married Michael.

And that was ridiculous, because there had been a time when Annie herself had almost done the same thing. There'd been a time when she had thought it necessary to marry him.

What had she been hoping to find here? Roaring alcoholism, insanity, drugs, perversion? Her honesty forced her to admit she had been hoping for something like that. Anything to justify forbidding them any association with Jason.

But she'd learned, this past week, that Jason had a mind of his own about this. Besides, there was nothing here to object to. She felt defeated, old and tired.

She got to her feet, holding her body stiff against the accelerating pain in her shoulders. "When do you want to see him?" Her voice was a monotone.

Michael had risen, his arm around his wife. "As soon as possible," he said, giving Lili an exuberant squeeze. "Thank you, Annie."

Lili's face was shining with happiness, her eyes soft and liquid when she looked up into Michael's face. Obviously there was love between them, and that was more reassuring than anything they could say.

"Sunday, then." Annie forced herself to set a date and make the whole thing official. Jason would ask her anyway, first thing—when, when, when?

Best to get it over with quickly, now that it was decided.

"Perhaps you would come with Jason and share dinner with us on Sunday?"

Annie was touched by Lili's invitation, but she shook her head. "I think it would be best for him to meet you alone. I'll drop him off here around noon, and you can bring him home."

It was done. Annie drove home, and Jason met her at the door. His face was one large question mark, and when Annie told him, he threw his arms around her and squeezed until she winced.

"Thanks, Mom. Hey, thanks. And, Mom?"

"Yeah, Jason. I'm here."

"I went to see the manager of those theaters. I'm gonna run errands and clean up junk for them, starting next weekend."

"That's a good idea. Did you also talk to your teacher and get the work you missed yesterday?"

He nodded. "Yeah. She gave me a detention for skipping school. And, um, Mom?"

Annie recognized the tone, the determination combined with uncertainty. "Did you, uh, did you tell my, my...dad...about what I did, about the, the...cops and all that?"

Shock went through her that he would even think of such a thing. Worse than that was the fact that he would call the man he'd never even met yet "dad."

"Of course not, Jason. I wouldn't do a thing like that."

His shoulders slumped with relief.

"It's just that I'd like him to sort of, kinda, well, develop his own opinion of me, know what I'm sayin', Mom?"

The enormity of the boy's vulnerability overwhelmed her. It ripped her heart to shreds because she'd been so certain all along that the environment she provided for Jason was all he'd wanted or needed.

As it had been doing with increasing regularity, Annie's world and the security she'd always found in it seemed to shift and re-form like the images in a dream.

CHAPTER TEN

THE TELEPHONE RINGING on the nightstand beside the bed finally penetrated deep, thick layers of sleep, and David rolled over and lifted the instrument to his ear.

"Yeah, hello?"

He cleared his throat and pulled himself into a sitting position, squinting with bleary eyes at the darkness outside his bedroom window. The clock read two forty-five.

The middle of the night. Saturday morning?

It was his answering service.

"Sorry to bother you, Doctor, but an urgent call just came through long-distance from a Mrs. Vance in Enderby, B.C."

David swung his legs out of bed and grabbed the pen and pad from the night table. "What's the message? And give me her number."

"Message reads, 'Charlie running a high fever.'"

David scribbled down the number and dialed it the instant the line was clear.

The young mother's voice was strained and thin when she answered the phone. It rang only once before she came on the line, and it was obvious from her voice that she'd been wide-awake, waiting.

"Thanks so much for calling me back, Dr. Roswell. I'm sorry to wake you up but I'm awfully worried. Charlie seemed to have caught a little cold two days ago. I took him straight to the doctor here, and he put Charlie in hospital just to be sure." She gulped in air, and hurried on. "But about six last night, his temperature started going up, and now he's running a fever and I'm not sure what I ought to do. Our doctor will be phoning you later this morning, but I couldn't sleep all night. I had to talk to you and see what you think."

David thought hard for a moment. Charlie was listed as urgent on a North America-wide waiting list of possible liver transplant recipients. When a suitable organ became available, he would be flown by special plane to the Pittsburgh hospital where such procedures were performed.

David would check immediately, but it wasn't likely anything would happen within the next day or two, either, so sending Charlie down to the U.S. medical center was probably useless at this time.

Charlie's situation, although it was urgent, was not yet life threatening; the liver disease he suffered from would slowly cause his death, but David had believed it would be some months, perhaps a year, before that happened.

Time. They needed time to get all the details in order, time to find a suitable organ for Charlie.

The question was, what exactly was wrong with Charlie now, and how equipped was the tiny medical facility in the small town the Vances lived in to cope with Charlie's problem?

"I'll call your doctor immediately, Mrs. Vance, and see what he says. Do you have his home number handy? Thanks. I'll ring you straight back, and we'll decide what's best to do."

When he'd finished the second call, he got up, pulled on a pair of sweatpants and a top and walked across his cluttered bedroom to the window, trying to make the wisest decision.

Streetlights cast a faint glow over the peaceful neighborhood. The streets were deserted, and a feeling of intense loneliness came over David. Since Annie had come into his life, he found himself longing to have her with him at times like this.

The young doctor he'd just awakened and spoken to was bright and anxious to help, but he stated in no uncertain terms that he felt the tiny hospital was out of its depth should Charlie become seriously ill during the next few hours. His temperature was still high, but not dangerously so.

If the child were to be moved to Vancouver, where sophisticated help was available should the situation get worse, now was the time to act.

David weighed the possibilities and made a decision. He dialed the Vances' number again, and gently, trying not to upset the young mother more than she already was, instructed her to make arrangements for bringing Charlie to Vancouver.

David knew the trip would be harrowing for Mrs. Vance, and for Charlie as well. It would involve an hour's car trip just to reach the nearest airport, and then another hour of flying time.

It meant arranging care for her baby daughter, as well as coming up with the money for the trip. It was a major upheaval, and that was why David had hesitated over whether or not it was necessary.

He'd have an ambulance waiting at this end, David assured Mrs. Vance, and he'd instruct the airline that serviced her area that this was a medical emergency, so there would be no problem getting a seat on the first flight out that morning.

He'd see her about noon, he promised, at the hospital.

It took him another hour of phone calls to make every possible arrangement, and when he was finished, it was just past five in the morning. He was wide-awake. There was no point in trying to fall asleep again.

He went into the small galley kitchen and boiled water for instant coffee, still going over the decision he'd made and hoping he wasn't disrupting the Vances' life and causing them financial problems if it wasn't absolutely necessary. But how the hell could he know for certain? Making judgments like this one was by far the hardest part of being a doctor.

Sitting drinking the bilious liquid he'd made, he came to the sudden conclusion that he was fed up to the teeth with living alone. He wanted Annie's warm body next to him in that damned bed, he wanted her to talk to at times like this, to sit with him here in the kitchen in the gray dawn and tell him he'd made the right decision, even if he hadn't.

He wanted Annie in every way a man could want a woman. He wanted to share the rest of his life with her. He'd known that on some level, ever since the afternoon he'd taken her home and watched her while she slept.

The trouble was, more and more obstacles seemed to get in the way of their romance. There were the demands of his job, the new drain on his time that all these damned meetings and social engagements were creating, and on Annie's side there was her reluctance to commit herself to any relationship. Of course part of that reluctance involved her son, Jason.

The boy had made it crystal clear that David was unwelcome in his life. David couldn't help feeling irritated with the kid.

He made toast and ate it, hoping that, despite the way the day had started, it would smooth out enough so that his date with Annie tonight worked the way he wanted it to.

THE MORNING BEGAN GRAY and rainy, but by afternoon it had cleared. Annie spent most of the day in her study, although she was careful to allow herself plenty of time to get ready for her date with David.

The ritual of grooming and dressing was drawn out and delightful when the entire purpose was to be lovely for him. She bathed and shaved her legs, rubbed perfumed lotions into her skin, slipped on satin underwear and the simple lime-green dress she'd decided on. She spent forty minutes making her mass of hair look as if she'd just stepped out of bed.

Her reward was the open admiration on his face when she opened the door at his knock. His eyes roamed over her and his mouth pursed in a silent whistle. He had a bouquet of violets and small yellow roses in one hand, and a huge box of chocolates in the other. He half bowed and handed them to her with a grin.

"You didn't have to bribe me, but I love it," she told him. Her gaze went to his hair. "You didn't get a haircut," she said with a catch in her voice.

"This lady I know told me not to," he teased and they stood and smiled at each other.

The truth was, David had forgotten all about a haircut. He'd spent most of the afternoon at the hospital running tests on Charlie. The boy was still feverish, the tests had been inconclusive, and David was carrying a beeper in his jacket, just in case there was any change in the child's condition.

Jason was watching television. He waved a hand at them when they left; he was expert at being polite to David while making it clear he'd rather not bother.

The restaurant was one Annie had only read about, new and trendy, welcoming and expensive. It overlooked the ocean, with a view of freighters and the promise of a spectacular sunset over the North Shore mountains. David had managed to secure a table by the window wall.

The background music was soft, the tables far enough apart for private conversation, and Annie felt pampered and full of anticipation for the evening ahead as David carefully seated her, his hand caressing her arm and lingering on the soft skin bared by her lime-colored summer dress.

"How lovely you are," he said, a note of quiet wonder in his voice. The wine was poured and he'd approved it so the waiter would leave them in peace. His eyes seemed to caress her, and a lovely tingle of awareness and pleasure traveled down her body.

The problems and tensions of the past several days faded as she sat across from him, and they chatted and laughed over inconsequential things as their dinner was served, admiring the view, speculating over where the boats outside were heading.

"I followed Dr. Kendrick's advice and went to see the hypnotherapist he recommended," Annie finally confided over dessert. "His name is Steve Munro. You probably know him. It was sort of a weird experience."

She rattled on for several minutes, relating details of the hypnotic session before she realized that David wasn't saying anything. He was frowning a little, so she stopped the free flow of words.

"What's the matter, David?"

"I should have guessed that Kendrick might suggest something like hypnosis. I remember now we got in quite an argument about it one day. I have to admit it's not a treatment I agree with, Annie. And neither do a great many medical people. There's a lot of controversy surrounding its use, outside of strictly controlled instances."

Annie felt a twinge of irritation. "Well, it's far too soon to tell whether it'll help my neck or not, but certainly the doctors didn't have much else to recommend, except good old painkillers. My attitude is, if hypnosis will help, I'll use it."

"The problem is," David began to explain, "they're starting to use all sorts of questionable hypnotic techniques, like..."

The raucous sound of the beeper in his pocket startled them both. David got to his feet. "Annie, excuse me. I'll have to find a telephone."

She was aware of the sudden tension in his body and voice as he asked directions of the waiter and hurried off.

THE NEXT FIFTEEN MINUTES were frenzied. David strode back to her, and explained that there was an emergency and they'd have to leave, right away.

He paid the bill and they all but ran to the parking garage. Once they were in the car, he sketched in what had happened earlier that day, explaining the problems Charlie was having. "With kids like this, poisons build up in the bloodstream as the liver malfunctions and enlarges. We figured we had a bit of time with Charlie, but now it seems the process has suddenly accelerated, heaven only knows why." He reached across and touched her arm, caressing it lightly with his fingertips.

"Honey, I'm sorry about this, but the resident feels the little guy's in serious difficulty. We've been in touch with the medical center in Pittsburgh. They're frantically trying to locate a donor organ, and we have a plane standing by. Our Canadian centers have nothing suitable. Anyhow, we have to stabilize Charlie before he can even be flown down. I'll make arrangements for a taxi to take you home once we're at the hospital."

An hour later, Annie knew she ought to have done what David had suggested and taken a cab home, but still she lingered in the bright waiting room on the ward, where a young resident had been waiting for them.

He and David had hurried down the hallway and disappeared, and Annie had been about to use the phone for a taxi when she saw an impossibly young woman come out of the intensive-care unit into which David had disappeared.

Annie watched as she stood in the hallway for a few moments, leaning against the wall with her head down. Then she made her way into the waiting room and took a seat on the lounge where Annie was sitting.

Her pale blond hair and thin face and body made her seem fragile. She looked the way Maggie might in a few years, with her round blue eyes and pretty, dainty features.

She wore a faded cotton skirt and a pink shirt, and she was crying silently, her face an impassive mask as the tears dripped down her cheeks and off her chin. She sniffled once or twice, and swiped at her face with her open palm.

Annie dug into her purse and produced a small pack of tissues. She extracted several and handed them over. The girl took them without looking at Annie, wiping her face and blowing her nose like a dutiful child.

A nurse appeared in the doorway. "Mrs. Vance, it's going to be a while before you can go in again. The doctors are busy with Charlie just now. Why don't you go to the cafeteria and get a bite to eat? I'll come down for you if there's any change at all."

Mrs. Vance shook her head. The fear in her eyes was naked and horrifying when she looked up at the nurse. Charlie's mother.

She didn't look old enough to be anyone's mother, but her utter aloneness made Annie want to reach out and put her arms around her. She felt an overwhelming affinity for the young woman, a deep sense of kinship and a helpless need to do something...anything...to help her, comfort her.

She was a mother, too. What if it were Jason, or Maggie, or Paula, in that room down the hall?

Annie shuddered and swallowed hard. Her own eyes were damp.

"Excuse me," she said at last in a soft voice, after the nurse had gone. "My name is Annie. I came with Dr. Roswell. I'm not...not a medical person or anything, but I'm a mother, too. Won't you let me get you a coffee, maybe, or a sandwich?"

The woman looked at her, and tried for a quavery smile. She failed, and reached for the tissues again to mop her face more thoroughly this time.

"Gee, I can't stop crying. I'm so scared. You, you're Dr. Roswell's wife?" Her voice was soft but full of reverence for anyone who knew David.

"He's such a wonderful doctor," she went on, gulping her sobs back. "He's been really good to us. I'm Linda Vance. I don't think I could stand all this, with...with Charlie, I mean, if Dr. Roswell weren't here for him. I just have so much faith in him. But it's so hard to know what to do. Like I keep thinking I should have seen that Charlie was sick sooner, y'know?'' She bit her lip hard before she could continue. ''I should have brought him here to Dr. Roswell right away...''

Annie hurried to explain that she wasn't married to David, but was a friend. She added that she, too, thought he was a great doctor, and that he'd told her what a fine boy Charlie was, what a personality he had.

Linda did smile at that, a tender, maternal smile. She drew a dog-eared photo out of the pocket of her skirt and held it out to Annie.

''This is him on his second birthday. I swear he was born smiling that way. He's so spunky, that little kid. He's had to go through so much in just two years.''

Her face crumpled, and Annie saw the cost of love and fear and worry in the deep marks beside the wide eyes, the ridges around the tender mouth.

''Charlie can be hurting real bad and yet he's always got a smile for everybody. Dr. Roswell says Charlie has what it takes to come through all this. He says if we can only hold on till there's a liver available....''

For the first time, Annie truly understood the frightful burden of trust placed on David. *This is my beloved child. Please, Doctor, make him well. I know you can, I have to believe you can, because I have nothing else to cling to.* How did David stand it, the wordless haunting plea in eyes like Linda's?

Shaken, Annie could only encourage Linda to talk about Charlie, and then about her new baby girl, Angela.

It was significant that Linda didn't reveal what David had already told Annie, that Angela was in the same danger Charlie was. Instead the pale young woman talked about Enderby, the small interior town she came from.

Linda had been born there, gone to school and married her high-school sweetheart, Rudy Vance. Rudy was a truck driver, but was taking night school courses to better himself, she said with pride.

A tiny bit of the awful tension in the young woman's body eased as she talked in a steady stream. ''Rudy's mother offered to keep Angela, so Rudy's coming down. He's driving. We couldn't afford for both of us to fly. He won't get here till late tonight. It's so much easier if he's here with me,'' she sighed.

Annie went for coffee and sandwiches, and brought them back on a tray. Linda drank the coffee and barely nibbled at the sandwich. There were huge dark rings under her eyes, and finally she nodded off to sleep while Annie was telling her about the books she wrote.

Annie got up and found a phone in the hallway. She called Cleo, outlined what had happened and asked her friend if she'd mind checking on Jason.

"I'm sure he's fine. Probably he's already gone to bed. But I'm liable to be lots later than I planned."

"I'll bring him over here for the night. He likes sleeping in a sleeping bag down in the TV room. Don't worry about him, Annie."

Annie made her way back to the room where Linda was now slumped in a heap across the arm of the sofa, still asleep.

Picking up a magazine, Annie flipped through the glossy pages, hoping that Linda would rest for a while. But it was only fifteen minutes before the nurse who'd been in before appeared, hesitated and sighed, and then gently touched Linda's arm.

"Mrs. Vance, Dr. Roswell wants you to come back in now."

Linda leaped up and staggered, her eyes wild, and the nurse had to hold her arm until she regained her balance.

"Is...is he better?"

Annie noted that the nurse avoided the question, listing instead what was being done for the boy in medical terms that Linda obviously found familiar.

It sounded formidable.

Linda hurried down the corridor, and Annie waited.

Time passed, more than an hour.

Then, activity increased. Nurses and several doctors swept past, disappearing into Charlie's room.

It was much later when a flurry of activity startled Annie out of a half doze. Dread filled her when a nurse half ran down the corridor, and another accompanied her back through the swinging doors. After an interminable period, doctors and other medical personnel began to pass the waiting-room door. They were leaving the intensive-care area where Charlie was.

They were all ominously silent, shoulders slumped, expressions strained, and now there was no urgency to their gait.

Annie felt nauseated and her blood pounded in her ears. She paced the hall as more time passed and it seemed she couldn't get air deeply into her lungs.

It was after three before David appeared. His curly hair was on end, and his face looked haggard. "One of the nurses told me you were still waiting," he said, his voice was rough and strained. "You shouldn't have. Anyway, let's go now."

Annie could hardly make the words come out.

"Charlie Vance? Is— How—"

She stopped and looked at David's face. It was stiff and unyielding, as if the muscles underneath were frozen in place.

"We lost him," David said with awful calm. "Nothing we did helped. It's like that sometimes."

The terse words knifed into Annie.

"Oh, God, David, that's terrible. But Linda, his mother. I was talking to her a while ago. I should go talk to her."

And say what? What words or actions could possibly help that fragile girl now?

"We had to sedate her. One of the nurses is with her. Her husband should be here soon." David's harsh tone softened a little. "There's nothing to be done, Annie. Absolutely nothing, believe me. Let's go now."

He walked ahead of her toward the elevators, and stood, hands thrust into trouser pockets, jingling his keys, during the ride down. He didn't say anything, and he didn't look directly at Annie even once. He seemed lost in his thoughts, faraway and impassive.

It had started to rain outside, a dismal, typically Vancouver downpour that obscured the windshield when they pulled out of the underground garage. The lighted parking areas around the hospital looked forlorn and eerie; the gray streets were nearly deserted in the early dawn.

Annie thought about Linda's husband, young and frightened, driving alone through this wet darkness, perhaps getting lost in the strangeness of the huge city, still unaware that his baby son was gone.

She remembered a time when Jason was about three, and she'd just moved from one apartment to another. She didn't know anyone in the new building, and the first night there, Jason had run a fever that had gone higher and higher despite all her frantic sponging with cool water and dosing with baby aspirin. Her telephone wasn't connected yet, and she had had to bang on a neighbor's door and ask if she could use theirs. The neighbor was old and angry at being awakened.

She'd called her doctor, but he was away. The doctor taking his calls was obviously at a party, and considered her a panicky bore.

"If you think it's necessary, take the child to emergency," he'd finally directed impatiently when she tried to explain how frightened she was.

She'd spent the night holding Jason in an apartment where everything was still in boxes, bathing him, agonizing over whether or not to awaken the neighbor again in order to call a cab. It meant taking her baby out in the freezing rain, and probably waiting for hours in the chaotic frenzy of a big city emergency unit. What if she did, and Jason got a chill?

What if she didn't, and he died in a convulsion?

That had been one of the loneliest nights of her entire life, and it came to symbolize for her the magnitude of being solely responsible for a child.

Linda and her young husband must be feeling just that way about their children, Annie knew, except that their problems were much greater than Annie's had been with Jason.

David drove the sleek gray car fast, braking hard at stoplights, squealing the tires around corners, making Annie's heart race as he dodged recklessly around even the few cars that were on the streets at this hour.

She bit her tongue and swallowed the words of caution she longed to say.

He pulled up in front of Annie's house and left the engine running. "Won't you come in, David?" she asked. "I'll make you coffee or something to eat." She needed to talk.

He shook his head, one decisive shake.

"Can't, Annie. Sorry. I'll call tomorrow." He reached across and touched her cheek with his fingers, but that was all. No eye contact, nothing except the controlled quiet voice.

Defeated, let down, Annie got out and made her way up to the door. As soon as it was unlocked and she had stepped inside, David roared away, his taillights disappearing as he careened around the corner.

Annie felt empty. She slumped against the door, tears burning behind her eyes. But then a mixture of total frustration, sorrow and nameless rage began to build inside of her.

How dare David close her out this way? How could he pretend to care for her and then the first time something like this came along, something terrible that affected him deeply, how could he just lock her out of his emotions, drive her home and tear off the way he'd just done? Didn't he think she had any feelings about what had happened that night?

She tore up the stairwell and into her bedroom. In a kind of frenzy, she stripped off her dress, her high sandals and her panty hose. The delicate hose ripped and she threw them violently to the floor.

She was shaking with the force of her anger. She tore off her bra and panties, stormed into the bathroom and started a tub of water running. Her eyes were hot and dry, and her breath came in short, angry gasps.

He'd done this before, hurried off and left her to deal with her emotions alone.

She didn't stop to wonder when.

It took several moments before she was aware that someone was leaning on the front doorbell. She turned the water off and listened.

Then she grabbed the worn blue robe hanging on the hook behind the bathroom door and wrapped it any which way around her.

She didn't remember going down the stairs, or unlocking the door so David could burst in. She only knew that he was kissing her all over her face, wild kisses that tasted of her tears and his agony. The smell and feel and taste of him engulfed her.

He used one arm to shove the door shut behind them.

"Annie, my Annie, I need you." The words were torn from him, raw and full of pain.

"Jason's next door for the night," Annie managed to whisper.

Somehow they climbed the stairs, his arms still locked around her.

CHAPTER ELEVEN

ANNIE LED THE WAY into her bedroom, his hand in hers.

The small lamp she'd turned on earlier revealed her clothing, tossed at random across the bed and on the floor, ivory bikini panties, matching lacy bra, satin slip...she'd forgotten about tearing them off and throwing them everywhere.

It was embarrassing.

She made a move to gather some of it up, but David's arms came around her from behind, holding her with fierce strength against his body, shoving her loose hair aside and bending his mouth to her neck. His lips burned a trail across the tender flesh, and his breath was hot and urgent in her ear.

"Love me, Annie. Just love me, please love me...."

She turned into his embrace, her lips opening to him, longing to heal the damage this night had inflicted on each of them.

There was reassurance in the surging heat that traveled through her body, in the answering passion conveyed by his hands, his mouth, the hard pressure of his erection against her abdomen.

The edge of the bed was pressing against the back of her legs, and Annie allowed herself to collapse onto it, squirming backward until her whole body was stretched out, waiting.

"Come to me," she whispered, and David seemed to strip in one graceful motion. Shirt, pants, shoes, underwear came off and joined her own discarded garments on the rug.

She gazed at him, reveling in his beauty, remembering...

He was finely made, long, sinewy bones knit together with elegant grace, overlaid with smooth muscle and tawny skin. His chest had a curly, dark mat of hair, and his need for her was evident in the swollen, pulsing maleness that thrust from the apex of his thighs.

He knelt over her, cupping her face in his palms, and the tip of his tongue closed each eyelid in turn with a soft, exotic caress that then traveled down the length of her nose, and outlined her lips with careful, erotic attention to the deep indentations that bracketed her mouth. He nuzzled her chin, trailed his mouth, hot and wet, down her throat, and made her wriggle and sigh with impatience before his mouth again captured hers, tongue promising.

Her body filled with hot liquid desire. She could sense the female parts of her swelling, opening, lips parting to welcome him. But he forced her to wait.

He unknotted the belt at the waist of her robe, and when the garment fell free of her heated body, he slid his hands under the lapels, his long, sure fingers exploring her swollen breasts with tender, teasing strokes and easing the robe off at the same time.

She gasped and he lowered his head, again using his tongue and his lips to suckle and tug and tantalize.

"Annie, my dearest Annie, beautiful Annie...."

He knew exactly when her nipples began an agonized throbbing, linked in some invisible fashion to the burning pulse hammering at the core of her body, and he slid his hand down to the soft nest at her thighs, his fingers parting her with gentle intent and finding the bud that at first seemed too sensitive for even his sure touch.

She cried out, and he gentled her with soothing noises that made words unnecessary.

He released her wetness and stroked it up over her, making the movement of his fingers like satin slipping over velvet. He knew the exact pressure she needed at all the right moments, slow, soft, indistinct; then firmer, more direct, faster...and all the time his mouth rehearsed the movement of his fingers, drawing the hardened tips of her nipples one by one deep into his mouth, flicking with his tongue, wetting and drawing, releasing, until she felt the knot of orgasm beginning to come undone deep within her.

She wanted him to go on, more than she could ever remember wanting anything. She needed him to suck the engorged nipples, torture her until release came.

Her body thrust up toward him, helpless with hunger, and she moaned, out of control. It was her turn to beg, "David, please, love me...."

"David?"

She opened her eyes and stared up at his face, unable to form other words that would tell him of her delight, of the burning need that soared in her.

His eyes seemed to have become darker, the pupils huge and almost drowning out the surrounding blue. Deep lines etched his face into stark and bony elegance, lines which might have been agony but were instead the marks of rapture.

In the midst of her craving she felt replete, because he'd forgotten everything but her. In the universe, there was only the two of them.

She moved her legs farther apart, inviting him, and in one surging motion, he lowered himself and thrust high and deep into her body. She drew him still farther with her muscles, enclosing him with her legs. And almost at once, she felt the scalding spurt of his fluid begin. Now his motions were also without control, his body taut and melded with her own, his sobs echoing those rising from her throat. His wild and savage thrusting exactly matched the depths of her hunger, and finding the elusive pinnacle they sought was the easiest of tasks.

He sought her mouth at the last instant, locking her lips to his so the primeval sound they made seemed to issue from one throat.

After an endless time, he rolled them to one side, cradling her.

"Annie. I love you more than I dreamed possible," he murmured, and for a long while they rested in silence, floating in and out of sleep.

She could tell exactly when the tension began to build in him, when the euphoria of their lovemaking faded a bit and the devastating memories of Charlie's death crept back.

"I'm ashamed," he finally said, just as if they'd been involved in a long and complex conversation.

"Ashamed of what?" She waited, feeling the tension build in her as well.

"Oh, of being a doctor, and not being able to do more than I did tonight." He smashed a sudden, violent fist into the mattress, and she jumped.

Rage and grief and impotence mingled in his low, passionate words. "If we just had a damned transplant center here in Vancouver, the way we ought to. We've got an organ bank.... Maybe the boy would still have died, but I'd feel as if I'd done more for him and his parents than just promise and not deliver. I'm ashamed of our limitations, Annie, because they're not necessary. We could do better. We have to do better."

He sat up, shoulders slumped forward, still holding her hand, but alone now with his thoughts, his mouth curved into a bitter, sardonic line. "I failed those people tonight. I failed Charlie."

Annie sat up beside him. "David, you did everything possible for him. No one can work miracles. Those parents are aware of that."

Beneath the reason and the quiet assurance she offered him, a torrent of emotion was building inside her, feelings Annie didn't want to explore, couldn't explore just now.

David was telling her he felt like a failure. He'd been Charlie's doctor, he'd had a long-standing relationship with the boy and his parents, and he had every right to be this disturbed over the boy's death. Annie felt that her role ought to be simply that of comforting and loving David.

But the truth was, she felt like a failure, too. Charlie's death had affected her, bringing to the surface feelings that had been building in her for days, and striking at the fragile framework of her love for Jason, her role as a mother, her thoughts about death, her feelings about life.

The deepest fear a parent had was that a child would die, because death was the final loss, the cruelest of all. But Annie realized there were other losses besides death. There was, for instance, the pain of having a son transfer his love and loyalty to a stranger, a man who'd accidentally fathered him fourteen years before.

The truth was, Jason's eager joy at meeting Michael was tearing Annie to bits. She felt betrayed, deserted. She felt the same sense of failure that David was feeling, and she tried to stifle it because it seemed trivial in comparison to his.

"We train ourselves not to become emotionally involved with patients, because of this very thing," David was saying. "But damn it all, it happens anyway. I cared about Charlie, I..." His voice broke, and he cleared his throat gruffly, reaching out with a tortured groan and pulling Annie into his arms.

"I'm sorry, love, going on like this. I never intended our first time together to be anything but joyful. I've dreamed of holding you, making love with you, laughing together. Not this way."

Annie pressed her cheek against his chest, willing away the storm building inside her.

"Tears count every bit as much as laughter," she managed to say, and then the burning ache in her chest erupted, and violent sobs tore from her throat.

"Annie, don't." David clasped her tight against him, cursing aloud as she wept on and on. "Sweetheart, I shouldn't have let you stay there tonight. I should've seen to it you went home. It wasn't fair to expose you to all that. It's my work, I've had more experience at handling it than you." He swore again.

Annie pulled herself away from him, drawing the sheet up and locking her arms around her knees against the torrent of emotion.

"It's not...it's not—just—Char-Charlie," she managed to choke out. "It's...oh, damn, it's Jason, and all...all the things that have been happening."

Unable to stop herself, she blurted out how the past hours had made her feel—her awful, helpless compassion for Linda, and her realization that her own role as a mother was changing, that she was losing Jason.

As if a dam had burst, she spilled out the problems of the past few days, the awful way Jason had been acting and the reasons for it, her own reluctance to let Michael be involved in his son's life.

David listened.

He stopped her several times to ask puzzled questions, and Annie realized how little she'd confided in him. She found herself having to go back to the beginning, describe in detail the battles she'd had with Michael over custody, her very real fear of him, the horror of the court battles fought to keep her son.

"Now Michael's taking Jason anyway, without any effort. Jason's made it plain he wants to be with his father, and it hurts." She knew she sounded hysterical.

"Come here," David said, and she allowed herself to be drawn into his embrace.

"Love isn't a limited quantity, Annie," he said with quiet assurance, holding her and stroking his hand up and down her back in a soothing gesture. "Just because Jason wants to know his father doesn't mean he's going to stop loving you."

She nodded. She knew with her brain it was true. Her heart didn't seem to agree.

"It's just that seeing Michael again reinforced all the bad feelings I have about him. I still don't trust him, and I don't like the thought of him being around me or Jason. The feeling hasn't changed even after all these years. He gives me the creeps."

"Give it time, Annie."

They were quiet for a while, exhausted, empty of emotion.

Gradually David's stroking became more purposeful, and once again shivers of longing soared in Annie. This time, their loving was less desperate than before.

As the hours of the night gave way to dawn, they loved again and again, and with the physical joining came peace and a measure of self-forgiveness.

"How come Dr. Roswell's car was out in front of our house all night?"

Annie was making toast, and Jason's question caught her unawares. David had left shortly after five that morning because Annie had wanted to avoid this very thing with her son. David had seemed to understand.

It was now ten-fifteen, and Jason had been home for an hour. Why hadn't he said something before now?

"His car was here because David spent the night here, Jason."

"So I guess he's gonna be around here all the time from now on, then. Are you gonna live with him or just have an affair?"

Annie held on to her patience, forcing a reasonable calm in her voice that she didn't feel, and doing her best to ignore the aggressive and insulting tone Jason was using.

"We're just close friends, Jason. For the moment that's about it."

"You wouldn't marry him, would you, Mom?" There was plaintive appeal in his voice. "I mean, then I'd have a stepfather. Yuck."

Annie's patience slipped a bit. It wasn't easy to vocalize something she hadn't allowed herself to even dream about.

"Adults do get married, Jason. Just because I never have doesn't mean I'm never going to. But at the moment, I haven't any plans."

"Well, I hope if you ever do, it's not Dr. Roswell I get as a stepfather."

Annie's control snapped. "Jason, that's enough."

Knowing he'd gone too far, Jason slid out from the table and headed for back door. "I'm gonna cut the grass until it's time to get ready to go meet my father."

"Right. That's a good idea." Annie smeared apricot jam on her toast and felt like collapsing as she slammed the door behind him. She heard him whistling as he rummaged in the shed for the push mower.

She took one bite out of the toast, and dropped the rest in the garbage, resting her head in her hands and fighting tears.

The events of the past night had left her drained. The lovemaking she and David had shared was overpowering, frightening, because it marked the beginning of a drastic change in their relationship.

Before, Annie could still pretend that her soul wasn't linked with David Roswell's, that the insistent sense of destiny she had about him was just the product of a writer's fertile imagination.

This morning, that rationale was impossible.

She belonged to David, heart, soul and body, and that was that, which raised a whole lot of questions she didn't have answers for.

Questions such as whether or not she could override the convictions she had about staying single, and marry him. What kind of father figure could David be to Jason when Jason made it clear he hated him?

What the hell was she going to do about that kid?

"SO THE POOR little boy died. God, Annie." Cleo's eyes were swimming with tears, and Annie felt herself choke up again at the painful images the conversation was evoking. She'd been telling Cleo what had happened the night before at the hospital, and the telling was painful.

It was afternoon. Annie had dropped Jason off at the McCraes' around noon, and it had been traumatic, not only for her, but also for Jason. He'd showered without being nagged, changed his striped rugby shirt twice before they left the house, and made a touching effort to smooth down his unruly shock of hair. The boy was in a state of near hysteria on the long drive across town.

Michael had been waiting out in front of the apartment, and Annie didn't want to see any more than she had to of the first meeting between him and Jason. She dropped her son off and drove away, tears blurring her vision.

It was stupid, but she felt as if she were delivering her beloved son into the hands of the enemy.

Now several hours later, she was peeling apples in Cleo's kitchen. The mother of one of Cleo's day care youngsters had given her a bushel of late apples, and Annie had offered to help peel and make applesauce.

It was therapeutic, the kind of mindless busywork that Annie welcomed today. She'd tried and failed to write even one page of her book. Images of Michael, of Jason, of Linda Vance, and always, superimposed on everything, of David loving her, intruded between her and the computer screen until she'd turned the machine off and escaped next door.

"The thing is," Cleo said now, "the whole time you were talking, I've been thinking about this organ donor thing. It's really tough to figure out whether or not I'd be able to donate my kids' bodies for organs if something happened to them. My own body, fine. But my kids? I'm not sure I could carry through with that."

"I know. Reason tells you it's the only ting to do, but I'd find it hard if it were Jason. But then last night, I saw it from the other side, from the point of view of a child needing the transplant if he were to live."

"I'm gonna have to give this lots of thought. It's exactly like the emergency fund I started," Cleo said. "It's something you ought to set up ahead of time. Heaven forbid we'd ever have to make the decision about organ donation, Annie, but it's better made when you're calm."

Annie couldn't help but consider all the decisions she'd had to make the past week; meeting Michael again, dealing with Jason, taking the final step in loving David. She couldn't say she'd been calm about any of them.

And then there was the pain in her neck. It was driving her nuts again this morning.

They worked in silence for a time, slicing and peeling.

"Cleo, what do you know about hypnosis?"

"Hypnosis?" Cleo shrugged and tossed a long strip of apple peel into the garbage bag, then dumped her basin of apples into the huge kettle steaming on the stove. "I've read the odd thing, and once a couple of years ago I went to see that show—you know the guy who hypnotizes people on the stage? It was kind of scary. Embarrassing and silly, too, because the people he called up out of the audience sang and did dumb things they'd never have ordinarily done.''

"I'm going to that hypnotist they recommended for my neck pain," Annie admitted. "Actually he's called a hypnotherapist. I've only been once, but I'm going again next Tuesday. He says that stage hypnotists abuse the real power of hypnosis, and exploiting it as a game can be dangerous."

"Ask him if it's possible to hypnotize a person into believing that the cellulite on her butt is actually an aphrodisiac to a lover, and I'll make an appointment."

"You're a hopeless case," Annie said. "Truthfully I'm not at all sure if I want to try this, but there isn't anything else, and I'm sick of this miserable pain."

"So if there's a chance it will help, like I told you before, go for it. But I want to know every last detail of every last visit, starting with the one you already made. Start talking, pal.''

Cleo's blatant curiosity made Annie smile, the first time she'd felt like smiling all day.

"This first session, did it help at all?"

Annie shrugged. "It's too soon to tell, but my neck has felt better until this morning. I just started treatments a couple days ago.'' She explained in detail exactly what Dr. Munro had said and done and Cleo listened with avid attention.

"Is this Munro good-looking?"

"Nope, and he wears a big fat wedding ring as well, and his wife works in the office. But he's the easiest person to be around, really laid-back and accepting of everything. Open. He makes you feel safe and secure.''

"Lord, I wish I'd meet an eligible man who's uncomplicated and offered me security and sex. The ones I fall for are so damned unreliable.''

"So who have you fallen for lately, Cleo?" Annie's question was flippant, teasing.

Cleo tossed the paring knife down on the pile of apple peelings and slumped back on her chair with a morose expression on her face.

"It's the cop I told you about, Don Anderson. The one whose wife left him to care for their baby? He came by that day and we had coffee. I figured Don would go on and on about this bitch who walked out on him, real bitter, you know, but he never said a word beyond mentioning that he's started divorce proceedings. We got talking about his work instead, the people he meets.... He's got a great sense of humor, and he's kind of shy and gentle. He's maybe six feet tall, and really strong—big muscles. And he's got this thick blond hair and green eyes. And I fell in love with the baby. He's the sweetest little guy! His name is Ben. He smiles at you all the time. And now Don's asked me out for dinner next week."

Annie felt out of breath just listening. "So where's the problem?"

"There are two dandies. One, Don's twenty-four years old and you know I'm thirty-two. Now I know Mary Tyler Moore's made a success of the older woman, younger man relationship, but she's cute and petite and rich. I am none of the above. By the time I'm forty I'll probably look forty-five. I don't have money or time enough for maintenance stuff like collagen creams or, heaven forbid, plastic surgery." Cleo's litany was humorous, but underneath it Annie sensed real turmoil.

"And he'd be what when I'm forty?" Cleo continued. "The age I am now, thirty-two. Sexy, macho, dealing every day with bimbos who trade off sex for a canceled parking ticket."

"Cleo, that's ridiculous."

"Maybe so, but that's not even all. See, Annie, I don't want to get mixed up with a cop, for Pete's sake. Have you any idea how many cops have been shot in the line of duty over the past year or two? Granted, Vancouver isn't Chicago, but there's still a high element of danger. I had one exciting, dangerous, disappearing man in my life and I don't want another one, for any reason. I couldn't stand it." She pursed her lips. "Why I couldn't have married a nice steady, reliable, boring guy the first time is beyond me, but no, I had to have excitement. Next time, I want a marriage that I can count on. I couldn't stand sending a man off to work and spending all day worrying over whether or not he's getting shot at."

"So when did this Don ask you to marry him?"

Cleo stared at Annie as if she'd gone berserk.

"He didn't, you imbecile. I've only known him a week. He hasn't even kissed me, although once there we were breathing pretty hard when I handed Ben over."

Annie held out sticky hands, palms up. "I rest my case. The poor guy asks you out for one innocent, enjoyable evening, and you've got him married off to a forty-year-old hag who lost her bottle of moisturizer as well as her sense of humor."

Cleo threw a handful of peelings at Annie's head, and they both started to laugh.

It felt wonderful.

ANNIE WENT HOME SOON, but that conversation with Cleo lingered in her mind.

It was ironic, but she was guilty of doing exactly the same thing she'd accused Cleo of, crossing bridges before they even appeared.

She was anticipating all sorts of problems with Jason over this meeting with his father. Instead she ought to just go along and deal with problems as they arose, instead of creating them in her imagination, she lectured herself.

And she ought to do exactly the same thing with what was happening between her and David.

HE CALLED just as she was about to drop off to sleep that night. She'd listened to the tapes Dr. Munro had given her, so her body was limp and relaxed, her mind in neutral.

"Hi, gorgeous," David said when she mumbled hello. "I wanted you to know I've thought of you all day. I was over at the hospital with the Vances most of the morning. I called this afternoon but you weren't home."

"I was over at Cleo's. I thought about you too, David."

"Listen, I've got two heavy days at work, Monday and Tuesday. But I wondered if you could take Wednesday afternoon off and spend it with me?"

"I'd love that."

They chatted on. David asked about Jason's visit with his father.

"He was really quiet when he came home tonight," Annie related, a trace of worry edging her voice. "I thought he'd be going on and on about what a wonderful time he had, but he didn't say very much at all, except that his father seemed 'okay,' Lili seemed 'okay' and the dinner they had was 'okay.'

Annie hadn't known what to make of Jason's reticent mood.

"It's pretty difficult, meeting someone you've only imagined. Maybe Jason's having a tough time adjusting to the real person."

It made sense, and it relieved Annie's concern somewhat.

They talked then about the night they'd spent together, lovers' words that they both needed to hear and say, affirmations that what had happened between them was new in both their experiences.

Before they hung up, David said, "Annie, I love you very much. I'm so glad I found you."

"I'm glad, too. I love you, David."

She hung up and began the slide down into sleep, warm and full of emotion.

I'm glad I found you, he'd said. She was glad, too, that he'd found her...again.

ANNIE'S APPOINTMENT with Dr. Munro was for 9:00 a.m., Tuesday morning. She was there ten minutes early, and this time it felt easy to walk into the cluttered office. Edith greeted her like an old friend and offered her a cup of coffee, which Annie accepted gratefully.

Steve Munro was just as disheveled as he'd been the first time, and just as easygoing. He was finishing a Danish pastry when he called Annie into his inner office, and his shirt—yellow today—had a small coffee stain down the front. He brushed crumbs off his jacket, missing half of them.

"We'll try age regression again, Annie, and see if we can find the specific time in your life when this bothersome pain first affected you."

Annie took her place in the reclining chair, and was guided through the relaxing techniques, which were becoming familiar from the tapes.

"Let go. Relax. Permit all tensions and anxieties to flow out of the body..."

Steve's voice droned on, and Annie felt herself letting go, slipping into a detached, floating trance.

"Relax more deeply..."

Annie felt herself dropping easily into a deep and utterly peaceful state.

"Imagine yourself getting on a train, Annie. Take a seat facing the rear."

Annie could see herself stepping up the high step, she could smell the faintly musty smell of the coach. She sat down in one of the seats, facing the back of the train.

"Outside the window is a sign with today's date on it."

Annie looked, and the sign was there.

"The train is starting to move. Now there's another sign with yesterday's date..."

The signs flashed past. The train built speed. The past dates went by faster and faster.

"Stop at the scene where the problem with your neck originated, Annie."

She could hear the instructions, coming from a great distance. But she couldn't stop.

The signposts were blurring, the train was hurtling her through time and space at a speed she couldn't control.

And then Steve's voice faded, and she was falling head over heels, down and down a long, dark tunnel.

CHAPTER TWELVE

STEVE MUNRO FROWNED as Annie gave a frightened, drawn-out cry and then was silent.

"Annie, you're perfectly safe. Stop at the time the pain in your neck began," he repeated again, watching her with a frown.

She gave no sign that she'd heard him.

She'd dropped spontaneously into what was known as third-stage hypnosis, where the subject has no memory of what is said by the hypnotist. Annie was proving to be a deep-trance subject.

Watching her every moment, Steve leaned over to the nearby desk and pressed a button, turning on the tape recorder he kept there.

Wherever Annie was, she'd likely be interested in hearing about it when she awoke. As he turned back to his patient, he was startled to find that her eyes were open and she was sitting up, although she was obviously not seeing him or the office.

Instead her gaze was inward, staring hard at some scene invisible to him.

"Annie, tell me where you are." He repeated the demand several times with no effect. But what happened next sent a shiver of excitement down Steve's back.

The voice his patient replied in was deeper and more throaty than that which she normally used, and her diction was different as well.

"My name's not Annie, it's Bernadette. Bernadette Desjardins. How is it that you don't know my name?"

There was a trace of irritation in the statement.

Steve studied her, uncertain of what was happening or exactly how he should proceed.

"My mistake. From now on it will be Bernadette," he apologized.

She nodded, and settled herself with precise little movements, more comfortably on the couch. There was a subtle difference now in her body movements. Annie was graceful and moved with deliberation. Bernadette had a quick, impatient way of moving.

"Now, umm, Bernadette..." Steve debated what to ask that would best reveal where the scene she was obviously watching might be taking place.

"Can you tell me what clothes you're wearing?"

She was aware of the voice, coming from a distant place. She felt a need to answer it, although she wasn't certain why. "What I'm wearing? Why, my everyday clothing, of course," she said. "The old brown skirt with the pockets, this pale yellow blouse that I made, oh, two summers ago. It's faded now." She looked down at her feet, and noticed the heavy work boots she hadn't taken off yet.

"Oh, these boots, soiled from the barnyard. I must take them off." She bent and went through the motions of tugging them off, grimacing at the dirt that clung to her fingers. She appeared to peel off some stockings and rubbed her hands down her skirt before pulling something soft over her feet.

"How old are you, Bernadette Desjardins?"

Such strange questions. She thought about it. Strange, not to be certain of her age. But it came to her after a moment.

"Well, I was born in 1892, and this is 1917. So I am twenty-five, yes?"

"Where do you live?"

Really, this was quite ridiculous, and her voice reflected her irritation. "I'm at home, here on my farm in Normandy, where I've lived since I was born."

"You're not married, then?"

The questions were disturbing, and for an instant, she tried to juggle the two realities occupying her mind, the dreamlike knowledge that it was Steve asking her these things, that Bernadette was the vision and Annie the reality. But the effort was too great.

Bernadette triumphed.

"Of course I'm married. I have a child."

"How long have you been married?"

She sighed. "Oh, forever. It seems forever. I was just eighteen. Too young to marry."

There was a deep sadness in the response. She hadn't really wanted to marry Jean Desjardins, but what choice was there? Her parents were old and poor, and there was no chance of going to Paris, to art school, as she'd dreamed of doing. When she finished all the schooling the tiny village could offer, there was little to do except work on her parents' farm and marry. It was what girls were expected to do, in this place.

She explained it as best she could, and Steve encouraged her to tell him more of the story.

"Jean was always around. He was ten years older than I, a neighbor who helped Papa when the old man couldn't manage the heavy farm work on his own anymore. Finally Papa became too sick to manage at all, and then he died. I had no brothers or sisters to help, you see, so Jean took on the full responsibility of the farm for me and my *maman*. She was difficult, *Maman*, as she grew older.''

Bernadette's face was somber as she related her history.

''She became helpless, like a little child. Her mind was gone toward the last. She wandered away, and she had to be watched every moment. And—'' she paused and shrugged, an expressive movement Steve was beginning to recognize as distinctive of Bernadette ''—and Jean was always there to help me, a strong, quiet man, never saying much.''

''You fell in love with him?''

She frowned and shook her head. ''He represented security to me. He proposed, and with some reluctance—I'd hoped like any romantic girl that there would be more than this—I accepted.''

''Was it a mistake?'' Steve asked, caught up in the story.

That shrug again. ''Yes, and no. How was an innocent girl to know what the needs would be of the grown woman?'' Bernadette portrayed stoic acceptance. ''It wasn't always good for me, no.''

She brightened a little, and with a half smile added, ''But how many marriages are perfect? At least I have my daughter. I was fortunate. Nicole was born after only a year, my beloved little girl. She's a joy to me. I have so many dreams for Nicole. I want her life to be different from what mine has been.''

''How old is Nicole now, Bernadette?''

''Seven, last month. Lorelei...she's my friend, the village mid-wife...she brought me sugar so I could make Nicole a cake. We don't have much money for such things. Times are difficult. France has been at war for a long time.'' She shook her head. ''All of Europe is at war.''

1917. Steve remembered sketchy descriptions of the devastation the First World War had wrought on France.

''Is your husband home with you, or did he go off to fight?''

''Oh, he's gone. I thought you knew that. Jean resisted, but finally he had no choice. He had to go. He hated to leave us alone here. He believed the work would be too much for me.''

''And is it?''

There was scorn in her voice. ''No, of course not. The truth is, it was only a matter of weeks after Jean left that I began to realize I'm not nearly as lonely with him gone as I had been living with him. There's more work, but I don't mind.''

She paused and added contritely, ''It's probably a blessing I feel this way, because he's almost certainly dead, poor Jean. A telegram came twenty-two months ago. He was reported missing in action and by now he's presumed dead.''

"Do you think you'll ever marry again?"

"Never." The denial was swift and absolute. "I've had enough of marriage to last me a lifetime. Oh, I feel bad inside, that I can't grieve properly for Jean or long to have him back again. The child misses him, and for that I'm sorry. But for myself, marriage was a mistake I'll make only once." Her mouth set in a determined expression.

"How do you live? How do you earn enough money for your needs?"

She shrugged again, that delightful Gallic shrug.

"Oh, the farm provides most of our food. There are apple trees out there in the orchard. See, through that window?"

She gestured, and Steve was so caught up in the story he almost looked where she pointed.

"There's the garden, the chickens, and the cow, of course. I sell eggs to the inn at the village, and butter as well. And I go out and do housework, cooking, cleaning, when someone has a baby and needs help for a time. I earn a bit of money that way. Lorelei gets me those jobs."

It was a scanty living at best, and making ends meet was a constant worry to her.

Steve decided to carry her along to something besides the day-to-day running of the farm.

"I want you to go ahead in time, Bernadette, to an event that's important in your life. You're moving ahead in time..."

It was confusing to her. Her thoughts seemed to blur, and when they cleared again, she was sitting in the rocking chair in the early summer evening, in the large front room of the stone cottage, singing to the freshly bathed little girl on her lap.

The child was sleeping, her dark head curled in sweet innocence against Bernadette's breasts, and outside, darkness was beginning to overcome the soft summer twilight.

Bernadette cradled the child, burying her nose in the warm, moist perfume of Nicole's hair.

She jumped, startled, when a sharp knock sounded on the front-room door, and fear made her heart beat fast.

No one she knew ever came to that door. Everyone used the kitchen door at the back. With so many soldiers around, one had to be careful.

She got to her feet, balancing Nicole's slight body, and went into the little ground-floor bedroom where the girl slept. She laid her on the narrow cot and covered her with the sheet. Bernadette smoothed her own dark brown hair back—wild curly tendrils always escaped the thick braid she fashioned each morning and coiled at the back of her neck. Then she took the steel poker from the grate and moved nervously to the door where the knocking sounded again, more insistent this time.

She opened the door only about six inches, holding the poker behind her, concealed in the folds of her skirt.

The tall young man standing there looked at her with a gentle expression, studying her for a long, silent moment before he smiled, and any fear she'd felt was gone in an instant. But her natural wariness lingered, and she peered out at him without widening the opening or dropping the poker.

A woman alone with a child couldn't be too careful.

"Excuse me, *mademoiselle*. I'm sorry to disturb you..."

He was wearing an army uniform, not French, though, with the chevrons of rank on his shoulder.

He had a delightful, crooked grin, and he snatched his hat off and held it in his hand. His face was craggy, with deep lines beside his eyes and mouth, but there was a tired grayness to his complexion.

In fact, Bernadette thought as she went on looking, his skin was pasty underneath. Exhaustion? Illness?

"I'm afraid I've managed to lose myself thoroughly..."

His French was good, but he had a strange accent, and she couldn't help but be amused by several of his expressions as he explained that he'd taken the train to Rouen and then arranged to borrow a car, planning to spend his leave at a remote country inn.

"There were a dozen crossroads, however, and I must have taken several wrong turns somewhere back there," he added, gesturing over his shoulder with his cap.

"My name is Paul Duncan, Dr. Paul Duncan," he added, smiling again. His efforts at being cheerful didn't alter the pale, sickly color that showed through the faint tan of his skin.

"American, Monsieur Duncan?" It was the first thing she'd said, and she knew she sounded wary.

"Yes, although I'm with a British medical unit, number twenty CCS. We're stationed at the Somme. I had a couple weeks leave coming, and I wanted to get completely away. It's a—" He broke off what he'd been about to say, substituting, "Call me Paul, please."

A doctor. Certainly, Bernadette was cautious about soldiers—any respectable woman living alone was—but there was something reliable about Dr. Paul Duncan.

There was also an awareness, from the beginning, that he was male and that he thought her attractive. It was in his shy, honest glance.

She made an uncharacteristic quick decision, stepping back as she opened the door wide, setting the poker on a stool before he could see she held it.

"The inn you're looking for is quite a long distance away, Monsieur Duncan. If you come in, I'll draw a map that might help." She stood back from the door, and he came into the room.

His hair was golden and curly, mussed from the hat, cut short in the military manner. He pushed his fingers through it, setting it on edge. It gave him an endearing boyish look.

"Thank you so much." He drew in a deep breath and added, "It smells delicious in here."

She smiled up at him, shy but pleased. She was cooking a stew for her dinner, and the fragrance filled the small stone house.

He was the most handsome man she'd ever met, and it made her more nervous than ever.

"Please, sit down." She gestured toward the broken-down sofa in the corner, and he folded his long body down to the seat, still holding his cap in one hand. He seemed to dwarf the furniture and the small room.

"You have a comfortable home, *mademoiselle*."

"*Madame*. My name is Bernadette Desjardins. My husband's name is Jean."

It was probably wise to tell him that she was married. Was she still married?

He made a polite move to get to his feet, acknowledging the introduction, but she waved him down again. "I will find a paper. Excuse me...."

She hurried into the kitchen, to the drawer where the paper and pencil were kept. The stew she'd been simmering for hours bubbled on the wood stove in the corner, giving off the savory, rich odor he'd commented on, and she gave it an absent-minded stir as she passed.

It would be outrageous, unthinkable, to ask him to share her simple meal.

But how wonderful it would be to sit across the table from him and talk. She loved the way he spoke, with that strange accent. Apart from Lorelei, she seldom had company for a meal.

He had the bluest eyes she'd ever seen.

Perhaps he'd tell her about America, describe it for her... No. What was she thinking?

She took the paper and went back into the other room.

He was standing at the window, his hands folded behind his back, gazing out over the fruit trees that marched in orderly rows down to the banks of the Seine, their branches laden with the promise of a good harvest in another month or so.

There was just enough of the sunset glow left to illuminate the orchard and turn the water of the river the color of brass.

"*Madame*...Bernadette, please, may I call you Bernadette? Your farm is the most beautiful thing I've seen in weeks. It's so peaceful here, I can hardly believe it's real. I feel as if I'm dreaming. It's hard to believe this exists, after..."

Again, he didn't finish the sentence. His voice died, but she knew what he meant when she looked into his face.

Horrible stories of the war and the battles of the Ypres Salient filtered through every day, even to this backwater area.

She felt her heart contract as she looked fully into his face. His eyes held an almost desperate appeal, a pain that reached past her thoughts of propriety and decorum, reached the loneliness that was her silent companion as well as his.

"It will be a long journey to the inn you want to reach, *monsieur*. Their kitchen will undoubtedly be closed. Would you..." She stumbled over her words, desperate and shy all of a sudden, horrified at her boldness. A blush crept up her neck and suffused her face. She could feel it burning all the way to her hairline.

What would he think of her? Would he think she was suggesting more than just a meal to him, here all alone as she was?

She hadn't yet told him Jean was gone.

"It's only stew, not at all fancy," she stumbled on. "Would you like to...to share supper with me before you drive on?"

His face lit up, and his tone was sincere. "There's absolutely nothing I'd like more. Thank you."

Because his pleasure was evident, she relaxed a trifle.

He took his tunic off and tossed it over the back of the sofa. In his shirtsleeves he came into the kitchen, offering to help set the table, and she handed him the plates and cutlery, careful first to spread her best embroidered cloth on the battered wooden table.

"Your husband isn't here?" He was placing the two plates and cups she'd given him on the cloth.

"No. No, he's...Jean's been gone for two years now, missing in action. I'm not—I haven't heard if he's...alive. Or not. The authorities think not. I think not, either. I would have heard before now."

"I'm sorry." The simple words were sincere. "It must be hard for you, alone here."

She shrugged. "It's not always easy, but I have my little daughter."

She told him of Nicole, and made him laugh with a funny anecdote about the child.

"Where are you from in America?" she ventured next.

He described what he labeled a medium-sized town in a place called Ohio, where there were lots of farms. "My father-in-law and I have a small medical practice there."

So he was also married. The strange twinge in her chest couldn't be regret...could it?

She sliced a loaf of her heavy, dark bread, and was thankful that she'd churned earlier that day, so they had fresh, sweet butter to smear on the thick slices. Soon they were laughing and talking together like old friends over the simple meal.

In every way, they were different: language, homeland, education, experience. Yet something between them meshed to perfection. And between them was that ever-increasing awareness of each other, male to female.

The slightest brush of his hand against hers, passing a bowl, caused quivers in all the nerves of her body. And while he spoke of Paris, of the chestnut trees, of how he'd gotten hopelessly lost in the complexities of the Métro system, his wonderful eyes were telling her he found her attractive. Desirable.

It was new to her. She'd never experienced anything like this with Jean. Coupling with him had been a marital duty performed without much feeling on her part, and she'd sometimes longed for the sort of love depicted in the romantic novels Lorelei loaned her.

Every cell in her body reacted to this man. Sensations that had been dream remembrances surged into forceful reality.

She leaped up to clear the table and he helped with clumsy goodwill. "I must go and shut the door on the henhouse. I forgot earlier. There's a fox, and he's already had two of my new pullets," she explained.

"I'll come with you, and then I suppose I should be going," he said.

She checked Nicole. The child was sound asleep, and Bernadette pulled the handmade quilt higher under her little chin, pressing a kiss on her forehead.

He was waiting by the kitchen door, and they walked through the summer darkness to the shed. She secured the door, aware every moment of him, not touching her, but close at her side.

There was a moon, spilling liquid silver over the countryside. Birds called from one tree to the next. A dog barked on a neighboring farm, and the air smelled of growing things.

"Bernadette." His voice was hesitant. "Would you walk with me down by the river, just for a short way? I'd like to remember this idyllic place, when I have to go back to the front lines.''

He reached out and found her hand, and the simple touch of palm to palm made her shiver.

Hand clasped in his, she guided him down through the orchard, to the path that traced the loops of the Seine, a trail she sometimes walked along in the evening.

They walked without talking, absorbing the peace and tranquillity of the silver ribbon of river and the dark trees silhouetted by the moon.

''Would you mind if I dropped by to see you on my way back from the inn?'' he asked after a time. The words were polite, questioning, but there was a desperate intensity in his tone.

She ought to say no.

''I think I should like that, very much,'' she answered with prim decorum, while her heart beat a frantic tattoo.

And then he stopped, and put his hands on her shoulders.

''Bernadette, I have no right. We've only just met. But I think I'm falling in love with you. It happened the moment you opened that door tonight, and I saw your face, your huge gray eyes, so frightened of me.''

He made a low, lost sound in his throat as his arms came around her, drawing her in to him, and then he kissed her.

It was inevitable. It was what she'd wanted from the first moment she'd laid eyes on him.

His lips opened and encompassed her, tugging at her soul, and she wanted all of him with a sudden, fierce passion she'd never dreamed existed in her traitorous body. If he'd gone on kissing her, and lowered her to the moist earth, she'd have welcomed him.

But he didn't. He drew away, and she understood the effort of will it took. She resented it.

And when he drove away a short time later, Bernadette knew that he'd be back. Soon.

HE APPEARED the very next forenoon, a trifle shamefaced when he confessed that he'd gone no farther than the nearby village, where he'd taken a room for the duration of his leave.

''How many days?'' She didn't try to disguise the eagerness in her voice.

''Fourteen.''

And one was already gone.

Nicole was playing with a doll when he came, and she ran to hide behind Bernadette, clutching her mother's skirt in both hands, her dark eyes huge with apprehension.

He'd brought a bottle of wine and—unheard of luxury—packets of chocolate and fancy biscuits. He set them down on the table, and then bent down so that he was at the child's level.

"Look what I've found, little one," he said, voice full of excitement, and to Bernadette's amazement, and her daughter's delight, he skillfully made it seem as if a bright red hair ribbon had unfurled from inside Nicole's ear.

"A ribbon for your pretty hair, hiding in your ear."

"How did you do that? You are a magician?" Bernadette clapped her hands with pleasure. She was as thrilled and amazed as her child.

"It's my hobby, magic," he confessed. "And I'm afraid I'm very limited at it, so don't expect much."

But the females made it plain they thought he was wonderful, and for the next fifteen minutes, he performed other tricks, using a pack of cards and ordinary things from Bernadette's kitchen to astonish and delight them.

Bernadette tied the ribbon in her daughter's hair, and from that moment on, Nicole adored him. Watching Paul with Nicole, she saw the love he had for children, the pleasure in his eyes when the shy little girl put her arms around his neck and kissed him.

Grace, his wife, was fragile and often ill, Paul explained, and so terrified of childbirth there had never been any question of their having a family.

PAUL AND BERNADETTE became lovers the second night. After that, he didn't bother going back to the inn. Time was far too precious to waste.

There was always work on the farm that had to be done, and he helped Bernadette, seeming to welcome the earthy tasks, shoveling out the manure or putting out fresh hay. He mended the door to the stable, and nailed new perches up for the chickens. Bernadette helped and Nicole ran errands, bringing a drink or more nails from the shed.

And the three of them, man, woman and child, laughed and teased and played childish games, so the work seemed nothing at all.

In the long, twilight evenings, after Nicole was asleep, they strolled along the Seine, drinking in the sunset, glorying in the growing love between them.

They made love there, under the sheltering branches of a huge old tree, cushioned by the mossy earth. All around them was the smell of growing things, and Bernadette marveled at the aching fulfillment he brought her, holding himself back until she arched and cried out.

Later, Bernadette and Paul would go up to her bedroom under the eaves. She didn't think of it as Jean's bedroom anymore, she'd been so long alone.

It belonged only to her and Paul. There they held each other and made passionate love, and they talked, hour after hour, about secret things from the depths of their beings.

She told him of her convenient marriage to Jean, and how she hadn't known what to wait for. "But then, you might never have come at all, and I wouldn't have had Nicole, so probably it was all for the best," she added with the French practicality that made him laugh.

His marriage was complicated. Grace's father, Martin Oakley, was Paul's dearest friend, an older doctor who helped Paul through medical school and then made him a partner in his practice. And somewhere along the way, it became understood that Paul would marry Grace.

"It was a mistake," Paul said with sadness in his voice. "But when there's no one you truly love, it doesn't seem to matter as much, marrying someone for other reasons. It's only later..."

"I know, my dearest. How well I know."

His arms came tight around her, and she pressed herself against him and thought of the innumerable nights spent sleeping in this bed with Jean, hoping that he wouldn't turn toward her.

"I felt as if part of me was dying, withering away in that tidy house, with dinner always at the same time, formally set in the dining room, and conversation that never touched on anything remotely personal. When the war began, I couldn't wait to go. That's why I volunteered with a British medical corps."

"And your father-in-law? He was not happy?"

Paul laughed, but there was a bitter undertone. "Understatement of the century—he was not happy. He was furious. We had our only serious quarrel ever. But there was nothing Martin could actually do, and eventually he agreed to run the practice until I go back."

His words evoked thoughts of his leaving, and they turned to each other yet again, searching in the solace of their passion for forgetfulness. Already, neither could bear the thought of that eventual parting, although both knew it was inevitable.

Even the days of Paul's leave were dwindling: seven, five, then three. Bernadette slept locked in his arms, and it seemed to her she'd stolen more happiness in these few days than she'd had in the rest of her life. She wanted them to go on forever.

But there was a voice in her dream...

"ANNIE, ANNIE PENDLETON, I'm going to count backward from fifty to zero, and with the descending numbers, you will slowly return to the present. You will leave behind the personality of Bernadette Desjardins. You will remember what has occurred, and remembering will be a positive impression. Fifty, forty-nine..."

She was far away and reluctant. She snuggled closer to Paul, trying to ignore the summons, but at last she was compelled to obey the voice.

"Thirty-eight, thirty-seven..."

It seemed a long time before she was aware of the office couch, her body, the figure of Steve Munro standing over her.

"Three, two, one...."

For an undecided moment, she wanted only to return to the bedroom of that cottage in France, to the arms of her lover. She could still feel the hot length of his body close to her. His unique male scent lingered in her nostrils. And she felt bereft, as if part of her soul had been torn away....

"Zero. Annie, are you here?"

Then, distance intervened. She was fully Annie again, and she was trembling in violent spasms and starting to cry. Tears cascaded down her face, and Steve offered tissues and took her hands in his in an effort to console her.

"It's fine. You're doing so well, I'm proud of you, Annie."

There was raw excitement in his voice. "Annie, how exciting. You regressed spontaneously into another life. You're a terrific hypnotic subject, for this to happen the way it did today, and after only one other session. I don't know what your views are on reincarnation—but the scenes you described were certainly vivid and real to me. Hey, you need some tea. How do you feel?"

Annie controlled the tears with a great effort, mopping her face and blowing her nose before she attempted an answer.

"I feel weird. Shaky. And cold. And I don't...I don't even believe in this reincarnation stuff, so how could this happen to me?"

She shivered, and Steve brought a flannel blanket and draped it over her lap, then handed her a steaming cup of sweet tea.

"Believing isn't necessary. Annie, do you understand what happened to you?"

She shook her head. "Only that I was someone else. But not really someone else, because that woman, Bernadette...I felt I was Bernadette. I know I was."

Steve nodded. "I believe you were, too, in another time frame. I do believe in reincarnation, and I've deliberately age-regressed patients before with varying degrees of success. But you surprised me. You did it so fast and all by yourself. You were phenomenal."

Annie took grateful sips of the tea, using it to wash away the tears that clogged her throat.

Steve took the tape out of the small recorder.

"When you feel up to it, listen to this. I know you remember what was happening, but it's interesting to hear yourself as you sounded to me."

She accepted the tape and tucked it into her purse. The emotions Annie had experienced as Bernadette were still vivid in her mind, and in fact seemed more important and urgent than the events occurring now.

"Why, Steve? Why do you think this happened to me?"

He was his relaxed self again, sitting at his cluttered desk drinking his own tea.

"Because I told your subconscious to go to the scene where the neck problem originated." He shrugged and grinned at her. "Obviously it didn't originate in this lifetime, so you just did as you were told and went to the one that mattered."

Annie sat up straighter, setting her cup on the couch beside her. She was angry and confused, and she opened her mouth to deny what he was saying, to tell him that the whole thing was ridiculous.

Preposterous. Unbelievable.

But being ridiculous, or preposterous, or any one of a dozen different adjectives she could apply to this experience didn't change what had happened.

The fact remained that it had happened.

And deep inside, she had to face the fact that it was real. She knew every detail of Bernadette Desjardins's life to the point when she'd obeyed Steve and come back here. She knew how the French woman felt and thought, she knew how she made love, and how it felt to have Paul inside her.

Annie flushed at the memory. She swung her legs over the edge of the sofa and got unsteadily to her feet.

"Here's an assortment of books on reincarnation, and on how regressive therapy unlocks the memory of other lives. Remembering allows us to heal old wounds, Annie. Read these. I brought you out today before you had a chance to explore what happened to your neck in that lifetime. But I feel sure that if we pursue this, if we keep going with it, we'll discover the root cause of your problem. And once that happens, I can almost guarantee that you won't be bothered with neck pain ever again." Steve handed her a bag stuffed with books.

"And Annie, more memories will probably come to you spontaneously over the next few days. Don't let them upset you. Remember that whatever happened back then is part of history. It can't be changed, but neither can it hurt you any longer. Accept the memories as a valuable learning tool about your own psyche.''

She left in a daze, astounded when she found the same sunshine outside that had been there at nine, when she'd gone into the office.

Now her watch read twelve-fifteen.

Three hours. She'd wandered through time for three hours. She shuddered and walked off slowly to find her car.

The significant thing was that she'd stopped of her own free will at Edith's desk and made another appointment. After all, she couldn't just leave Bernadette there, without knowing what had happened to her and to Paul. Had they found any sort of future, or was their love as doomed as Bernadette had seemed to think it?

Annie unlocked her car and slid in behind the wheel. Her lips twisted in a grim smile. *Tune in again next week, folks, for the dramatic conclusion.*

Then she put her head down on the steering wheel and started to cry all over again.

CHAPTER THIRTEEN

ANNIE DROVE HOME, took one look at her empty house and headed straight toward Cleo's back door, carrying the shopping bag full of books Steve had loaned her. If ever she'd needed a friend to talk to, she needed one now.

"I stopped off on my way to the bridge," she joked in a shaky voice as she came through the door.

"Good thing. I sure don't feel like raising all these kids plus Jason on my own," Cleo quipped. "C'mon in and sit down."

She was feeding babies, one in a high chair and one cradled on her lap. She stopped long enough to toss a pile of magazines off a kitchen chair for Annie, and both babies instantly began to howl.

"Boy, are you guys single-minded," she accused, making a face at the wailing infants.

"Sit down here and tell me what's up, pal," she ordered Annie over the din, spooning mashed peas into both tiny mouths, stopping the racket in midcry.

"Well, I went back to that hypnotist I told you about, and after what happened this morning, I think I know why I had that feeling about David the first time I saw him, at the magic show. Remember I thought I knew him?" Annie began.

"Sure I remember. I'd never seen you that way about anybody before. So where did you know him from?"

Annie put her elbows on the table and rested her chin on her palms while she tried to figure out how to best explain what had happened to her. Then she just went ahead and blurted it out. There was no best way with something as bizarre as this.

"I think he was someone I met in another lifetime, Cleo. He was a doctor then, too," she began, realizing as she went on with the story what it was about Cleo that made her a wonderful friend.

Cleo had the gift of active listening; instead of the understandable, vocal skepticism Annie might have expected, Cleo just blinked once with surprise and didn't say a negative word. She leaned forward in between spooning, her entire body alert, eyes wide and waiting, expression eager.

"And did you love him then, too?" she prompted.

Annie nodded. "This is how it happened," she began, and through it all, Cleo tended the babies with absent, practiced ease and listened, nodding and asking questions now and then, but allowing Annie to finish the story before she said much.

"Lord, that's amazing. The only other thing I've read about something like this was a book a long time ago called *The Search For Bridey Murphy*," Cleo finally commented when Annie reached the point where Steve had called her back to reality.

Cleo used a washcloth on both dimpled chins and planted a smacking kiss on two tiny faces before she set each roly-poly baby on the floor with a stack of plastic toys to play with.

"I figured it was just a story somebody dreamed up. But come to think of it, there's lots of stuff now about parapsychology and channeling and all that in the bookstores. I just never wanted to know much about it."

Cleo plugged in the electric kettle and made tea. "Same thing as the organ transplant donations we talked about—it only gets to be a personal issue when you do more than just read about it, when you know about someone like little Charlie and his mother. Your ideas change fast when you get involved."

She slapped together two fat egg salad sandwiches, despite Annie's insistent claims that she couldn't eat a thing.

"Eat. Even people heading for the bridge can die prematurely from starvation. Could I borrow a couple of these?" Cleo was shuffling through the bag full of books that Steve had sent with Annie.

"Sure, take as many as you like. I'm not ready to get into reading about this right away. It was enough to have it happen to me."

Cleo shuddered. "I guess. Tell you the truth, I'd rather not know if I lived before or not. There's enough to worry about with one lifetime, never mind two. Eat your sandwich. It'll make you feel better."

Annie did, and Cleo paged here and there through one book after the other. "There're books here about life before life, life after life, using hypnosis to access past lives. Pretty esoteric ideas, but it looks as if this regression thing happens to lots of people."

Cleo closed the books and concentrated for a moment. "When you were, ummm...when you thought you were in that other woman's body, Annie, did it feel as if you were eating real food with this guy Paul? Remember you said you invited him for supper?"

Annie swallowed a mouthful of egg before she answered.

"Cleo, it was so real I can remember the exact taste of that stew. It was seasoned with garlic and thyme, and I added lots of parsley just before I served it, and a handful of what smelled like sage. I liked to cook then just as much as now, but now the ingredients are easier to come by. Digging them out of the garden was a heck of a lot harder than buying them at the supermarket. I remember looking down at my hands, and they were all stained from the earth, and my nails were rough."

Cleo stared at Annie. "Garlic and thyme, huh? Well, even now you're a kook about spices." She thought for a moment and added, "I don't suppose you remember having to go to the bathroom while you were this Bernadette woman?"

Annie giggled, the first time all day she'd even come close to laughing. Trust Cleo to get down to absolute basics.

"As a matter of fact, yes, I went out behind the house to a privy. It had two holes and a sort of wooden platform. It wasn't very pleasant. There wasn't any proper paper, just ripped up rough stuff."

Cleo's mobile features lit up with excitement and she snapped her finger and thumb together.

"Annie, as far as I'm concerned, that does it. You were there, all right. That one detail convinces me more than anything else could, more than any of the rest of this professional garble in these books. I'll bet you never used one of those kinds of toilets in this life, right?"

"Right," Annie agreed with feeling. "And from what I remember, I'd just as soon not use one again, then or now."

"When do you go to see Munro again? Because I think you're on to something that's really important to you here."

Annie groaned. "Getting used to outdoor privies and visiting the twilight zone have to be high points in anybody's life all right. I made another appointment for next Tuesday."

"Y'know, it might be neat to find out that what's happening in our lives made sense on some grand scale, that it was all linked to the past in a pattern instead of being just a big, ironic accident. If you did know David back then, well, maybe there's a good reason for knowing him again now," Cleo mused.

"What if the people we meet and fall in love with are all people we loved before? If we found out where we screwed up in the past, would we still agonize so much about whether it's right or wrong to fall in love with somebody again?"

Annie studied her friend, recognizing something under the surface of the words, something that was disturbing Cleo.

"Did you go out with Don Anderson yet?" she hazarded, knowing she'd struck a nerve when Cleo's face flushed crimson.

"Yeah, last night. We took all the kids to a drive-in movie. It felt like a family, with the baby in the car bed and the girls asleep in the back seat. We ate popcorn and laughed a lot."

"And?"

Cleo got up and began to scrub the countertop hard. "And what? He's a super guy, he's still as young as he was a week ago and he's still a cop."

There were tears glistening in her eyes when she turned and gave Annie a helpless look. "And I'm afraid I'm falling in love with him, damn it all to hell."

Annie got up and wrapped her arms around her friend.

Before today, she'd have advised Cleo to be careful, to hold herself back in an effort to avoid hurt.

But the memory of Bernadette, the power of the love she'd shared with her Paul were still so fresh in Annie's mind that all she could say was, "Give it a chance, Cleo. Who knows? Maybe this is the guy you've been waiting for."

She went home shortly afterward, but she found she wasn't able to concentrate on her book at all, even though her editor had called with an excited message about going straight ahead with it, that she was mailing a contract immediately.

Normally that news had Annie on a high for days. But now she felt as if a vital part of her belief structure had been turned upside-down. Selling a book was exciting, but finding out she'd maybe lived before was earth-shattering.

SHE WAS STILL OFF BALANCE when Jason breezed in from school that afternoon and announced that his father—Annie still had difficulty with that label—had promised to come and watch his rugby game later that afternoon.

"When did he promise, Jason? You know I explained that arrangements like that have to always be made with me, so that I know ahead of time. Your father hasn't called. I was out this morning, but there's no message on the answering machine from him because I checked."

Jason's face fell, and he gave her the pleading look she had such trouble resisting.

"I called him from school at noon today. My friend's father is coming to the game and we thought it would be excellent if my father could come, too. Jeeze, Mom, it was my idea. Don't blame my father, okay?

I wanted the guys on my team to meet him. Their fathers are around all the time.''

There was a deliberate plaintive note in his voice when he talked about other boys' fathers. This kid of hers was getting adept at heavy guilt, Annie concluded, glancing at him narrow eyed.

The whole issue of Michael was getting more and more complicated. Now she'd seem out-and-out mean if she said no about tonight. And anyway, how could she? A rugby game wasn't exactly limited admittance. If Michael wanted to turn up at the field where Jason played, she couldn't stop him.

"All right, Jason," she said with obvious disapproval. "But from now on, talk to me first, understand?"

He agreed with apologetic enthusiasm, and the telephone rang.

It was Michael. He told her word-for-word what Jason had just related, adding that he was concerned about not letting her know ahead of time. Then he asked if he could possibly take Jason and his friend out for hamburgers after the game.

"I'll make sure he's home at a reasonable hour."

What was there to say? It was a logical thing to want to do, and Jason had stood three inches away during the whole conversation, eavesdropping and making excited faces, nodding with wild enthusiasm each time Annie looked at him.

Annie repeated to Michael what she'd just said to Jason, using the same tone, stressing that she needed to know about things like this ahead of time, that it was inconsiderate and unacceptable at the last minute.

Michael agreed with the same apologetic enthusiasm Jason had used. "Also, Annie, he's going to be asking you if he can start spending some weekends with us, staying over from Friday till Sunday. I was firm about him having to ask you first, but of course we'd like it if it's possible."

Her first reaction was to scream no, no, and no again. But now that she'd allowed the relationship to begin, how was she to say that three hours was acceptable, but two days wasn't?

Her brain told her that the sensible thing to do was to allow Jason time with Michael, as much time as he seemed to require. But every one of her insecurities hurt like a toothache at relinquishing her son to this man.

Annie swallowed hard, said it would be all right and hung up in total defeat as Jason went charging downstairs to gather his rugby equipment.

Her son had just left when David walked in the open kitchen door a half hour later, and Annie's flagging spirits went soaring just at the sight of him.

"I've been thinking of you all afternoon, and I got out of the last meeting earlier than I figured," David explained as he wrapped her in his arms and kissed her. Their love and mutual need for each other blazed out of control as their lips met again and again.

"Jason?" David whispered as the spiral of desire began to soar between them in a pulsing arc.

"Out, until nine-thirty," Annie murmured, and they hurried up the stairs to her bedroom.

But as David undressed her and then himself, using his lips and hands to caress her pulsing body, Annie couldn't stop the images that crowded her mind, images of another man and woman, making love just the way she and David were now.

And when her climax began, it was as if she and Bernadette rode the tumult together, their bodies one, just as the men loving them were one. And at that moment, it didn't matter where or when the eternal bond uniting their souls had begun. To Annie, the only thing that mattered at that moment was that their love be truly eternal.

DOWNSTAIRS AGAIN, Annie made them each a drink, and then she related the details of her hypnotic session to David.

He listened without any of Cleo's responsiveness, and Annie grew more and more ill at ease, beginning to stumble over her words as his face set in stiff, disapproving lines.

Finally she gave up trying to describe the occurrence and instead simply slid the tape Steve had made into her recorder and pushed the play button.

The moment she did she found herself wishing she'd never brought the subject up at all with David. Steve's deep, resonant voice filled the room, instructing her, reassuring her, and Annie, glancing up at David's frozen expression, began to tremble.

She hadn't realized what an effect the tape would have on her, or him. She was frightened, so frightened her insides felt cold and empty. Why was she so afraid to hear this? Was it only David's presence that inhibited her? She fought the sudden, irrational impulse to reach over and switch the machine off.

It took several moments before the sound of a woman's voice registered as having had to come from her own throat, and the profound shock that voice gave Annie rendered her immobile.

The voice was deep and musical, the timbre and quality very different from Annie's, and yet she knew it was her. Or someone who had been her. She stole another glance at David. He was rigid, his mouth a long, hard line, eyes narrowed as the woman who called herself Bernadette described the scenes that even now Annie could see as well in her mind's eye as she could see the pattern of the shawl on the back of the sofa where they sat.

Annie began to shake as the tape continued, and a pulse throbbed in her forehead. She wanted to move over closer to David, press her body against his warmth and know the reassurance of his smile, his arm around her.

She longed to have him give her some logical, medical explanation for what was happening on that tape.

But for the first time since she'd been with him, David was somehow closing himself to her, holding himself away even though they sat just a few feet apart.

What Annie found most disturbing about the tape was the emotion, the depth of honest feeling in Bernadette's voice as she talked about her lover, her child, matter-of-fact yet somehow eloquent in her simplicity, with an undercurrent of hope and desire and longing.

The sentiments expressed were very like those she felt for David, or Jason, and they struck a deep responsive note inside her. Her voice and Bernadette's might differ, but their souls were one.

At last a whirring emptiness filled the room and then, with a sharp click, the tape recorder shut itself off.

Annie was the first to speak. "Well, what do you make of that?" she asked in as normal a tone as she could manage. Her voice shook anyway.

David was still seated on the sofa beside her. He reached for the glass of Scotch Annie had poured him earlier and took a long, hearty swig.

"David, what do you think about all this?" Annie asked again.

He set the empty glass down on the coffee table, still without saying anything to her or even looking at her, and Annie felt as if she were shriveling up inside.

He turned at last and gave her a long, searching glance, one she couldn't interpret. Then he stood and picked up his glass, heading for the kitchen where Annie had left the Scotch bottle on the counter. She heard the liquor splash, the gulp of sound as he added water.

She waited for him to come back, every nerve ending alive.

He didn't sit down. He walked over to the window and stood as if he were staring out at the twilight.

When he did speak, his voice was careful and controlled at first. "I wish you hadn't gone along with this nonsense at all, Annie. I have to say I not only believe it's absolute hogwash, but I also think it could be harmful to you.'' The control disappeared, and he sounded angry and disgusted when he added, ''I've never heard such a bunch of garbage in my life.''

The condemnation in his voice shocked her.

''But Steve explained to me...''

''I don't give a good goddamn what this Munro told you.'' He whirled around, his blue gaze icy and hard.

She flinched as if he'd struck her.

''I'm telling you I don't approve, Annie, from either a medical standpoint or a personal one.''

Annie shuddered. He'd never looked at her in quite that way before, as if she were a stranger he didn't consider quite bright enough. ''Why...why are you reacting this way, David? I just wanted you to hear what happened to me, and give me an opinion on what went on today.''

''That's exactly what I'm doing, Annie. I'm a doctor, and I'm telling you I think this nonsense has gone far enough.''

Annie was shocked and angered at the harshness that had once again crept into his tone. Her hands knotted into fists, but she kept silent as he went on talking, striding up and down the room in an agitated way.

''I'm willing to concede that hypnotism has its place as a tool in modern medicine. I've seen it used effectively with children when they have to undergo painful procedures. But what you're fooling with here is preposterous. Surely you understand that after listening to the garbage on this tape. All that's happening is that you're dredging up some buried memories from a movie you've seen, a book you read, a conversation you overheard as a young child. And because you're vulnerable, and innocent, you believe it's happening to some person who lived seventy or eighty years ago, some woman you think was you. You're far too gullible, Annie.''

He thrust one hand and then another through his hair, setting it on end in wild clumps.

''I want you to give this up. If you feel that ordinary hypnosis helps your neck in any way, I'll be glad to find a therapist who doesn't carry the procedure to the extremes this Munro obviously does.'' His voice was hoarse, filled with passion and anger. ''The man's a fanatic. I don't want you near him again.''

Annie stared at him, at a loss as to what to say.

He stopped in front of her, reached out and clasped her shoulders with his palms. She felt the warmth that emanated from him, the texture of his skin through the thin blouse she was wearing. She also felt his agitation in the almost painful bite of his fingers on her flesh.

"Annie, love, I want you to promise me that you won't go along with any more of this," he begged. "Will you do that, for me?"

She felt as if she'd ended up in a conversation with a stranger. The overwhelming love she felt for David, the desire to please him, the respect she had for his ability as a doctor, were all at war with an automatic, deep-seated conviction that what he was asking her to do wasn't based on logic, and also wasn't something that should upset him this way.

David was reacting from some deep emotional level she didn't understand. She suspected he really didn't understand it, either.

She summoned up all the logical words she could think of to try to explain that to him. "But what happened to me was real, David, whatever the reason or the cause. It wasn't fraud, or imagination, or something I read. I can't explain it except to say that just as I know I'm alive now, this minute, so I also know I was alive then. I remember the emotions very strongly. There were things I didn't or couldn't explain on that tape, the way there are emotions inside of me I can't explain now." She frowned up at him.

"I don't understand exactly what you're warning me against, but I don't like it. Dr. Munro is a competent person, or he wouldn't have been recommended. What's more, I like him a lot and trust him. There's no physical danger, he assured me of that. Are you...afraid that I might get trapped somehow and not be able to come back?"

That sounded so much like science fiction it embarrassed her.

David let her shoulders go and stood straight, staring down at her. His words were passionate and again, angry. "What you're doing is mentally dangerous in my opinion. Already you seem to be fully accepting some ridiculous explanation for all this, willing yourself to believe it's all valid. Why do you really want to go on with it, anyway? There wasn't one single reference in all that—" he gestured toward the tape recorder "—about the real problem this Munro is supposed to be treating, namely your neck spasms."

She swallowed. Her throat felt parched and fear was clutching at her stomach. In this mood, David was intimidating.

"Steve felt that the reason I ended up back there was that something happened at that time that caused the pain I'm having now. He says I've only begun to explore the reasons."

"Ahh, hogwash," he said in a tone of absolute disgust. She could see he thought her explanation ridiculous, and helpless frustration welled up in her.

Lord, she loved this man. The intensity of that had never changed, never lessened one iota over the time she'd known him.

She didn't want to quarrel like this, didn't want tension or bad feelings between them. For an instant, she considered doing what he wanted, canceling her next appointment, trying to forget the powerful emotions she'd experienced as Bernadette.

But she simply couldn't do it. Somewhere between the time she'd left Steve's office and now, the decision to go on with the hypnotic regression had firmed and stabilized in her thoughts. She had to explore the astonishing possibility that somewhere in the annals of time, she'd lived before, and she would do that research with or without David's approval.

It didn't seem a decision she'd had any choice in making, anyway. The regression to Bernadette had been automatic, as if she were being led toward an experience she needed to remember. Just as she had to know what would happen next.

"David, I'm sorry, but I have another appointment in a week, and I plan to keep it," she said with conviction.

She could see the effort he put into controlling his reaction. She knew that he was forcing himself not to reveal the true depth of his anger, not to lash out at her in rage.

She didn't understand his objections now any better than she had when he first made them.

"Then there's no point in discussing it further, is there?" he said in a clipped, distant tone that she'd never heard him use before. He glanced at his watch, and her heart sank. She'd driven him away.

"I'd better be going. I told Calvin I'd drop by and have a drink with him tonight if there was time. There's some committee planning meeting he wants to discuss."

"Are...are we still spending tomorrow afternoon together, David?" Annie hated having to ask, hated the feeling that she was begging him for reassurance.

"Of course. I'll come by and pick you up just after one. We'll have dinner out, if you can arrange something for Jason."

It should have made her feel better, but it didn't. Neither did the perfunctory kiss he planted more or less on her mouth before he hurried out, closing the door firmly behind him.

DAVID DIDN'T GO to Calvin's, however. Instead he drove in the direction of the ocean, braking with a jerk each time a light was red, pulling away with an angry squeal of tires and accelerating with reckless abandon when he reached the long stretch of road that bordered the water.

An irrational need to get away drove him, but what was it he needed to escape?

Annie? He loved Annie.

Whatever it was, it possessed him, kept him from stopping and parking on the all-but-deserted beach. He needed to go on driving, putting distance between himself and the scene he'd been through back there.

Anger and puzzled frustration mingled inside of him, and driving fast released only a tiny portion of the tension that had been building inside of him ever since Annie had played that damnable tape. The moment it started, he began to feel physically ill.

What had caused the deeply rooted fear, the terrible anxiety and sense of failure and frustration he'd experienced when he listened to the damned thing? To her, that woman who called herself Bernadette.

Chills had gripped him when her voice first sounded, and then foreboding and regret had knotted his gut as that haunting familiar voice with its lilting French intonations went on and on. He knew that voice, damn it, knew it in the depths of his pores. It was a voice in a dream he never remembered on waking. He couldn't explain it, and neither could he control the reaction it caused.

He'd channeled his feelings like an idiot into the harsh things he'd said to Annie, but they expressed exactly the way he felt about this whole process she'd bumbled into.

It had to be garbage, didn't it? It had to be a clever fraud perpetrated by her subconscious, or his, or by this jerk Munro. By somebody, damn it, because there wasn't any other explanation.

He'd had to tell her how he felt, he rationalized. *But you didn't have to hurt her doing it, Roswell.* Her soft eyes had widened and then filled with hurt, and it tore his gut apart to see what he'd done with his tirade. What made him act that way, for pity's sake? She was the one person he never wanted to hurt.

All at once a sense of utter desolation rolled over him. He loved Annie, as he'd never loved another woman in his life. But sometimes, sometimes like now, this minute, but also during the entire time it had taken that hellish tape to run its course, he had the feeling he'd lose her somehow. He became convinced he'd eventually end up spending a large portion of his life without her—empty years, lonely years. Long and straight and dusty, leading only to the grave. Who the hell had said that, anyway?

He was past the beaches, back into a suburban area near the university.

All at once he wheeled the car into the parking lot of a small pub he'd never been in and before he could change his mind, he walked through the door into the smoky noise.

He took a stool at the bar and ordered a Scotch.

What he had to do was somehow find more time to be with Annie, put more effort into breaking through the wall Jason had erected to keep him out, and through Annie's own reservations and doubts about their relationship being permanent. He needed time to court her, time to let her get to know him and trust him.

Time. With Calvin pulling strings to get him invited to every bloody business meeting in the western hemisphere, time was the one thing David didn't have.

The bartender put a glass and a pitcher of water in front of him. David ignored the water, lifted the glass to his lips and shuddered as the liquor burned its fiery way down his gullet.

It was sad and ironic that a man with as little spare time as he had should be wasting that precious little sitting alone in a pub trying to drown the haunting memory of a voice he could have sworn didn't belong to Annie, and yet did.

And if it didn't sound like the woman he now loved, then why the hell should it affect him at all? Why should it make him feel as if nails were scratching in slow motion down the blackboard of his nervous system?

"Bartender, another Scotch, please. Make it a double."

He was going to have one bitch of a headache in the morning. With savage intent, he drank the second whiskey and ordered again.

ANNIE WAS READY when David drove up in front of the house the next afternoon. She'd been ready for a nervous half hour, and she didn't wait for him to get out of the car and come to the door.

Instead she hurried out and slid into the seat beside him.

The events of the previous evening and the long, dream-thick night that had passed since their quarrel had given her time to think, time to plan some sort of strategy.

She'd decided the best thing to do was avoid the whole topic of regression and hypnosis with David, and that's what she intended to do this afternoon. They had little enough time together, she reminded herself over and over, and she wasn't about to spend the afternoon quarreling. She only hoped David felt that way, too.

"Isn't it a great day? We're having a real Indian summer this year," she remarked with forced cheerfulness, turning to smile at David as she looped the seat belt across her and fastened it. He was looking out the side window, away from her, staring at two children tossing a ball on the sidewalk.

"Bet this is some sort of record for the Coast. We've had so many days without rain." My gosh, it sounded like the type of conversation she might have with a perfect stranger.

It was hard to read his expression even when he finally turned his head toward her. He was wearing dark glasses that shrouded his eyes, but he attempted a polite smile and agreed before he pulled the car smoothly away from the curb.

"I thought we might take a drive out to Steveston," he said in the same polite, impersonal tone she'd been using.

"There're lots of places to walk beside the river, and the village is fun to explore. Also, someone mentioned a great seafood restaurant where we could have an early dinner later on."

Annie agreed with enthusiasm, doing her best to fill the awkward silences that fell between them as he maneuvered through traffic and over bridges, heading south of the city toward the municipality of Richmond.

There had never been these silences before between them, and it bothered her that there were now. It tore at her, and she wondered if the entire afternoon would be this way.

She'd take a bus home if it didn't improve, she told herself. She couldn't stand being with him, loving him, and having this tension between them.

He was an impossible, pigheaded man, she fumed.

They were driving past fertile vegetable farms whose silt-rich fields were dotted with workers in conical straw hats, crouched along the long straight rows weeding the healthy-looking plants. It might have been a scene from Bangkok.

"...and my editor called and said she loves my proposal, and I finally hit some sort of breakthrough with the character of the boy," Annie heard herself chattering, filling empty air with senseless words. "I was up really early this morning..."

She'd wakened with a violent start at half past four out of a dream she couldn't remember, unable to go to sleep again. So she'd gotten up and gone into the study, turning to her work to stop the parade of confusing images that had marched all night through her dreams.

"...and all of a sudden, I realized what needed to be done..."

She stopped, because David had pulled the powerful car out of the speeding lines of traffic, steering over to the shoulder of the highway and braking with an urgent jolt.

The engine idled and cars sped past as he turned toward her, releasing his seat belt and stripping the dark glasses from his face, revealing bloodshot, weary eyes.

"Darling, I'm sorry." He reached out to draw her into a rough embrace.

His arms encircled her, but the seat belt stopped her. It took her a moment to fumble it open, and then she moved deeper into his arms with a mixture of relief and happiness and overwhelming love for him flooding through her like liquid sunlight.

It was going to be all right, after all.

"Annie, my dearest." His mouth was close to her ear, and his gruff words tickled. "Whatever happens between us, remember that I love you. I'll always, always love you," he said, holding her against him with a ferocity that made breathing difficult for her. "Annie, I'll love you till I die."

And afterward, a still, small voice inside of her whispered.

She lifted her head and put her mouth on his, drinking his feverish kisses, running her hands over his face and chest and shoulders, reassuring herself that he was really there for her again.

She wanted to forget the harsh words he'd used the night before, the resentment she'd felt when he walked out the way he had.

"I love you, too, David, more than I can ever tell you."

As they wandered hand in hand through the quaint Japanese fishing village of Steveston and ambled along the shoreline of the Fraser River that day, he wanted to tell her about the dream he'd had the night before.

Nightmare, he corrected himself. He'd never had a nightmare in his life, he'd never understood how unsettling they could be, but if anything was to be labeled nightmare, it would be this infernal demon, which had left him shivering and icy cold with sweat at 3:00 a.m. It must have happened as a result of the whiskey he'd consumed. It had to be the liquor that had caused it.

Maybe if he talked it over with Annie, and they laughed at the ridiculous power dreams seemed to possess in the lonely hours just before dawn, it would lose its importance, fade from his consciousness. But he couldn't bring himself to talk about it, even to Annie, and it settled into his awareness like an invisible albatross.

He'd left the pub just after midnight the night before with enough sense to know he'd had far too much whiskey to make driving possible. So he'd called a cab from the pay phone out front, hoping his car would be safe in the lot till morning.

During the taxi ride home, the alcohol he'd consumed had caught up with him, and by the time he reeled into his apartment, it was a major task just to get out of his clothes and tumble into bed and blissful oblivion.

Drugged sleep enveloped him in an instant.

He wasn't sure when the dream began. He only knew with sudden clarity that he found himself in a large, gracious old house. He wanted to buy it for himself and Annie. They'd be happy there, and he felt excited and eager because now that he'd found them a suitable place to live, there couldn't be any more obstacles between them. More than anything else, he wanted that, needed that permanence.

This house was perfect, he was sure of it. He toured the ground floor, reveling in the gleaming old wood, the size of the rooms, the huge old-fashioned kitchen. Annie would adore this house.

He started up the winding staircase to the upper level, and the first tiny threads of illogical fear began to weave their way into his sleeping mind, but he ignored them, shoving them aside as he moved through the bedrooms and bathrooms, noting the fine polished oak floors, the wide casement windows, the large east bedroom that would serve as a perfect writing studio for Annie.

Then, all of a sudden, he came upon another stairwell, hidden in a shadowed corner, and David knew it led to the attic above. He knew, too, that the time had come to explore that area, and the tiny licks of fear he'd experienced earlier became stronger as he stood at the bottom of the narrow steps looking up at a closed door a dozen steep steps away.

Behind that door lurked horror.

For some unaccountable reason, he was terrified of that door, and of whatever ghastly, unmentionable menace lurked in wait for him behind it. He knew there was something unspeakable up there, and he wanted to escape, leave the house without finding out what it was. But he couldn't go anywhere but up.

The dream twisted, confining him as he forced himself to take one step up those attic stairs, and then another. He was frightened, but he didn't want to acknowledge that fear even to himself. He was a man, and deep shame filled him. Men shouldn't be afraid. Especially of a thing he couldn't even see.

He felt his heartbeat accelerate. *One. Two.* One step after the other, he forced himself to climb. The dream atmosphere was now heavy and ominous: an unimaginable terror held him in its grip, making it hard to breathe. His chest hurt as he inhaled and exhaled. And he could smell his own fear, rank in his nostrils.

The steps narrowed as he neared the top. Now his heart was thundering, and cold sweat broke out on his body.

David had never before believed he was about to die, but he believed it now. With every ounce of willpower he could manage, he reached for the door handle to that attic, forcing himself to turn it....

His scream was still echoing through the apartment when he awoke, and the paralyzing fear took several moments to begin to fade. He was sitting bolt upright in bed, and his body was trembling, drenched with sweat.

He couldn't breathe at first. His heart thundered hard enough to make his chest ache, and the relief he felt at getting out of the dream before that attic door opened made him weak.

Dawn was barely a suggestion in the sky outside his window, but he didn't even try to fall asleep again. He didn't dare chance falling back into the dream, even though the whiskey he'd consumed made him long to throw himself back on the bed and sleep until his eyes and head were better.

Instead he perked coffee, and after the first mouthful, bolted to the bathroom and threw up.

He'd been awake ever since.

ON THE SURFACE, the day Annie and David spent together was a success.

They wandered like carefree lovers, laughing together at nonsense, stopping in secluded places to kiss and hold each other.

David insisted on buying her a teardrop-shaped crystal on a silver chain in a strange little jewelry store hidden down a lane in the village. "It will bring happiness and much luck in love," the Japanese proprietor promised.

Annie figured she needed all the help she could get as David fastened it around her neck, letting his fingers trail across her neck and shoulders.

They ate a delicious seafood dinner in a restaurant overlooking the pier, where dozens of fishing boats rocked at anchor. Annie fed David bits of her lobster and smiled into his eyes, pushing aside the sad knowledge that, despite all their efforts, there was new tension between them now, tension that hadn't been there before the previous evening, tension that must remain unresolved because now there were subjects they simply couldn't discuss without quarreling.

Subjects like hypnotism, regression, reincarnation: offbeat subjects that only a short time ago, Annie wouldn't have thought of discussing anyway. And of course there was the ever-increasing drain on David's time and energy. They couldn't be rational about that, either, because Annie was anything but rational when it came to a situation she felt Calvin Graves had engineered.

Now these matters loomed large and ominous, important, in her life, in her brain, in her subconscious, and she had to be very careful about not mentioning them at all, because they were right there every minute in her thoughts. They put an invisible barrier between her and the man she loved.

DAVID DROPPED HER OFF at dusk. He had to check on a small patient at the hospital, and they both felt a little cheated at not being able to make love that evening.

Jason had had dinner with Cleo and the girls, and he was engrossed in an episode of *Star Trek*.

Annie turned on the answering machine. There was a message from her editor, two hang ups, and then a pleasant voice with a slight accent said, "Annie, this is Lili McCrae. I wondered if you might have lunch with me, perhaps Friday this week? Call me."

Annie frowned down at the machine. Did she really want to put herself through still another awkward situation?

But Lili must have a good reason for wanting to invite her to lunch. Perhaps she and Michael were having some problem with Jason, and Lili wanted to discuss it?

In slow motion, Annie lifted the phone and dialed the number that was becoming all too familiar to her.

It was a small relief when Lili answered instead of Michael, and Annie agreed to meet the other woman Friday at a restaurant on Broadway.

When she hung up, Annie reflected that her life was beginning to resemble the description of plotting she'd once heard a well-known writer deliver at a seminar.

"Plotting a book," he'd said with a beleaguered sigh, "means having one damn thing happen right after another."

It fit the pattern Annie's life was taking, all right. One damn thing happened to her right after another.

CHAPTER FOURTEEN

ANNIE HURRIED in to Lothario's Bistro on Friday at twenty past twelve.

Lili was already waiting at a table near the window.

"Sorry I'm late," Annie apologized as Lili stretched out an elegant, slim hand in greeting.

"But you're not at all," Lili smiled. "I'm compulsive about appointments. It's only by the greatest act of will I avoid getting anywhere two hours too early."

Annie took the chair the waiter was holding, feeling a bit apprehensive about what was to come.

Lili was sipping a glass of white wine, and Annie ordered the same. Once the waiter was gone, she took a moment to study the woman across the table.

Lili was wearing a brightly-patterned narrow skirt and a rose-shaded silk blouse. She had silver hoops in her ears, and her hair was styled as Annie remembered, a dark glossy mass drawn into a high dramatic knot. She wore subtle makeup, but it was her eyes that commanded attention, deep and soft and gentle. Lili was ageless. She'd probably look much the same when she was eighty.

"You must wonder why I asked you here today," Lili said with the forthright manner Annie remembered from their first meeting.

"I know we share a delicate acquaintance, but I thought it wise for us to know each other at least well enough that phone calls and the necessary communication we must make because of Jason might be comfortable instead of strained between us, no?"

The old resentment rose in Annie for a moment, the feeling that these people, Michael and this wife of his, were usurping her place with her son.

But hard on that thought came the realization that the whole situation wasn't exactly easy on Lili, either. It was a wonder she didn't bitterly resent both Jason and Annie because of their ties to her husband. Yet she didn't seem to at all. Her words were positive and totally free of undercurrent as far as Annie could tell.

"I have had little to do with growing boys, you see, and I need to

ask you questions about Jason, so that I won't undo through my stupidity things you have set in place. He'll be coming to spend the weekend with us soon, and I need to know what foods he likes, besides
hamburgers—'' both women grimaced ''—and also what rules you feel
are important for him.''

Before they could talk further, the waiter brought the wine, and they
studied the menu, trying to ignore his ongoing litany of what was delicious today.

Annie ordered a croissant stuffed with crab, and Lili decided on lin-
guine with seafood sauce.

Lili leaned across the table when the waiter left and confided in a
low voice, ''Food is my great weakness. Do you know I have almost
seventy cookbooks? I read them like novels. When I was learning English at school I used to study cookbooks, so instead of being able to
say—'' she frowned, trying to remember ''—oh, things like 'my uncle's
dog is staying with my cousin'—instead I was spouting 'separate the
eggs and whisk in cream.'''

Annie laughed. ''I can't resist cookbooks, either. Jason literally drags
me past displays of them in the supermarket.''

Until their food arrived they talked about cooking and recipes, and
Annie found she was enjoying herself.

Lili was intelligent and quick-witted, with a wry sense of humor and,
just as she'd admitted, a healthy appetite. She attacked her food with
honest hunger.

''I think I must have died of starvation in some other life, to be such
a glutton in this one,'' Lili sighed, spooning up the rich creamy sauce
and buttering a thick slice of fresh hot bread.

Annie suddenly lost her appetite, but her attention was fully on the
other woman. ''Do you believe in reincarnation, then?'' she managed
to ask.

Lili swallowed a mouthful of food and then raised her wineglass and
sipped. ''I never give it much thought. It's part of our Eastern belief
structure, of course, but—'' she said matter-of-factly ''—I'm afraid I
neither believe nor disbelieve. We weren't a particularly religious family, although I was taught the basics. Reincarnation is linked with
karma. You understand the concept of karma?''

Annie shook her head. ''Not really.'' Over the weekend, she'd
skimmed through one of the books Steve had loaned her, but her emotions were still too ragged to allow her to concentrate on theory. She
was still feeling rather than thinking.

''Doesn't it have to do with—'' Annie searched for a cloudy
dictionary definition ''—with destiny?''

Lili reached out and refilled their wineglasses.

"In a way. It's simply cause and effect, a belief that our lives have purpose and we come back each time to learn lessons that have escaped us the time before. Karma can bring happiness or sadness, depending on the results you've learned by your choices."

There was something that was concerning Annie more and more. "Do you think, Lili, that when—if—we do reincarnate, that we come back here with the same people?"

Lili shrugged. "It makes sense, of course. The theory is that we're here to learn lessons of love, and if we love the same people again and again, we'd be able to work out problems that defeated us the last time 'round."

Annie wanted to ask if Lili had ever felt that she'd known Michael before, but the complexities of the relationship between her and Lili and Michael and Jason stopped her.

Annie leaned forward, about to ask one of the dozens of other questions Lili's words had evoked, but she was interrupted by the cheerful young waiter.

"Would you ladies like to see the dessert menu? We have the most amazing selection today." He rattled off at least a dozen choices, and Annie met Lili's amused glance and rolled her eyes.

"I can't remember all that. Perhaps I'd better see a menu and study this decision properly," Lili teased him.

When the young man had left again, Annie remarked, "I have a friend who says things always go from the sublime to the ridiculous. Here we're talking about karma, and he's talking about dessert."

Lili's eyes sparkled with humor. "Isn't that true? But perhaps it's a warning that if I keep eating this way, I'll come back with a serious weight problem."

The waiter appeared yet again and placed huge menus in front of each of them. "The chocolate cheesecake is divine, and there's *crème brûlé*..."

Somehow, by the time they'd each chosen, the plates had been cleared, the dessert served and coffee brought, the conversation had turned to Jason and the matter of karma wasn't mentioned again.

Annie found that Lili already had a perceptive understanding of her son, and what seemed to be an honest and growing affection for the boy. She asked questions about school, about what special areas Annie was concerned with, about his day-to-day schedule. It was obvious that Lili cared how the relationship progressed, and wanted to conform to any firm rules Annie had.

"The incident with the rugby game concerned me. It's important we have a clear-cut understanding about these matters,'' Lili said, and Annie agreed.

When the luncheon ended, Annie was the one who offered her hand to Lili. "Thank you for arranging this. You're right, you know. It makes it much easier now that I know you a little."

"For me also. Thank you for coming."

Under different circumstances, Annie thought, she and Lili might have been good friends. But it was impossible, because of Michael, because of the resentment and fear he still sparked in Annie. Neither woman had mentioned him at all today, intuitively aware that he was an invisible presence anyway at the luncheon. Because of him, they'd never be close friends. Instead they shared what Lili had aptly labeled a "delicate acquaintance." Lili loved Michael, and Annie came near to hating him. It left precious little room for a meeting place.

DAVID HAD CALLED while Annie was out, and his rapid-fire message resulted in a lonely weekend.

"Annie, Phyllis just reminded me that I signed up for a seminar in Los Angeles this weekend. There are a couple of doctors attending whom I especially want to talk to about this organ transplant thing. I thought of asking you to come, but these things are a big bore if you're not involved, and you'd spend most of your time alone. I'm booked on a seven-thirty flight out tonight, so I'm hitching a ride to the airport with another guy who's going. Be back Monday. I lo..." The tape ran out before he could add what Annie considered the most important part of the whole thing.

When she thought about it afterward, Annie wished he'd asked her to go anyway. At least they'd have had the nights together.

Jason spent Saturday playing rugby and Sunday with the McCraes, and Annie tried to devote most of her time to her book.

David didn't phone until late Monday night. He was at his apartment, and he sounded tired and out of sorts. His flight had been delayed for over three hours in Los Angeles, and he'd missed the connecting flight from Seattle, so he'd just gotten home.

"Damned hotel beds. I couldn't get much sleep at all. I missed you, Annie. Tomorrow's frantic. I've got a surgical conference first thing and one of my patients, a kid I operated on for ruptured appendix late last week, has started hemorrhaging so I'm heading straight down to the hospital now."

GETTING READY for her appointment the next morning with Steve Munro, Annie worked herself into a nervous state. She felt cold and hot by turns, and she was shaking with apprehension as she dressed and drove over.

No one could stay uptight long around Steve, however. He was so relaxed himself, it simply rubbed off on anyone around him.

"How's your neck pain been?" he asked, taking a seat as he talked and tipping his chair back as far as it would go.

He wore what Annie now recognized as his uniform: baggy, wrinkled navy polyester trousers, a tweed sport jacket much the worse for wear, and a shirt, gray today, with several indecipherable stains down the front.

"It comes and goes. It was good after my last appointment, but yesterday and today it's there again, as bad as ever. I've been using the relaxation tapes."

"Good. Now about this session. When I hypnotize you, I'll strongly suggest you return to the same time frame you visited before, Annie, but I have to warn you, sometimes it just doesn't work. We'll do our best and see what happens."

Annie was alarmed. "But I want to go back there, to France," she told him as she settled more comfortably on the couch. "I want to find out what happened to Bernadette."

She added in an urgent tone, "I have to find out, Steve. She's haunting me."

"Have any more memories come back to you, in dreams or just in flashes of awareness?" he asked.

Annie nodded. "That man I loved, Paul. He's someone I know now. Someone I'm in love with now."

Steve nodded, not at all surprised. "That's quite usual, recognizing people from the past as part of your present life. Did you have a chance to read any of those books I gave you?"

"I looked through them. I plan to begin studying them this week."

"I think you'll find in your reading that it would be highly unusual not to recognize at least some of the same people you knew in that other lifetime. If the purpose of rebirth is learning love in all its complexities, then we probably need a lot more than one lifetime to do it in."

He grinned, which made him look like a friendly leprechaun. "Unless everybody's a lot better at learning than I am, that is. I've been regressed numerous times, and I've remembered a whole series of different lifetimes."

Annie thought of the tangled web of relationships that surrounded her, the tangled memories she'd already relived as Bernadette, and she shuddered.

"Reliving just one is quite enough for me," she decided.

"Shall we begin, then?"

Her courage deserted her all of a sudden.

"Steve, I'm scared...."

"It's natural. What you're experiencing is a whole new frontier. You're like an explorer without a map, Annie. And I can't promise that the memories won't hurt. All I can promise is that I'll do my best to guide you through them."

Her heartbeat accelerated, but she leaned back and closed her eyes as Steve's voice began the now-familiar relaxation procedure.

SHE WAS AWARE first of all of the river, the constant, soothing rush of water flowing close to where they lay sheltered beneath the overhanging branches and leaves of a huge old willow.

Much time had passed. The awkwardness of first love was gone for her and Paul, but not the intensity. Paul was no longer a stranger; they knew each other well by now.

The number of days they'd managed to spend together was pitifully few, but every chance he'd had, Paul had somehow managed to find a way to come to her.

It was autumn and the leaves were falling. They formed a thick, crackling carpet that both cushioned and prickled Bernadette's nearly naked body through the thin folds of the old blanket she kept hidden behind a fallen log for just such times as these.

She lay curled in Paul's arms, head resting on his shoulder, and she was staring up at the blue sky and white clouds dancing across the heavens through the lattice of branches overhead.

They'd made love only moments before, and her body was still throbbing from the joy of fulfillment. Even after all this time, it still amazed her that she'd performed this act all those years with Jean without ever feeling once the way Paul made her feel every time.

"My love, we have to talk," he was saying, and she wished he wouldn't. She knew what he insisted on discussing, and they never managed to reach a solution. "The war is nearly over," he went on.

His deep voice rumbled through her head, a sensation felt rather than heard, using sounds she didn't want to make sense of.

"I'll be leaving soon, first back to England and then, eventually, on a troop ship to the States."

She lay without moving, and he reached a finger to stroke the line of her jaw.

"Bernadette, I can't bear the thought of leaving you behind. Please let me begin to make arrangements for you and Nicole to emigrate."

His tone was persuasive, insistent, the way it was each time this subject arose between them.

It had come up more and more often in the past two months.

"There are certain people I know here who could help, who'd speed up the whole process for me. Once I'm back in the States it'll take longer, be more complicated than if we push things from this end, now. After the war ends, there'll be chaos and confusion. Paperwork won't get done as quickly."

Bernadette's heart sank. It was a subject they ended up arguing over each time they were together these days, and she hated hearing him bring it up now while her mind was still floating from his lovemaking. She tried to distract him by nibbling at his chin, but it didn't work.

"I'll start divorce proceedings as soon as I get back, and when I'm free, we'll marry," he persisted. "In the meantime, I'll support you and Nicole, you know that. Lord knows it's not an ideal solution, but it's the best I can do at the moment."

Silence fell, and she could see a lark winging high overhead. After a moment, he grasped her chin gently and turned her head so he could look into her face.

"Bernadette? Do you hear me?"

She pulled away and sat up, pulling her dress on over her head, tugging on the rest of her clothing, avoiding his eyes.

"I cannot," she finally said in a soft, sad voice. "This farm, this land...it's all I have, Paul. It's my home. It's a big decision, what you ask of me. I need more time than this. I would have to try to lease the land, or sell, and in these times it's difficult."

He grew angry, cursing her stubbornness under his breath.

"Damn it, Bernadette, be reasonable. Once I'm gone, it'll take months, perhaps years, to arrange visas and do all the bloody bureaucratic nonsense they'll require. I've looked into it. While I'm here I can pull strings for you, but afterward..."

Afterward. She tried never to think about that. On her knees, she moved close to him, wrapping her arms around him, breathing in the musky scent—her scent—that lingered on his skin.

Words didn't work when they talked about this. She couldn't explain that the real reason for refusing what he wanted was fear. With inborn French practicality, she knew that here, he belonged totally to her. Here, love overcame all doubts.

The only people she and Paul had any contact with here were Lorelei, and occasionally, Marc Cerdan, the doctor Lorelei worked with.

Dr. Cerdan had asked Paul to assist him several times with patients from the village, once with a difficult cesarean birth, and twice more with injured farmers.

The villagers gossiped, and knew the handsome young foreigner stayed with Bernadette, but she had little to do with them, so it really didn't much bother her. Nothing bothered her as long as she had Paul's love.

But once he was back in the United States, then more people would become involved. Paul was a married man with deep financial and emotional ties not only to his wife, but also to the shadowy, ominous father-in-law, this Martin Oakley, to whom Paul felt he owed so much. And because of his skill as a doctor, Bernadette realized he would be well-known in his town.

How would these foreign people feel about a French woman and her child?

Going with Paul as he wanted her to do meant trusting him totally. Here, he was simply an army doctor, doing his best to repair the frightful horrors that war produced.

But back there...ahh, back there his life was unknown to Bernadette, with responsibilities and pressures she couldn't begin to imagine, people by the score she didn't want to encounter.

Trusting someone completely was a thing she'd never been able to do. And ever since the war had begun and Jean had left, she'd had to be self-reliant and strong. She'd made this small acreage support her and Nicole. The land was her only security; it was literally all she had in the way of worldly goods.

"My marriage to Jean was a mistake, and you say the marriage you made is the same, a mistake," she said now, holding Paul, feeling the strong muscles in his body knot with frustration and anger, anger she knew was directed at her.

It wounded her, and she shuddered. They had only a brief time left. She couldn't bear having him angry, and struggled to make him understand.

"Paul, listen to me, please." He began to protest, but she laid her fingers over his mouth, insisting. "What if I'm the type of woman who shouldn't marry, what if once we're able to be together all the time, we find we've made yet another error? Have you considered this? Marriage is not a thing that should be decided in haste. Both of us know that. We've had only scraps of time together, days and hours here and there, not enough yet to base a lifetime upon."

It wasn't quite the truth. The fact was, she knew in her soul that being with Paul for the rest of her life was all she wanted, all she longed for.

But she'd come to understand him in the months since they'd met. Paul was an honorable man, a man with a deep sense of commitment and a powerful compassion for those weaker than himself.

He'd told her his wife was frail, that he owed a great deal to his father-in-law, and that their business partnership was complex.

If she and Paul were ever to be truly happy together, Bernadette knew that he would have to settle his other life in his own way, without the influence of herself and Nicole hanging like millstones around his neck.

Here, she was independent. There, she would be totally reliant on Paul, and Bernadette sensed that was dangerous.

She tried again. "If there was only myself, perhaps, but I have Nicole to consider. She's in school, and uprooting her is hard. Paul, my darling, I love you with every fiber of my being, but this...we cannot do this in haste. Surely you can see that?"

He couldn't, though. He was furious with her. He took her clinging arms in his and peeled them from his body, getting to his feet with the easy grace she admired even now.

His face was etched in harsh lines as he yanked his clothing on— the yank of each garment betraying his anger.

Bernadette watched, her stomach in knots. She tried twice to reason, even to beg, but as soon as he was dressed, he stalked away from her down the river path, each long stride taking him farther away from her.

She knew he had to return to his unit by evening, that he had to leave soon in any event. But to have him leave this way, angry, hurt; she couldn't bear it.

"Paul, please, Paul, come back, just for a moment, my darling, please..."

He didn't turn.

Bernadette dropped her face into her hands and allowed the pent-up sobs to explode from her throat in a torrent of anguish.

WATCHING HER CRY, hearing the agony in her harsh exclamations of grief, Steve intervened.

Drops of sweat had formed on his forehead, mute testimony to the tension of the scene she'd been describing. Steve wiped his head absently with a tissue, watching his patient every moment, noting the gamut of emotions on her features as she related to him what was happening to her.

Regression as successful as this was an eerie experience, even for a therapist who'd witnessed it many times before. No one watching and listening to Annie could doubt that the places and the things she spoke of were less than real. And most touching of all was the emotion she evinced.

She was still sobbing as if she'd never stop, deep gut-wrenching sobs that had to hurt her chest.

It was time to move her forward, to explore the consequences of her decision to remain in France despite Paul's desperate efforts at changing her mind.

"Annie, move ahead, away from this sad time. I'm going to count to three. At three, you will move ahead in time, move ahead to another major occurrence in the life you're experiencing as Bernadette. One, two, three..."

The sobbing gradually abated, and Steve said, "Now can you tell me where you are, what year it is?"

Annie sighed, and seemed to take a long time to assimilate whatever she was experiencing. "The war is over, just as Paul predicted. It's spring, it's...I guess it's April now."

Her voice was subdued, lacking the vibrancy that had been evident up till now. "The calendar on the wall says 1919. Apple trees outside in the orchard are in bloom again." She sighed, as if the beauty was no comfort, and her whole body slumped.

"He's gone, you know. Paul's gone," she confided. "Since last December. He managed to stay a little longer because he volunteered to stay with the worst of the injured soldiers, the ones who couldn't be moved. But finally, he had to go."

"And how are you managing without him?"

The voice seemed to be inside her head. Bernadette tried to figure out where the questions came from, but she felt muddled, as if her head were full of cotton wool.

She was tired of being weak, of feeling drained and ill. She had little patience for all this talk. Who was this, asking questions? She looked around.

Lorelei Dupré was seated on the chair across the kitchen table from her, and Bernadette thought of asking her if she heard the voice, too, but it seemed too much effort to explain.

Anyway, Lorelei knew that Paul was gone. She knew everything. She was like a sister.

Bernadette was pregnant with Paul's child, and Lorelei came by almost every day, riding her rusty old bicycle along the lane. The two women were closer than they'd ever been, perhaps because Lorelei, too, was in love, and the relationship was complex.

Lorelei was married to a man much older than herself. Years before, she'd come to the village from Paris to live with an old aunt. Her

parents had died that year, when Lorelei was twelve, leaving her pen-
niless and terrified of being sent to an orphanage. She'd told Bernadette
many times how grateful she'd been to her aunt for bringing her here
and caring for her.

Pierre Dupré was a wealthy shopkeeper in the village, and he'd
courted the teenage girl despite the fact that he was forty years her
senior. Encouraged by her aunt, Lorelei had married him when she was
barely fifteen, and she'd been a dutiful wife.

But the war changed everything, just as it had for Bernadette, and
Lorelei fell in love.

His name was Tony Briggs, and he was English, a squadron com-
mander who'd crashed his airplane during a thunderstorm one evening
in a rocky field five miles out of the village. It happened during the
final days of the war.

Dr. Cerdan had been called to treat the injured man, but as usual
lately, the doctor was far too drunk to respond. Lorelei had gone to
administer whatever help she could, and she talked a local family into
taking the unconscious man into their home.

Dr. Cerdan eventually sobered up enough to set his broken arm and
leg. Lorelei went on nursing him, and by the time Tony could have
been shipped back to an English hospital to recuperate, he and Lorelei
were lovers. He stayed on in the village as the war came to an end,
and lingered during the confusion that surrounded the military afterward.

Tony was single, and he urged Lorelei to leave her aging husband
and come away to England with him. Lorelei was torn, wanting to go,
but at the same time feeling responsible for Pierre, who loved her like
a child and relied on her more and more as he grew older.

Tony finally was forced to leave, but he'd managed to come across
from England twice since in order to see Lorelei.

Bernadette thought it would have been wonderful if Paul could come
back, even for a day. She said as much to Lorelei.

"If he were the one pregnant, he'd be back for longer than that,"
her friend declared with typical cynicism. "Is the nausea any better?"
Lorelei had poured them each more of the herbal tea, which seemed to
be the only thing Bernadette's stomach would tolerate these days.

"I think so," Bernadette lied, turning aside for a moment to admire
a picture Nicole had drawn with one of the colored pencils Paul had
brought her on his next-to-last visit.

"Look, Maman."

"It's a beautiful drawing, *chérie*. I see the trees, and the river. What is this, here, then?'' She pointed to an uncertain group of shapes in the center of the paper.

''It's Paul, Maman, coming here to see us, in a wagon. See the horses pulling him? When will he come again to see us, Maman? I miss Paul. I miss the magic tricks he used to do. And he made my head better the day I fell down.''

Nicole had been climbing on a fence once when Paul was visiting, and she'd fallen and split her head open. The blood had terrified Bernadette.

Paul, with infinitely gentle skill, had stitched the child's head and then spent all day acting as a willing slave to her, carrying her around and doing all sorts of magic illusions to amuse her, even making one of the farm rabbits appear out of an old hat. He'd rocked her to sleep that night, humming a bawdy American folksong instead of a lullaby.

Pain overcame Bernadette, and her eyes filled with the easy tears that seemed to hover all the time behind her eyes these days.

''I miss him, too, *chérie*. Go draw another—one for Lorelei, perhaps?''

The little girl trotted off, and the women were silent for a moment.

''I shouldn't be hard on him. He really had no choice, and you were far too stubborn. You should have gone with him when he asked. Have you had another letter?'' Lorelei added in a softer voice.

Bernadette nodded. ''Yesterday. And money, as usual.''

''Thank heaven he's generous. At least you can rest the way you need to, instead of having to do laundry and scrub floors for sour-faced old bats, the way you would have to if he didn't send money.''

''He's generous, as you say. From the very beginning he brought me food, books for Nicole I couldn't have bought. And when he left, there was that account.''

Paul had thrust the bankbook into her hand a moment before that final leave-taking, his face contorted with the effort of holding back his own tears. And the balance in the account had staggered her. It had also given her a measure of security.

In postwar France, there was no room for false pride. Life was difficult, supplies, apart from the barest essentials, almost impossible to obtain, and the money Paul left allowed Bernadette to relax from the constant weary struggle to make ends meet.

It was fortunate, because she couldn't have worked hard, no matter how desperate the need. Paul's child was making her sick in a way she'd never been with Nicole.

''You still haven't told him, in your letters?''

Lorelei disapproved of Bernadette's firm decision to keep the pregnancy a secret from Paul. Lorelei felt Paul should have been told about the baby before he left; Bernadette had known for several weeks by then that she carried his child.

Bernadette shook her head. "It would be wrong to tell him now. He's far away. He couldn't come racing back here. And there's nothing he can really do. As sick as I am, I'll probably never carry this child to term anyway."

Lorelei said nothing, but her soft green eyes met Bernadette's in a telling glance. They both knew that miscarriage would be a blessing in these circumstances.

When Bernadette first knew she was pregnant, Lorelei had offered help if she wanted to abort the child. It was proof, if Bernadette had ever needed it, of the other woman's love for her, because Lorelei adored children. Her job was bringing them safely into the world, and Bernadette knew her friend would never consider doing such a thing for anyone but her.

"This last letter is disturbing, Lorelei. Paul's father-in-law, this Martin Oakley, has had a slight stroke, and Paul's...wife, Grace, has fallen ill with flu. Apparently she's very sick indeed. Paul says this flu is causing many deaths in North America just as it is here in Europe."

Lorelei made a disgusted noise in her throat, and Bernadette didn't have to add that discussion of divorce between Paul and Grace was obviously out of the question at the moment.

"This Grace won't die, worse luck," Lorelei fumed. "From what Paul told you about her, this is a woman who can become ill whenever it suits her. Such women hold their men with yokes of guilt and duty." Her face grew rebellious and a little guilty. "Not only women are capable of that. Pierre, too, keeps me tied to him that way."

"Even now Paul begs me to come to America," Bernadette said in a soft, choked voice. "How I long to do exactly that."

Now she tossed and turned through the lengthening nights, cursing herself for not making the decision to go with him when he had asked. The loneliness she felt was like a cancer eating at her heart. Sometimes it overcame her, and she had to creep into Nicole's tiny bedroom and crouch beside the child's bed during the black night hours, reassuring herself that she wasn't really alone, holding the sleeping child's hand for comfort.

Now, of course, it was too late to go to Paul. She was far too ill to travel even to the village, let alone begin the complex machinations that were necessary if she were to emigrate to the United States.

But after the child came, she promised herself with fierce intent, then she would go.

Nothing would stop her after the child was born.

When the retching was too severe to allow her to even lie down, she would sit propped against pillows with paper and pen, and write long letters to Paul, to the work address he'd instructed her to use.

She wrote cheerful fantasies, little anecdotes about herself and Nicole, regards from Dr. Marc Cerdan, reports on the farm animals, the latest story from the postman, who cursed about everything.

She told him of the late produce from the garden he'd helped her plant, of the kittens the barn cat produced, and always, of how she walked daily along the river path where she and he had walked, thinking of him, pausing under the tree where they'd made love.

Here, she felt closest to him. Here, too, she missed him with a desperation close to madness. She'd left the blanket behind the fallen tree, where they'd folded it the last time they'd made love there.

She never told him that she seemed to have become a bottomless well of tears that flowed in endless rivers down her face as she followed their path and imagined him at her side. Her eyes burned and stung from crying, and she felt sick all the time.

TEARS WERE AGAIN POURING down Annie's cheeks, and Steve, with gentle care, blotted them away using a handful of tissue.

It was once again necessary, he decided, to suggest she move ahead through time.

"You carried the baby to full term?"

She nodded.

"Move ahead to that time, then. What are you aware of now?"

Her tears stopped, and her voice became thin, as if she were tired, very weak, and worried. She didn't talk about the child right away.

"The letters have stopped, you know—Paul's letters. I've had no word from him for over three months. I'm insane with worry. Do you suppose he's forgotten me? I can't bear to think he's forgotten me. It must be something else, don't you think?"

The pathos in her voice touched Steve's soul.

"I was ill after the baby came. I truly thought I would die and I didn't care. I suppose I might have died, without Dr. Cerdan and Lorelei. She moved in here with Nicole and me, and nursed me and the baby. But I did such a stupid thing then, while I was sick. I wrote Paul. I told him everything, about the baby, about how ill I was, everything. I sent the letter to his home address."

Annie's breath caught in a gulp, and she wrung her hands.

"I told him that I couldn't go on without him, that I'd come to him as soon as the baby was old enough, if he would arrange it. I love him.

I love him so much, I can't bear to live like this, without him. I would rather die than live my life without Paul.''

The vehemence faded and Annie's body became still in the reclining chair. "Lorelei posted the letter, and I waited. I waited week after week, but no answer ever came. I've stopped waiting now. Inside of me, my heart is dying. I should never have told him. Perhaps he thinks I'm trying to trap him. Or he's simply forgotten me.''

Steve's own voice was thick with emotion. "What about the baby? Is your baby healthy?''

She didn't smile, but there was tenderness in her tone this time, and she gazed down at her lap as if she were looking down at a baby.

"My son is very tiny. How could one this tiny cause such difficulties? Lorelei says it was the hardest labor she's seen. She was furious with Dr. Cerdan. He was drinking all that day and was no help to her at all.''

Steve's face twisted with compassion, and he swallowed hard as she went on, "I lost a great deal of blood. It seemed to go on forever, and then, this small one decided to be born, after all.''

She clucked her tongue the way all mothers do at their babies. "Nicole adores him, she's like a little mother herself with him. His name is Marcel, after my grandfather. I wanted at first to name him Paul, but Lorelei said the child needs his own name, not one that reminds me every second of...'' Her voice broke, and her face crumpled. Then she seemed to muster her strength, becoming almost businesslike, although her tone was still weak and reedy.

"He's five weeks now. I'm feeding him, although sometimes there's hardly enough milk...'' Her voice trailed off, and she tipped her head to one side as if she were listening.

"What is it?'' Steve asked. "What's happening now?''

"I hear someone, at the door. Someone...''

She sounded puzzled and a little apprehensive. Steve waited, curious about this new development.

The fearsome cry that came from Annie resounded through the room, and Steve bolted from his chair, staring down at her.

"Whatever it is has no power to hurt you any longer, do you understand?''

He forced himself to sound calm and persuasive. She was breathing rapidly, cowering on the couch, an expression of extreme fear on her face.

"Ann...Bernadette, whatever is occurring is already over. Move through it. It can't hurt you because it's over. Do you hear me? Move to the other side of the experience.''

Her hands were trembling, and every faint trace of color had fled from her face.

"What is it? Can you describe it to me now?"

She tried to speak and couldn't. Finally moistening her lips, she managed.

"My God! My God, it's my...it's Jean Desjardins! He came walking through the door just now. He has come home. And I was...was sitting here, nursing this child." Her voice dropped to a whisper. "It's not Jean's baby. He couldn't have known about him. I was... nursing...Paul's baby...and the man...who was my husband came... came...home."

She spoke in staccato gasps, and Steve was concerned about the violent emotion Annie was reliving. He debated whether or not he should allow her to continue, and decided against it.

"Leave the emotion back there where it belongs, Annie. It has no power to hurt you anymore. You are Annie Pendleton again. You're waking up now. At the count of three, you will awaken, and you will remember these things with understanding, without pain, knowing how they relate to your present life. Coming out now, one—two—three—"

The total silence was marked only by the faraway ringing of the telephone in the outer office and Edith's muffled voice as she answered it.

Steve waited, apprehension knotting his gut.

After what seemed an eternity, Annie opened her eyes, the anguish and fear slow to fade from her features.

"Now I know who he was," she said at last, looking up at Steve with eyes still half in another world. "I know who he is in this life, and I know why there are bad feelings between us. I know now—I understand why I couldn't marry him again."

"What do you understand, Annie?" Steve smiled at her, reassuring her, relieved more than he could say that she was back. The depth of the trance she attained was worrisome at times like this.

"I know," she said again, drawing in a ragged breath, "that my husband back then, Jean Desjardins, is someone I know well in this life. His name—" she swallowed and tried again "—the name I know him by in this life is Michael McCrae, and he's the father of my son, Jason."

CHAPTER FIFTEEN

"STEVE?" Her voice was urgent and her eyes begged for reassurance.

"Yes, Annie, go on. I'm right here, listening."

Her breath caught in a sob. "I'm terrified of him. I always have been. Jean, Michael, whichever name he has. I was afraid back then, at that dreadful moment when he walked in the door, but I've felt that way about him in this lifetime, too."

She drew in another breath, and Steve asked, "Can you tell me exactly what happened to you? You were frightened, and I felt there was a great deal of the story missing."

Steve hoped that the telling would let her release the pain of the memory.

She stared at the opposite wall, but he could tell she wasn't seeing it at all.

She was seeing Jean Desjardins. Her voice was almost a whisper when she began. "He was so angry, he looked quite insane. He stood there clenching and unclenching his fists and staring first at me and then at the poor tiny baby, as if he hated us both."

Annie shook her head, trying to explain to Steve the rest of the traumatic scene she'd just experienced, which still seemed powerful and real.

"I was breast-feeding the baby. I couldn't move when he came toward me. I sat there as if I were paralyzed, and he came across the kitchen, step by slow step."

She shuddered, and cold drops of perspiration dotted her forehead. Even with Steve's suggestion that she move beyond the emotion, all the feelings still lingered, mixtures of fear and sorrow and terror, and worst of all, that deep, maternal protectiveness toward the tiny infant she'd held in her arms.... It seemed only moments ago.

Her breasts still ached with the fullness of the milk. She could smell the clean baby scent, see how the fine hair on the top of the fragile skull whirled into a peak beneath the blue-veined skin. She could feel the overwhelming mother love for the child she held. It almost choked her, even now.

And she could see that threatening man...her husband...coming toward them.

She began again, trying to keep her voice steady and failing. "Jean, he—Jean looked barely human, skeleton thin, hair shaved off, dirty." She shuddered again. "I learned later that he'd been in a prison camp, close to death for many months, and he had suffered a sort of mental breakdown there. When he saw me with the baby, I believed for a moment he was about to kill us both, Steve. His eyes were bloodred, and his whole body shook as he came toward us." Annie shuddered, clasping the welcome cup of tea Steve handed her.

"Nicole came running in just then, and the expression on her little face stopped him. 'Who is that man,' she kept asking me. 'Is he going to hurt our baby? Don't let him hurt our baby, Maman.' And I couldn't answer. I couldn't tell her it was her father. I couldn't even seem to get it through my own head that this awful creature could still be my husband. It didn't seem possible."

Annie's eyes closed as the horror of the situation rolled over her. "You see, I felt that I belonged, body and soul, to Paul Duncan, regardless of whether we were married or not."

Just as she felt she belonged to David, here and now, whether he was with her or not.

"I know them all again—that's what's so awful," she burst out. "I know both my husband and my lover from that other life, Steve. I'm involved with them all over again in this one. I love David just as passionately as I loved Paul, and years ago I was involved with Michael. He fathered my son, and I gradually began to hate and fear him. I always believed it was illogical, my deep-seated feelings about him, and yet now I see that what happened before had bearing on what I feel for him now."

Steve nodded. "Of course it does, Annie. Remembrance can bring new insights into our lives, and it can also bring the memory of great suffering. Understanding is the true benefit of all this, because with knowledge comes the power each of us has to change the outcome this time around. Perhaps we can prevent further harm, or make up for old wrongs. It all comes down to choice."

Annie listened, not just with her ears, but with her whole being. Because of what she'd experienced, she understood as never before the reservations she'd had about marrying Michael years ago.

She poured it all out to Steve. "I was married to him once already, a hellish marriage, that lifetime ago. It was a monstrous mistake. At least I had sense enough not to do it again this time."

Steve waited. When she didn't go on, he said, "But this time you had his son, didn't you?"

And, her relentless mind prodded, wasn't it a kind of divine justice for the son to be Michael's this time, having to adjust to David much the same way he must have had to adjust to Jean in another lifetime?

And why did Paul desert her back then? The devastating sense of loss and heartbreak she'd experienced as Bernadette lingered in her very pores, and when she thought of it a sore knot formed in her chest, and resentment grew.

Resentment toward David?

Yes, she admitted silently. Knowing what she knew did make her resent him, however illogical that might seem. No matter what, he shouldn't have deserted her the way he had.

There was a pattern forming again, of strong influences in David's life that pulled him away from her. It was his same deep-seated sense of responsibility, of needing to help those who depended on him, that was tearing David away just as it had done with Paul.

Would it happen again, here and now? Would David leave her this time, too? Their love was under severe strain, just as it had been then, and the problems weren't only on her side.

She often felt as if she and David were worlds apart emotionally, as they had been physically in that other life. She listed to herself the other concerns that nagged at her day and night. David was totally dedicated to his work, to the exclusion of all else at times. More and more, she was convinced there wasn't room for her. And what about Jason, who stubbornly went on rejecting David? And then there was Calvin Graves and his ambitions for David that didn't include her.

Somewhere too deep for rationality was the conviction that no matter how much she loved him, David would abandon her again.

The echo of that tragic life in France was haunting her. It was haunting all of them, whether they realized it or not.

Were they fated to relive that other sad time? If only David would listen to the story, she could perhaps somehow convince him that they'd destroyed the love they'd shared once already, and that they mustn't let it happen again.

"How can a person persuade someone else that it's really possible to experience this, Steve, and to learn from it?"

Surely Steve must know of a way that would work. She stared up at him, begging for an answer.

But he shook his head. "Annie, only personal experience works. If I'd told you the first time you came here that this was going to occur, you'd probably have walked out in disgust, and labeled me a fraud.

There are books, like the ones I loaned you, but they have to be read with an open mind. If the other person has a strong enough block against such material, there really isn't any way I know of to make him think otherwise. He has to come to it on his own. We all do." He added after a long, silent moment, "There's an old adage that says, 'When the student is ready, the teacher appears.'"

That was no consolation at all. She folded her arms against her chest, trying to hold in the agony inside but failing.

"Steve, I won't be back after today. I can't go through this any longer. I can't stand the pain. I'd rather not know if it's all going to happen again, or how it all ended back then."

She looked at him, her eyes swimming with tears so that he seemed shimmery and insubstantial.

"I just can't do this anymore. I can't stand this feeling that lasts even after I come out, as if the only person I've ever totally loved has—" her voice broke again "—has deserted me forever. See, Steve, it makes me certain that he'll do it all over again, and I can't bear that."

Her face was ravaged, a kind of agony contorting her features.

"Now that we've found each other, I can't stand the thought of living another lifetime without him, and yet deep in my heart I'm afraid that's what's going to happen. But I can't be absolutely certain, you see, because I can't see the future. I'm so glad I can't. At least I can dream. I can hope."

Her eyes met Steve's, and his heart contracted with pity for her.

"Back there, there wasn't even one shred of hope. And that's why I can't go back again. Oh, Steve, I'm such a rotten coward."

Steve reached out and took her hand. "You're a brave woman, Annie. Few of us have the courage to look at ourselves the way you're doing."

She made herself unknot her fists.

"Isn't this ironic? We go through life wishing we knew more about ourselves, and now I'm scared witless because I think I do." She gave a laugh that sounded more like a sob.

Steve came and took her shoulders in his hands. "Annie, I have to say I think it's a mistake to come this far and not see it through. We haven't reached the core of the problem with your neck yet, and I know it's buried back there, in that awful time. Annie, don't make a final decision now. Wait a few weeks until the memories are easier to handle."

She shook her head. "They never will be. They're burned into my brain and they just go on hurting. Nope, I'm finished, Steve. I should have listened. David told me I was fooling with stuff I didn't really understand. Now I'm inclined to believe him."

"Does it help to tell yourself that everything that happened back then is over now—it's part of your personal history?" Steve pleaded. "You can't alter the past, Annie. But you can change the present. If you choose to stop now, that's entirely your decision. You're entitled to do whatever you think best. But if you ever feel you need to come back, remember that I'll help all I can."

Steve watched her gather up her purse and sweater.

"Goodbye, Steve. Thank you."

ALL THE WAY HOME, Annie thought about what had happened.

She had to try again to talk this over with David—she simply had to. She'd tell him of her decision not to go on with it, but she had to confide in him, let him know what she'd learned about their common past, because she was convinced it was his past as well as hers.

Jason would be spending next weekend with Michael and Lili.

If she made a special dinner, and she and David had time together, if she introduced the regression logically, without negative emotion or pressure, maybe it would work?

She called David at his office as soon as she got home, and her heart sank when she got Phyllis on the line.

"He's not available at the moment. He's in an important meeting," Phyllis said with more than her usual brisk impatience. "I'll give him your message, but his schedule is tight today, Ms Pendleton. He has several late appointments after this." She was both snippy and dismissive, and made Annie feel like a teenybopper hounding a movie star.

"Well, this is important, too," Annie forced herself to say. "Just tell David I called and that I'd like to speak to him as soon as possible."

The secretary's manner never failed to put her on the defensive. As she hung up, Annie mentally added Phyllis to the list of obstacles that loomed between her and David.

AS ALWAYS, when he appeared at her door later that day, every problem seemed insignificant in relation to the love between them. She flew into his arms, and he held her for a long, silent time as the invisible bond uniting them strengthened with the contact of their bodies.

"I missed you so much, Annie. Want to come away to a desert island with me?"

How she wished it was possible.

They settled on Sunday evening for a quiet, home-cooked dinner, because, predictably, David was committed to various appointments and dinner meetings for the rest of the week, including both Friday and Saturday.

Of course, they'd spend some evenings together before then, but it was always late by the time David was finished with his workday.

"How's the child you told me about who was hemorrhaging?" Annie asked.

"Took us most of the night, but we got him stabilized. He was a street kid, thirteen years old, and he waited too long to come in, so his appendix had burst. Then he developed stress ulcers in his stomach, and the ulcers bled. We nearly lost him. I was at the hospital at five this morning."

For a fleeting moment, Annie had considered trying to talk with David that night about the regression session, but she gave it up fast as a bad idea. His eyes were bloodshot and he moved as if he were exhausted.

She made him hot chocolate and a thick ham sandwich, and they talked about pleasant things.

"You will come with me to this luncheon deal on Saturday, love?" David coaxed. "It's the only damned thing all weekend that might not bore you to death."

Annie agreed to go.

Beggars can't be choosers, she reminded herself. If she wanted to share in his life, she'd better learn to look as if she enjoyed chatting to people she hoped to never see again.

The luncheon on Saturday was held at one of the huge downtown hotels, and during the social hour, David became engrossed in a technical discussion with three other doctors.

Annie listened for a while, but when the terms became indecipherable, she moved through the crowd to the wall of windows, to admire the breathtaking aerial view of the city and the nearby park.

A tall, older man with pepper-and-salt hair and kind eyes stood near her. He, too, was gazing out with a wistful expression.

"It's a pity to be trapped in here when we ought to be down there in the sunshine, don't you think?" He motioned with a stemmed glass toward the walkway that bordered the ocean.

Annie agreed, and they chatted for a few moments about Vancouver's weather.

"I'm from Seattle, and our climate is much like yours. My name is Abraham Caldwell." He glanced around the room at the groups of people intent on being social. "And medical gatherings are much the same everywhere. Are you a physician, Ms...uh...?"

His eyes scanned her shoulder for the name tag that wasn't there.

"Annie Pendleton, and no, I'm not a medical person. I write books for children." She half expected his eyes to glaze over before he moved away, searching for a more kindred soul to chat with. But instead he stayed and asked intelligent questions about the publishing world and being a writer.

"You're a doctor?" she inquired after ten minutes or so. He was a good-looking man, she noticed now, tanned and fit, with an appealing open smile.

"I have a medical degree, yes. I work as a professor, however. I'm here today to give a short luncheon address on holistic health."

"Which is…?" Annie felt enough at ease with him to reveal her ignorance about most things medical.

"Quite simply, the healing of the whole person, mind, body and spirit, using techniques such as acupuncture, visualization, therapeutic touch as well as more mundane methods. Our attitude is, if it works, use it, regardless of how unusual it might seem. Our success rate is our best advertisement."

He smiled again, and there was a touch of irony in his tone. "Medical science values the scientific, provable approach to problems. There's usually a fair amount of dissension and resistance among medical people when it comes to alternate methods." His eyes were full of gentle humor. "In fact, it might be wise not to sit too close to me at lunch, in case some good doctor throws a tomato or two during my address."

Annie felt a shudder of recognition go through her. She'd wanted more than anything to forget the regression last Tuesday. Yet here was Caldwell reminding her once again that all things were possible.

"What are your views on regressive hypnosis as a method of treating psychosomatic problems?" Annie's heartbeat had accelerated, and now her full attention was centered on the tall man at her side.

"I'm very much in favor of it. I feel we've only begun to explore the possibilities it affords. I refer a great many people to trained hypnotherapists, and the results are positive in an astonishing percentage of cases. In fact, I'll be mentioning that particular method in my talk later."

Annie had an eerie feeling that the powers that ran the universe kept leading her, like the proverbial horse, to water and daring her to drink.

DAVID WAS AWARE OF ANNIE every minute. He knew exactly when she became deeply engrossed in conversation with the distinguished professor, and he could feel his blood pressure rise.

Irrational jealousy stabbed him, tore at his guts, making him want to rush over and plant a fist in the professor's face and then drag Annie away, to a place where there were just the two of them.

His mouth twisted at the thought of Calvin's horrified reaction to a spectacle like the one he was contemplating. In fact, David had the uncomfortable feeling these days that Calvin was subtly turning him into a far too civilized version of himself. He also had the distinct impression that Calvin's plans for him didn't always include Annie. David was going to set Calvin very straight on that at the first opportunity.

Why was he haunted lately with this fear of losing her? He wasn't altogether certain, but it seemed to have something to do with that infernal nightmare that had torn him from sleep more times than he cared to count.

IT WAS AFTER MIDNIGHT, and they were wrapped in each other's arms, bodies still joined after loving, sweaty and slick from love's fervor.

"You made a real conquest at that luncheon today," David murmured, nibbling her ear. "Professor Caldwell was obviously longing to take you back to Seattle with him."

"Jealous?" she teased, raining kisses down his cheek and keeping her legs tight around him.

"Damned right," he growled, and she giggled, sobering when he added, "The professor's taste in women is first-rate, but his talk didn't impress me at all. Medicine is medicine, and magic is magic. I'm well qualified in both, and believe me, they don't belong under the same shingle. I get furious when I'm tricked into listening to garbage like he was spouting today."

Annie's heart sank. She'd been hopeful that Professor Caldwell's talk might open the door just a bit for her own discussion with David.

Passionate words sprang to her lips, defense of all the things David was denying. But she remembered that she had a good reason to keep silent, to save all her arguments and convictions to use where they'd do the most good; in an effort to get him to listen, really listen and absorb, the things that were important to both of them. And now was not the right time.

So she curled tighter against him, sliding a wicked hand down between them and cupping the part of him that gave her such pleasure.

He drew his breath in and covered her mouth in a kiss that was a prelude, and soon Annie forgot everything except his body, invading hers, joining with hers in an ancient dance that made them one flesh. The act of love allowed her the balm of forgetfulness for a tiny stretch of time.

SUNDAY MORNING, they got up early and rode bikes down to Granville Island and the huge farmers' market that was centered there. They breakfasted on croissants and fruit from stalls in the covered market, and Annie carefully shopped for the freshest produce and meat she could find for the dinner they'd share later that evening.

They rode home, puffing and laughing their way up hills because of the loaded string bags of groceries Annie had bought. At home, David helped her unload and shortly afterward left for his appointment.

He hadn't been gone fifteen minutes when Cleo gave her distinctive short rap on the back door. She was carrying two of the books she'd borrowed.

"The girls have gone to a birthday party, and I saw David drive away. You busy? If you don't feel like company just say the word."

"I'm about to do a massive cook scene here. C'mon in and help me prepare vegetables."

Annie put fresh coffee on, and together they scrubbed and chopped produce for the stew Annie planned.

"So how's it going?" Cleo raised an eyebrow and waited.

"Which particular 'it' are you talking about? There's David, there's Jason, there's Dr. Munro. My life is a mass of 'its' at the moment."

"Start with Munro. Don't you call him Steve? Have you learned any more with the regression?"

Annie quickly sketched in the latest developments from her last session, able to control her voice and minimize the trauma of what she'd gone through.

It was like a dress rehearsal, she told herself. She'd have to keep it light if she wanted David to listen to the whole thing. She concentrated on telling the story, trying to divorce herself from the emotion as much as possible, concluding by explaining the link between Michael in this lifetime and Jean in that.

Cleo listened. When Annie was done, her friend whistled in amazement.

"So there you were, with a husband back from the war and a kid who wasn't his. And when you think about it, it's obvious that Jean would turn up again as Michael. No wonder you feel the way you do about him."

It was absurd, but finishing the story had made Annie choke up with emotion all over again. She bent her head over the carrots. "I guess it was pretty hard on him, too, come to think of it."

"You know, these books explain a lot of things I've always wondered about," Cleo remarked. "Such as why bad things like that happen to us, and why the same damn situation keeps popping up over and over again in our lives. Apparently all we're here for is to learn lessons we've been too boneheaded to learn before. Which puts paid to my idea that we're here to have a good time. Anyway, what I still don't understand in this regression you've had is how it's related to the pain you get in your neck. Nothing's come up about that, has it?''

"Not yet," Annie admitted. That lack was beginning to seem the weak link in the whole thing. "I asked Steve about it, and he seems to think there has to be an incident of some sort in that particular lifetime that was the root cause of my neck problem, because my subconscious returns over and over again to that experience. Whatever it was, we haven't gotten to it yet. And we're not going to, either." She scooped up the neat carrot strips and dumped them into a bowl.

"What do you mean, 'not going to'? I'm waiting with bated breath for the next episode."

Annie shook her head. "Nope. I've decided not to go back for any more of this stuff, Cleo. I—I just can't handle remembering anymore, I guess."

Cleo studied her a moment and then nodded. "Yeah, I sure can see that. It must be scary. I don't think I'd ever have the guts to go through it. I still figure I'd rather not know who I was or what I didn't do last time around." After a moment she added, "Besides, I'd say having this Jean guy turn up like that is enough to give anybody a pain in the neck, wouldn't you? A pain in your backside as well."

Annie smiled a shaky smile and attacked the onions, holding them as far away as possible as she stripped off the papery skins.

"Ain't it the truth? But seriously, the pain is lots better. I've been using the relaxation tapes and the meditation exercises Steve recommended, so the whole thing was worth it."

They peeled in silence for another few moments while Annie wondered whether or not to reveal something else that had become apparent to her after the last session.

"I know you said you don't want to know, but you were my friend back then, too, Cleo," Annie ventured. "I'm pretty certain you were Lorelei Dupré."

Cleo tossed some celery into the bowl. "I sort of thought so myself," she mumbled, not looking at Annie. "I had a funny feeling each time you mentioned her." There was a long pause, and then Cleo asked in a small voice, "If you find out anything bad about her, don't tell me, okay? I mean, part of me would like to know if she ever got up enough gumption to take off with that young pilot, but another part doesn't have the stomach for it, see?"

"I understand, only too well. Why do you think I can't bear going back and finding out anymore?"

Cleo tossed her knife down and slumped back in her chair. "I probably didn't do anything but mope around like a sick cow back then. That's typical of me. I'm not any braver this time around, either."

"Do you mean Don?"

Cleo nodded and bowed her head. She hesitated before she answered.

"I really like this guy, y'know, Annie? He's intelligent and sexy and sweet. And he's interested in me. But for all the yapping I've done about finding a guy I could love again, now I'm scared of getting involved. That's what's underneath the noise about his age and being a policeman and all that. That's not the reason at all. I'm simply scared of getting hurt again."

"Well, you got really hurt when your husband walked out," Annie reasoned.

"Yeah, but wouldn't you think I'd be over that by now? I thought for sure I was until Don came along. I really wish I knew how to stop feeling this way."

"Give it time, Cleo," was all Annie could find to say. Who was she to advise anyone on matters of the heart? She felt just as uncertain about David as Cleo did about Don Anderson.

And in an eerie fashion, it was for the same reason as Cleo.

She'd had her heart thoroughly broken the last time around, and she was scared spitless it was going to happen again. It didn't matter one bit that the last time had happened to her over seventy years before.

THE DINNER was going to be a triumph, she told herself as she made the final preparations after Cleo had gone home.

She'd put together a thick, exotic stew with beefsteak simmered in red wine, herbs and fresh vegetables. She baked a loaf of crusty bread, and made a crisp salad, with apple pie and thick cream for dessert.

She placed the regression tapes in the machine. They would need only a touch to turn them on.

The problem was trying to figure out just when it would be best to broach the subject with David.

Perhaps before dessert? Or after, when they were having coffee?

She set the table with extra care, opened a bottle of fine French wine to let it breathe and dashed upstairs at the last minute to shower and change into a pair of silky black pants and a blue jersey top that hugged her breasts. She brushed her hair up and twisted it into a knot, then fastened the crystal pendant David had given her around her neck, adding a pair of tiny pearl earrings.

"Annie? Hey, darlin', get down here and kiss me." David's voice was full of exuberance, and she bounced down the stairs to greet him with the long, passionate kiss he'd requested. David held her tight, and words poured from him.

"I stopped off at my apartment to pick up the phone messages, and there was one to call Calvin. Apparently he's managed to get me on the finance committee, which means I also become an advisor to the Board of Directors. Annie, my love, it looks as if I might get a chance to have my say, after all."

He held Annie around the waist, and she looked up into his eyes. They were like blue flames, full of light and animation and love for her, with a touch of self-mockery. He announced his news.

"Calvin was as close to gleeful as I've ever heard him."

Annie thought that would really be something from a near cadaver like Calvin, and then felt ashamed of herself.

"This is the all-important first step toward eventually becoming a full board member, Annie, and being able to really carry some weight when it comes to decisions such as whether or not we need an expanded transplant facility. I feel as if I'm actually doing something at last instead of just making empty noises nobody hears."

"Oh, David, I'm happy for you. I'm thrilled, darling." She hugged him and soon the kisses they shared grew heated and full of desire.

"Maybe ... we ... should ... just ... go ... upstairs ... and..." With each word, he walked her backward toward the stairs, kissing her face and throat wherever his lips landed, pressing his hips against her with urgent need.

Annie finally tore her mouth from his and resisted his backward path by going limp in his arms.

"Stop, you lunatic." She grabbed his hand and tugged. "Come in the kitchen and behave yourself. Dinner's all but ready, and you can have a drink while I put the finishing touches on the food."

"But man doesn't live by liquor alone," he teased, pretending to ruffle her hair and then managing to make it seem as if he'd pulled a long-stemmed red rose out of her upswept knot.

He looked comically amazed at his own sleight of hand, and then bowed and handed her the flower. She was thrilled and amused; she couldn't figure out where he'd had it hidden, and of course he wouldn't tell her.

"Sorcerers never reveal their secrets, my pretty one," he hissed, pretending to twirl an imaginary moustache. "However, if you should change your mind and come upstairs with me, I could probably be seduced into..."

She tossed a tea towel at him.

He made her laugh all during dinner with gross, exaggerated tales of the women's auxiliary meeting he'd addressed.

When she served the warm apple pie with thick slices of cheddar cheese and a bowl of cream, he reached across the table, took her hand and brought it to his lips.

"Annie, this is a meal fit for a king. Thank you, sweet, for going to all this work for me. I wish we could have evenings like this more often. The schedule of committees and meetings that Calvin has me roped into isn't my idea of how a person spends his free time, and I promise you it won't always be this way."

"Will the meetings ease off now you're an advisor to the Board?" Annie was pretty certain they wouldn't, but there was no harm in hoping.

He grimaced and shook his head. "It's unfortunate, but no."

For the first time that evening, a look of strain came over his face. "I've said I'll do this, Annie, and I will. But if I'd known what a drain it was going to be on our relationship, on my time, even on my job, I'm not sure I'd have gotten myself into it..." His voice trailed off.

"David, are you dead certain this is what you really want?" The question popped out, probably because it had been hovering under the surface for a while. "Or are you going along with it because it's what Calvin Graves wants for you?"

Whispers of another time, of a man named Martin Oakley, rose in the back of her mind. Although she couldn't be sure, she had the feeling that Oakley had had something to do with Paul deserting Bernadette.

"What do you mean, because it's what Calvin wants?" There was harshness in his answer all of a sudden. "That's a rotten thing to say, Annie. Of course it's my own choice to do this. I thought you knew that without having to ask.

"After all, the committees I'm on now are just learning tools," he rationalized. "I plan to head one in the near future that studies the feasibility of an extended organ transplant unit and devote all my spare time to that one issue. The rest of all this is unimportant."

Unimportant? Then why was he doing it, she wondered? Was never having time with her unimportant? Irritation grew in Annie until she couldn't stifle it.

"But David," she burst out, "it's eating your life just the same, and affecting my life, as well, because I love you. I want to spend time with you, and there isn't room for that. How can I share what's happening to me when I never see you?"

Damn it all, this wasn't what she'd planned to talk about. But now that it had surfaced, maybe it was important that he know how she felt.

He sighed. "I know it seems impossible just now for us to have much time together, and believe me, I want time with you, Annie. I want us to spend the rest of our lives with each other."

Annie felt her heartbeat accelerate, and she knew what he was going to say. David was about to propose to her. And what was she going to answer when he did?

His words were quiet and emphatic. "Annie, I want to marry you." The statement was matter-of-fact, purposeful, and as if he read her mind he added, "You may not be ready for that yet, but I am."

His blue eyes seemed to pin her to her chair, blazing with intent. "See, I want to come home each evening and find you there for me. I want to be around when you need me. It drives me nuts, not having enough time to court you the way I want to. It's a real problem, and I take full responsibility for it."

His tone took on a harder edge. "But there's a hell of a lot more to this than just the demands on my time. The problems aren't all on my side. You know as well as I do that Jason resents me, that there's no way in the world he'd accept our being together without causing us both a great deal of trouble. And believe me, a thirteen-year-old boy can make life pretty miserable if he decides to."

She did know that. She'd been hoping that Jason would improve, but he hadn't.

"I've tried to be reasonable, tried to explain to him that adults need relationships, but he's just not ready to accept..." she began, but David slammed his hand down on the table, silencing her.

"There's a point where a boy Jason's age needs more than sweet reason, damn it. He's manipulating you, doing his best to control the situation. Don't you see that, Annie? He's a bright kid, and he's strong. Right now he needs a stiff dose of tough love, ultimatums about behavior and consequences. Stop shielding him, stop letting him make you feel guilty for loving me. He's good and jealous of me. He's had you to himself far too long. It's natural, but it's as dangerous for him as it is for you if you let him win."

His harsh criticism wounded and angered her. She knew there was truth in some of what he said, but his absolute assurance that he knew all the answers enraged her. Jason was her son. David had never had a child, had no idea of the pitfalls involved. Yet here he was, lecturing her on how it ought to be done.

"Is that what this is, David?" Her voice was dripping with sarcasm.

"Some sort of competition between you and Jason with me as the prize?"

She was trembling. She folded her hands in her lap so he wouldn't see.

"Don't be ridiculous." He scowled at her. "I'm just telling you it's wrong to let the boy run your life."

"Run my life? He's a huge part of my life. We've been alone together since he was born, and I know him better than I know you."

Annie saw David flinch at that, but she was far too angry to back off now.

"Don't you think that it might be a good idea for you to get to know Jason before you make all these assumptions about him? You're full of suggestions, but you're never around to spend any time with him."

"Damn it, Annie...."

She knew he was about to say that time was one thing he didn't have, but they'd been over that already. Besides, that was his concern, not hers.

He looked exhausted all of a sudden, and maybe ashamed of his bad temper.

But what she said was right, Annie reassured herself. He had no right to criticize Jason if he didn't also put time and effort into helping the boy.

As if they'd conjured him up, a car door slammed out front and Jason's voice hollered a cheerful goodbye. A moment later, he came in through the back door. Annie and David waited, tension thick between them. Jason appeared in the dining room doorway, sports bag slung over his shoulder, red hair on end.

"Hi, Mom, I'm home. I'm going downstairs to do homework." There was much less enthusiasm as he added, not looking at David, "Hi, Dr. Roswell."

His negative attitude was palpably evident.

"How was your weekend?" Annie's voice sounded strained even to her own ears.

"Ace, just ace. My dad and Lili—I guess I should call her my stepmother, eh Mom?—well, we went hiking up in North Vancouver, by the reservoir, and there's this suspension bridge, and she was scared to go over it. My dad and I had to take her hands and lead her across. And then we made all these weird things for dinner—*chapatis* that you fry, like flat bread. Man, they're good. Maybe you oughta get the recipe, Mom. Well, see ya."

He clattered down the stairs to the basement, whistling tunelessly. There was silence for a long time after Jason disappeared.

Annie's shoulder and neck were throbbing all of a sudden. She felt as if her face were frozen with the effort it took not to show she was in pain.

David studied her expression. Then he swore and got to his feet, knocking his chair over behind him. He ignored it and drew Annie into his arms, stroking her back.

"I'm a rotten-tempered ass, darling. I haven't been sleeping well lately, probably—" he held her away and looked down into her eyes, making a joke of it "—probably because you're not lying there beside me. Anyhow, I'm sorry if I hurt you with what I said. I sounded like a know-it-all."

"But you were right about a lot of it," she said in a small, dreary voice. "It's just that I'm defensive when it comes to Jason, I guess."

"Well, in the next few weeks I'm going to do what you suggested— try to get to know him and let him know me."

She didn't ask when he'd find the time for it, because she simply didn't believe him. His intentions were without doubt the best, but she knew from experience it wouldn't work. After all, there were only so many hours in a day or a week.

David helped Annie tidy the kitchen and load the dishwasher. They both did their best at being cheerful and they even managed to laugh a little, but David left early.

"I've got surgery first thing in the morning, and I'm beat," he explained, kissing her at the door, and Annie felt only relief when his car sped away. The strain was obvious between them, and tonight she didn't feel able to cope with it any longer.

Annie knew it was ridiculous, but she felt wounded and threatened by Jason's account of the weekend with his father and Lili, coming as it had on the heels of David's criticism.

All in all, the evening hadn't been a success. In fact, it had come near to being a total disaster. And she hadn't even mentioned the hypnotic tapes to David the way she'd planned.

That, she decided as she dragged herself up the stairs to her bedroom, was most likely a blessing. They sure didn't need one more thing to argue about, and she didn't have one shred of energy left to do it with anyway.

It wasn't until she was almost asleep that she realized the meal she'd made for David tonight was almost a replica of the one Bernadette had shared with Paul. The more things changed, the more they stayed the same.

HALFWAY THROUGH the following week, David called and asked to speak to Jason.

Annie could tell by the monosyllabic answers her son gave that David was asking him to go somewhere, and she held her breath until Jason finally, grudgingly, agreed.

"What was that all about?" Annie couldn't help asking when the boy hung up.

"He wants me to help him at a magic show he's putting on next Saturday," Jason said with such nonchalance that Annie knew Jason was thrilled despite his animosity toward David. He'd never break down and admit he was pleased, though.

Annie wanted to throttle him.

"Is it okay if I go practice with him tomorrow after school? He said he'll teach me a couple of tricks to do on my own."

"Sure, that's fine." Annie was as careful as her son to sound offhand about the whole thing, but she felt a warm rush of love and gratitude toward David for keeping his promise about getting to know Jason better.

Maybe Sunday evening hadn't been quite the disaster she thought it had.

CHAPTER SIXTEEN

"Now, Jason, this next illusion is called 'Dozens of Eggs from a Hat.'"

They were in David's apartment, and the entire living room area was a carefully congested mass of different magician's equipment that David had been demonstrating for Jason.

"Because the show we'll be doing is for kids of about six to ten, they ought to love this trick," David went on. "If you and I are adept enough to pull it off, that is, without scrambling the eggs ahead of time."

David grinned at the boy, and began to explain the secret.

"What we do is call somebody up from the audience to examine this top hat inside and out, and of course they won't find a single egg anywhere in it. Then you, my trusty assistant, walk casually out from stage back holding a huge piece of oilcloth, which you hold up boldly to convince the audience there's nothing in it, either—it's just to protect the floor from the eggs. As soon as you walk on stage, I'll pass behind you to stand at your side...and remove the silk bag of eggs pinned to your back. Then just as you hold up the oilcloth, I'll slip them neatly into the hat. Let's give it a try."

Jason's face was radiant, and he grinned as David walked him through the procedure.

"Hey, this is bad."

It took David a moment to realize that bad meant great.

"This is real bad," Jason enthused. "We're gonna pull this off like nothin'."

"Right you are. Just don't make any sudden moves with those eggs hanging down your back, partner."

They both laughed.

"Y'know, magic is weird, isn't it?" Jason commented. "I mean, it all seems too easy when you know the secret of the trick, right?"

During the drive over and the first ten minutes there, Jason had been sullen and silent. But David had set the stage for this meeting with extreme care. He'd selected books about magic that would fascinate any boy who had the vaguest curiosity about the art, and had scattered them on the table and the arms of the sofa.

And he'd decided on some not-too-complex illusions that needed an assistant—with a bit of showmanship and sense.

He was beginning to suspect Jason had both traits in abundance, and by now David was enjoying himself just as much as Jason was.

"I want you to perform a trick on your own in the middle of the program," David told the wide-eyed boy. "It'll act as a filler while I'm getting ready for the more elaborate act to follow, but the one I have in mind is punchy and surprising. It's called 'The Glass of Water and the Hat.' This is what you do."

Another two hours sped past without either of them realizing.

"Well, that's about it. I'd better get you home," David said at last. "How about a burger and fries on the way? I'm starved."

"Me, too! I'd really like that, thanks."

The conversation flowed now, centered mostly on magic, and by the time they pulled up in front of Annie's house, David felt there was a new warmth between them.

He soon realized he was mistaken, however.

"You're not comin' in to see my mom tonight, are you?"

There was a less-than-subtle change in the boy as he asked the question.

Open resentment came through in his tone. It was clear that any understanding between them didn't include Annie as far as Jason was concerned.

David sat with his hands on the wheel for a long moment, feeling defeated, and then he decided that win or lose, the time had come to talk to Jason.

He turned and looked at the boy—a long, thoughtful look.

"There's a few things you and I have to get straight between us concerning your mom," he said. "So we might as well sit out here and hash it out right now, Jason. Man-to-man."

David kept his gaze on Jason. "The bare facts are, I love your mother, and I intend to marry her someday soon, if she'll have me. You don't like that idea one bit, and you're putting up a fight."

David stated the facts, keeping his tone as neutral as he could. "I warn you, I'm going to win, regardless of how you feel. But I'd rather have you as a friend than an enemy, Jason. After all, we both love the same lady, don't we?"

Jason's face was stiff and remote, as if he'd removed himself in spirit. It was like giving a speech to an empty room, David decided, trying to talk to this boy. He forged on anyway.

"One of the things we have to learn to do as we grow into men is to begin to think about the consequences of our actions."

Damn. That sounded pious and superior enough to make a kid want to vomit, although Jason didn't look nauseated; he looked more like a marble statue.

David tried again. "What you're doing, see, is agreeing to take on full responsibility for your mom as long as she does what you want, which is dump me and go on with the safe and comfortable life you've shared up till now. You think that's what you want, but there's always a price if we get what we want, Jason."

The boy was staring out the side window, a study in boredom.

"That price is usually our freedom," David said, wondering why the hell he was bothering. "You're growing up. You'll want to be out on your own eventually, living life your own way. If you win this fight with me and get your mother all to yourself again, you'll always be aware that Annie's alone not through choice, but because you manipulated her into it." David made the words emphatic. "And believe me, that's going to bother you a whole bunch."

"That's a big fat lie." Jason had suddenly come to life. Now his face was scarlet, and he was glaring at David with unconcealed anger. "I never manipulated my mother into anything. She can do what she likes. She's an adult. I'm just a kid."

A kid far too smart for his own good, David thought.

"You're her son, and she loves you. What your mom wants is to make certain you're happy, and you know that better than anybody. That's your ammunition in this fight," David said with firm emphasis. "Now if you and I really didn't get along, if we hated each other's personalities, that's one thing. But the fact is we do get along. I think you're a fine guy. The only time there are any bad feelings between us is when your mom's involved. And," David concluded, angry now, "at the same time you're doing your best to restrict her life, you're demanding freedom in your own life. Is that fair?"

"I don't do that. I do not!" Jason objected, sounding close to tears. "I'm just a kid. Kids can't go around demanding things."

"Come off this 'just a kid' nonsense," David said with disgust. "You've got lots of clout and you use it all the time. Of course you demand things." David was remorseless. "You wanted to get to know your father, for instance, and you were pretty adamant about getting what you wanted."

"That's different. That's personal. And lay off my father, you hear?" There was a note of near hysteria in Jason's tone.

David knew there was no point in coming this far and then backing down. "We're not talking about your father, we're talking about you. I'm criticizing you, Jason Pendleton. Think about it. You wanted a relationship, your mom wants a relationship. What's so different about the two situations?"

Their voices were both loud by now, as words flew back and forth. They glared at each other for several moments, both breathing hard.

"You finished this lecture, Dr. Roswell?" Jason's voice dripped venom, and he made a move to get out of the car. "'Cause I've gotta go in now."

David gave up. There was no more he could say that would help. He dropped his head back on the padded headrest for a moment, wondering why he'd tried at all.

"Yeah, I guess that's the whole business." He added with no hope at all, "After this, are we still on for next Saturday?"

The answer would determine a great deal on whether he and Jason would ever be friends.

A long, tense moment crept past, and then Jason surprised him. With a visible effort, the boy nodded. "Yeah, I suppose so." As if every word were a tooth being extracted without freezing, he added, "I'm not saying you're right about any of this, Dr. Roswell, but I guess I'll think it over. Maybe."

David could hardly believe his ears. He forced himself to keep his voice noncommittal. "Great. That's all I want you to do. So now let's go in and see your mom. And Jason?"

"Yeah?"

David had to hide a smile at the boy's world-weary tone. It seemed an echo of David's own just a few minutes before.

Obviously Jason was expecting a continuation of the lecture.

"How about calling me David from now on?"

SATURDAY'S MAGIC SHOW was a resounding success. Annie took Cleo and the girls, and they sat up front, close to the stage.

Maggie and Paula were nearly incoherent with the excitement of seeing David as The Sorcerer with Jason as his assistant.

When David called for volunteers to check out his hat in the Dozens of Eggs illusion, Maggie went forward, and Cleo and Annie had to smile as they watched her check out the hat in her own thorough fashion, holding it upside down and reaching her hand inside several times to make certain it was empty.

She was such an earnest child.

"There was nothing in it. I saw with my own eyes it was empty,"

Maggie told her mother. And then she watched in utter disbelief as David pulled one egg after another out of the tall silk hat.

"He really is magic, isn't he, Mom?" Maggie sighed in ecstasy.

After the show, David invited everyone to McDonald's, where he and Jason refused to reveal any of the secrets of their act, and the laughter and teasing at their table made half the restaurant look their way and smile.

Annie watched her son and the man she loved, noting the warm camaraderie that seemed to have sprung to life between them, and she allowed herself to half hope that the complications of her life were all going to sort themselves out the way this one seemed to have done.

That hope died during the next weeks, however.

David became more embroiled than ever in the endless meetings and dinners that went along with his new appointment.

Annie went along to two of his business dinners, but it was evident that the only person who wanted her there was David. She ended up being seated at the opposite end of the table from him on both occasions, and the time spent on social niceties with strangers seemed to her to be a total waste. Her book was due in another month, and she felt irritated at spending precious hours socializing with people she'd probably never see again.

Calvin Graves was present at that second dinner, and he reinforced all of Annie's misgivings. He was suave, charming and, Annie concluded later, not subtle at all in his dismissive attitude toward her.

"He's a young man on the move, don't you think?" he purred into Annie's ear as David made some clever remark that caused an outburst of laughter from the group around him. "I feel David has the makings of an excellent politician in years to come."

"Yes, I suppose he has," she said with little enthusiasm.

"And how is your little book coming along?" he asked next.

He was both patronizing and as phony as a three-dollar bill. She also had the distinct impression that Calvin felt he could afford to be magnanimous toward her because David would soon be out of her life permanently. Trust Calvin to sense the widening gap between herself and David.

Annie certainly did, no matter how she tried to deny it. Their lives were moving in different directions, and she told David exactly that when he drove her home after the second dinner.

He was silent for a long time, and when he answered it was obvious to Annie that he was impatient with her attitude.

"These affairs aren't exactly fun for me, either, but I thought spending the evening together was worth it."

"David, I hardly had a chance to say two words to you all night. I don't consider that spending the evening together. And half the time I don't even know what those people are discussing. I'm a dead loss when it comes to politics and stock market deals, you know that. I simply don't give a damn about those things."

"I know. But this happens to be the best I can do at the moment socially, if we're going to see each other at all," he said with icy precision, and misery filled her.

"I'd rather you attend these things alone from now on. I'm under pressure to finish my book, and I just don't enjoy this."

He didn't answer, and he didn't ask her to go with him again.

AFTER THAT the time they had together, always limited, seemed to dwindle until most of their contact was on the telephone.

Annie worked hard on her writing and tried not to mind the long evenings alone, tried not to recognize what was happening between them.

Or not happening, she corrected with black humor.

They managed to spend four nights together out of fourteen, and on each occasion David arrived near midnight when they both were exhausted, and all either of them wanted was to lose themselves in the glory of loving and then fall asleep in each other's arms.

But on one of those nights, Annie was startled awake in the dark hours before morning as David flung himself to a sitting position and cried out in such a lost, terrified way that Annie felt paralyzed by nameless dread.

His entire body was soaked with sweat, and she could feel his heart pounding in a frenzy as she touched his chest with her hand. She fumbled with the bedside light and at last its soft glow illuminated the scene.

"David, darling, wake up. What is it?"

Her own heart was pounding with fear. He brushed her arms away with a violent movement, and although his eyes were open, it was obvious he was still unconscious.

"David, wake up! Please wake up."

When she finally managed to awaken him, he looked at her with crazed, staring eyes, terrifying her for what seemed an eternity before he realized who she was and what was happening.

"David, good grief! What were you dreaming? You scared me half to death."

Annie was close to tears, and her entire body was shaking.

He gathered her close, full of apologies, but refused to say what the nightmare had been about, and Annie felt like a stranger.

It happened the next time they slept together as well, and that time David insisted on getting up and going home at 3:00 a.m. when it happened.

That heralded a new and even more disturbing pattern between them. David still stole hours at night to be with her. He made passionate, wonderful love to her, and he assured her he loved her. But after their lovemaking he didn't stay the night as he'd done before. Instead he got up and dressed, using the excuse of early surgery or breakfast appointments so that even their stolen half hours over coffee in the early dawn, and the conversations they'd shared in those intimate morning moments became a thing of the past.

Annie was resentful and angry, puzzled and helpless as well as lonely.

What was haunting David? What demon caused the violent nightmares, and why wouldn't he talk about it with her? The strange new problem was one more wedge in the gulf forming between them.

ANNIE AND JASON were having supper one evening, both lost in their own thoughts, when Jason broke the silence.

"Mom, did my dad talk much when you knew him in the old days?"

The question dropped into the pool of quiet, surprising Annie with its intensity as well as its content. She looked at her son, trying to see him as a stranger might.

Jason was changing. Meeting his father might have matured him in some indefinable fashion, but he was changing physically as well. The traces of little boy softness were disappearing from his features. His face was taking on more angular lines, and where his hands and feet had seemed too large for his frame just months before, now it was his nose and ears that were out of proportion. His hair had darkened to an auburn shade, closer to the color of Annie's.

"Well, Mom?" His voice was impatient. "I asked you if my father was very talkative when you used to know him."

"Yes, I heard you, Jase. The answer is no, he never talked a whole lot. Michael was...I guess you'd say he was always a quiet man."

Sullen, Annie added to herself. Michael was sullen. The same as Jean had been....

"Yeah, well, I don't know how to take him sometimes, y'know? I'll be talking away, and it's like he doesn't hear me or something. It really bugs me. I mean, you'd think he could answer me at least. I mean, he wanted to get to know me, right?"

Annie couldn't believe her ears. This was the first whisper of criticism she'd heard about "my father."

Jason had been spending every other weekend with the McCraes, and the reports till now had been glowing, so much so that Annie had begun to wonder in her darker moments if the time might come when Jason would decide to live with Michael and just visit her.

"Lili says Dad's paying attention all right. She says that's just how he is, and in families you have to accept differences in people's natures. You figure that's how it really is, Mom?"

"Yes, I think she's right," Annie agreed after a moment's thought.

"Lili's pretty smart, isn't she, Mom?"

Lili was bloody brilliant, mediating between her husband and his son with such tact. Annie nodded reluctant agreement.

Jason gave her a measuring look, and then added, "Lili and my dad are pretty close, y'know, Mom? Kind of like best friends or something. It kinda made me feel left out at first, 'cause I'm used to there being only me and you—y'know how we are with each other? But Lili noticed I felt left out, and we talked about it, and now she always makes me feel part of whatever's going on. It's real strange, though, to be around a place where there's two adults, and they talk and laugh and stuff. And even kiss, sometimes." The disgust in his voice was patently phony.

An ache began in Annie's chest. Jason was describing a union based on love, she suddenly realized. He was describing a family—man, woman, child. Complete.

Not like here, with just the two of them.

What harm had she done to her son, denying him that family feeling?

He was staring at her, and he seemed to somehow know she was hurting. "Don't get me wrong, Mom. I figure we have lots of fun, just you and me," he assured her.

She met his concerned glance and forced herself to give him a jaunty wink. "Let's really have fun and get these dishes cleared away," she teased.

When they were clearing the table, he said, ultracasually, "What do you do all the time I'm gone to my father's anyway, Mom? And tell me the truth."

The truth. Careful, Annie. It would be so easy to sow the seeds of guilt here. And, Lord, it was tempting to admit she was lonely.

"The truth? The truth is I can't wait to boot you out the door, kid. I'm on a deadline with this lousy book. You know that. So I work and don't worry about the human food machine and what it's going to eat for supper, and I actually find there's hot water because some shower maniac hasn't used it all up, and I tidy the house and no teenage earthquake disrupts it."

He wasn't fooled. "But you don't see much of David anymore, huh? How come you don't spend much time with David, huh, Mom?"

It was revealing that Dr. Roswell had become David.

Just when she almost needed an introduction to the man because she saw him hardly at all, here was her son, on intimate first-name terms, asking where he was, no less. There sure as hell was no justice.

"Oh, I see him now and then. You know he spends the occasional night here. He's a busy man."

"You gonna marry him, Mom? He told me you guys were gonna get married."

Annie stared at her son, all her defenses up.

"He did, did he? Well, maybe he was a bit premature telling you that. We haven't settled it between us, and it's customary for the lady to make her own decision about things like that."

"Jeeze, Mom. Don't get all huffy, okay?" Jason frowned at her. "He told me he'd talked it over with you, and if you wanna know what I think, I figure if he asks you again, maybe you'd better go along with it. It's not a bad idea, y'know. Like, you're not exactly twenty. How many more chances are you gonna get?"

Annie opened her mouth to blast him and realized that his brown eyes were dancing with mischief.

"Rotten brat," she said with feeling. "I work my fingers to the bone for you, and what do I get?"

"Bony fingers," he sang, off-key.

He danced out the door ahead of the dishcloth she aimed at him, but for all the fooling, Annie recognized her son's real concern. He was worried about her. He felt guilty about leaving her alone on the weekends.

Because he wasn't around to bring her breakfast in bed on Saturday or Sunday the way he'd always done, he had started getting up early some weekdays and making her a tray.

Their roles were becoming reversed in some subtle way. It pointed out as nothing else could have how fast Jason was growing up.

And that remark about her and David getting married. Annie sank into a chair and closed her eyes. Utter desolation swept over her as she admitted how unlikely that possibility had become. She and David didn't have time enough together to discuss the weather report, much less marriage.

With every passing day, it was becoming more obvious that David was out of her league, part of a different world and, therefore, lost to her. It was only a matter of time before he left her.

DAVID STRIPPED off the mask and gown he'd worn in the operating room and, after a long conversation with the parents who were waiting to hear about their son, forced himself to exchange a few cheerful comments with the staff about the success of the tricky operation he'd just completed.

As he washed and dressed again in street clothes, bone-deep weariness and a bleak sense of depression overcame the exhilaration of the operation's success.

"Good work, David." The surgeon who'd assisted clasped a hand on David's shoulder to congratulate him. "When I saw the size of that mess, I figured you'd never get it out clean."

The patient had been an eighteen-month-old boy with a large tumor in his abdomen, a neuroblastoma that turned out to be malignant. It had taken hours of meticulous work, as well as a good dose of luck, to get the thing out intact.

He ought to feel exuberant, but more and more often these days, David just had the feeling his life had gone out of control when he wasn't looking.

"See you at the Parking and Safety Committee meeting this afternoon?" The question came from a man he passed in the hall, a man David couldn't for the life of him identify.

He nodded, smiled and hurried on.

The ever-increasing demands the new appointment made on his time plus the social tap dancing that Calvin insisted upon were wearing him down. He must have six meetings lined up just in the next couple of days, and heaven only knew what Calvin was planning after that.

Worst of all, he was haunted by the sick feeling that he was losing the woman he loved.

There was now a subtle but disturbing difference in Annie. He felt as if she were watching, waiting for something inevitable and final to befall them. She was withdrawing from their relationship. And although he knew it was happening, there didn't seem to be anything he could do to stop it.

He didn't have any energy to stop it. He felt as if he were moving through his days in a slippery thick fog, barely avoiding disaster in every area.

And he knew why he felt that way: he could no longer get a good night's sleep. As a doctor, he understood better than most the dangers of sleep deprivation over a long period, and the very real prospect of a mental breakdown if it went on too long.

The dream that turned to nightmare, the door he couldn't open, now waited for him each time he relaxed into deep slumber. It didn't take a genius to figure out the symbolism of that dream, the fact that there was something in his subconscious he was terrified of facing.

He'd done his best to delve into areas he wasn't too proud of in his life, in an attempt to uncover whatever it was. But try as he might, he couldn't reveal it to his conscious self.

It was obvious something was buried deep in his subconscious that was haunting him, demanding to be examined, yet hiding behind that infernal door. And whatever it was scared him witless when he encountered it in his sleep, so much so that he was avoiding going to bed.

He was ashamed of such weakness, but also unable to pinpoint whatever it was he was blocking.

He was going to have to do something about it, soon. He was still functioning in top form at his work, but even a system as strong and healthy as his would break down eventually unless he managed to get more rest than he was getting.

Phyllis looked up when he walked in the door of his office and handed him a handful of messages.

"You're late, Doctor," she greeted him. "Dr. Graves has called at least four times. He told me to tell you it's very important you speak with him before noon. He'll be at the Faculty Club at the University most of the morning, and you're to call him there the moment you come in. And—" Phyllis tilted her head a trifle higher and managed to convey disapproval, as she always did whenever Annie was involved "—your Ms Pendleton called, as well."

Emphasis on the "your."

David suppressed an exclamation of annoyance with Phyllis's attitude and went into his inner office, shutting the door with a bang and dialing the phone as soon as he sat down. Phyllis had a divorced daughter she'd been trying to interest David in for years now, and he knew that was why she resented Annie.

Annie had her answering machine on, and when her recorded voice asked for messages, he said, "This is my answering machine calling your answering machine. In the words of a long-ago song, has it told you lately that I love you?"

He cleared his throat and crooned the rest of the message, well aware that he couldn't carry a tune to save his life. "Well, darlin', I'm tellin' you now."

He added, "If you're still there, I'll be here in the office this afternoon. Give me a call, darling, and I promise I won't sing anymore. I miss you, Annie." He hung up wishing she'd been there to really talk with.

Then, with a lot more reluctance, he dialed the Faculty Club and had

Calvin paged. The other man sounded almost jocular when he finally picked up the phone after a long delay.

"Hello! Hello there, David, my boy. I'm in the midst of a rather important brunch meeting, so I won't keep you."

I'm busy, so I won't keep you. Calvin's reasoning brought a rather grim smile, but it faded when the monologue continued. "I simply need you to stand in for me later today at the Lions' Club annual luncheon, my boy. It won't entail more than just showing up for an hour and saying a few brief words about their support for one of my projects. If you have a pen handy, I'll give you the details."

It was probably a result of already feeling pressured and exhausted at barely ten in the morning, but David suddenly found Calvin's manner irritating, as well as his bland assumption that David would drop whatever plans he might have and race off to do Calvin's bidding. Was it his imagination, or had Calvin Graves become much more demanding, telling David what he ought to do instead of asking the way he always used to?

Steady, Roswell. Remember you're not hitting on all cylinders here. David scribbled down the things Calvin was dictating and held back the sharp rebuke on the tip on his tongue. *Calvin Graves is working hard to get you what you most want for this hospital,* he reminded himself, but it was difficult. *Don't be a bastard just because you're turning into a psychotic idiot.*

But when he hung up, he was aware that Calvin never had said just why he couldn't go to the damned Lions' Club meeting himself that afternoon. And he hadn't once asked David to go in his place, or even questioned whether it was possible. He'd just told him to go, and that was that.

ANNIE LISTENED to her answering machine later that day and smiled at David's nonsense. She dialed his office number again, and was told in a haughty tone that the doctor wasn't in, and wasn't expected back that afternoon, and no, Phyllis had no idea where he could be reached.

Annie bit her tongue to stop the pithy swearword that best described Phyllis, and then dialed David's apartment, knowing as she did that he wouldn't be there, either.

Damn it all, she wanted to talk with him. A feeling of urgency had been growing in her all week, a need to settle their relationship one way or the other.

She still wanted to talk over the regressions with him. Instead of fading as each new day passed, the memory of that other life they'd shared became more real, more vivid. Details that had escaped her before came to her now with spontaneous impact, in dreams at night but also like misplaced wisps of memory when she was wide-awake.

If they discussed it, David would see the connections, the parallels between then and now that were recurring. Maybe together they could figure out how to avert the parting that Annie sensed was becoming inevitable.

But the phone rang and rang, and finally she hung up.

David might turn up late that evening, for an hour, maybe two or even three. But stolen hours late at night when they were both tired didn't leave time to properly satisfy the body hunger between them, much less allow room for discussion of anything serious. And he was so tired all the time.

DAVID CHECKED with his answering service when he finally managed to escape the Lions' Club meeting late that afternoon. He was frustrated, embarrassed and more than a little furious with Calvin Graves.

Far from being the lightweight social event Calvin had led him to expect, the members of the service club had asked difficult and penetrating questions, and David, naturally, hadn't been prepared. Besides, he'd overheard two members speculating as to why Calvin himself hadn't appeared. One of them seemed quite certain it was due to a golf tournament being held that afternoon at the University links.

The two hours David had counted on for the meeting had stretched to four, and there were urgent matters at his office he'd still have to contend with before he could think of going home.

"You've had calls repeatedly from a boy named Jason Pendleton, at this number," his service reported.

David frowned, and his fingers knotted around the receiver. The number Jason had left wasn't Annie's.

Anxiety knotted in his gut as he dialed. If something had happened to Annie, and he wasn't even there to help...but the jaunty excitement in Jason's voice when he finally came on the line was reassuring.

"Hi! Hey, David, I've been trying to get you all afternoon. I'm at my friend Jeff's. There's something I need to ask you, David, and it has to be kind of a secret, so I didn't want to call from home."

David felt his muscles unclench, and the adrenaline that had spilled through him drained away, leaving bone-deep weariness behind. He slumped against the rough cement wall beside the phone, trying to keep his voice from revealing how he really felt.

"Fire away, Jason. I'm good at secrets."

"Well, there's this fund-raising fair at my school the end of November to get money for our rugby team to go on tour, see. And I sort of told Mr. Albright, he's the coordinator, that you and I had done that magic show and it turned out ace, and maybe if I asked you we could put on one for the fair?''

Jason's voice went up the scale and back down, his eagerness and uncertainty painfully obvious to David.

"We'd be the main attraction. Well, you'd be, of course. I'd just be helping like last time, but Mr. Albright said it would be terrific if we could do it. And the reason it's a secret is, I thought maybe I could invite everybody at the last minute—Mom and Cleo and the kids and...and maybe my dad and Lili, too—and not tell them we were the main attraction till they got there, right?''

Wrong. David screwed his eyes shut and shook his head from side to side. Wrong, wrong, wrong.

The idea was impossible. A magic show performed with any degree of professionalism would require untold hours of practice, especially if Jason were involved to the degree that was necessary here. David didn't have time to go to the bathroom properly these days, much less spend hours on magic. It was out of the question and that was that.

When David still said nothing, Jason recklessly added, "See, I figured you and my mom sort of got together at a magic show, right? And now you don't see much of each other anymore and I feel bad about that, so maybe...'' Jason's voice trailed off, and David could hear him breathing into the receiver as if he'd been running.

It took a long moment to register, and then the words hit David like a blow in the chest. Unless he was mistaken, this crazy, wonderful kid was actually trying to put him and Annie back to the beginning, when they'd first fallen in love, when things were near perfect between them and a future seemed possible.

After months of stonewalling, Jason was playing matchmaker.

David thought of the gut-wrenching meeting he'd just bungled through, of the appointment calendar so full it depressed him just to think about it. And he thought of Calvin and the cavalier way he'd sent David off to fill in for him today, just so that Calvin could play golf.

"What do ya think, David?''

He thought he had to say no. He had to let Jason down because there was no way humanly possible to fit this into his life.

Was there? And then he heard himself saying, "Tell Mr. Albright he's got himself a magic show, Jason. The Sorcerer and his Apprentice. But we'll have to set aside several hours at least twice a week to practice, you understand that? We don't want to look like a couple of bumbling fools up there, do we?''

The victory yell that came over the line almost deafened David, but for the first time since surgery that morning he actually felt good about something as he hung up the phone.

If he could only sleep one whole night through, he might start feeling better about the rest of his life as well.

ANNIE'S BATTERED green Volvo was parked across from his apartment building when he arrived home just after ten that night, and for a moment he was elated at the thought of having her there waiting for him.

He was surprised, as well, because in all the time she'd had keys to his apartment, she'd seldom used them.

When he'd called her from the hospital an hour before and gotten her answering machine, he'd smashed his phone down in a rage when her recorded message began, and then reflected how the slightest frustration seemed to make his temper flare these days.

As he fitted his key into the lock, he tried to overcome the overwhelming weariness that plagued him like a virus.

She'd made tea, and when she heard him rise in one graceful motion from the armchair where she was sitting, and put her mug on the side table so that she could fold herself into his arms for a kiss.

"I needed to see you. I hope you don't mind my coming here," she blurted before he could say anything, and the hint of apology in her voice brought home to him as nothing else had how far they'd drifted away from each other. Only a short time ago, no explanation would have been needed for wanting to be with him.

"I decided to wait here all night if I had to, because we have to talk, David." She tipped her head back so she could look up into his face, and the deep lines and dark shadows there made her lose the resolve that had brought her there in the first place.

"You look exhausted," she murmured, putting her hand along his jaw. "Maybe I'd better go after all...."

His arms tightened around her. "You're staying, love. I'd planned to grab a quick shower and then come over to see you anyway, so this just gives us an extra hour." He held her against him for a long moment, wishing he could absorb some of the fine vitality that always seemed to surround her.

"How about pouring me a drink while I get out of these clothes and put on—" he made an attempt at a leer "—something more comfortable?"

She smiled, but he sensed that she was preoccupied.

"Want to come and talk while I change?" he suggested, but Annie shook her head.

"I'll wait here," she said, and apprehension flared in him.

It was obvious she was there for a specific reason, and he cursed under his breath as he stripped his suit off in the bedroom and stepped into a cool shower.

He wasn't up to a heavy scene, damn it. He was off balance, wiped out from nights with little sleep and days like today when one frustration piled upon another until he felt he balanced the weight of the world on his shoulders.

He toweled off and pulled on worn jeans and a T-shirt. The shower had refreshed him, and a drink might help as well. He began to feel more cheerful about everything.

Annie was once again curled in the armchair, and she smiled as he came in. She'd mixed him a Scotch with just the right amount of water, and he flopped down on the battered sofa and took a long sip, feeling the liquor flow through his veins in a comforting stream and admiring the long, tantalizing length of her legs, bared by the skirt she wore.

"Lord, Annie, I love you." The words were spontaneous, and a sense of well-being he hadn't experienced in days welled up in him, just from the primal joy of being with her.

"I love you, too, David. It's because I love you this way that I have to talk over what's been happening to me. I want you to listen, please, David, with an open mind, because I'm convinced we're making the same mistakes together now that we made once before, and I'm frightened."

Annie's eyes seemed to overshadow the rest of her features, and David could feel the intensity of her emotion like an electrical force field vibrating between them, compelling him with its power.

Instinctively he knew what she was about to bring up, and with every fiber of his being, he rejected another discussion about hypnotic regression and past lives.

He wanted to jump to his feet and roar like a wounded animal would, as the last fragments of his newfound optimism shattered like shards of crystal. He tossed the last of his drink down his throat and grimaced at the raw fire in his chest.

There was a small tape recorder on the side table, and he watched, keeping his features impassive, as she reached out and pushed the button. She'd set it all up ahead of time, and David felt anger and resistance of this whole charade overwhelm him.

Almost at once, that haunting, familiar woman's voice wormed its way into his ears, into his soul, while every fiber of his being rejected the unfolding tragedy that voice revealed.

CHAPTER SEVENTEEN

"DAVID, THAT MAN I LOVED back then was you."

The tape had ended, and Annie's urgent voice filled the silence with still more words David didn't want to hear.

"You were Paul, and I loved you and had your child. Then, for some reason you deserted me. And the man I was married to, Jean Desjardins, came back. David, Jean was Michael McCrae. He was the man who walked in and found me nursing your son."

David's head was throbbing, and the headache seemed to penetrate every muscle in his body as he got to his feet and walked over to stare out the window. It took every ounce of control he possessed not to bellow at her, not to pick up the infernal tape machine and smash it against the wall.

"What you've done here is create an elaborate fantasy, Annie. You're a writer, and you're unusually creative," he began, and every word drove the pain in his head deeper.

"But to blame our current situation on this...this daydream of yours is preposterous. I know things between us haven't been ideal lately, but I promise you they'll get better. I'm trying my best to..."

She was on her feet when he turned toward her, and she was tucking the tape in her handbag. He moved toward her, but she avoided his arms and walked to the door.

"Damn it, Annie, sit down." His voice was almost out of control.

"I won't argue with you about this, David," she said softly. "You don't believe it, and I do. I guess I was hoping you'd be more honest than this with yourself and with me."

"Sit down and try being reasonable about this garbage," he roared, flinching at the ugly flaming bolt that shot through his brain when he raised his voice.

The door closed behind her, and he took two long strides toward it, more angry than he'd ever been with Annie. He'd bloody well drag her back in here, force her to listen to reason...

He slumped against the door, aware that he was thinking like a maniac. Sleep. Damn it, he needed sleep.

He staggered into the bedroom and dug through his medical bag in a frenzy. The sealed packages contained samples of a new pill, one that the pharmaceutical companies assured in their brochure would bring deep, restful sleep with no ill effects to even the most dedicated of insomniacs. He ran a glass of water and swallowed two capsules.

HE DROVE OVER TO ANNIE'S early the next morning and apologized.

"I'm too tired to think straight," he told her, and then he lied. "I'll give this whole regression thing a lot of thought and we'll discuss it another time."

Thus, they made a sort of strained peace between them, but both of them knew they were avoiding any real issues.

The next two weeks stretched David's endurance to the limit. Long, haunted nights when he tried to sleep without the aid of the pills were shattered as he climbed those stairs in his dream and shocked himself awake by screaming. He used the capsules with care at first, aware of how soon dependence could occur, but he was soon swallowing three, and then four.

The nights ran into long grueling days of surgery, office hours and endless, eternal meetings. He stole time from an overloaded schedule to practice magic with Jason several nights a week.

David missed three meetings during those two weeks in order to keep his evenings free for Jason. It was ironic that spending time with Jason meant even less time to spend with Annie. Jason had told her they were planning a surprise, and she accepted that. She was working long hours, as well, finishing the first draft of her book.

The evening David skipped the meeting of the Finance Committee, Calvin called.

Jason and David were perfecting an illusion called Doves in a Box, which involved making two live doves vanish using a folding box. Jason's job involved carrying offstage the flattened box, behind which was suspended a zippered bag in which David had secreted the doves. Like all stage illusions, the success of this one relied on Jason's smooth and innocent removal of the evidence, and the rehearsal wasn't going well.

David knew why. The fault wasn't Jason's; it was his. Magic required perfect timing and quick reflexes, and he was just too tired to be adept. When the phone rang, he was feeling frustrated with his own clumsiness.

"Have a Coke while I answer this, Jason. There's a pack in the fridge," David called as he lifted the receiver and said an impatient hello. His mind was still on the illusion.

"My boy, you are aware that today is Thursday?"

Calvin's smooth voice was sarcastic, and being called "my boy" grated on David's already raw nerve endings.

"Yes, Calvin, as far as I know it's been Thursday since early this morning." He was even more sarcastic than Calvin had been, and it gave him great satisfaction.

There was a discernible pause.

"This is also the third Thursday of the month, David, which heralds the regular meeting of the Hospital Finance Committee. I take it you aren't planning to appear?"

"No, Calvin, I'm not. I had Phyllis call the committee chairman and tell him I wouldn't be there. Is there a problem?"

"The problem, my friend, is the simple matter of your absence from a group that is most influential, and in which you should at this moment be highly visible. Now I had to call in a fair few debts to get you installed on that committee, David, and I'm afraid I don't understand what's going on. You're not ill, are you?"

It was like being caught playing hooky from school, and David resented the implication. His answer was abrupt and his voice revealed his irritation.

"No, I'm not sick, Calvin, although I am fed up to the teeth with meetings. However, we can discuss that another time. I'm busy at the moment, so if you'll excuse me, I'll get back to you tomorrow."

Calvin hung up in his ear with a decisive bang, and David stared at the receiver for a long moment before he set it in its cradle.

Hell. Maybe Calvin had every right to be angry. He had no right at all to be condescending.

It was beginning to sound at times as if David was a property Calvin Graves had invested in rather than a friend he valued.

DESPITE THE PILLS, every time David fell asleep that night the dream recurred, and he jerked himself awake only to fall back into a drugged stupor and have the whole scenario repeat itself.

At last he swallowed two more pills...did that make four? Six? His befuddled brain tried to add and failed. Finally oblivion descended, a black unhealthy nothingness that was a parody of restful sleep.

He dragged himself out of it knowing the alarm had been buzzing long ago. In fact, he was almost an hour behind schedule, and the residue from the powerful sleeping drug made him feel as if he were swimming underwater. His eyes were almost glued shut and his tongue had a furry, foul coating. When he raised his head from the pillow a zigzag jolt of pain shot through his skull, a hangover from the narcotic effect of the drug. He must have taken plenty.

He made black coffee and while he choked it down and shuddered at the bitter taste, he admitted to himself that had he been scheduled to perform surgery that morning, he wouldn't have been fit for it.

Hell, he wasn't fit for office routine, either. He dialed Phyllis and canceled his morning appointments.

You're a sorry mess, Roswell, and now you're swallowing pills like some kind of junkie.

If only...if only he could sleep.

If you were one of your own patients, you'd prescribe psychological help about now, wouldn't you?

Physician, heal thyself? Something had to be done, and fast.

An idea began to form, murky and flawed, but just maybe possible. Maybe he could kill two birds with one stone here, lay two demons to rest with one blow.

David forced himself to locate his address book, find a number and dial a colleague he liked and respected. David and Mike Dresko had interned together, and although they hadn't been close friends, they shared a mutual respect for each other's ability. Mike was a clinical psychologist.

"SO THAT'S THE PROBLEM, Mike, plain and simple. I can't sleep because I can't make myself open that damned door in my dream. I know the door symbolizes a problem I'm blocking, and I know if I ever manage to face whatever the hell is there, I'll feel better. Just don't feed me your Freudian mumbo jumbo and suggest years of analysis, because I don't have any time for it."

Mike was a tall, gaunt scarecrow of a man, prematurely balding. He'd poured them each a cup of coffee that tasted rather like ammonia, and he gulped his with relish, giving David an amused glance as he took one sip of the vile concoction and nearly gagged.

"You don't recognize good coffee, and you don't listen to what your doctor has to say, either. I guess we'll treat your symptoms by giving you stronger and stronger sleep medication, and just go on hoping the problem disappears before you OD, since obviously you've already decided nothing I can do will work anyway."

Mike's voice was level, but his irritation was obvious. "Why bother coming here if you aren't going to agree to treatment? You can prescribe your own damn sleeping pills, Roswell. You don't need me for that." He shook his head and took another long pull at his coffee.

"I swear doctors are the very worst when it comes to problems of their own. I ought to know by now never to let another doctor in that door in the guise of patient," Mike grumbled. "Every last one of them starts off just like this, telling me what not to do."

He gave David an astute look. "Actually you look like hell, Roswell. If you haven't done any better than this treating yourself, maybe you'd better decide to trust me a little, fill me in on what's going on in your life, and stop telling me how smart you are about psychology. I'd never tell you how to take out my gallbladder."

He was right, and David gave him what passed for a grin and relaxed as much as he could. "Your gallbladder's in danger if this is what you call coffee."

For the next hour, Mike painstakingly found out most of what was happening both on the surface of David's life and below, without seeming to pry too much.

David tried to be as honest and open as he could, within limits. He told Mike about Calvin, about the hopes for the transplant center, and all about Annie, including the fact that they were having various problems, outlining most of them and putting much of the blame on himself. But he left out any mention of Annie's experience with regressional hypnosis.

"Mike, I know the most direct means of breaking down a barrier like this one of mine is by trying hypnosis, right?"

Mike sighed and nodded. "Here we go again."

"Well, I want you to try hypnosis on me, but I want you to go one step farther. If there doesn't seem to be any basis for this nightmare in my past, then I want you to regress me, take me back to birth and before if you can."

Mike frowned and shook his head. "Look, David, it's one thing to come in here and tell me what treatment you expect. But to get into this regression stuff... Hell, as far as I'm concerned, the jury's still out on all this reincarnation material, memories of past lives and all that. I've read some of the books, and I know a lot of people are jumping on the bandwagon, but I've never put much faith in it."

"I figured not. Which is exactly why I came to you, why I'm asking you to do this for me. I don't believe either for one second it's possible. But the only way I can be certain is by trying it myself. The fact that you don't believe it, either, is the very reason I'm even suggesting it."

Mike gave him a long, measuring look. "I take it you have a good reason to want to do this, something you're not telling me, and it's connected in some way to this sleep problem you're having?"

"Yeah, Mike. I can't explain how or why, but I know in my gut this dream of mine is connected to the feeling I've always had about hypnosis. It goes way beyond skepticism. I've got a total block about the whole subject."

"Which doesn't exactly qualify you for the procedure," Mike groaned. "You're lucky I enjoy a challenge once in a while. As you know, even under hypnosis, your own subconscious mind is in complete control anyway, so I can't see any harm in trying."

"I probably can't be hypnotized anyhow," David snapped. "I really don't believe in this garbage. And don't ask me to lie down, either. I'm staying right here in this chair."

"For crying out loud, David, this was your idea, not mine. Sit wherever the hell you please—I don't care. I can only try." Mike sighed, adding under his breath, "Sometimes I wish to heaven I were a dentist."

MIKE'S VOICE DRONED ON in a relentless monotone, and at some point David stopped fighting.

He was tired, so tired. He'd tune Mike out, let him say whatever the hell he wanted, and maybe just take a short nap. This had been a total washout from the beginning anyway. He ought to have known better than to get himself into it.

He allowed himself to relax, and the sensation was delicious. He let himself sink into oblivion....

He was in an office. Not the office he had now, but one that he recognized from somewhere. It belonged to some practice he'd had in the past. He was standing in front of a file cabinet. He pulled out a drawer and selected a yellowed folder.

He opened it, following Mike's instructions.

David's heart thundered in his ears, and he wondered with clinical detachment if he was about to have a heart attack as he stared down at the contents of the docket. Inside was a bundle of letters with foreign postmarks. French postmarks.

David knew he wasn't having a heart attack. His heart was breaking instead, crumbling into dust inside his chest, and he didn't care. He knew only that he truly wanted to die....

MIKE WAS FEELING SMUG and satisfied as he watched David's wall of resistance fade and disappear. This was going far better than he'd anticipated, considering David's attitude. Far from being a poor subject, Mike was beginning to suspect that David was one of those rare people who entered the deepest levels of mind quickly and easily once their initial reluctance was overcome.

"Go to the door in your dreams," and then "Open the door without fear,'' he'd instructed after careful preliminary cautions were in place. He wanted to explore the cause of David's sleep phobia before attempting anything else. David's suggestions about regression could wait until the major issue was resolved. Then, if he still wanted to pursue it, Mike would help.

They'd agreed on taping the session, and Mike couldn't wait for David's reaction when he brought him out and proved to him how simple the hypnotic procedure had been.

"Are you reading the file now, David?" he queried. What happened next was unexpected. The hopeless, desperate sound that erupted from David rose in volume and became a tortured scream, and what was left of Mike's hair felt as if it were standing on end with horror. A cold shudder ran down Mike's body, and he leaped to his feet and came close to the slumped figure in the leather chair.

"David, move away from this scene. Move back in time. The scene is receding now," Mike instructed urgently.

David's face was contorted, agonized, and the sounds coming from him were desolate, animal-like in their terror.

Mike swallowed hard. "Leave the scene, David. Move back in time. Leave the folder in the drawer and go back, far, far back...to the cause of the pain you're experiencing. Go back, David, and find the cause. The pain is gone now, it's receding, and you're going back and back..."

The dreadful cry faded and as David relaxed, Mike dragged a chair over close to his patient and sank into it. He hadn't had a scare like this in a long time.

"Tell me where you are, and what's happening to you," he instructed. "Where are you now, David?"

This time, David's voice was controlled, but it held such anger, such sadness and depths of futility that Mike was chilled, listening.

"In a...in a tent. Hospital tent. At the front. It's a casualty clearing station. We work in these tents," David said in a weary monotone.

"Dismal, dirty tents set in a sea of mud. Men are screaming. I hear them even in my sleep. They found this man I'm working on this morning. He'd been lying out there in the barbed wire."

Mike frowned and shook his head. Whatever was going on here was outside any knowledge he had of David's life. As far as he knew, David hadn't been involved in Vietnam.

"Are you a doctor, then?"

"I'm a surgeon." The weary voice was full of irony. "A surgeon— that's a joke. This place is more like a butcher shop than anything else. A lot of the time there's damned little anyone can do." There was anguish in his voice for a moment, but then David's tone became authoritative, as if his attention were elsewhere and he was instructing a medical team.

"Gangrene's set in here. We'll have to amputate. Make sure there's plenty of chloroform handy." He raised his voice and called, "Nurse, inject these men with five hundred units of ATS. And we need morphine." His voice dropped and he murmured in helpless fury, "He's not a man, you know, he's just a boy. Doesn't even shave yet. Must have lied about his age, because he's only a kid. And he's going to lose both legs. If he even lives. So many of them don't."

Compassion washed over Mike, pity for David, and for the terrifying, vivid scene he was describing.

"David, what year is it?" Mike was perplexed with the sudden change of scene, the depth of emotional intensity his patient was experiencing.

"Year? How the hell can anyone forget the year? It's 1918. I'm thirty-six years old. Thirty-six, going on ninety." He gave a caricature of a laugh.

"The war's supposed to be over, according to the politicians here in France and everywhere else. They mouth that, but they're still sending these boys out there to die. It's all numbers to them. They figure on so many casualties for so many feet of useless mud."

Mike stared at the man before him, unable to speak for a second.

The First World War. David was reliving a scene from the First World War. David had regressed to not only another time, but what had to be another life...a situation which he'd already firmly rejected as a possibility.

Mike had strong doubts about it as well. But no one listening to David right now could possibly doubt that what he was recounting was a segment of his past, a past in a body long dead and buried.

Mike struggled with his scientific beliefs, searching for an explanation he could accept. He knew of Jung's theories about a universal unconscious, of the concept of extra cerebral memory.

But when he thought it over, he realized he shouldn't be as concerned over where these memories were coming from as he was about where they were leading his patient at this moment.

After all, he reminded himself, he wanted David to find the key to whatever was causing the disturbing and dangerous sleep disorder that had brought him to Mike's office.

He'd best use his energies to try to uncover the source of David's problem right here and now, because he was pretty certain when his stubborn, opinionated friend came out of this, he'd never turn up next Tuesday at three for another session. One way or another, this was it.

Mike moved to his desk and punched a button on the intercom.

"Margie, better cancel my next two appointments this morning," he instructed in a soft tone that grew impatient when Margie objected. "No calls or interruptions until I give you the word."

This was going to take time, but it was fascinating. His practice was lucrative, but he did get bored with upwardly mobile women and their sex problems.

He moved back to the large man slumped in the leather office chair. "David. Can you hear me, David?"

There was silence, broken only by the sound of traffic on the street outside the office window. Brakes squealed and a horn honked.

Mike asked again, and David frowned and moved his head from side to side.

"I hear you. Different name," he murmured, a puzzled frown creasing his brow. "Can't remember my name. Now why is that?"

Mike cursed his own stupidity and said, "At the count of three, you'll know your name. Someone will call you. You'll hear them call your name. One, two, three..."

"Lord, this hellhole must be getting to me. Of course I know. I'm Paul, Paul Duncan. Colonel Duncan." His mouth curved again in the ironic smile Mike was beginning to recognize. "They've just made me a colonel. The army's obsessed with having the proper rank doing the proper job. Major, Colonel, as if I give a damn about it. As if these soldiers I'm treating care, either."

David's forehead creased again and his fingers curled into fists. "I only wish I could really make a difference here, really do something for these poor suckers."

The more things change, the more they stay the same, Mike thought, remembering David's crusade for a transplant unit. David's need to make a difference for his patients was just as urgent then as it was now.

"If the war's technically over, will you be going home soon? Where's your home, Paul?"

"I'm a Yank, an American, from Columbus, Ohio."

Mike asked questions, and David answered.

"I'm married back there. My wife's name is Grace. Her father, Martin Oakley, and I have a medical practice together. There's talk of shipping us home you know, before Christmas."

Mike watched as his patient frowned, a worried expression creasing the handsome features. "I don't want to go back to the States, but I have to. I have to get things settled once and for all."

"You don't want to go home? Why's that, Paul?"

There was silence for a moment, and then the response came in a rush of words and feelings.

"Because I've fallen in love with a woman here. I never dreamed I'd love anyone the way I love Bernadette. Going back home means leaving her over here until I can arrange a divorce, and I hate the thought of leaving her behind. It tears my guts apart. Oh, I tried writing Grace and telling her, but I couldn't do it properly on paper. I didn't mail the letter."

There was a pause, and then he said with a sigh, "It's complicated because of my relationship with my father-in-law, Martin. I owe him a great deal. He paid for most of my medical training, and I dread telling him what my plans are. I hate hurting him, but it has to be done. And there's my wife. Grace has never been strong. Martin's always protected her." His head moved from side to side in a despondent motion, and his tone became vehement.

"We should never have married—I know that now. She wants a husband who plays bridge, makes a lot of money, knows the right people. She doesn't want kids. I'm wrong for her. I don't care about any of those things, especially not now, after what I've seen here. It all seems frivolous, unimportant to me now."

He was breathing fast, overwhelmed with feeling. "I'd like a kid of my own. Bernadette has a daughter, Nicole." He seemed to be seeing the child in his mind's eye, because he smiled a little. "I love that little girl."

A sad smile creased his mouth and then was gone again. "Children. They're our hope for the future, when this hell is over. Maybe I'll specialize after this, work only with kids. I'd like that."

"And this French woman, Bernadette. How does she feel about your leaving?"

He became agitated again. "I love her more than life itself. I don't want to leave her even for a day. She's so strong, full of life and laughter, yet there's something wistful about her as well. Meeting her, being able to spend a few days or, if we're lucky, a week together, has made this bearable, you see, this...carnage, this squandering of human lives. She helps me, she makes me feel there's still beauty and peace in the world."

"Where is she now?" Mike was trying to place the characters in this drama.

"On her farm, in Normandy. By some miracle, the place has escaped pretty much untouched. It's a small farm. Her husband was a soldier, but he's dead. He disappeared early in the war. Her life is hard. I spend as much time as I can with them. It's like a different world. I want to marry her, take her back to the States.''

Mike listened, and a strong presentiment of tragedy overwhelmed him as he instructed David to move ahead, to a time after the war. He knew it was ridiculous, but Mike almost hated to ask the next questions.

How the hell could he become emotionally involved in a romantic tale seventy years old? And yet he was involved, in a way he seldom experienced with his patients. This was real, and vivid.

''Months have passed, the war is over now. Tell me what's happening to you.''

Moments passed again as David oriented himself in his invisible reality.

''I'm back in Columbus. I've been sick.'' He coughed, a harsh, empty rattle in his chest. ''This rotten flu. Everyone has it. People are dying as if it were the plague.''

Mike was flabbergasted at how David seemed to change. Even the voice, which had been vibrant and strong was now thin and reedy, almost a whisper at times.

''Grace caught it first, the very week I arrived home. She was dangerously ill, and Martin...good Lord, it shocked me, how old Martin's become while I was away.'' Silence, and then he burst out, ''It's a trap, you know—Grace's illness, Martin's aging. It's an insidious trap, and I'm caught in it.'' David's fist knotted all of a sudden, and he pounded on the chair arm in frustration. ''This place, this place is like a prison to me.''

His voice dropped to a near whisper of despair. ''Every day, every hour, I feel like walking out of here, taking the first ship back to France, back to Bernadette. But how can I, the way things are? How can I leave now?''

He shook his head in absolute despair. ''You'd have to be heartless to walk out on them the way they are. And then, I caught this damned flu, and pneumonia afterward. It was weeks before I was even strong enough to hold a pen and write to Bernadette.''

His features contorted with pain. ''What did she think, my beloved, all those weeks without a letter from me? Martin took care of me here at home. The hospital is overflowing with flu cases. I was delirious. I remember calling out for Bernadette again and again. Heaven knows what Martin thought. He's never said a word about it, and I know I babbled. I worry about the letters that come from her. They're addressed to the office, and Martin must see them—he's taking care of the mail.''

David was silent for a time, his face a mask of despair. When he spoke again, there was a dry and hopeless desperation to his words.

"It's hard to accept this, you know. I was always physically strong, but I'm not strong any longer. I can't even walk to the office, just a few short blocks. It's humiliating to me. I took my health for granted. I'm not yet forty years old, but the muscles around my heart were damaged by this flu. Martin called in a specialist yesterday, and he says it's irreparable. I'll be a semi-invalid the rest of my life."

He struggled for a long moment, the struggle of a proud, strong man who wouldn't give in to tears.

Again, Mike moved the scene ahead, half expecting to be told that Paul had died.

"Move ahead in time. Tell me how old you are now, Paul."

"I'm sixty-three."

"And where are you now?"

There was more strength in the voice than there had been, as well as world-weariness and perhaps just a touch of pomposity.

"Still here in Columbus, still running the practice. I've been successful in my career. I'm director of the hospital, you know. Martin got the town to build a new and better hospital. I'm also a member of the town council. The place is growing."

"What about your wife? Do you have a family?" Mike posed the questions with intense curiosity.

"No family, no," the dry voice related. "I live alone." He gave a dry and bitter chuckle. "Grace divorced me several years ago. She got involved in social work and women's rights. Martin was horrified. He came close to disowning her." A stiff little smile came and went.

The irony of it all, that the woman both men had protected had turned against them, brought a wry grin to Mike's face, but he sobered when he asked the question bothering him.

"And what of Bernadette? Did you ever see her again?"

Paul shook his head from side to side and seemed to struggle with his feelings.

"I wrote, but she never answered again. Finally I contacted a friend I'd known in her village, a doctor. He was a chronic alcoholic, but a nice guy. His name was Marc, Dr. Marc Cerdan. I begged him to write and tell me what had happened to her."

An enigmatic smile played over David's features. "He wired me back, a short and cryptic message saying that the lady was well, she was now living with her husband, an injured war veteran, still in that same tiny hamlet in Normandy. She had another baby, Cerdan said. He suggested that I chalk up the experience to wartime romance and forget about it. Leave her alone, he all but ordered."

"How did you feel about that?"

Anger sparked, the first real sign of emotion Paul had shown for some time.

"How the hell do you think I felt? I was half insane with jealousy and grief. I was hurt, betrayed. She'd assured me her husband was dead. Had she lied, or was this some new man she met and married after me? Was he the reason she refused to come to the U.S. when I begged her? I couldn't stand not knowing, so I decided to go to France and confront her."

"And did you go?" Mike felt deep compassion.

A huge sigh. David seemed to slump. "No. No, I never did. There was always something, work, meetings, illness, never a time when I could get away easily. Martin expanded our practice about then. He had high ambitions for me, and I got caught up in local politics. As time passed, I began to feel that I really had no right to interfere in her life, just as Cerdan said. She had a husband now, and another child. I could only cause trouble for her."

He sighed again. His voice was heavy and sad when he added quietly, "But I never forgot her, either. I never could stop loving her. I love her today, this minute, as much as I ever did. Not a day passes that I don't think of her. For some people, there's only one love in a lifetime, and she was mine. I think of her, and I remember everything, every detail of our time together. I dream of her at night. Ahh, I remember."

He seemed to be lost in memories for a long moment, and Mike didn't interrupt. At last, with a visible effort, David resumed the narrative.

"Martin Oakley died two days ago, you know. I'm in his office now. There's an old file cabinet that needs cleaning out."

A warning bell went off in Mike's mind. They'd come full circle, back to the office, the file. He sat forward on his chair.

Sweat suddenly appeared on David's forehead, and lines of tension deepened on his face.

"I don't want to open it," he said abruptly, fear evident in his tone, each word an effort. "I have to do it, but I don't want to."

His clenched fists strained against the chair arms and every muscle in his body seemed to stiffen. Cords stood out in his throat and blood vessels bulged in his forehead.

David was again at the hidden door in his nightmare, and terror was building. Mike prayed silently for the skill he needed to guide his patient through the next few crucial moments in safety.

"David, I want you to remove yourself from the scene and just observe what's happening. Watch without feeling. Allow yourself to move away from the fear, move back from it and observe. Can you do that?"

Sweat streamed down David's face, and his eyes opened, unfocused and wild. It took several seconds for Mike's suggestion to take effect, and then gradually, David relaxed a little.

"Are you feeling safer now? Can you tell me what's happening?"

"Opening...the...drawer, taking out...the...folder."

Even with the strong hypnotic suggestion, David still showed signs of extreme stress as he related what was occurring.

"Inside...oh God, oh God...letters." David's hands were trembling visibly, his face contorted in agony.

"Bernadette. Letters from her, my letters to her. Martin must have stopped them. I gave them to him when I was ill, but he never mailed them... How could he do this? How could he?"

A charged silence followed, as if David were examining the contents.

"They're open. He must have read them all. And hers to me. There's one addressed to me at home! She'd never have done that unless she was desperate.... Here, she says...she writes..."

David's moan of anguish and heartbreak echoed through the room, but now the terror was gone, leaving only a depth of pain that made Mike feel helpless and inept.

"God, I have a son. Our son—the child was mine. Martin knew how much I wanted a child, and yet he never let me know...and in every letter, every single one, she tells me she loves me. She...she needs me. See here, this final letter, she's begging me to come to her...oh God, she needed me. She needed me, and I never went back."

Tears poured from David's eyes, and anguish contorted his features.

"I've wasted all these years. I've wasted my life. I always knew I shouldn't have given up. I let Martin pull the strings that kept me here. Our son, I'll never know my son...and oh, my Bernadette..."

Mike's own eyes were damp as he watched and listened to the powerful play of emotions rocking David.

Then to Mike's alarm, David flinched violently and groaned.

Mike snatched up his patient's wrist, monitoring his pulse, and was astonished to find it thready and weak.

"What is it, David, what's happening?" he demanded, but there was no reply. David slumped over in the chair as if he were dropping farther and farther into oblivion.

CHAPTER EIGHTEEN

HE'S ONLY REACTING to a powerful memory, Mike reassured himself. A patient in hypnosis is safe from actual physical harm. Still, in another minute he'd have to bring David out, and to hell with theory. A person couldn't actually relive a heart attack or anything like it, could he?

Of course not.

Mike felt beads of anxious sweat form on his own head and drip down the sides of his face as David gasped, "Heart...always weak, white-hot pain, in my chest, down my arm..."

"David, your inner mind will let go of these memories now. This is happening in another time. Let them go, become calm and relaxed, very relaxed. The nightmare is gone. It will never recur because you know now what's behind that door. You will be able to sleep long and restfully from now on, with no disturbing dreams. You will come back to the present. You will wake up now with full recognition of what's happened here, and you will understand and examine these memories and the messages they hold for you in your present life."

Thank the Lord something was inspiring him, Mike thought with relief. The words, the reassurances, were there when he needed them.

David was slow in coming out of hypnosis. He was wet with sweat, and his shirt clung to his chest. He looked gray and weary, and at first he avoided Mike's eyes. He sat immobile and silent, staring with blind concentration at the window, his face a controlled mask.

Mike knew David was struggling with what had occurred, because Mike himself was. He felt as if he'd just witnessed an event that radically affected his professional life and every last one of his personal beliefs. Of all the dramas that had ever been played out in his office, this was the most memorable by a country mile.

At last, Mike couldn't help but ask with gentle curiosity, "David? You remember all that?"

David gave one emphatic nod. "That, and more." He sounded as if his throat hurt.

"Did you die from that attack, David? Your pulse actually had me worried for a while there. There's nothing really wrong with your heart, is there?''

"Nothing. And no, I didn't die right then. Not from that one," David answered. He seemed to be drained of emotion; his voice was matter-of-fact and without inflection.

"It was the first of several. I didn't really give a damn about living any longer, see. I remember thinking I only wanted time enough to write one last letter to...to her. To, ummm, to Bernadette."

He raised haunted eyes to meet Mike's gaze, and in a low, strangled voice he said, "Lord, I loved her, Mike. I love her now. Isn't that a hell of a thing, to love a woman who's been dead a long time?"

The ghost of a smile came and went again. "Except I know her again. I told you about Annie. I know deep inside of me that Annie and Bernadette are the same person. I think I've known a long time, but I kept denying it. It meant facing a version of myself I didn't like much. Mike, I love Annie the same way I loved Bernadette."

A strange, sad envy was born in Mike at that moment. He thought of his pragmatic schoolteacher wife, Sarah, of their three children, their lavish house in Kerrisdale and their secure and predictable life.

He thought of the shoddy affair he was having with Margie, a romance he'd convinced himself was torrid and exciting.

And for the first time in years, he remembered being young, and having dreams of a great and memorable love, the way all idealistic young men do. But he'd never found it.

He was an impatient man, greedy for instant reward, and he admitted to himself that he'd never come close to knowing the kind of love David was describing. Was it really out there, for everyone, if they searched hard and waited long enough?

With an immense effort, he brought his thoughts back to David, to what had occurred.

"You had me on pretty strange ground there for a while, partner. Lucky thing I keep up with the journals. At least I had some idea what was going on."

He hesitated, and then asked, "Do you think it was fantasy or actual memory, David? It sure as hell sounded authentic to me. But if it was a legitimate regression, you and I have a lot of revising to do in our belief systems."

"It happened all right." There wasn't a shred of doubt in David's voice. Disgust filled his voice. "Jeeze, Mike, I was a sorry excuse for a man back then. I let my father-in-law coerce and bribe me into becoming what he thought was a success. Why the hell didn't I take charge of my own life?"

David got up from the chair, feeling drained of energy. He walked to the window and pulled back the blind. The traffic outside had accelerated, and the sun's angle indicated that somehow the morning had become afternoon. But inside the office, time had somehow stopped being a factor. In the midst of their clock-regulated lives, Mike and David had created a warp, and neither man felt urgency or pressure or even curiosity about the changing numbers on their expensive watches.

Instead Mike thought about all the things David had experienced, and his wide mouth twisted in a sad, sardonic grin.

"Then or now, how many of us ever take charge of our lives? Life seems to happen, and we're along for the ride. Which makes this reincarnation idea pretty scary, because it throws responsibility back on us. Who the hell else can we blame if we create our own destinies?"

David considered the life he was leading now. He shuddered as he remembered Paul, the tragic man he'd been, and perhaps still was, somewhere deep inside David.

"I chose my life back then, regardless of how much I'd like to blame the whole thing on Martin or war or fate. I could have made a different decision at any time, gone back to France, turned my back on my career. What happened was my choice, mine alone." He was talking more to himself than to Mike. He felt dizzy and light-headed for a moment, and he grasped the back of a chair and bent his head until the giddiness faded.

"I've got the same options now as I had then."

"The thing is, do you figure you'll be able to sleep now without nightmares?" Mike queried.

A weary grin twisted David's mouth. "Nightmares won't be a problem anymore. I know that. I've got some waking horrors to get through, though."

Mike watched as David straightened, reached for the jacket he'd hung on the back of a chair and shrugged into it. He held a hand out and Mike clasped it hard.

"I'm grateful, Mike. You'd better bill me in installments, or sure as hell I'll really go into cardiac arrest when I get your statement for this one." David tried for a light tone and a grin, but he was sweating and shaking again. The session had taken its toll physically. It was all he could do to hold himself upright. Some shred of macho pride in him didn't want Mike watching while he fell flat on his face.

Mike went to his desk drawer, extracted a set of keys and held them out to David.

"Listen, the only thing you're fit to do is rest, and nobody knows better than me how impossible that is at home, with the office or your service calling every fifteen minutes. Besides, you probably shouldn't be driving either. If you go out the front door of this building, you'll see a small apartment complex halfway down the next block. I, ahh, rent a unit there nobody's gonna be using today. Why don't you go over there and sleep for a few hours?''

David gave a good imitation of a grin and shook his head. ''There's somebody I need to see right away, while I'm still raw enough to swallow my pride and admit I was wrong about a lot of things. I'll sleep at her place. Thanks, buddy. I owe you one.''

As the door closed behind David, Mike mumbled, ''Maybe you do. And maybe you don't.''

DAVID DROVE with extreme caution along the busy streets, forcing himself to think only of the traffic until he arrived at Annie's house and parked at the curb. He'd never felt more relieved at getting anywhere as he dragged himself out of the car and made his slow way up to the front door.

It was locked. Annie was out somewhere.

For a moment, David contemplated lying down on her front lawn and just staying there until she came back. Then he remembered that she seldom locked the kitchen door, and with slow, dragging steps, he made his way through the side gate and around the back.

That door was unlocked. He went in, and with a slow, single-minded shuffle, he headed across the kitchen to the hall that led to the stairs.

The small watercolor, the pastoral scene of the stone cottage with the river in the distance, hung on the wall by the doorway. David stopped and looked at it for a long time. Waves of recognition rolled through him, along with a sense of grief so overwhelming it was all he could do not to cry.

No wonder Annie had bought the picture. It could have been a sketch of Bernadette's farm in Normandy. He could almost smell the scented air, hear the larks singing in the trees beside the river.

He moved down the short hall to the stairs, taking them the way an old man would, one laborious step after another.

At last, he was in Annie's bedroom. He took off his coat and his shoes and gave up the struggle, collapsing on the unmade bed and rolling on his stomach so he could bury his nose in the scent of Annie that pervaded the pillow. Or was it the clean-washed lemon scent of Bernadette's hair?

Oblivion was immediate.

ANNIE HAD WRESTLED with the increasing pain in her neck for three days, and she'd reached some kind of crossroad during the night while she tossed and turned, trying to find a position that eased the burning sensation.

One of her decisions had to do with David. She couldn't stand one more day of indecision, of sitting waiting for him to make room in his life for her. She was determined to search him out, and force him to spend at least enough time to say goodbye with dignity, if that's all that was left for them.

The other decision was out of her control. She would go back to Steve and undergo regression one last time. Her neck hurt enough to overcome her fear of the past.

She tried to settle the issue with David first, but the problem was the usual one; she couldn't locate him to tell him anything.

Phyllis snapped at her even worse than usual when Annie called the office just after nine.

"The doctor hasn't been in this morning, and I don't expect him."

"Well, do you know where he might be?" It galled Annie to have to ask, but she did anyway. The answer was abrupt and final. "No, I don't."

"You know, Phyllis, it doesn't cost anything to be polite," Annie said.

Click.

At least this time she'd said it, and it made her feel good.

Annie hung up, dialed again, left a second message on the machine at David's apartment and then wondered if perhaps he was with Calvin Graves.

To hell with it. She didn't feel intimidated by anyone any longer. She located and dialed Calvin's home number and actually got Calvin on the phone after the first ring.

If anything, he was in a worse temper than Phyllis had been. "Unfortunately I have no idea where our good doctor is, or where he can be reached, or even when he might again be available, my dear." His voice was frosty and heavy with sarcasm as he added, "Ironic we should both be ignorant of David's whereabouts, don't you think? Perhaps there's some little thing he isn't telling either of us."

Annie's bravado deserted her. She swallowed the furious retort that Calvin deserved and hung up again, but his vicious innuendo stung.

Did she really know whether or not David was involved with someone else? He certainly wasn't seeing much of her.

Is this what had happened in that life long ago as well? Did the sudden ending to Paul's letters mean that he'd found someone else to love? Maybe, her confused brain suggested, Calvin had given her the real reason for David's absences.

That's absurd, Annie, she reasoned. *You know that's absurd.*

But she could no longer tell what was logical and what wasn't. The shafts of pain in her neck accelerated until they were agonizing. She switched on the relaxation tape and tried to concentrate, but the pain was now uncontrollable. In desperation, she picked up the phone while she could still function, and dialed Steve's office.

She'd spent a great deal of time in the past weeks reading the books he'd given her, learning more and more about the strange phenomena of past life regression, and more as well about the lessons to be learned from understanding reincarnation.

The message that came through loud and clear was that there were no accidents in the universe, that each person chose every detail of the life they lived: past, present, future. Hiding from the truth was impossible. Sooner or later, every challenge had to be dealt with, every pain expiated, no matter how many lifetimes it took.

During those weeks of reading, she'd resisted what she knew was necessary, but now the time had come for her to learn the ending of that other life, regardless of how painful it might be.

She might as well get it over with this time around. She might as well find out once and for all why Paul had deserted her.

"Come right over, Annie. I know Steve will see you right away," Edith said immediately.

Within an hour, Annie was lying back on the now-familiar battered couch, and she knew it would be a simple matter to find the familiar tunnel that led into that other life. Whatever scenes awaited there would be anything but simple, however.

"I'm petrified, but I want to know what became of me, of all of us back then," she told Steve, and he agreed.

"I'll take you over the years that intervened, but I'll try to have you view them as an observer, so the experiences aren't as painful. Then I'll guide you to the last day of your life as Bernadette," he promised. "Relax, Annie. It'll all be over soon."

WITHIN MOMENTS, Annie once again saw herself as Bernadette. Years had passed since Paul left, and she never heard from him again. She never forgot him, either. As long as she lived, her heart would belong to Paul.

She lived in two worlds all those years, and in halting, pain-filled phrases, she explained it all to Steve.

"In one way, I was Jean's wife. I worked hard, cared for my family.

But in some other reality, in my dreams, Paul and I walked hand in hand forever along that tree-lined path by the Seine, the way we had so many times when we were together. Every day, after my work was done, I'd go there.''

"Wasn't your husband jealous? He must have known you thought of your lover."

She shrugged. There was a touch of disdain in the movement and in the tone of her voice when she said, "What could he do? He thought he owned my body, but he couldn't control my mind, could he?"

Jean Desjardins had grown physically strong again. Lorelei had used all her considerable nursing skills to help him recover in the weeks after he came home, and she was a positive influence on his mental state as well.

After that first terrible encounter the day Jean arrived home, Bernadette fled with her children and went to stay with Lorelei and Pierre Dupré, desperate to escape Jean's presence and his rage. Lorelei had reasoned with Bernadette, convincing her that she should go back and make the best of it. Inside herself, Bernadette knew she really had no choice in the matter, with a new baby and little money left from the amount Paul had given her.

And she couldn't go on staying with Lorelei and Pierre. Lorelei, too, lived a married life far from ideal. Pierre Dupré was a sad, dependent old man, clinging to Lorelei like a child, and just like a child he was jealous of his wife's attention.

There was really nowhere else for Bernadette to go but back home.

"To give him credit, Jean did his best to accept what had happened. Basically," she admitted with some reluctance, "I suppose he was a good man in some ways."

But living with Jean and loving Paul was slow agony for her. Gradually Bernadette compensated by lavishing her affection on her children, particularly on her son...Paul's son, Marcel.

Jean's daughter, Nicole, was a serious, responsible child. She looked like Jean, and the physical resemblance reassured and pleased him. He set out to win the little girl's trust and affection in the weeks after his homecoming.

A frown came and went as she tried to explain the complex relationship among the four of them. "It wasn't that I didn't love Nicole," she said at one point, as if defending herself against an accusation. "But Marcel was conceived of the love Paul and I shared, and there was a special feeling for him. Jean knew this. I kept the boy away from him as much as possible."

Jean at first ignored Marcel completely, the hurt of having another man's child around almost more than he could bear. But as the years passed, he did try his clumsy best to form a relationship with the boy. He never succeeded, and Bernadette had to accept much of the responsibility for that failure.

Marcel was very much like his father, Paul, in appearance and in disposition. Thus, he seemed totally foreign to Jean. The boy, bright and charming, handsome and quick-witted, soon was aware that he always had his mother's support in any dispute with Jean. As a result, Marcel became headstrong and willful.

As Marcel grew, Bernadette was aware that her son was a constant, visible reminder to Jean of her love for another man. Marcel caused a great deal of trouble in the family by his very presence, but also because of his actions. He was rebellious from an early age, and at times his mischief sparked an insane, blinding rage in his stepfather, Jean, and then Bernadette would come rushing to her son's defense.

"Several times, Jean goaded me, telling me that my American lover had deserted me and my bastard son, and now he was stuck supporting us. I hated him when he was like that."

Annie recounted these situations for Steve in a matter-of-fact way, but there were undertones of both growing fear and increasing sadness in her voice as she again took up the story. Steve noted that the role of impartial observer had disappeared, and once again, Annie was Bernadette.

"Marcel is now twenty and two weeks ago, against my wishes, he ran off to join the army," she said in a quavering voice. "We are once again in another war, you know."

"And your daughter? Where is Nicole now?" Steve prodded.

"Gone away as well, to train as a nurse." Weary desolation filled her voice. "I'm more lonely than I've ever been before. It's like a cancer in me."

"What about your friend, Lorelei? Don't you have her to talk to?"

She shook her head. "Lorelei's dead. She left here years ago, two years after Jean returned. Her young lover, Tony Briggs, gave her an ultimatum, and she went off to be with him. But it didn't work out. He fell in love with another woman and left her, and it broke Lorelei's heart. She stopped writing after that. The last letter I had of her, she was working in an orphanage in Paris. Dr. Cerdan went to find her, and he brought me the news that she had died. Consumption, he said. I miss her so."

Steve decided the time had come to move forward.

"You will go now to the last day of your life as Bernadette. You will remember without pain what occurred that day. You will exorcise the soul memory once and forever...."

The words penetrated her deepest consciousness, but even powerful hypnotic suggestion couldn't defeat the horrors of that awful day as she allowed herself to remember.

At first, excitement and apprehension seemed to overcome her.

"What's happening now?" Steve asked, curious at the sudden change in her body language.

"A letter." Her voice was breathless. "A letter from the United States. From—" tension filled her "—from a lawyer?" There was a pause, and then her hands clasped and she slumped as if in pain.

"Paul. Somehow I knew it," she whispered at last. "It says here that Paul is dead. My love is dead, forever gone from me." Her arms folded around herself in a lonely, pathetic gesture that wrung Steve's heart. "The lawyer encloses a letter Paul gave him for me, and a bundle of faded envelopes...."

"Open the letter," Steve instructed with gentle insistence.

She shook her head, her breath coming in short, agitated sobs.

"You must open the letter Paul wrote, Bernadette," Steve said again, "and read it to me."

"My...my dearest love..." she began at last, so low Steve had to lean forward to hear.

In a few terse phrases, the words described Paul's life, how circumstances had prevented him from coming back, the maze of complications and errors of judgment that finally prevented him from returning at all.

"His father-in-law hid these letters, all of them," she said dully. "At least now I know—I know he didn't stop loving me."

And then, with heartbreaking tenderness, she began to read aloud. "The memory of the love we shared is etched indelibly into my soul, beloved. How I long to see you just once again before my life ends. How bitterly I resent the accidents of chance that have kept us apart." Her voice broke, and she reached a finger up and rubbed away a single tear that trickled slowly down her cheek.

"I realize now I should have put everything aside and come to you, Bernadette. I know that now, when it's too late."

A deep, silent sob shook her, and she bit her lip before she could go on. Steve was shaken and deeply moved by the scene.

"Bernadette," she read on, "I have the strangest conviction that we've loved many times before now. Remember how we used to talk about the feeling that we'd known each other before? And so I can only hope that we'll meet again, in another time, another place. Until then, my darling, hold me in your memory the way I've held you all these long empty years."

Her voice broke again, and she choked out the final words. "Dearest Bernadette, remember me. Remember me as I do you. Yours eternally, Paul."

Tears were flowing down her cheeks, and once again she raised her hand, brushing the wetness away with her knuckles. "You see, Jean?" she cried out all of a sudden, with a passion and a depth of anger that startled Steve. "You see? He loved me after all, during all these years he loved me, and that's all that matters to me now."

Listening, Steve was appalled, and a foreshadowing of awful tragedy overcame him.

"Bernadette, is Jean there with you? Did he hear what was in that letter?"

When she nodded with proud defiance, Steve felt his stomach clench with fear. Despite it, he instructed, "Move ahead now. Tell me what happened next."

"I can't stand the pain of knowing what might have been for Paul and me. It's tearing my soul apart, and Jean is watching with that awful burning look on his face."

Her words came faster now. "I run from the house. I run to the path by the river...where Paul and I...made love under the trees." She was panting, and her breath was coming in short, sobbing gasps.

Then, for an instant, the anguish contorting her features seemed to be smoothed away, and she said in a lilting, girlish voice, "Paul? Is that you, Paul...?"

Her tone was full of wonder, her expression one of surprise and joy that changed in an instant to a look of horror as Steve watched and waited.

"Jean," she gasped, her eyes wide open and filled with horror. "Jean, don't, I..."

"Tell me what you're experiencing," Steve ordered firmly. "Try to stay relaxed and calm and tell me what's going on."

"He...I...I thought it was Paul, but it was Jean," she gasped. "Only a step behind me, and I turned and...oh, his face! Jean's face is full of rage...and I'm frightened. Oh, Lord, he's got my arms now and he's shaking me...shaking me back and forth, and...I'm struggling...he's strong...my body, my head, jerking...back...forth...can't..."

Steve crouched down beside her and took her hand, but there was little more that he could do but listen and try to comfort.

This was it at last. This was the buried moment from long ago, the traumatic moment that Annie had carried with her through death, through birth, through her entire present life. This was where the pain had originated.

"Stay very calm and very relaxed, and describe what happens next," Steve said.

"Pain," she gasped. "Terrible, burning pain in my neck, my neck... Stop him, oh, stop...God, help me...shaking and shaking me...I can't stand it...ohhh, this cracking noise...filling my head..."

The last wailing cry she then made rose to a peak, filled the room and then faded, and Steve knew with sick horror that somewhere in the past, and eerily again here in his office, Bernadette Desjardins was dying of a broken neck.

SHE FELT HERSELF TUMBLE to the earth.

The red-hot agony in her neck and upper back engulfed her, but soon it passed into darkness, and she moved up, into a brilliant tunnel of light. A tiny part of her was aware of the tormented figure of Jean, far below, shaking the body she'd left behind, roaring out his fear and pain and grief like a wounded animal, then running toward the riverbank and plunging into the swollen spring waters of the Seine.

Steve took charge again as her whispered words ended. He had to swallow several times to make his voice behave.

"You're going to receive more and more insights into this other life during the next few weeks, but now I want you to come back to being Annie. I'm going to count from ten to zero and I want you to come back, remembering what you've learned today."

"My neck hurts," she moaned, still deeply hypnotized.

No damn wonder, Steve thought, awed by the power of the scene she'd recreated. You've just had your neck broken. No damn wonder it hurts....

"This is the last time it will ever hurt this way, Annie," he assured her. "You now know the reasons for the pain, and you can leave it behind forever." With care, he brought her out of the trance.

The pain in her neck began to ebb, pain from a long-ago tragic death. The last burning traces faded along with her tears, and Annie knew with deep conviction that the problem she'd had all her life would never trouble her again.

She knew as well that the neck pain had become a secondary issue in this search for truth. She'd begun the journey with single-minded purpose, to help with a physical problem. Now she'd ended it, and the physical relief seemed minor in comparison to the emotional knowledge.

"I understand now the feelings I've always had about Michael, the fear and distrust, and even why I was both attracted and repelled by him when we met again in this lifetime.''

Annie shuddered as she thought over the mistakes she'd made as Bernadette, the countless small ways she must have wounded Jean over the years. And the selfish way she'd clung to Marcel and spoiled him, excluding any relationship the boy might have formed with Jean.

Steve listened as she verbalized her experience.

"As Bernadette, I was unfair to my husband, you know. He was basically a good man, and I knew deep inside myself that he loved me, even though his nature wasn't expressive. I shouldn't have stayed when I couldn't love him back. It was almost as if I taunted him at times with Paul's son, with the enduring love I felt for Paul and not for him.''

It was ironic, this feeling of regret, and even shame, for the way another version of herself had acted so long ago.

"Maybe through Jason, we can learn to forgive each other this time around,'' she mused. "I feel easier about Michael now. You'd think knowing what he did to me would make me hate him, but instead it's myself I blame. With Jason,'' she went on, "I've come close to making the same selfish mistake again, keeping Jason from Michael. This time Michael is his natural father, and yet I've resisted the idea of letting the two form a bond.''

She thought for several moments. "How strange, and yet how just that David...'' She'd been about to say that David would be the boy's stepfather this time, but she stopped before the words were out.

Familiar anxiety filled her as she admitted that it was far more probable that David would disappear from their lives forever, just the way he had the last time.

She could alter only her own reality, but not David's. He had free will, and she couldn't influence the choices he'd make. Judging by the way things were going between them, it seemed unlikely he and Annie would ever make a life together.

How that hurt. Her mouth twisted with pain as she thought of living the rest of this life, too, without the man who seemed to be the missing half of her soul. *David,* she thought in agony. *If only I could make you understand these things, see them as I've been allowed to do.*

"Do you know what became of Marcel and your daughter, Nicole?'' Steve's question was a welcome distraction.

Annie closed her eyes and nodded. "It seems they died in that second war. Those were terrible times, for us, for France, for all of Europe. When I left that body, it seemed to me that I could see both the past and the future, and my children didn't survive the war.''

Tears filled her eyes again, and regret filled her heart. She hadn't been the best of mothers to Nicole or to Marcel. She'd spoiled Marcel, allowing Nicole to take a secondary role. The girl had been sweet and undemanding. Annie felt stricken with guilt while realizing how fruitless the feeling was.

"Do you have any idea if Nicole is part of your life again this time?"

Annie shook her head. "I've thought about all of them, trying to place them in this incarnation. I can't figure it out for sure, except for Paul and Marcel. And Lorelei, of course, dear Lorelei. She's Cleo, my best friend all over again. But the others..." She frowned, puzzled.

"Give it time—it'll all come clear. The important thing is not to agonize over what happened, but to learn from it and apply the lessons here and now. I believe that's why this gift of memory is sometimes granted to us, to help us along the path to knowledge a little faster than we'd progress otherwise."

They talked a long while over the usual cups of hot, sweet tea. The cycle was at last complete.

He took both her hands in his when she said goodbye, and his ageless eyes met hers with compassion and deep caring. "May this life be filled with love and happiness, Annie."

"Thank you, more than I can say. Goodbye, Steve."

This time, they both knew she wouldn't be back.

"MAY THIS LIFE BE filled with love and happiness." Steve's words lingered like a benediction in Annie's mind as she shopped for groceries, returned library books and went through all the mundane activites she had to get through during the remainder of that afternoon.

Jason was going to a friend's house for supper, and then to an exhibition basketball game, so there was no real reason to hurry home.

Annie drove to a stretch of beach deserted on this cold October afternoon, parked and locked her car and went for a long walk along the shore of the inlet. The brisk cold air and the rhythmic sound of the waves gradually overcame the turmoil of her thoughts, and a strange sense of peace filled her.

Nothing in her complex life had really changed, and yet everything seemed clear to her now. Not happy. Just...clear.

She drove home just before darkness fell. Astonishment filled her when she recognized David's car parked at a crooked angle in front of her house. She couldn't remember the last time he'd come by this early to see her. And she hadn't been home.

She raced up the stairs and fumbled with the lock.

"David? David, I'm back."

There was no answer, and no lights on anywhere inside. A deep stillness surrounded her as she hurried from one room to the next, searching for him.

She found him fully clothed except for his jacket and shoes, and for an awful moment she was frightened. He was limp and still. He hadn't even heard her come in. He didn't hear her now.

But then she saw the almost imperceptible rise and fall of his chest. He was asleep. It had been a long time since he'd slept in her bed, and an aching tenderness came over her, as well as the strangest feeling that everything was going to be all right now.

She had no idea why he was there, but as always, just having him with her was enough.

She tiptoed back downstairs and scribbled a note to Jason, asking him to be quiet when he came home, since David was resting. Then she went back upstairs, stripped off her clothing and slid her naked, chilly body carefully into bed beside him.

He still didn't awaken, but he turned in his sleep and mumbled, hooking an arm around her and drawing her into the curve of his body, warming her, holding her as if he would never let her go again.

"Bernadette," he murmured, burying his face in the spill of her hair. "I love you, Bernadette."

Annie let the words sink deep into the raw wounds in her soul, and she felt them beginning to heal. "I love you, too," she whispered, folding her hand inside his.

Then she let the balm of sleep wash over her, secure in the arms of the man she'd loved through many lifetimes.

CHAPTER NINETEEN

THE SCHOOL AUDITORIUM was packed that late November evening, and the variety show was drawing to a close.

Jason and the other members of the rugby team had done a fine job recruiting an audience for the benefit, Annie decided as she glanced around the crowded, stuffy room.

Still, if all the other boys had as many people to bully into buying tickets as her son did, the size of the crowd was understandable.

Jason had high-handedly reserved the best seats in the house for his "family." They occupied an entire front row of folding chairs. Annie was flanked by Cleo on one side and Maggie on the other. Don Anderson was at Cleo's other side, holding a sleepy Paula on his knee, and somehow managing to hold Cleo's hand at the same time. They'd left the baby with a sitter tonight. And beside them, Michael and Lili were also hand in hand.

The young master of ceremonies, resplendent in top hat and tails, bounded out on the stage and the room grew quiet. "It gives me great pleasure," he boomed into the microphone, "to introduce the grand finale of the evening. Ladies and gentlemen, our feature attraction, an act that has amazed and delighted royal audiences all over the world, and which we are proud to have here tonight at Kitsilano High. May I present…"

The school band, heavy on brass, gave a drumroll that Annie felt reverberate up through the soles of her feet.

"Jason and The Sorcerer."

A tall figure and a shorter one strolled out of the wings, one from each corner of the stage. Both were dressed in casual jeans and matching rugby shirts, but each wore a magician's signature top hat on his head.

In unison, they met at center stage and turned toward their audience, swept their hats off, and bowed low.

David looked astonished when out of his hat jumped a live rabbit and then another. Jason peered at the rabbits, nodded and winked at the crowd, and nonchalantly produced a bundle of huge carrots from his own hat.

The audience roared with laughter, and the two performers began a quick routine that combined humor with clever variations of the usual stage illusions magicians performed.

They were good. Annie's nervousness faded and her heart swelled with pride.

"Annie, look what they're doing now. Jason's taking a balloon out of David's ear." Maggie's freckled face was alight with wonder, and she clapped her hands and giggled, making her blond braids bounce. "It's blown up, too. How could it come out of his ear, Annie?"

A small, timid girl cowered behind her mother's skirt in the warm farm kitchen. The tall, uniformed man with the deep blue eyes bent down and seemed to draw a bright red ribbon out of the little girl's ear. Then tied it in a clumsy bow in her dark curls....

Annie's heart seemed to turn over, and she reached out and squeezed Maggie's hand.

The memories came when she least expected them, these moments of recognition she was learning to trust. David had them, too, wisps of memory that came and went like dreams. They'd been able between them to piece together the jigsaw of that lifetime in France. There were only a few pieces still missing, and this was one.

So the earnest little girl who'd been Nicole was now Cleo's daughter, Maggie. And Annie was being given a second chance with her, not as her mother this time, but as a beloved friend.

Maggie leaned her head against Annie's shoulder for a second and whispered, "I'm glad you're gonna marry David, Annie. I like him a lot. He's the best magician, isn't he?"

"Yes, Mags, he is," Annie said through the lump in her throat. And the best doctor, and the best lover...and she had not a single doubt that he'd also be the best of husbands.

It would be a Christmas wedding, small and informal, in the living room of Cleo's house with all the children present.

Jason had asked for and been given permission to invite Michael and Lili, which, along with the prospect of Jason giving his mother away in the traditional ceremony Annie planned, appealed to Cleo's sense of the unorthodox.

"Jason can give me away, too, when the time comes," Cleo insisted. "It's only fair, having had to go through adolescence with me. But just don't try to locate that rotten ex of mine to invite to the wedding. I'd rather not have him there when Don and I get married."

Cleo laughed at the scenario, but Annie's smile was always strained. Annie wondered a lot about Pierre Dupré and Tony Briggs. What roles were they now playing in Cleo's life? Which one had returned as the young and handsome Don? And as Lorelei, which man had Cleo deserted?

THE MAGIC SHOW was almost over. The audience watched with delight as Jason carried a small wooden table out from the wings and put it center stage. On the table was a bird cage, and Annie raised her head and met David's eyes.

"They're gonna make the bird cage disappear. 'Member how David did this at that magic show before, Annie?"

She hadn't known until this moment that David had taught Jason his special illusion. She remembered David's refusal when she'd asked him long ago to explain the secret of the trick so she could use it in her book.

"The bird cage is unique, Annie. Sorry, but it's a trade secret, sort of a magical legacy, the sort of valuable secret I'd hand down to a son if I had one. I can't let you use it in a book. It's the only trick I never explain to anyone. I'll find another illusion for you, though...."

Here was tangible evidence of the bond that united David and her son.

David was asking for young volunteers to come up and help with the illusion, to hold the bird cage down.

"I wanna go up. It's okay if I go, isn't it, Annie?"

Maggie raced to the stage, and soon a ring of children had their hands on the cage containing the canaries. In unison, Jason and David raised their hands high over their heads, and with perfect timing, brought them down. The bird cage and its contents disappeared.

A magic incantation was recited in tandem, and the cage and its contents were back again.

The audience roared its appreciation. Jason and The Sorcerer had them under their "fluence."

"WASN'T I JUST EXCELLENT, Mom? Did you hear how we made people laugh? It was awesome, just awesome. We were ace, right? And how about that one we did..."

Jason and David had done a quick job of packing their equipment after the show, and now they joined the group waiting for them in the hallway outside the stage door.

"You were totally awesome, all right, kid," Annie agreed. "And not only are you an ace performer, you're so modest as well," Annie teased, rumpling his thick hair.

"Ahhh, Mom."

Michael and Lili moved up just then to give him hugs and extravagant compliments, and Annie could return Michael's proud glance without a trace of resentment for either the man or his affection for the son they shared.

Annie's inner reaction to Michael was not exactly one of friendship. It was rather a deep and compassionate recognition of the law of cause and effect. It was one of tolerance, forgiveness and peace. As far as she was concerned, they'd settled the debts and credits between them.

David slid an arm around Annie, and she felt the warm rush of joy that filled her whenever they were together, the sense of unity that bonded them.

"How about a hamburger, everybody?" David suggested. When they all agreed, Annie noticed David slip folded money into Jason's hand, and the two exchanged a conspirational glance as arrangements were made about where to meet.

"WHAT WAS THAT all about?"

Somehow, Annie and David had ended up alone in David's car. Jason had decided to ride with his father.

"Just a gentleman's agreement Jason and I made," was all David would say. But Annie noticed they weren't going in the direction the others were. They were heading for David's apartment.

"I CAN'T BELIEVE you did all this by yourself."

Annie was relaxed on the couch with a glass of wine in her hand. A fire blazed and crackled in the fireplace, and on the low table in front of her sat an assortment of fresh fruit, pâté and cheese. The food shared space with a mass of daffodils and tulips jammed any which way into a plastic pitcher.

David was in the galley kitchen, adjusting the oven with the same intensity he must apply to major surgery. He had a list tacked to the fridge, and he consulted it several times as he slid a pan of rolls in and took a covered casserole out, swearing under his breath each time he burned himself.

"Ahh, you underestimate me. I'm a magician, remember?" He swore again, out loud this time, and almost dropped the casserole before he got it safely to the table. "Dinner's almost ready," he announced with enormous relief.

Annie glanced at the assortment of containers jumbled on the counter, all bearing the logo of Vancouver's most elegant catering service.

"Bet you're a rich magician at that," she teased, watching the performance he was going through just to serve her dinner. "You've gotta be rich to afford Lazy Gourmet."

"I once promised you dinner, dancing, wine, flowers, and choco-lates," he'd explained when they arrived. "But unfortunately, the eve-ning didn't turn out as I planned. So I'm going to keep my promise tonight."

She was thrilled to the core, and touched that he would somehow find time to make these arrangements in the midst of what was still a brutally busy agenda.

Not quite as busy as it had been, however. David had resigned from most of the committees during the past weeks, and there'd been a dra-matic showdown with Calvin. Annie didn't know all the details—David had just told her he was no longer a candidate for any sort of office, and Calvin was raving mad at him as a result.

"Can you salvage your friendship with him, David? After all, he's been part of your life for years."

"A lot more years than he realizes. It's up to him now. Annie. I'm not certain Calvin understands friendship as well as he understands manipulation and power. It's a lesson he'll have to learn on his own."

Knowing Calvin, Annie wondered how many more lifetimes that was going to take.

"How's your wine, pretty lady? Time for one more small glass, and then we'll eat before this mess gets cold."

She held out her glass for him to refill. He reached over and plucked a card from a pile of mail on the stereo stand and handed it to her.

"This came yesterday. It's from Mrs. Vance, Charlie's mother."

The message on the outside of the card just read, Thank You. Inside was a note and a snapshot of a little boy with laughing eyes and a smile that reached out from the picture and wrapped itself around Annie's heart. It was the photo Linda Vance had shown Annie with such pride that long-ago night at the hospital.

"Dear Dr. Roswell," the note read. "We want to thank you for all you did for us. Like you said, you can't promise things will be different for our baby girl, but we have complete trust in you. We know you will do everything possible for her, just like you did for Charlie. Wher-ever he is, I know he thanks you, too. I thought you'd like to have his picture."

Annie slid the card back in the envelope and handed it to David. "They'll have to take her to Pittsburgh, won't they?"

David nodded. "I've accepted the fact that a full transplant unit is still very much in the future. But we're making progress here all the same. There's the Organ Retrieval for Transplant facility, and the pub-lic's becoming more aware of the need for donor organs."

He poured himself a glass of wine and perched for a moment on the arm of the couch as he drank it.

"I feel differently about it now than I did before. The sense of desperation is gone," he admitted. "Part of it is understanding that a lot of the frustration I feel is linked to that poor bastard doing surgery in a tent back in France, trying to patch up young soldiers as best he could and failing more often than not."

It still amazed Annie, having David accept and talk about this concept of other lives.

"But the biggest change is knowing for certain that life is eternal, that little old Charlie is out there somewhere right now, and that maybe the next body he gets will work better than the last." He smiled down at her, that wide, crooked smile that always reminded her of Paul.

"It's knowing, too, that kids like Charlie choose their bodies for a reason—that there's a rational purpose to it all. It makes my job a little easier, understanding that."

Her heart full, she reached up and wrapped her arms around his neck, pulling him down on top of her, spilling what was left of his wine all over her dress and not caring at all.

He let the glass fall to the carpet and settled her more comfortably beneath him.

"David, you're such a fine man, such a good doctor."

"Not yet, my love. But I will be, even if it takes another dozen lifetimes. With you."

He kissed her, and profound peace and soaring joy filled Annie's heart. She and David had been born again, to find a way to be together, and now at last the sad and lonely images of Bernadette and her Paul could be laid to rest. Yesterday's debts were paid. There was only love on time's ledger now, to look forward to. To remember and enjoy again, after this lifetime was ended. Love was eternal; yesterday, tomorrow, forever.

She wriggled underneath him.

"Enough, woman. My dinner is gonna be ruined if you distract me this way."

"Woman does not live by food alone," she breathed in his ear.

"I heated it up, and you're going to eat it," he insisted, and kissed her again.

"Food now, love and dancing later," he promised.

There was plenty of time.

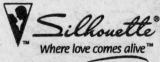

AVAILABLE IN OCTOBER FROM SILHOUETTE BOOKS!

THE
HEART'S
COMMAND

THREE BRAND-NEW STORIES BY THREE
USA TODAY BESTSELLING AUTHORS!

RACHEL LEE
"The Dream Marine"

Marine sergeant Joe Yates came home to Conard County ready
to give up military life. Until spirited Diana Rutledge forced him
to remember the stuff true heroes—and true love—are made of....

MERLINE LOVELACE
"Undercover Operations"

She was the colonel's daughter, and he was the Special
Operations pilot who would do anything for her. But once
under deep cover as Danielle Flynn's husband, Jack Buchanan
battled hard to keep hold of his heart!

LINDSAY McKENNA
"To Love and Protect"

Reunited on a mission for Morgan Trayhern, lieutenants
Niall Ward and Brie Phillips found themselves stranded at sea—
with only each other to cling to. Would the power of love give
them the strength to carry on until rescue—and beyond?

Available at your favorite retail outlet.

Silhouette

Where love comes alive